ACCLAIM FOR

Burridge Unbound

"In electrifying prose, by turns violent, manic, and deeply sad, Alan Cumyn charts Burridge's lurching, rubble-strewn, chaotic, and strangely heroic course."
— Jury Citation for The Giller Prize by Margaret Atwood, Alistair MacLeod, and Jane Urquhart

"*Burridge Unbound* is a thrilling piece of literary fiction. Cumyn has taken an explosive subject and made a fine novel out of it." — *Edmonton Journal*

"Cumyn's writing is breathtakingly good. . . . He develops Burridge as a darkly humorous Everyman. . . . The novel is a beautiful and painful slice of reality. . . ." — *Ottawa Life*

". . . his convincing portrait of Burridge alone, in all his psychological complexity, is highly original and no small feat."
— *Toronto Star*

"The book takes on the dimensions of a thriller, taut, mesmerizing, horrific." — *Quill & Quire*

"The pain, suffering and chaos of a world turned topsy turvy is superbly mediated through the sardonic voice of Burridge, and the result is a novel which both moves and educates."
— *Amnesty International*

"Powerful. . . . Hard to put down." — *Windsor Star*

BOOKS BY ALAN CUMYN

FICTION

Waiting for Li Ming (1993)
Between Families and the Sky (1995)
Man of Bone (1998)
Burridge Unbound (2000)
Losing It (2001)

NON-FICTION

What in the World Is Going On? (1998)

BURRIDGE UNBOUND

ALAN CUMYN

EMBLEM EDITIONS
Published by McClelland & Stewart Ltd.

First published in trade paperback with flaps 2000
First Emblem Editions publication 2002

National Library of Canada Cataloguing in Publication Data

Cumyn, Alan, 1960-
Burridge unbound

ISBN 0-7710-2488-6

I. Title.

PS8555.U489B87 2002   C813'.54   C2001-903821-6
PR9199.3.C775B84 2002

We acknowledge the financial support of the Government of Canada through
the Book Publishing Industry Development Program for our publishing activities. We further acknowledge the support of the Canada Council for the Arts
and the Ontario Arts Council for our publishing program.

This novel is a work of fiction. Except for historical references, the names,
characters, places, and incidents are the product of the author's imagination and
their resemblance, if any, to real-life counterparts is entirely coincidental.

The author would like to gratefully acknowledge the financial assistance of the
Canada Council for the Arts, the Ontario Arts Council, and the Region of
Ottawa-Carleton Arts Grants Program in the preparation of this manuscript.
Thanks too to the many friends, family members, and colleagues whose
comments, suggestions, and support have been invaluable. Finally, thanks to
Ellen Seligman for her inspirational editing. The deficiencies that remain are
entirely mine. Thank you! A.C.

SERIES EDITOR: ELLEN SELIGMAN

Cover image: Les Szurkowski
Series logo design: Brian Bean

Typeset in Janson by M&S, Toronto
Printed and bound in Canada

EMBLEM EDITIONS
McClelland & Stewart Ltd.
The Canadian Publishers
481 University Avenue
Toronto, Ontario
M5G 2E9
www.mcclelland.com/emblem

1 2 3 4 5   06 05 04 03 02

For my mother and father

I

This is the moment people remember: the sudden intake of breath, the shift of attention. It's Geneva or New York – for now I'm not sure which. If I thought it through I'd know. I haven't entirely lost my mind. Things just fade in and out sometimes. I'm learning to live with it, as with so many other parts of my condition.

We're a small group, just me, Derrick Langford, and Joanne Stoddart, the complete staff of Freedom International. Derrick has all the files, Joanne her nurse's bag. I walk empty-handed. I'm the point-man, the face and mouthpiece; my job now is to not fall over. I try to stand straight, to do my breathing, to turn my elbows out a bit (for energy – everything is for energy). Derrick walks ahead because he knows where we're going. Joanne stays a half-pace behind, her right hand free in case I stumble. If I stick to my breathing (abdominal; slow sips of air) and watch the horizon I'm usually all right. The table is grand, not the circle I expect but a huge rectangle, and the chairs have high sweeping backs and swivel soundlessly. The windows are high so nothing outside can distract us.

They're all watching me. Men mostly, senior, overweight, distinguished, from two dozen different countries. They don't rise, just stare. The special rapporteur – his name escapes me though I've met him before – half-rises and holds out a hand, which I grasp momentarily as I pass. He's a Chilean with tiny, intense eyes and too firm a grip; every pore reeks of nicotine and worry. There are few smiles. One woman, the only female I notice besides Joanne, pales when she sees me but doesn't look away. I'm the man who walked through the valley of the shadow of death. I didn't succumb and yet I didn't entirely survive either. I *became* the shadow of death. Despite the suit, the vitamins, the best efforts of modern medicine, damnation is written in every jutting bone of my face.

We reach our seats finally and I clutch the armrests like life preservers. So often people are struck by how still I appear, and yet my heart labours as if stuck in the wrong gear. Joanne reaches to touch my arm. "Breathe," she says softly and I do, and it makes things better for a bit.

Derrick pours me a glass of water. I drink, close my eyes, try to focus. It's New York. The United Nations. I threw up in the cab on the way here. My leg is already feeling uneasy. Shit for that. I've been fooling myself. Too much pressure. I shouldn't have come.

More water. The special rapporteur speaks in solid, professorial paragraphs – long, structured thoughts laid like paving stones, the designs careful, crafted without wobbles or loose dirt or unexpected outcomes. He holds up my book, speaks of its "integrity of voice," "passionate detail," the "honest and personal account of horrors beyond our imagination." The book has sent my voice around the world, I suppose, but mostly it sent my face, the dark ragged stare, the eloquence of the unexpressed.

It's turning into one of the most famously unread documents of the decade. Briefly I did some talk shows, put up with interviews from young media people who didn't seem to know what to ask or how. There have been prizes from humanitarian organizations, too many to remember – not that my memory has been much to rely on. I dwell on too much of what I need to forget, and have a tenuous grasp of everything else. Derrick has managed to spin the prizes into grants. I stole him from Amnesty International. I don't know why he came, really; I couldn't offer much money, and I'm not all that pleasant to deal with. Maybe this puts him more in the limelight. I'm the face and the name but everyone knows Derrick does everything. Don't they know that?

Drifting again. I have to keep my mind focused. Especially in public. Everyone is clapping and I don't know why. What did I miss? I look to Derrick but he's clapping too. A large black man from Nigeria thumps the table with the palm of his hand. The special rapporteur stands and so does everyone else. I start to stand too but Joanne puts a hand on my shoulder. Of course. I'm three-quarters stupid half the time. It's my condition. That's what I tell myself anyway.

When the ovation is over Joanne passes me a note. The paper has the blue U.N. symbol in the top corner with HUMAN RIGHTS COMMITTEE in large black letters. Joanne's writing is spidery, with thin pointy letters designed to be packed onto an airmail sheet. "*Why does the Pope keep his eyes up when he's in the shower?*"

I start to laugh as soon as I read it. Our oldest joke. Near the end of the interview in my sparse apartment, when she'd reviewed the long, daunting list of my ailments and had talked about her nursing stints in Rwanda, Sudan, Mozambique, I'd suddenly asked her to tell me a joke. Without a second's thought she asked about the Pope, and delivered the punch-line with genuine glee. "Because he doesn't want to look down on the unemployed!" Her great bush of red hair shorter then, skin deeply freckled from so many stints in the tropics. Just the slightest shadow in her gaze, a tenseness in her shoulders and jaw, otherwise she looked untouched from her years of dealing with refugees. I told her most of all I needed someone who could say something funny on command. It doesn't have to be new or in good taste or even particularly humorous. Just an attempt to lighten the mood.

The Spanish delegate is speaking. Again, I haven't been following. Derrick has been taking notes. He has brown curly hair, intense eyebrows, an enormous head on quite a young body. His doodles range from the margins to the middle of the page, at times blocking out sections of his notes. Sometimes I've turned his pages upside down to look at what I'd swear were sexual organs, male and female mixed, pendulous testicles and breasts, a storm of pubic hair and vagina lips angling into a thigh that narrows phallic-like. Or maybe it's just my mind.

On and on he goes, this Spanish fellow. If I plugged in the earphones, if I found the right setting for translation into English, I suppose I could follow what he's saying. But I know already, have heard too many of these sorts of speeches. The words are careful, diplomatic, righteous in safe ways. They weigh in against torture, extrajudicial executions, disappearances, defend the individual from tyranny without naming the individual or the tyranny. Words we all can support without risking anything at all. I don't need to hear them but I nod my head, giving the impression, perhaps, that I'm following in Spanish.

People will believe almost anything about a torture survivor – that I have a greater consciousness, a more developed sense of conscience, a supernatural refinement of the higher emotions. That I don't have a back passage. But I do, and the Spaniard has been talking too long. I clench, but everything about my bowels is delicate. I forgot my breathing. I deserve diarrhea. I forgot my fucking breathing! I try now to get it back against the panic. I'm going to shit my pants in the United Nations. The Spaniard goes on and on and the shit is coming sure as a train on greased rails. I knew I wasn't ready. I could've just sent Derrick. He wrote the brief and he can read it better than I can anyway.

Joanne has a whole drugstore in her bag. Sometimes one little pill can make all the difference. I ought to know. Amitatriphyline for stress, insomnia, and depression. Cisapride for heartburn and my various digestive disorders. Furosemide and metoprolol for high blood pressure. Aspirin for my weak heart. Those are the ones I remember. Joanne keeps track of when and where and how much. I can't keep it all in my shrinking brain. The metoprolol and aspirin work against the cisapride and mess up my digestion. Almost everything ruins my sex drive, and my heart is too weak for any new anti-impotence drug. Then there's all the chemically induced laundry lint in my brain. Daily reality for a human-rights defender.

Still the Spaniard speaks on. I've been so preoccupied keeping back the mudslide that I haven't paid attention to the crawling, itching, pulling in my leg. Now I squirm. Sweat seeps down my face, onto my shirt collar and jacket. Why did I agree to wear a tie? Respect for the goddamn United Nations. Stupid, lame, impotent organization. Begging for money. They don't even have air conditioning. What a travesty. I was clear with Derrick and he was clear with them. No fucking speeches. I don't need to hear this Spanish crap. It wasn't on the schedule and I don't have to put up with it. My leg burning now, I can't keep it back. I should've videotaped my testimony and stayed home.

This is my last thought before my leg jerks out and slams the underside of the table. Everyone's water jumps and Derrick's pen flies out of his hand. At least the Spaniard stops talking, but the damage is done – my pants are now full of runny, toxic, smelly shit. Joanne knows exactly what's happened and knows too she can't do a thing about it. Derrick gets out of his seat to retrieve his pen. The Spaniard finishes up. My leg slams the table again and another jet of shit surges to freedom. In my incarceration, in the closet in the hood with my limbs shackled, I learned to be still as a rock under a lizard. But no more. I have control over nothing.

Everybody's staring. *Now* it's my turn to speak. But if I stand up the shit will run down my trousers. If I stay seated my leg will just keep jerking up every thirty seconds – Restless Leg Syndrome.

Joanne leans in. Everyone is watching. "Do you want to leave?" she asks in a voice as soothing as flannel sheets on a winter's night. I think that's why I hired her. For her jokes, her voice, and her eyes, a thousand shades of green and brown. I can imagine those refugees staggering into the holding camps, rubbing the dust from their vision. We soak in energy from people and sometimes it's cleansing and sometimes it frazzles and defeats.

"We can come back and do this another time," she says. "It's just talk."

It is. Just talk. Talk can happen now or later. Talk changes nothing. Words are written on paper. Sounds vibrate eardrums and the words go onto different paper, are printed up and mailed to libraries and offices around the world where they sit largely unread. Nothing actually changes. Helicopters still arrive in mountain villages and huts are still set ablaze and children are gunned down as they flee. I'm not the only one who has seen it and talked about it. But I *suffered* and I'm an ex-diplomat. I come from the moneyed part of the world, so prizes have been bestowed upon me for that and for my useless bloody words.

I get to my feet before my leg jerks out again. Maybe they can't see. Maybe they're all diplomats, so they purposely don't notice. It's only three or four steps. My hands can't keep still to hold Derrick's speech, so I just set the papers down and grip the sides of the lectern. Breathe and breathe and breathe. Look to the horizon. I jiggle my leg to stop the jerking and more shit slides down, now onto my socks and shoes. The scent of my own rot. So familiar. Let them smell it. The reek of a life coming apart.

"In the mountains of Santa Irene," I read in my quavering voice, using the Spanish pronunciation, *Ee-ray-nay*, "government troops are carrying out a systematic slaughter of villagers suspected of harbouring guerrillas of the rebel resistance group Kartouf. They arrive sometimes in broad daylight, but usually at night, two or three helicopters in a pack. They rake the village first with machine-gun fire and then they set fire to the huts and the surrounding jungle. The villages are small but often thirty to sixty people die at a time, sometimes as many as two hundred."

I lose my place briefly. Derrick has triple-spaced and used a large font, but when I'm tired my vision can't be trusted. Sometimes the world goes blurry. No doubt the pause makes the delegates wonder if I'm overcome with emotion. I'm just trying to see the words. I blink and look, blink and look. Breathe and breathe and breathe.

"As many of you know," I say finally, abandoning the text, "the Kartouf are a terrorist organization. As a junior diplomat only three weeks in the country I was kidnapped and suffered their hospitality, longed for death every moment under their care. I harbour no protective feelings for the Kartouf. But the government of Santa Irene is committing cold-blooded murder of largely innocent people. They have used my incarceration to step up their campaign, which infuriates me no end. I'm personally involved in this struggle. My organization, of course, advocates peace, justice, and human rights around the world. Blood is flowing in so many parts of the planet. But I've come to add my voice to this one small struggle for the human soul. I'm asking you to add your voices as well. Create an international outcry. Use my name as much as you wish. Our report is in front of you. You don't really need to hear the words from me. You already know the right thing to do. *Do it.*"

I've said enough, but for a time I look back at Derrick's notes to try to see what I've left out. The sources of documentation. The names of the villages. The letters from survivors. What was it one of them said? *They eat us like locusts and our blood becomes the soil.* I know these words are there but my eyes are blurry still.

I don't sit down, don't wait for the clapping, for questions. My leg has to move anyway. I think it's this way. In a moment Derrick and Joanne are back with me. I feel smaller, bent like an old man, though not yet forty. I feel like I'm walking up an endless hill. "I'm sorry," I mutter over and over.

Joanne finds the washroom. Derrick goes back to deal with the committee. He knows the details anyway. I feel so humiliated. The washroom is finely appointed, as they say, everything mirrored and gleaming. I lean against the counter – marble? certainly cold, hard, and smooth – and I fail to look away from the mirror soon enough. That haggard face, the doomed eyes, the sparse greying hair. It's me. I look like a street person. Two years after freedom and I'm still so far beyond the bandwidth of normal human experience.

Joanne peels me down and wipes me. Slowly, calmly, rinsing her cloth from time to time, soiling the beautiful sink. Does the world know what expenses have been lavished on the United Nations' washrooms?

"I was travelling once in India," a voice says. I hear it as in a dream. "On a train, in Maharashtra. Third class. I thought it was all I could afford." Such a voice, I'm thinking, my head down, my eyes shut tight. Joanne daubing me clean. What if someone comes in? I don't even know if this is the men's wash-room or the women's. I didn't notice urinals. I wasn't looking for them.

"It was alarmingly hot, and we were wedged in like cattle. You know those trains, the peasants riding on the roofs with all their bags. I actually had a seat inside, but I didn't dare get up to pee because five different people had been standing for a hundred miles staring at me and my seat. I was twenty-one, I didn't know any better. I just crossed my legs. Sometime in the night my period came, and I still didn't want to get up. I thought everybody knew. They could smell me. Some of them slept standing up. One little man fell asleep on the floor with his head under my seat. I thought I was going to drip on him."

Daubing, wiping, cleaning the cloth. Cool on my legs. Of course the voice is Joanne's.

"It was so hot. I'd sweated through my clothes, I thought everyone could see right into my underwear. The train eased along at about twenty miles an hour and we were stewing. I felt like the frog in the pot that just keeps heating up. Why didn't I buy a first-class ticket? I had two hundred dollars' safety money sewn into my bra. I was saving it for a real emer-gency. But something happens to your brain in the heat. After a time I knew I was going to die but I decided I'd go nobly. Without a word. I'd just . . . *expire* in my seat."

The cool cloth on my legs, bum, testicles. Those silly, useless ornaments. A beautiful woman is washing my body. If I were a teenager I would've exploded already. Now – sagging meat. Pitiful.

"Somehow I lasted the entire night without moving. I willed myself into another state. I think I was seeing angels by the morning. I finally got up and went to the bathroom. My God. The door was broken. There was absolutely no privacy. I didn't care by then, I was in such need. But from where I crouched I could see in a cracked mirror a Hindu woman performing her morning ablutions. She had almost nothing – her sari, her fingers, a bit of saliva. But in five minutes she'd washed herself completely, had wiped away the dirt and fatigue, the grinding desperation of that journey. Just rubbing herself here and there. She emerged the most beautiful creature I've ever seen: refreshed, radiant, like she was floating a few feet above everything."

Joanne tosses my underwear in the sink. I tell her to just throw it out, but she soaps and rinses it instead, wrings it with her strong, competent hands. "Whenever things got really bad in the camps," she says, "I thought of that Hindu woman. And I always made sure that I cleaned myself at the start and end of every day."

She fits me with an adult diaper. There's another name for them. She'd suggested I wear one in the first place but I told her I wasn't going to the United Nations wearing a diaper. Idiot. It feels bulky and completely conspicuous. Everyone will know instantly. Why does such a skinny man have such a huge butt? But it doesn't matter. "Thank you," I say, again and again, as she rinses out my trousers.

"Did you hear about the bombing in the New York City police department?" she asks gravely.

"No. There was a bombing?"

"In the washroom," she says. "They've just started their investigation. *So far police have nothing to go on.*"

Her smile. That's the best part of any joke she tells. Like a sly bend of a creek in sunshine, heading back into shadows. It's such a slight and ridiculous straw, you'd never suspect it could hold the weight of a grown man's life, through days like this of sewage and despair and worse, I'm afraid, far worse.

"How many surrealists does it take to screw in a lightbulb?" she continues, now using the hand-drying hot-air blower to dry my pants.

I shake my head.

"One to nail the bicycle to the wall, and three more to put the giraffe in the bathtub."

"Yes," I say, standing in a diaper in the United Nations, waiting for the streak of sunlight on the bend in the creek.

2

Dear Bill Burridge,

Punjab police came for me yesterday morning it was about 6:30 am in Chandigarh I was visiting friends of my father's. It was exactly as if they were coming for him they burst in swinging lathis destroyed my friend's television and then I was on foot out the back way I hid behind a vegetable stall and some friends came by and sped me away. I don't know why they would bother with me now except we have pressed for action on the disappearances cases especially Khalra. So much for this being the peaceful Punjab. I have heard that the police took my friend's wife for questioning about me and I am fearful for what the brutes have probably done to her. Please do your magic like the last time and maybe the dogs will be loosed from our necks.

Thank you, your friend in need, Jaswant Kashmir Singh

Sometimes when I sit in my corner office in my apartment, twenty-seven flights above the ground, I have the illusion of flying. Not as in an airplane, but like an eagle, soaring over the city at dawn, the sun reflecting purple on the Gatineau Hills, pouring liquid light into the Ottawa River. The whole world stretches before me. It doesn't look like a wounded place, but large, big-shouldered, impassive in the face of what we're doing to one another.

Bill –

We're in a state here after the bombing. Police are back to cordon and searches of entire neighbourhoods. My cousin stammered at a roadblock on his way to work and they decided to take him in even though he had all his papers and has been going through that roadblock every morning for five years. My sister phoned me at work and I went straight to the police station. They disclaimed all knowledge of him. "But I have five witnesses who saw you take him to this station!" They gave me a form to fill out, which I did, in triplicate. The station clerk said I should come back tomorrow. I refused. "I want to talk to the SSP!" Impossible. The SSP could not be disturbed. I said I would wait. The clerk said I could do as I wished. And so I sat in that sweaty police station for sixteen hours, praying that they would not light into a prisoner knowing that his relative is waiting outside.

Finally enough was enough. "If you do not let me see him this minute I will get the Minister to fry you on a stick!"

"Which minister?" the clerk asked. Cheeky lad. Bloody Sinhalese bastards.

"What is your name?" I screamed, pulling out my pad. He would not tell me. I reached across the counter and started launching files into the air. Three police goons suddenly had me twisted on the floor in agony. I thought I was destined for a cell myself. But they pitched me outside instead.

It has been three days now. My sister is beside herself. The last time Vijay was arrested he came back swollen and blue and did not talk for two months. He is an innocent boy. He works in a photocopy shop.

If you do not hear from me in two more days please post this as widely as you can. I am afraid the police will not appreciate my efforts to free my cousin. Most probably they are looking for a large bribe and I am raising the money now.

All the best to you and your family.

TJ Villaiparram

Clouds move in slowly and the light turns ordinary. The traffic starts to build on the bridges across the river, and the deep green of the trees surrounding Parliament Hill turns dull and unremarkable as the morning stretches. From where I sit I can even see the smog line and the blue above it. It's late August – no leaves have turned yet, but we know what's brewing.

dear mr burridge

it feels strange to write you cuz i feel ive known you all my life :-} i know what you went through was terrible and im looking forward to reading your book – my mom has it now and says its too violent for me to read so i really want to! im writing now tho because i saw on your website some information about sleep disorders for victims of ptsd and they really rocked me! i thought – no way! because this is exactly the type of dream i have :-[everything is great and then all of a sudden i cant move i cant turn over or lift my hand or wake up. i know im asleep but i want to wake up i just cant and its terrible its total sleep paralysis but as i think about it more and more i realize whats happening – you wont believe this but im remembering detailed episodes of alien abductions!!! cuz when i was a little girl my father disappeared ive never seen him in like twelve years and my mom says there hasnt even been a card or anything and he wasnt bad news before that i think we were both abducted and hes still being held while i had my memory erased only it comes out in sleep paralysis so maybe what you experienced wasnt terrorists holding you but these same aliens!! i cant really see them clearly but they have a weird smell and creepy long fingers with lights at the ends

its great to be able to write to you i wrote to Stephen King too but he never replied :-[

Cheryl Ann Tyson
Tulsa

Behind the flat screen of the computer words fly around the planet, pulsing with life and meaning. In seconds I can connect with Amnesty International in London, Human Rights Watch in New York, a State Department friend in Washington, a journalist in Karachi, an amateur human-rights observer from Thailand who now lives in Moose Jaw . . . and with thousands of people I'll never meet. Eight hundred and two logged onto my Web site while I was in New York panicking at the United Nations.

The world doesn't sleep. Bombs rip through U.S. embassies in Kenya and Tanzania and tear up a shopping district in Northern Ireland – places where peace was supposed to reign. The Russian ruble loses half its value overnight and Serbs murder Albanians with NATO looking on. Famine seeps sound-lessly through Sudan while Chinese doctors remove organs from condemned prisoners for use by aging cadres and Israeli guards legally torture prisoners for information. Indian and Pakistani generals ponder nuclear war over the mountains of Kashmir, and Aung San Suu Kyi sits on a bridge for endless days in Burma in a stalemate with the military.

The world doesn't sleep, why should I? Why should I submit to the degrading treatment of my own mind? Alien abductions! If only it were so simple, Cheryl Ann. I'd welcome those long fingers with light at the tips. My dreams are of cold darkness and they don't end with any sort of rosy dawn or willed waking of the mind and spirit. They last the entire period of my own abduction and include every electroshock, rape, hallucination, humiliation, starvation. My magnificent brain has saved and stored each morsel in sequence and can play them back, beginning at any time and ending only with the soul's near-total exhaustion, with Joanne wrapping me in sheets for my own protection and my body thrashed and wasted. If only I could have a nice alien abduction! Maybe I'd meet your father, Cheryl Ann, and we'd tell tales about our children and what the food is like in captivity.

Dear Daddy,

How was New York? Where you ok on the plane? I was afraide you might have bad memories and I prayed for you to be ok. The cottage has been fine. Buster got sand in the computor but it still works. Mommy works all the time on her art. There's a studio and all she does is stuff for her show. Buster and I run up and down the beach but he doesn't like going in the water.

I wish you could come to visit us but Mommy says your very sick still. Maybe you should stay in bed and not go to New York any more. I heard there was a big terror bomb there.

Write right away please so I know that your ok.

Patrick (your son)

Heat bakes the city most of the day and then strong winds bring a new front through, so that by the time the cars are stalled on the bridges for their homeward journey rain lashes my windows and we slide into a premature night. Derrick calls to remind me he's starting his two-week holiday and Joanne brings dinner and pills, but she can't stay – some friends from Médecins sans frontières are organizing a mock refugee camp downtown to mark the fiftieth anniversary of the Universal Declaration of Human Rights – as long as I'm all right, she asks, and I am. This is home, safe and aloof and connected at the same time. I haven't had a twister originate from this apartment in several months, and I can usually tell now when they're coming on – my anxiety level rises, my jaw clamps, my heartburn flares, my breathing races shallow and fast. I can almost believe I'm more or less a whole person, talking like this, the smell of stir-fry on the table.

She really must go, she says. Yes, but she stays while I tell her today's e-mails. I have her cellphone number. She's taken a room nearby so that she can be here in minutes. The stir-fry has ginger and garlic and strips of chicken and vegetables coloured with extra vibrancy as if auditioning for a spot in a glossy magazine advertisement.

Then Joanne leaves and I'm stunned by how completely she takes all vitality with her. In a moment the apartment is a cave of gloom. The storm outside intensifies and my insides protest the richness of the food just as a headache arrives and the walls start to close in. I settle back in front of my computer, my steady friend, my refuge. The night stretches in violent wonder pulsing around our planet at the speed of electricity. And so conveniently in English! Thank God for the British Empire and American know-how. *The South China Morning Post* and *Hong Kong Standard* publish pictures of the flooding Yangtze River, run stories on the villages officials have decided to sacrifice in order to save the large city of Wuhan. *Dawn* and *The International* in Karachi write about the suspect caught there in the African bombings of U.S. embassies, and about the MQM factions killing one another in the streets. The Colombo *Daily News* speculates on the standing of Clinton after the confession of his "inappropriate relationship" with Monica Lewinsky. And in Santa Irene, AP reports a protest of students about the tripling of tuition fees and inflation in general. The Asian economic crisis has even affected drug profits, the article says.

On and on I travel and read, but I'm one man against the night and the odds are ruinous. Eventually the screen dulls, my eyes tire. I breathe and breathe – little sips of air, but from the diaphragm, a *qigong* meditation that sometimes sends subtle waves of energy through my body. But tonight the air has a hard time passing my throat. And now my leg makes it impossible to sit anyway. I pace the short section of rug past the west window to the north and back, try to keep track of how many times I turn around (as if that statistic will somehow keep me anchored). I should have exercised today. Why didn't I? Everything was so good. I felt as if I could go forever. Who needs to eat, walk, touch the earth, talk to a human being face to face?

It all sours so fast. What kind of wonderland was I inhabiting? This is my true reality. Total exhaustion. But stay away from sleep. Sleep is torture. The Kartouf own sleep and Burridge has been banished from its gates. I dial Joanne. I should just let her have her evening but I can't. I need to know that she'll be able to come.

"Bill? Are you all right?"

"Yes." I breathe for a moment. It's true. Just having her to call has calmed my heart. I'm still pacing, but it's manageable now. I'm okay. "I'm sorry," I say. "I had some anxiety, but it really wasn't so bad and now it's fine. I shouldn't have bothered you. How's the refugee camp?'

"Soaked with rain," she says. "It seems like old times. Are you sure you're all right?"

"I seem to be fine. I think I just needed to know I could reach you. I'll do some more computer."

"How many feminists does it take to change a lightbulb?" she asks.

"I don't know."

"*That's not funny!*" she says. "You should put on Abbott and Costello."

I tell her I will. Slapstick suits me fine most of the time. Buster Keaton, Chaplin, Laurel and Hardy, the Marx Brothers. Nothing too lowbrow for my taste. I have a nice collection. They remind me of childhood Saturday mornings watching cartoons with my brother Graham. Bugs Bunny and Roadrunner. Woody Woodpecker. Popeye and Olive Oyl. Just reading the video titles starts to cheer me up. Suddenly I wish to God Patrick were here to watch with me. We'd snuggle on the couch and share a blanket, stuff ourselves with milk and cookies. Charlie Brown. *The Grinch Who Stole Christmas.* That little puppy pulling the huge sleigh, teetering on the brink of oblivion. *Butch Cassidy and the Sundance Kid.* The two outlaws trapped on the cliff. Sundance won't jump because he can't swim. Why does Sundance end up with Katharine Ross?

Katharine Ross. Whatever happened to Katharine Ross? I'm soaked suddenly in sadness about her. She was so beautiful in *The Graduate*, but why did she go for Dustin Hoffman? He was bad news for her in that movie. Bad news or good news? I would've crashed the church at her wedding too to get her. That final look as they pull away on the bus. *Now what?*

Now what? Now the night stands before me. I'm pacing again. I take the uneaten portion of Joanne's stir-fry and mulch it in the trash compactor. I'd go out for a walk, but the storm is blowing too hard. A cold rain like that could land me with pneumonia. Just what I need. I sit back at the computer but my leg jumps – *whack!* – within seconds. A hot bath. I head for the bathroom, change my mind, pace some more. If only I could sleep. It would make everything better. Maybe I'm on an even keel again and it's the lack of sleep that's throwing everything off. If I just went to sleep I'd be fine.

I try to clear room on the bed. It's covered in old newspapers, magazines, Action Alert printouts, Death Penalty logs, and the like. The slaughter of the Kurds. Ethnic cleansing in Albania. Sixty-three bodies with slit throats in Algeria. A crackdown on religious minorities in China. *The Silent Slaughter.* I push them all aside and lie with my face in my pillow.

This isn't how to go to sleep. I have a vague memory. I need to take off my clothes and put on pyjamas. Sip hot milk, take out and brush my teeth. Read something light before turning off the lamp. Any one of the above would be an improvement. But my body doesn't move. I need to take off my shoes and socks.

I think I'm rising to do some of this, but it turns out nothing like that. Part of me rises but my body stays immobile on the bed. I should've eaten more. Then I'd have the energy to get up and do all the right things and fall asleep properly. But now I'm split and watching myself, not properly asleep at all. My leg starts twitching. It's amazing to see. Still one moment, jerking out the next. Articles scatter every time. Soon there's going to be nothing else left on the bed. Everything will be out of order. (Is it in order now?)

There should be an order, but there isn't. I shouldn't be able to watch myself sleeping, but here I am hovering near the ceiling. Sometimes in the hood in the closet with the heat and insects and immobility and starvation eating me slowly slowly I'd hover like this above my body and feel a great sense of lightness because of how close to freedom it all felt. Release. This isn't the same. (That wasn't the same either. It was all wrong. Every bit of it.) This is disjointed. If not for the ceiling I'd just float off and never be heard from again. Now I want to be joined. I want to be part of that body and make it sleep properly again. Not articles on atrocities raining all over the bedroom.

I want to, but I can't. And now the ceiling is opening up into blackness. The ceiling opening up and I try to get back to my body. I try to turn and that works, I can turn, but I can't get anywhere. There's nothing to push against. I try but my limbs have no substance. No substance but all the pain of my wretched body. Who rigged the rules in this universe? If you don't have the substance you shouldn't have the pain either!

I need to call Joanne. If I could just get to the phone but there's no way to move and anyway they have the phone they pull the strings I couldn't even remember the number *just hit redial* a voice says clear as anything if I could just get to the phone and hit redial she'd know and she'd come but there's no hope of it they have everything attached and are asking me again in Kuantij I can't understand a fucking thing I shouldn't have gone I shouldn't have taken the damn car it was just badminton an accident a flat fucking tire and if I hadn't stalled the gears that one time when I was almost away I wouldn't I wouldn't I wouldn't . . .

Her voice again. Jesus. They've got Joanne. I can't believe it! I writhe now spit scream shit ache turn *not Joanne* she's the safe spot the warm voice *damn!* I can't move it's all pressing down *don't touch her!* a slope of earth turned mud and sliding now burying me take the house swallow the town your kids your life *not her!* I hear her voice now from way up on the surface shrieking God I know what they're doing I can't stand it I shouldn't have called I should've just let them kill me don't they know one shock too many and my heart bursts that's it end *fin* I'm free I didn't need to call Joanne I'm sorry so sorry I brought you into the trap *goddamn them* . . .

Hands now on my face going for my throat ripping into me burning fire arcing across my limbs and I need to go deeper into blackness down into the hood just further and it goes away it does they never kill me they never do it just will go like this and on until it doesn't until . . .

Breathe and breathe and breathe.

It's what you do after the twister has left. When you've been shipwrecked and lie on the beach seven-eighths dead with the cold waves washing you and your skull feels like cracked eggshells your skin tissue paper guts a mudslide trees upon houses and cattle corpses and dead cars and mud, mostly mud. . . . I open my eyes and for several heartbeats cannot comprehend what reality this is. Slowly the world returns. I'm wrapped stiff in bedsheets. Joanne is holding a warm cloth on my head. My tongue feels swollen, eyes beaten, pores exhausted. It's morning. Which morning? Sometimes I find myself days later. I was doing so well. Wasn't I doing well?

Joanne unwraps me, cleans me gently, draws a hot bath. I hobble out of bed, soak in the water, sip hot lemon-and-honey tea with the lights off. "When did you get here?" I ask softly.

"That night," she says. "I should've come when you called."

"I told you not to."

"Yes."

Soft music in the background. My eyes are so sore, but I don't want to close them. I lose so much when I do.

This is how it is after a twister: you're thankful to be breathing still. You don't know how you survived. It's internal, a savage storm that comes from nowhere, goes to nowhere . . . A virus injected with all the other drugs. The Kartouf virus. It shifts, lurks in my organs, my brain cells. Attacks now and again just to let me know: *you never really escaped*. I'm not free. I will be destroyed, any time they choose.

This is what terror is all about.

The water turns cool and I reheat it, turns cool and I reheat. Just want to stay here. One breath at a time. Scrambled eggs and more tea. Served in the bath. Sometimes months go by with nothing. Just the threat, the knowledge. The Kartouf is still inside me.

I get out finally and dry off, pat the towel gently against my aching skin. On with my thick robe. Joanne tells me to sleep, but I refuse. Gently. The only way I can now. Quite a blue sky. She tells me it's cooler, that the storm brought in a breath of autumn.

"What day is it?"

"Thursday."

I sort through the lint in my brain. The twister hit on Tuesday night.

The tears start. Everyone says I need to cry them. But two years later – two fucking years later? Do I still need to cry them? How long does this go on for? I cry the tears and then head back to my computer. Thursday! What time is it? 4:02. It couldn't be morning, it's too light. All that traffic on the bridges. It's Thursday fucking afternoon.

"What happened?" I call to Joanne. "Did anything happen while I was out?"

I like that word, *out*. It sounds so inoffensive.

"You need to rest, Bill."

"I know. I have been. Did anything happen?" This computer takes so long to boot up.

"Clinton bombed terrorist sites in Afghanistan and Sudan," she says. "It's classic wag the dog."

"Oh, for God's sakes!" I have a friend in Sudan. "Was it Khartoum?" This computer!

"I think so." She tells me the announcement came just as Monica Lewinsky was going in to testify again. And what she says next freezes my blood.

"There was one other thing. I think you should just go to bed, but I know you won't, so I'll tell you. Minitzh was assassinated last night. The whole of Santa Irene has been turned upside down. The phone's been ringing off the hook for you. I finally just turned it off. Bill?"

Breathe and breathe and breathe. Sometimes it's all you can do.

3

A reporter from the BBC calls, asking for a reaction. I tell him I'm like everybody else, stunned. CNN broadcasts a five-minute segment of amateur video of riots in the capital: blurry colour shots of a crowd overturning a bus and then setting it ablaze, of distant troops in ragged green firing at unknown targets, of a dog writhing and yelping in a muddy backstreet. That's it – on to Yeltsin overturning his cabinet and Angola sending soldiers into the Congo. The South Asia desk at Foreign Affairs doesn't know what's happening – who murdered Minitzh, what the army is doing, whether the Kartouf is behind it or how they're reacting, who will take over. The mission in Santa Irene was closed two years ago after they got me home safely.

Another reporter calls from CBC Radio. "Mr. Burridge, how do you feel when you hear that the country where you suffered so much is now in the throes of such confusion?"

"I'm concerned for people, obviously," I say.

"Do you fear that the rebel Kartouf, the group that kidnapped and tortured you, could now be on the verge of taking power in Santa Irene?"

"It's unlikely, I think, that the Kartouf would be in a position to take power. They really are a raggedy force. Their support is in the villages, which have been decimated. In the capital there's no love for the Kartouf, and the military is the real power. There could well be a struggle going on now within the army and some new strongman will emerge. We'll have to see."

"Reports are reaching us today from AP and other sources that the 'strongman' could actually be a woman, Suli Nylioko. What can you tell us about her?"

The question takes me by surprise, and my pause turns into a ponderous radio silence.

"Mr. Burridge?"

"Suli Nylioko," I say, "is the widow of the former leader of the Democratic Coalition, which was banned in the early 1980s. Her husband, Jono, was shot at the airport after being given a promise of safe passage from General Minitzh. Suli and her children were allowed to leave. The family was very wealthy, although I don't know how much money they were able to take out of the country. She studied at Oxford for a time. I had no idea she was back in the country."

"So she is like an Aung San Suu Kyi?" the interviewer asks.

"Or a Corazon Aquino," I say. "Or perhaps a Benazir Bhutto or Winnie Mandela."

"That's quite a range of possibilities."

"We'll have to see," I say.

There are more questions to which I give careful, not very informed answers. The urgency of it is somehow satisfying, though; it takes me away from thrashing about in my own personal swamp. Then just as I have this thought she asks the inevitable.

"Since returning from your captivity two years ago, Mr. Burridge, you've managed to build a human-rights organization that has won a strong international reputation. You've won the Olof Palme Award and the Sakharov Prize for Freedom of Thought, among others. But in your book you indicate what a tremendous personal price you've paid. How are you faring these days? Have the ghosts of your ordeal been put to rest, or does the new uncertainty in Santa Irene bring them back to life?"

My sigh at the question is audible, I'm sure, across thousands of kilometres. Another ponderous radio silence.

"I'm sorry, Mr. Burridge, if that's too personal a question. You don't have to –"

I try not to sound too impatient. "What I tend to say is this: On a good day, I work too hard to think about it. On a bad day, I haven't worked hard enough."

We say our goodbyes and I sit for a moment in silence. Then Joanne brings me toast and mushroom soup, and I find *The Islander* on the Internet. The coverage is remarkably detailed – a good sign that no one at the top is in enough control to muzzle the press.

RIOTS IN WELANTO

20 August 1998
Hulinga Kaliotu

Thousands of rioters and looters took to the streets of Welanto last night, burning large sections of the shantytown to the ground and looting shops and stalls. Reports also say many daughters were raped by roaming packs of police who were supposed to be protecting residents.

No one knows what set off the riots. One man who was taking cover in a ditch said that a mob had been turned away from Seaside Heights by private armies and so had vented their anger against their own neighbourhood.

A long line of limousines could be seen through most of the night heading for the airport, which remains closed today. According to foreign news reports, some of Santa Irene's wealthiest citizens spent the night on benches in the airport lounge, waiting for clearance to leave the country.

There were no confirmed reports of casualties from the latest Welanto riots. Riots yesterday killed 23 people and injured some 350 more, according to local hospitals.

Another article focuses on Suli Nylioko.

SULI DENIES CHARGES, CALLS FOR CALM

20 August 1998
Dorut Kul

Freedom Party leader Suli Nylioko, who remained in hiding last night, issued a statement through Island Radio that she had no part in the assassination of President General Linga Minitzh. She also called for calm and demanded the military rein in its own soldiers who are causing so much destruction in the capital.

"I don't know who is responsible for this murder. My sympathies are for the family of the General and my hope is that the assassins will be brought to justice. But there have been so many other unsolved murders that justice has become a stranger on this island. Do we want to invite her back? Or let fires of hatred consume us? It is time now for calm, for proper elections, and for responsible, peace-loving people to get at the truth and set us to healing."

Suli returned to Santa Irene last year to manage her family's estates. She was arrested briefly in February for filing registration papers for the Freedom Party, but was let out on bail pending trial. Till now she has refrained from comment on national affairs, saying that she wished to live peacefully and rebuild her family. However, some sources say she has been using her time to build party support among influential academics, human-rights activists, and union leaders.

A photo shows a tank with ragged children playing all over it while a soldier discusses something with an old man. The soldier's machine-gun is slung lazily over his shoulder and the chinstrap of his helmet is undone; the old man has barely enough clothes to cover his stick-like limbs. The caption reads, *Out of gas!*

SECURITY FAILURE BLAMED

20 August 1998
Islander staff

Military sources have blamed a security lapse among the president's elite personal guard for the assassination of President General Linga Minitzh, according to unconfirmed reports.

The sources say that lax security allowed the bakery truck to pull alongside the presidential compound and self-detonate as the president was leaving for a meeting. No body has yet been found among the bakery truck rubble and a transmitter device discovered near the scene indicates a remote-controlled attack.

Officials have so far issued no statements.

Sources close to the military indicate that there is a strong possibility that terrorists infiltrated the president's personal guard. Otherwise they would not have known precisely when to attack or have been able to deliver the truck safely into the presidential compound. The president frequently changed schedules and boasted as late as last week that terrorists had been routed on the island.

The Kartouf has been widely suspected in the attack but so far has claimed no responsibility.

Further down the screen is an unsigned editorial that would have brought troops into the newspaper office if it had been published while Minitzh was alive.

WHILE THE RATS FLEE

There is something at once appalling and fascinating about watching the *lumito*'s desperate scramble to escape their native land now that their friend and protector has been killed. To see them in their Pierre Cardin suits and Versace dresses herding fat, spoiled, scared children down the long, jammed corridors of Minitzh Freedom and Prosperity International Airport, tugging at overstuffed luggage, fighting with others over trolleys and bench space, waving now near-worthless 100,000 loros notes at anyone who might be of help.

No law, decree, or regulation has been passed, yet somehow the soldiers guarding the checkpoints along the Airport Driveway know to turn away anyone not in a private limousine, anyone not abandoning a Seaside Heights property or significant business holdings – in short, anyone who was not a personal friend or relative of the dear departed leader.

Officially all flights have been suspended, no tickets are being issued, and yet now and again, according to no known or published schedule, a plane does lift off for Hong Kong, Manila, or Bangkok. Who is authorizing these flights? Who decides who gets on? What price has been paid?

And where is Vice-President Barios? Why hasn't he stepped into the breach to assume his duties? The leadership vacuum has spawned so many rumours – that Barios has left on his private yacht, is drinking himself to death in the bowels of the Pink Palace, has already fled to Geneva to oversee the millions siphoned into secret accounts.

Another rumour was confirmed by a close relative of Minitzh: that the important "meeting" the president was headed for before his fateful encounter was actually a tryst with his favourite prostitute Gloriala, who can now be seen wailing in the VIP lounge of Freedom and Prosperity International. She looks a mess, and so do we all.

I read through every story, download, catalogue, check for new articles. Late in the afternoon Joanne drags me from the computer and we walk slowly along the shore of the Ottawa River, past the Rideau Canal locks to the bottom of Parliament Hill. It's a strange place of near-solitude beneath the seat of power – from a certain perspective the river looks as wild and fresh as it must have appeared to Champlain when he first poked his canoe past this point.

Joanne holds my arm and I feel like an eighty-year-old invalid. How many regular programs have I started? Weights, treadmill, rowing machine, bike, martial arts, swimming. A long walk every morning. I understand now why old people give up. To be this feeble, to know you can't push very hard. If

I hadn't been in such good shape before my abduction, I never would have survived. I would've checked out early and saved myself a lot of grief and pain.

Slowly walking, these quiet non-conversations.

"I think you should go see Wu," she says. Pleasantly. A policeman rides by on a bicycle and strains his head back to look at her, so radiant in plain jeans and an oversized T-shirt. She has too much life. That's it. I have too little, so just being with her I'm soaking some of it in. But not enough. I know in my head that Joanne is extraordinary; my body feels nothing. Me and my limp dead rat. What could be sadder? My batteries were drained close to zero and even now the lights are on but the engine won't turn over.

Wu is another with too much life. If I could, I'd hire him to treat just me. But he won't give up his practice. Good for him. I've turned into such a greedy bastard. I meant to go see him more often. But somehow the work took over.

"Yes," I say. "Maybe tomorrow."

"Maybe right now," Joanne says.

"I should check the news."

"The news will be there when you get back."

"Yes, but a lot has happened just while we've been walking."

"It isn't dawn yet in Santa Irene."

"But around the world. I need to read my e-mails. There was a new one from Jaswant. And I think Ravi sent me something about T.J.'s cousin –"

"It'll all be there when you get back."

"And I didn't write my son . . ."

She's led me into a trap. We cut up the steps to the Supreme Court parking lot and a taxi is waiting. She has already made an appointment with Wu. In ten minutes we're in his tiny, incense-laden waiting room.

"Yes, harro, Missa Burridge? How-you?" Wu is, as always, cheery, calm, and gentle. He seems to get younger every time I see him.

"Not so good, Wu. I've had some setbacks."

"You practise to you breathing, uh-huh?"

"Sometimes," I say. "When I can."

"Animulse?"

"When I can," I tell him, which he understands to mean no, I haven't practised my animals. There are twelve of them; I've learned only six.

"First animulse," he says. "Then treatment."

We head into his studio. Wu teaches *qigong* and martial arts to a very few students, usually other instructors in town. The studio is for his own practice. He told me about coming from Taiwan fifteen years ago, how he wanted to continue practising outside for the fresh air, the natural energy of the sun and earth. But then November turned to December and there were no warm sea breezes in this cold town. Hence the studio.

We warm up gently with breathing, stretching, and shaking exercises, the sort of thing I need to do every morning and every evening but can't seem to find the discipline. Doing them beside Wu I feel a tingle and warmth and general blanket of well-being that I never feel when I try it alone. The energy must be coming from him.

"Dragon," he says, standing back and gesturing to me. I assume my ready position, a cat stance: weight on my right foot, left toe pointed in slightly, hands open near my hips, as relaxed as I can manage. Then I lunge forward, my fingers aimed at an imaginary neck.

"Turn you heel!" he says, and I do it again and then on the other side. Then he stands opposite me and launches a slow punch at my face. I intercept it with my forearms as I lunge, turn him as I turn my heel.

"Slowly-slow. Relax. Keep going!"

The "keep going" part is me jerking his arm, then thrusting towards his neck again as I step back. These are nasty fighting techniques, these animals. The *lun*, a mythical creature with the body of a cow, the scales of a fish, and the head of a lion, intercepts a punch, snaps the arm, then chokes the neck as the victim falls forward. The *pang*, a great bird, snaps the arm in a different direction, chops the throat, then pecks the side of the neck when the victim tries to defend himself. The *mandarin*, a little bird, stops a low, hooking punch, whirls the arm around, and strikes twice at the neck. The snake cracks the neck and attacks from below; the ape breaks the arm then shudders the body with a terrible spasm. They're all part of *liu he ba fa*, water-boxing, which Wu says is a gentle but effective system of self-defence, especially good for overcoming opponents who are stronger, and for building internal energy. The theory is good and I enjoy practising with Wu, but the details are overwhelming: back straight, bum in, chin tucked, tongue on the roof of the mouth, weight distributed through the heel, elbows out, turn the heel, catch the arm with the side of the forearm, not the wrist or hand. Do this not that, that not this.

"For confiden. In case attack again!"

I think Wu gets a certain pleasure out of turning me into a pretzel while he shows me the various applications. It *is* for my confidence, but I can't think I'll ever be attacked again the way that I was. It was a once-in-a-lifetime event. For no good reason either. I was in the wrong place at the wrong time and I learned what none of us needs to know for sanity or happiness: how merciless and harrowing the universe can be. Once you know you can't stop knowing. You work and work but in the end you still know.

For a warm-down we do more breathing exercises, which Wu claims will restore my "manlihood and vigour." In one I swallow my breath and hold it for up to a minute while gently pushing it down to my testicles, then recuperate with bellows breathing before trying again. In another I imagine I'm pulling up my lifeforce from my sperm – what sperm? I think – and channelling it up my spine, into my head, then down through my nose, throat, and chest to circle my navel. Any energy flow is subtle at best, and probably all in my hopes anyway. I really would like to believe in Wu, in the possibility of using dormant lifeforce for revitalization. But I know that as soon as I leave his office my resolve will fall away. He talks about tapping into the energy of the universe. I feel like my molecules were ripped apart by unimaginable emptiness and cold.

The final part of my visit, the real reason for seeing him, is Wu's massage. This is what most people come for: the way his gentle fingers find and soothe every knot, stimulate those magical points in the neck and shoulders, down the arms and the spine, in the legs and feet. More and more I'm convinced that not only is he tweaking my feeble points, he's pouring his own energy into me. When he rubs my scalp the pressure eases; when he presses his thumbs along the arches of my feet heat rushes through my body. I could stay for hours, but the feeling is of timelessness, as if he has administered a drug to liquify the moment and stretch it beyond where it should be.

I hate to leave a session with Wu. I feel so sad, almost bereft. He brings me within close memory of what normal is supposed to feel like.

"Practise animulse. *Breathe*. Every day. Twice, three times!"

Yes, yes, I tell him. I'll breathe at least twice every day.

—

35

Joanne pays him, has a taxi waiting for us. I don't carry money any more, hardly do anything on my own – don't feed myself, don't shop, don't make my own appointments.

"Someday I'll buy my own diapers," I tell Joanne, and she laughs so beautifully, rich as water from a winter melt. I'd swear she can read my mind sometimes, knows all the inner dialogue that has led to a particular statement or idea. It's a wonderful thought, but turns sour even as we ride through quiet backstreets. She's as desirable as a woman could be, and here I am trapped in this deadwood body, unresonating, dying of cold and fear.

Sinking. Sadness. This always happens after Wu. I'm tired of this aching, this lack of fixative. There's no starch in life any more, nothing keeps its shape; it melts in my hands, press it as I might. I try to do the breathing. There was something there when Wu was beside me. Now my body is wooden and lost. I can't keep a good feeling in place except with the most crushing concentration. The shit of the world is my proper domain. Bombs and torture and *coups d'état*, dogs writhing in the street in far-off lands most people don't care about. These things stay fixed: régimes are replaced but men still get hung by their arms in the airplane position; international declarations are signed but banned groups are still hunted down; reports are published but mothers who ask about their sons in detention are still drawn aside and raped. Here is my permanence: sadness, disaster, impotence, indignation. They belong to me. They look like they must lead to something else, something better, but they never do. They stay fixed while everything else crumbles.

Softly, I think. Go softly. This is just a moment's blackness.

Joanne makes me dinner while I stare stonily out my apartment windows at the dark clouds of August. Salmon, with baked potatoes and fresh corn, cut off the cob for me because of my dentures. She hasn't served any for herself and I feel put out. She's going to leave. She gets paid for certain hours but she doesn't have to abandon me. She must sense my depression. It's particularly bad tonight. She's a smart woman. But she wants to escape me. Well, let her go. I don't need her. I'll be fine.

"If it's all right," she says, gathering her sweater, "I said I'd meet some people for dinner. You've got my number?"

"Yes, fine," I snap. The salmon is undercooked. What's she trying to do, poison me?

"I'll stay if you like."

"No. Go!" I say, not looking at her. She can't stand being with me. Who can blame her? I'm such a stupid, suffering, helpless bag of bones. Live your life. Grasp it. Don't let the drowning pull you under.

"I'll check up on you later."

"No. I'm fine." I put my cutlery down on the plate and the noise resounds like a metal garbage can clattering in an alley.

"You should try to get some sleep. You usually sleep well after Wu."

Like fuck I do. I'm usually depressed as hell after Wu.

"I'll be fine," I say, picking at my salmon again.

When she leaves I turn on my computer, but *The Islander* is still carrying today's paper even though they're well into tomorrow by now. Bloody incompetents! It strikes me as personal somehow – they're so inefficient that they can't post their news when the whole rest of the world is waiting for it and it's the only thing I personally want to read. What am I supposed to do now? A country is crumbling and it isn't being covered. Two other papers from Santa Irene have Web sites but they're in Kuantij, and anyway they haven't even posted today's paper yet, much less tomorrow's. Jesus!

—

I click onto my e-mail and wait, impatiently, for the messages to appear. But instead of messages I get a little screen apologizing: *SmartMail is unavailable. Try again later.* Unbelievable. I wait several seconds and click again, again, again. *SmartMail is unavailable.* I try again. I wait and I try and I wait and I can't believe it. The whole fucking world is going to shit. Everything I touch. I click again. Standing now. *SmartMail is unavailable.* Right. *Try again later.* Later. Later. Later!

It really doesn't take much to push a computer screen off a desk. A little shove will do it. Hardly anything. A gesture of impatience. Then the screen falls on the hardwood floor. If the cables are short, like mine, the computer starts to fall as well, then goes completely off when I decide to help it on its way. They bounce and roll badly and the screen goes black when the connections rip.

Then the phone rings. It sounds like an alarm. I stare in disbelief at what I've done. The phone rings and rings and I'll be damned if I'll answer it. The machine is supposed to pick it up after four rings, but of course being mine it malfunctions. Ringing, ringing, ringing. I have this sudden vision of computer police spying on me through the modem and knowing exactly what I've done to an innocent piece of electronics.

I grab the damn phone. "*Yes!*"

No answer. Of course not.

"Bill?"

"*Yes!*"

"Bill you don't have to yell. It's me."

Me. I don't know who *me* is. I don't have a fucking clue. Why don't people –?

"Bill, are you all right?"

"I'm fine." It's my wife, Maryse. I knew I shouldn't have picked up the phone.

"Bill, I'm calling because Patrick had a bit of an accident. It's nothing to get too upset about. He was hit by a car this afternoon –"

"*What?*"

"He was on his skateboard, but it really isn't serious. The car had slowed down. He bruised his shoulder . . ."

"*What hospital is he in?*"

". . . and he suffered a slight concussion."

"*Oh, Jesus! Can you not keep an eye –*"

"I didn't call you right away because I knew you'd react like this."

"Like WHAT? *How am I reacting?*"

She doesn't answer. I picture her standing with both hands on the phone, her shoulders shaking.

"He's staying overnight at the children's hospital. I know he'd love a visit but I think you should bring Joanne if you're going to come tonight."

"*Are you telling me that I can't see my son at hospital? Where the hell do you –?*"

"Bill," she says, and something gets through. I close my eyes and grip the edge of the table. "It's just me, Bill. He really is all right. But if you want to see him, bring Joanne."

4

"It looks like a refugee camp in here," Joanne says softly as we walk into the hospital lobby. She's right. There's an impressive mix of families here: African, Middle Eastern, East European, South Asian. A tiny Chinese-looking boy with tear-puffed eyes holds his arm and looks at us dully. A tall, deeply black woman in Muslim dress cradles a sleeping child. A Caucasian family – Russians? Czechs? – huddles around a chessboard.

I've yanked her from her dinner and friends, the tyranny of the cellphone. Not to mention the tyranny of the needy.

The nurse directs us to another nurse who takes us to Patrick's room. Maryse leans against the wall by the door and goes immediately to Joanne when she sees us. Standing apart, I catch strands of the discussion.

". . . just out the door for a moment . . . the tires squealed . . . told him to be careful . . ."

They're nearly the same height, which surprises me – Joanne seems too tall. Maryse got some sun at her parents' cottage, is looking healthier than she was before. When did I see her last? It must be two or three months. In the spring. Her hair so white, still a shock. My legacy.

While they talk I slip into the room and see Patrick sleeping, a bandage around his head. Otherwise no scrapes and bruises. A picture of serenity. He's clutching his black, ragged teddy bear. Maryse has let his curls grow quite long; they're matted against the side of his cheek.

I need to say something to Maryse. Something small and kind and uncutting. It's hard when all the knives have been sharpened from the separation. I needed a nurse and she couldn't be one and had a hard enough time dealing with her own and Patrick's nightmares, waking and otherwise.

She took care of Patrick while I was kidnapped, told him gentle stories and rubbed his temples and held him in the middle of the night. Then later, when I was back and it was all supposed to be so happy, she took him those several times to the hospital to see me in my self-inflicted agony. Where was I? Teaching him how to throw a football? Quizzing him on his spelling? Responding to his e-mail messages? All the time I was away she built me up in his imagination and then when they wheeled me off the plane I wasn't the hero he expected, I was a fuck-up and a coward. I could barely stand.

She finally said the words. That last time I was leaving the hospital. "I don't think you should come home, Bill." Her eyes strained, her thumbnail pressing into the white of her fist. I know what's it's like to do whatever you have to do. I could see it in her. "We need a separation for a time. I'm not helping you and we are tearing ourselves apart. If we go on like this none of us will survive it."

Saving her child. Cutting me loose. I remember the burn of rejection, the surprising gust of relief.

She saved all our lives. And now I need to say something nice, non-confrontational. *He's beautiful, Maryse. You're doing a good job with him. You look well.*

I step back out into the hall, the phrases labouring in my cobwebbed brain as if I were an adolescent trying to ask for a date. *You look well. He's beautiful, Maryse. You're doing a good job.*

Maryse and Joanne stop talking when I approach. Maybe it's the dull light, but Maryse's skin still looks like that of a twenty-year-old. Her eyes are as dark as ever, but harder somehow, on the edge of attack. The kind phrases fall out of my head. I need knives. It's a matter of self-preservation.

"I bet he wasn't even wearing a helmet," I say bitterly.

"Oh, Bill –"

"Aren't there parks for skateboarding? You probably should just make a rule with him –"

The dark eyes look down at her lace-up boots. At any moment the points might come right up into my groin.

"Did this driver give a statement? Are we suing? You probably didn't even get the licence number."

"*You just fuck yourself,*" she hisses, then her boots click-click down the hall.

"That was accomplished," Joanne says, and I nearly light into her as well. But something holds me back – some small thread of sanity remaining in my ugly mind.

"*What kind of parent –?*" I start, but she touches my shoulder and the thought evaporates.

"*Save it,*" she says. "Is Patrick awake?"

She goes in to see him and I stand in the hall, feeling like a tree somehow engulfed by miles of ocean. What did I do? It's not my fault. It's not my fucking fault. Any father called to the hospital in the middle of the night to see his son . . .

"He's a treasure," she says, tiptoeing out. "He looks like an angel."

Outside, waiting for the taxi, I say, "Maybe you could write her a note." She laughs, not a happy sound, but sudden and harsh, like cars colliding.

"All right," I say. "*I'll* write her a note. You just tell me what to say to make everything better. Some little graceful card. So she'll read it and know I was fucking tortured within an inch of my life and that inch is all I've got left and it's not much to work with. I've done a bloody good job."

"That would make a *handsome* card," she says.

"Yes," I say. "*Handsome*. It would fix everything, wouldn't it?"

"She'd come running back to you. Romantics the world over would flock to you for advice."

Breathe and breathe and breathe. How much longer do I want to put up with this? I have work to do. I can't let myself get sidetracked by these petty, insignificant . . . these *distractions*. They're fine for everybody else who has more than one inch of life left to work with. But not for me. I have to look out for me.

No one else will.

In the taxi. I watch the passing streetlights, headlights, donut-shop fluorescence all poking impotently into the black of this night. The driver is from Lebanon. His smudged photo ID makes him look like a drug smuggler. Husayn Awada. Before long Joanne has got him to tell us his life story. He came to Canada in 1982 in the wake of the Israeli invasion. He was an engineer in Beirut; in Canada he's been a baker, waiter, pizza deliveryman, school janitor, Christmas-tree salesman, and, mostly, a taxi driver. He has three grown sons, all engineers, and one daughter, now married with twins. His wife runs a restaurant. Neither of them has taken a vacation in sixteen years.

"The winter was the worst thing about Canada. When we arrived it was about this time of the year, not too bad, we said we'd be all right. Then it got cooler and we said it wasn't so bad as we'd heard. Then the snow came and the ice and it never stopped. It just kept building up. My wife would look out the window and say, 'I won't go out today. It'll get better tomorrow.' Then tomorrow it would be worse and we'd say, 'How does anybody *live* here?' We still say that. This winter, I swear, if I can make some money, we're going to Florida. That's it!"

If I can make some money. It's a nice line and Joanne tips him almost as much as the cost of the ride.

"Thank you," I say to her at the door of my building.

"Not at all," she says, waving goodbye to Husayn.

"No, I mean it. I'd be lost without you. I'm sure you know it. I'd be in my grave."

"Maybe not."

"No. Maybe I'd be an unmarked body without a grave. Put to death by my relatives. A mercy killing."

"I won't be here forever," she says carefully, and just like that the night turns cold, I can feel winter slipping under our guard.

"Are you telling me something, Joanne?"

"I'm not the kind of nurse who waits around on cancer wards while people wilt and die," she says. "I'll treat people at their worst, fix 'em up, then ship 'em out. You know? Vaccinate the kids. Give them a week of steady food, water to wash with, a roof over their heads. It's amazing to see them bloom. That's what I live for. The big hit. Some die, it's inevitable, but if there's no hope then I don't want any part of it."

"So I'm hopeless, is that it? You want out?"

"Some things are beyond my control," she says. "I don't want you thinking that I'm going to dedicate the rest of my life to –"

"What things? What's beyond your control?"

"I have a life, Bill. I have a family, I have elderly parents, my mother is ill. She has throat cancer. Right now I'm doing the very best I can for you. I just hope I'm not working so hard you figure you don't have to do anything."

Ah. The point is made. This is a buck-up speech. I'd best buck up. Ultimately it's up to me. No one else can do it. I have to decide I *want* to get better. Moreover, I should be further along. It's been two years. Lots of water under the bridge. Bad things happen, but people get on with their lives. Think of the Canadian POWs starved by the Japanese in World War Two. Some of them came back. They lived their lives. There are rapes, beatings, attacks, mutilations happening every moment of every day. I was lucky, I escaped. No limbs lost. Faculties intact. It could've been worse. I have medical treatment. My condition is manageable. People look up to me.

This speech rattles fully formed in my mind. I've been over every part of it endlessly before. Joanne says one or two sentences and the self-flagellation begins. It'll go on for days if I don't stop it.

"You're right," I tell her. "I have to help myself." And I do. I help myself up to my own apartment. I help my computer back onto the desk and then I help it off again to see whether it rolls any farther if I push it harder. It's a scientific experiment. Gravity pulls on us all, but does it pull harder if we're kicked or if we're pushed? How hard does it pull if the desk itself is kicked or pushed? What does gravity do to other household items if they're liberated from their positions of

—

rest? Which way do dishes bounce if flung against a wall? How much plaster is liberated if struck by the edge of a plate? The flat of a bowl? Why do glasses shatter most easily against hard surfaces as opposed to soft?

Here's a helpful experiment. Fill your bathtub with household appliances and then turn on the water. Do microwave ovens float? How long will a toaster bob before settling on the bottom? What if the Yangtze River overflowed your bathroom right now? Where would the water go? Down the hallway? Into the bedroom? How wet will the carpet get before the water gets bored and must flow elsewhere? Down, down to the point of least resistance. Study the properties of water, how smooth, gentle, flexible it is. Abuse it all you want. Boil the hell out of it, it comes back in fine rain. Freeze it all to hell, it scars and cracks and breaks, then melts and flows again good as new. Beat it with your hands again and again. No harm; it becomes a game. Child's play. Poison it and you'll poison yourself the next time you drink, and then when you pass urine the water will be okay again, back to normal, right as rain.

First comes rain, then thunder. Regular as the pounding on a door. "It's okay!" I call. They want to come in but I tell them it's okay. I just had a little flood. I've turned the water off.

Okay.

I say the word again and again. Through the door. *Okay. Okay.* No, you don't have to come in. It's all under control. It's *okay.*

They say they're going to call Joanne. Yes, *okay.* Joanne is *okay.* Everybody, we're all *okay.*

I find a spot by the windows, near where the desk used to be. It's not too wet. There's just enough room to do some animals. A man has to be able to defend himself. *Dragon.* Lunge for the neck, pull on the arm, attack the neck again.

Both sides. You might get attacked on the other side. Back straight, bum and chin tucked in, rounded shoulders, elbows out. A cat stance. Why does the dragon use a cat stance? A question for Wu. Lunge and pull, lunge again. Now *lun*. Intercept the blow. Break the arm and pull down. Choke the neck as he falls towards you.

Pang, *mandarin*, snake, and ape. All my animals. I do them again and again, my feet going squish-squish on the carpet. There's going to be hell to pay.

Dragon, *lun*, *pang*, *mandarin*, snake, and ape. Both sides. Again and again and again. It beats thinking. It brings the night along. Slowly. Squish after squish. The time is liquid but it's flowing. Slowly at first, then quicker, like sweat. Elbows out, turn the hips, don't lean too much on the knee. Dragon, *lun*, *pang*, *mandarin*, snake, and ape. Intercept the punch and break the arm. Thrust and jerk. One side and another. Eyes on the horizon. See everything at once but not in detail. The devil's in the details.

At four in the morning I drink long from the tap, gingerly step around the shards of kitchen casualties. Breathing and breathing. When you do the animals for a long time a warmth takes over your body. It's almost as if Wu is standing next to me. This is the first time I've felt this on my own. I find my squishy spot again and fall into more practice. The less thinking I do the better off I seem to be. Dragon, *lun*, *pang*, *mandarin*, snake, and ape. Break the arm and strike the neck. Stay relaxed. If there is danger most of all. Your body can interpret the energy coming at you, will know in the moment exactly what to do. But only if you stay relaxed.

At five in the morning I start picking up pieces of glass. I unhook the trash bucket from inside the kitchen cupboard and traverse the apartment on my hands and knees. When the bucket is full I find a box and when the box is full I use a double-strength brown paper bag. Then I drain the tub and mop the remaining water from the bathroom, leaving the appliances to drip dry. Joanne will be so happy to see what I've done. I've been making so much progress!

When she comes in I've nearly got everything back in order. There's a terrible shortage of dishes, of course, and the baseboards betray a recent flood mark, and the place smells awful. And I haven't righted the desk yet.

"What happened here?" she asks, quite restrained, I think, considering.

"I'm going to need a new computer," I say. "This one just can't fly."

"You're right there," she says, surveying the trash bucket, box, and bag, the dripping appliances, the sorry computer. "I thought Hurricane Bonnie was heading for the Carolinas."

I get to my feet. "Cato, attack!" I command.

"You must be joking."

"No, I'm serious. I've been practising most of the night. Attack me. Anything you want to do."

"I am not Cato. I'm your nurse!" She comes at me anyway, a big sick grin on her face. I take my cat stance. Relax, relax . . .

In an instant she whirls a wet cushion off the sofa and launches it at my head. I have no defence except to duck quickly, by which time she's launched the second cushion straight into my midsection. I fall in a heap, coughing, sputtering.

"Oh, Jesus!" she says, kneeling beside me. "Are you all right?"

I cough some more, slowly get to my feet. "I haven't learned the wet-cushion defence yet," I say. "It must be one of the six missing animals."

"Must be," she says.

—

I go back to poking the computer. She looks through the kitchen for a while, then steps back out. "So, I take it breakfast will be out this morning?" she says.

"Just punch me slowly," I say. "With your left hand."

"My left hand?"

"Just do it."

The fist comes at me slowly. I intercept, bend it against itself, clamp my fingers around her neck as she falls towards me.

"How's this for better?" I ask. "I'm getting better, right?"

"Write to your wife," she says when I've let her go.

5

TINTO DECLARES MARTIAL LAW

23 August 1998
Islander staff

Former Interior Minister Tinto Delapango, cousin of deceased President General Linga Minitzh, has seized power and declared martial law. In a brief statement Tinto also announced that Vice-President Barios was no longer in the country and that key elements of the armed forces have sworn allegiance to his rule. "Stability is now at hand and all are required to give their full co-operation as I bring the situation under control."

Tinto's statement comes among increasing rumours that the armed forces is split, with President General Minitzh's elite Third Battalion backing Armed Forces Chief Mende Kul, while the vice-president's naval units are said to favour the flamboyant Tinto.

Opposition leader Suli Nylioko stated that if either Tinto or Kul seize power "there will be a bloodbath to make Minitzh look like a saint."

"We have had enough dictatorship. We have had enough killing and looting and government corruption. How can the rest of the world have faith in us if we do this again to ourselves?"

Under the terms of Tinto's martial law, which according to the statement comes into effect immediately, police and armed forces personnel have the right to shoot looters or suspicious figures on sight, to detain suspects without trial or access to a magistrate for up to 48 weeks, and to search homes and businesses without warrants or notice. A curfew is also in effect from 6 p.m. to 8 a.m. in the capital. Anyone breaking the curfew could be shot on sight.

Tinto was not on hand to deliver his proclamation but rather announced it through simultaneous fax transmission to national news offices.

The photograph of Tinto shows up narrow and blurred on screen, a wiry man with a downturned mouth, his eyes hidden behind dark shades.

WELANTO ABLAZE

23 August 1998
Hulinga Kaliotu

For the third straight day fires raged through the shanty-town of Welanto. Volunteer firemen were again turned away by gangs armed with bottles, sticks, and *toragu* blades. In all

76 people have been killed and some 600 injured in Welanto in the crisis since the assassination of President General Linga Minitzh.

According to eyewitness reports, packs of police again entered homes and raped mothers and daughters. Several bodies could be seen lying in the backstreets. Rain last night dampened many of the fires but did not put them out. Street gangs reset the fires this morning, and so far police have done nothing to stop them.

Local residents have started calling the police "Tinto's cocks" and confronting them with homemade weapons. One man, who could not be identified, said he had fought a policeman off his wife's back by hitting him across the shoulders with a bamboo pole.

"He drew his pistol out. I don't know why he didn't shoot me."

So far the announcement of Tinto's martial law has done nothing to stop the rioting in Welanto. "We need the army," one local resident said. "We need someone to stop the killing."

CNN has no coverage – it's economic chaos in Russia and falling markets worldwide, and a special segment on the coming anniversary of the death of Diana. I flip open my e-mail.

Dear Bill Burridge,

I am writing to you now to thank you. I was in interrogation for three hours when word arrived that I was to be let go. I pressed them – let go because of my innocence? No answer. But my lawyer Mr. I.K. Singh told me that there was high-level foreign intervention, and for that I thank you.

Three hours with the Punjab police is plenty enough. I know that you know what pleasantries they engage in, so there is no need to reiterate them here. That Sikhs can do this to other Sikhs sorrows my heart immeasurably. But I must remind myself they are not true Sikhs. True Sikhs do not fight on the side of injustice.

I thank you and my family thanks you.

In peace, Jaswant Kashmir Singh

A victory! I let the moment shine, then flip through other disasters: a Catholic priest has disappeared in Guangzhou, probably detained for running an underground church; there's a new outbreak of riots against ethnic Chinese in central Java; in Kosovo, Albanians are disappearing at the hands of Serb police while Serbs, Roma, and Albanians are being abducted by the Kosovo Liberation Army.

Derrick calls then from somewhere in Algonquin Park. "Did you read *The Islander* today?" he asks.

"Derrick, you're on holiday."

"It doesn't matter. Did you read it?"

"Of course I read it."

"But just now –"

"Are you in a canoe or something Derrick?"

"I'm on dry land. Don't worry about me. Just read the news."

I flip over to the *Islander* site.

SULI HOLDS MASSIVE RALLY
BETWEEN TWO ARMIES

23 August 1998
Dorut Kul

Freedom Party leader Suli Nylioko is holding a massive rally this morning on Kalindas Boulevard. Joined by tens of thousands of supporters and ordinary citizens, she is standing between troops loyal to former President Minitzh's cousin Tinto and those following the command of Armed Forces Chief Mende Kul.

The tense standoff began early this morning when a rumour spread through the capital that Kul had ordered troops to prepare for an attack on the presidential compound, where Tinto has made his headquarters. Freedom Party supporters immediately mobilized over a hundred *tritos* which sped throughout the city, horns blaring, the drivers shouting at citizens to come out on the streets. It is not clear how the party was able to convince so many independent *tritos* drivers to participate so quickly, but the effect has been one of a mass movement. Adults and children poured out of their apartments and greeted the dawn between two armies stalled for now across a barrier of innocent lives.

One startling characteristic of the Kalindas demonstration is its silence. There are no loudspeakers, Suli is broadcasting no speeches, the tanks that are pointed across the civilians are still. A light rain greeted the dawn but then was replaced by brilliant sunshine, and the civilians are now kneeling and sitting in silent prayer. Suli is in the middle dressed in a simple but brilliant blue *saftori* traditional to the Upong tribe of central Santa Irene.

Neither Tinto nor General Kul have issued any statements on the situation, which is ongoing.

Derrick calls back. "Nobody's covering it," he says. "CNN, BBC, nobody's there."

"The airport's closed," I say.

"And the stock market is imploding."

"How are you getting all this stuff in the bush? You're supposed to be paddling around."

"And I am," he says. "But I bought a few toys. Don't worry, the budget can handle it."

I don't ask Derrick about money and he doesn't tell me. It's better that way. Dollars come to him naturally – he waves my name around and money arrives. If he wants a few toys it's all right with me.

"Derrick," I say, "you're brilliant but sick. Turn it all off. The world will still be here when you get back."

"Yes, yes. I can turn it off whenever I want."

I try calling a contact at the State Department, but just get his voice mail. So I wait by the screen, watching for an update. Newswatch isn't covering it, AP isn't there, no word from Reuters. A strangely invisible event. I call the reporter from the BBC who phoned me before – not at his desk. Same with the CBC reporter who was interested before.

Late afternoon turns into evening. No new report. Joanne has tried to get me out for a walk but I won't budge. It's already tomorrow in Santa Irene. The event has happened, whatever it was. The event has happened but I haven't heard the shouting.

"You didn't visit your son," Joanne says, and for a moment I don't know what she's talking about.

"He'd be home by now," I say finally.

"You should call him."

"Yes," I say without conviction. I feel like I could call the prime minister of India but not my son. "My brother Graham was constantly getting concussions," I say. "He rode his bike like a kamikaze. Eventually he fell off a building. He was all right."

"The voice of compassion!" Joanne says. "The conscience of the nation!"

I click on the screen. *Los Angeles Times* – nothing. *Christian Science Monitor* – nothing. *The Independent* – nothing.

Joanne is right of course. I need to get out of this chair. I should do some animals. Take a walk. Call my son. Write a letter to my wife. *Dear Maryse. Dear Maryse. Words and words and words together. Down the page. One thought after another. My dear Maryse. I have loved you so much and so badly. My dear. Dear Maryse. Dear wife. Dear. My wife. I have meant to write. I have meant to start. So many times I've started this letter. Dear Maryse. Do you know when I started writing this letter? I wrote this letter in the molecules in the air when I was stuck in the lower regions of hell. I had a way out and it was through this letter. My dear Maryse. For so long the sound of your name was my mantra. Ages upon life-times. Maryse. My dear Maryse. The sound of your name was sweet nourishment in the very worst moments of my life. Maryse. The very worst? Who could predict? The worst would fall away as I stepped off the plateau and headed for the abyss. And still falling. Maryse. My dear wife. I wish to God I could let you go and know that some-where, at least, far above in the bright blue sky, someone is flying. My dear. Dear Maryse.*

CP has nothing, although I do get sidetracked by a story about a gigantic Canadian weather balloon that has gone astray and is now threatening commercial airspace over the Atlantic. Canadian fighter jets pumped over a thousand rounds into the balloon but couldn't bring it down. Perhaps this could add a new chapter to aviation history: intercontinental ballistic balloons. Don't tell India or Pakistan.

My dear Maryse. Just a few thoughts I meant to share. We have journeyed so far into bitterness and yet are still both standing. I am sorry for it and yet somewhat in awe, too, of what we can do to one another. In the name of love? Survival? I keep moving my house back from the edge but then more parts of me fall away. Is that sick or what? My leg jerks up and I get up and walk around. I sit down again until it jerks up once more. I talk on the phone and send off letters and wait and wait to hear – about what? About the country that returned the empty skin to you saying it's okay, it's still your husband, here he is, just bring him back to life.

Tell your son I'm sorry. Tell him to wear a helmet. Keep his head up. Some people bounce and some people don't.

At ten-fifteen a flurry of new stories is posted:

SULI STALEMATE CONTINUES

24 August 1998
Dorut Kul

The stand-off between unarmed supporters of Freedom Party leader Suli Nylioko and armed factions supporting Armed Forces Chief Mende Kul and self-proclaimed President Tinto Delapango continued into the heat of the day today on Kalindas Boulevard in downtown Santa Irene.

Temperatures reached 42°C and several civilians were taken to hospital with heat exhaustion. A row of tanks supporting Kul parted to allow *tritos* to transport civilians to Kolios and Wengata hospitals. It was a tense moment: soldiers at first refused to allow the *tritos* to pass, but relented finally when Suli herself arrived to plead on their behalf.

Tinto publicly called on Kul to stand down his troops and disband his "rebellion." Kul, on the other hand, announced through Island Radio that Tinto's declaration of martial law was unconstitutional and that Third Battalion soldiers were only protecting the country. The Freedom Party supporters and civilians who flocked to Kalindas Boulevard early this morning were technically in breach of the curfew proclaimed by Tinto yesterday. However, no one has been arrested as yet and so far the stalemate has remained peaceful.

Suli, while remaining most of the day in prayer, released a statement late in the afternoon calling on both Tinto and Kul to stand down their troops and allow free and fair elections.

FESTIVAL ATMOSPHERE OVERCOMES CAPITAL

24 August 1998
Islander staff

Despite the tense stand-off in the middle of Santa Irene today, or perhaps because of it, a curious festival atmosphere enveloped much of the capital. Citizens mingled on the streets in a way they've been too afraid to do ever since the Minitzh assassination and the outbreak of violence. In Welanto the last of several fires set by roaming gangs was put out. According to reports, the gangs themselves helped volunteer fire brigades douse the flames.

Ritaga music could be heard on many streets, and some people even returned to work.

"I don't know," said Kati Tulungota, a shop clerk in the exclusive Wexfords mall, which has suffered looting in recent days. "My brothers have gone to help Suli and somehow today I feel really happy. It could all end badly but I don't think so."

Such spirit was evident was well in the Fort district, where street parties formed spontaneously as people listened for news on Island Radio and danced and drank between announcements.

"We are so happy that Minitzh is dead," said 89-year-old Lori, a former labourer who sat in the shade and watched his great-granddaughter dance with other members of his family. "It's like the end of a long bad dream and Suli is leading us out. If they are still there tonight I will go stand with her."

Several others also said they would join "Suli's army" this evening when the heat cools down.

"They can't shoot everyone," said Desu, a clerk with the Ministry of Labour and Industrial Relations. "If they did, then there wouldn't be any country left."

In a grainy picture Suli kneels in the middle of an ocean of people, wrapped in her blue cloth *saftori* with white trim, one small shoulder bare, her black hair short, hands clasped, eyelids closed. A waif in the midst of great forces. The people around her are also kneeling or sitting but most are looking at her.

THE FRACTION OF A MOMENT

24 August 1998

On Kalindas Boulevard this morning time stopped for Santa Irene and it remains stopped as I write. We are caught in a moment of historical import that will be discussed and debated for years afterwards in our country.

If we have a country, that is.

In this fraction of a moment no shells have left the muzzles of any tanks. No soldiers have launched any grenades, no mortars have been fired, no blood has washed the hot concrete of this boulevard built by Minitzh as the approach to his great palace.

No flies swarm around limbless and headless corpses. No wounded parents feel their life ebb into mud while their children wail. There is no stench of death, although a crowd of a hundred thousand bodies doing what healthy bodies must do in the heat of day is not odourless. It's alive, as alive as any of us have been in recent years. It moves as one animal, thinks, prays, sings as one body.

The singing especially has been remarkable. It began with Upong harvest songs, then turned to celebration songs from the Telde and Iluny tribes, one song turning into another into another. How did a hundred thousand differ-ent people decide which song would follow which song? No one seems to know. This is unscripted, happening bit by bit. We have come together as one and it is the fraction of a moment before any shell has left its casing, any more life has been separated from an earthly body.

It is the fraction of a moment before a country slides into chaos, and the more people who sit and sing and pray the longer the fraction might last.

Suli Nylioko

6

I used to love wearing a suit. Stepping out of the shower, fitting a firm, healthy body into a fine set of clothes that tells the world this man has a purpose, a career, a proper place. All those wonderful illusions. Believe them and it's just as good as if they were true. Now I feel like a stick man in a sack, throttled at the neck. My blue tie with pink splotches. Maryse will remember. Her sister's wedding. A hundred lifetimes ago. Maryse's father bringing that young thing, what was her name? Mercedes. With the drug problem. She kept ducking out to the washroom and then drifting back, enlightened.

"Where is it?" Joanne asks. She's standing by the door of my apartment dressed in a black silk shirt, burgundy bolero jacket embroidered in gold, and flared, 1970s-style pants. She's even in cloggy high-heeled shoes that make her tower over me. She's a bit like looking at the sun, she's so brilliant, and so I keep my eyes lowered. Not for me this beauty, not even if I wanted it.

She repeats her question and I say, "I have no idea where it is. Some things are beyond my shrinking brain."

"They don't have to be," she says. "What's it called? Wicked Ash?"

"I have no idea."

"If you don't use it you lose it."

"That's one theory," I say. "The one I'm operating on is 'Take it easy, don't wear yourself out.'"

Joanne eventually figures out where we're going. Wicked Ash Gallery in the Glebe. I let her explain it to the cab driver, Abrahim Abinulla from Nigeria. He drives with one eye on the road and the other looking back at Joanne. Normally she can wheedle a life story out of a taxi driver, but this time Abrahim has her talking about her one trip to Lagos.

"My friend was supposed to meet me at the airport. He was teaching in a village about three hours away and he said, 'If I'm not there on time you wait. Don't go off with any Nigerians.'"

"Careful, careful with Nigerians," Abrahim says. I expect a grin but he's serious. "Some of those guys slit your throat to get your passport."

"Well, I waited and I waited, no Jeremy," Joanne says. "I had no one to call. It got dark. These men kept approaching me, offering to bring me to a good hotel. I said my friend was coming to get me. The men said they'd bring me to stay at their aunt's house. She had an extra room and would give me a good price. I said, no thanks. They went away and came back, went away and came back. Soldiers kept looking at me. There were police too, walking by, staring. Not good. Finally it was midnight and I knew Jeremy wasn't coming. I picked up my pack and three soldiers started to trail me, two police, another bunch of men. The guy with the aunt. My God. I started to run. They followed. I felt as if I'd been separated from the herd by hyenas. I saw this taxi and jumped in and locked all the doors. Do you know why I'm so good to taxi drivers? Because of Charles at the Lagos airport. He knew exactly what was happening and he sped away even before I told him where we were going. He said, 'Sheraton Hotel, yes, ma'am?' and I said, 'Sounds good to me. How fast can you get there?'

"We hit a roadblock almost immediately. Soldiers, only they didn't act like soldiers. They wanted me to get out of the car. I said, forget it. I showed them my passport through the window. Charles talked to them and then some more soldiers came up behind us in a Jeep, the same ones from the airport. I slid down in my seat. Charles talked and talked. He wouldn't leave the car either. I don't know what he said to get us out of there, but he got me to the Sheraton Hotel that night. I paid him seventy-five U.S. dollars and told him to be back to get me at eight o'clock the next morning. I bribed my way left and right, flew all the way to Cape Town to get back to Kigali. Goodbye, Lagos! I've never felt so relieved to be leaving a place."

Abrahim says much of his family is still there. "I keep sending them money," he says. "I think I support half the country by now!"

Joanne tips him well. "This is for Charles too," she says, stepping out.

The gallery is small, glassy, new-looking, in an old building sharing a block with upscale coffee shops, boutiques, and stores with Third World crafts. Several people are already inside. I see my parents through the window, am surprised. Joanne has also seen some people she knows but stays outside with me for a moment. I ask her what happened to Jeremy.

"He had some story about a flat tire. I told him on the phone he almost got me killed."

"Did you see him for long?"

"Pretty hard to with him in Nigeria and me in Rwanda. My nerves were jangled by then anyway. I heard he's gone back to England."

Occasionally Joanne will talk about some of her old boy-friends. There was an American serviceman ("God, he was pretty"), a Dutch boy who wore his blond hair over his shoulders and brooded even on good days, a Frenchman who was too pure. "He didn't even drink wine, for God's sake!" Joanne said. "You have to wonder about someone who's so far removed from his own culture." She seems to me the kind of woman who never goes for long without a man – it takes no effort, they gather of their own accord. And yet she admits that she chooses badly. The flaws that later are so obvious hide in the heat of the moment or appear worth the gamble.

Heads turn as soon as we enter. Conversations lull or stop, the focus shifts to me and Joanne, the survivor and the striking beauty. My mother crosses the room and hugs me. "You haven't been eating!" she says. She glances harshly at Joanne, just the once then not again. Somehow she seems to have reached the conclusion that Joanne stole me from Maryse, is performing the duties a good wife should be performing. I tried to tell her that Maryse and I mutually agreed to separate, that I hired Joanne much later, that everything is strictly professional. It doesn't matter what I say. She believes what she believes.

"You don't look like you're eating so well yourself," I say. She has sagged visibly, is ashen except for two pathetic spots of rouge on her cheeks.

"I'm doing the best that I can!" she announces. "Say hello to your father before he wanders off."

He's hiding by a tall, skinny tropical plant. He looks worse than I do in a suit: his hands shake and his face wasn't properly shaved this morning, his eyes are sunken and glum.

"Hi, Dad!" I say, gripping his hand just to keep it still. "What do you think?"

She hasn't been trimming his eyebrows. They droop over his eyes. Is this what happens when your brain goes under? Things start growing out of control?

"It's quite a party, isn't it?" I say.

I let go of his hand and it resumes shaking. He doesn't look at my face but down at my shoes.

"My son painted these," he says, still looking down.

"Not your son," I say, too loud. "*I'm* your son. It's your daughter-in-law who painted these paintings. *Maryse.*"

"My son did," he says.

"*I'm* your son. I'm right here in front of you, Dad!"

"He painted all these." Still looking down at my shoes. He backs away from me, bumps into the skinny plant, knocks it over.

"Careful!" I say, grabbing him too hard. "Here, do you want to sit down?"

Maryse is with us in an instant. I smell her before I see her – the scent of her hand lotion. She holds him by his elbow and shoulder. "Come on this way, Dad," she says, and he goes with her meekly.

"Did you see my son's paintings?" he asks her, and she finds chairs then sits beside him for a bit while I awkwardly right the skinny plant. She's taken my place, I think. They love her like a child. I'm the one who has fallen out of the family.

Someone brings me a drink and asks me about the situation in Santa Irene. We talk about it while I hold the wineglass, which is too full, I have to be careful. The man is brusque and worldly, his grey hair so neat, like a carefully tended lawn. Do I know him? It's quite possible that I do, but I've forgotten entirely. He probes me repeatedly about Suli Nylioko.

"She really is a phenomenon though, isn't she?" he says. "The country seems to have fallen in love with her."

The news coverage was sparse for a time, overshadowed by the stock-market crash and Russia's woes. But the image of Suli Nylioko praying between the tanks is starting to garner attention.

"Do you think she has a chance? How long can Suli and her people last? Any feel about this from your sources?"

He pushes, but I'm stuck on trying to remember who he is. From the suit he looks like Foreign Affairs. Probably quite senior, from his age and confidence. What's he doing here? Has he just come to talk to me?

Patrick runs by then wearing orange goggles and I excuse myself. "Hey!" I say, spilling my drink. I put it down on a little table, try to see where he's gone.

Many more people have arrived now. The talk fills the few spaces not occupied by bodies, jams the air above our heads like a physical thing pressing down on us. Patrick squirms his narrow shoulders between the hipbones of two young women dressed in black and white. "That's the husband," a young woman says when I squeeze past, my ear not two feet from her mouth. She raises her voice so her friend can hear her above the din. *The one who was tortured!*"

Somebody asks me to sign my book. I haven't brought a pen, but he has, and I stand staring at the title page trying to remember his name. He's in international development, I knew him from before. He and his wife used to come to our apartment when there weren't any kids. A hundred years ago. We went to their cottage once and got eaten by blackflies. *Click, click, click.* The gears in my brain slowly turn over. He's on the West Africa beat, smokes cigars in the backyard and brews his own foul beer.

"Who should I sign it to?" I ask finally, looking him straight in the face. He hasn't changed a bit, is so dramatically unchanged that he looks like an old photograph fallen out of an album. That sense of ages having passed.

"Just sign it to me," he says, unhelpfully, and I stare back down at the page, the pen poised.

"To me and Cecile," he adds to complete my bewilderment. Cecile? Do I know anyone named Cecile?

Finally I leave out both names but write this quote, the one thing that stayed with me from my time in the hospital.

> *Flatten and pave a field,*
> *the grass still pokes through,*
> *water widens the tiniest crack.*

It was hand-printed in careful block letters in the margins of a handout called "Keep a Good Thought." The hospital stamp was in the top corner of the cover page. There was one good thought for every morning – something short and sweet for lint-brained depressives on medication. I can't remember any of the standard-issue ones, but when I saw this one I made a project of holding it in my head. It only took a week.

And it takes some time now to get it all down. When I'm finished I look at my scrawl – the scribblings of a madman. My signature especially has become a black storm of meaningless scratches.

I hand the book back and look now for my son's orange goggles, wedge myself between bodies. Suddenly no one is familiar. Joanne has disappeared, as have my parents, Maryse, Patrick. Replaced by these young chattering souls in their black and white clothes. How can they all be wearing the same thing? "Sorry. I'm sorry!" I say, fumbling. More wine spills. "I'm sorry!"

Finally I see Patrick crouched in the corner beside my father, who sits on the floor with his knees drawn up close to his chin. The two are looking at something in front of them. A spider dragging a broken leg, scurrying from Patrick's corralling hands.

"How are you, son?" I ask, and he looks up at me, eyes bulging behind the goggles.

"Dad!" he says, and for a moment I'm transported to somewhere light and joyful. A spontaneous and utterly unreserved hug. "I hurt my head and went to the hospital!" he blurts.

"I know, I saw you."

"You *did*?"

"I was there. You were sleeping though. Didn't your mother tell you?"

The spider steals his attention and in a flash he's back after it. "I'm trying to get it outside before someone else steps on it."

It seems a dreadfully important mission. Patrick herds it towards me and I scoop it up in my hand, then the three of us head for the door across the crowded room, Patrick pushing his little body between the adults, me and Dad following in his wake.

"Is everything all right?" Joanne asks.

"Fine. We're saving a spider."

"You're what?"

More spilled drinks. What a night. Patrick gets white wine on his sweater and I get soda splattered on my shoes. We don't stop. "It's a wounded spider!" Patrick announces, pushing on. "We're saving a wounded spider!"

Outside, in the fresh air, I walk a few paces and then release the prisoner. My father stays right at my elbow. He seems happy to follow along. Look at him quickly, in a certain light, and he just seems odd, not addled with Alzheimer's. Patrick says, "Dad, you ate spiders when you were captured."

"Did I?"

"You told me. You used to eat them for protein."

"It must be true then."

"Well, didn't you? You said!"

"I said it, so it must be true," I say.

"Can't you remember?"

"Some things I don't want to remember."

"Grampa can't remember anything. He calls me Graham."

"It's because you fall down all the time," I say. "Just like Graham."

"He fell from a roof," Patrick says.

"When does the game start?" Dad asks. Here but not here. Patrick says, "*What* game?"

Dad says, "You know. What you were talking about."

"We weren't talking about a game! I said you always call me *Graham*."

"Where's the fire, for Pete's sake," Dad mumbles, his hands shaking, shaking. It's always been one of his great stock phrases, delivered not as a question but in affirmation of the chaotic state of the world. *Where's the fire, for Pete's sake.*

Patrick tells me about school and soccer, about being in the hospital and how important it made him feel, just like his famous father. "I didn't remember a thing!" he says about the accident. "Just like you!"

I've told him this story many times, to keep him from asking for details. And he's just young enough to still buy it, even though he knows that I've written a book about it all.

"What are the goggles for?" I ask.

"Mommy gave them to me," he says. "They're all steamy and I can't see a thing. She told me I could wear them tonight so it's all right."

Yes. It's all right. We could all use a steamy pair of goggles tonight. I return indoors, talk and visit and sip soda and the clock swings round. Eventually I have to look at Maryse's exhibit: *Shards*. A series of luminous acrylic paintings of women in ordinary scenes: standing in a kitchen at night, washing dishes in the sink; reaching for a bottle of ketchup in a hyper-coloured supermarket aisle; in a white slip brushing thick black hair in the bathroom mirror while a baby examines a red rubber boat; stepping onto a bus with a briefcase, a purse, a skirt twisted in the wind; sitting in the sun by a flower garden, a white blouse rolled off the shoulders, face lost in the shadow of a huge sun hat. In fact, the face is obscured in all the pictures – turned away, looking down, or the figure shown only from the back. The light is intense, dazzling, the colours radiant, almost overwhelming; the skin especially approaches translucence. And it's only when you get quite close that you realize that it *is* translucent in some areas – that bones are showing underneath, naked to the world, white and ghostly in some pictures, darkened slightly in others, with fracture lines and small brownish growths.

I can't look for long, can't help noticing that after viewing them for a time most of us turn away and chat, avert our eyes as much as possible.

Mom collects Dad and takes her leave. I tell her I'll visit them but don't say when. When I'm better. It's understood. I'm still getting better.

I need to leave too but can't think of what to say to Maryse. The age-old problem. If I just go she'll be hurt. If I open my mouth the same old crap will pour out.

She has been swarmed by friends and supporters all evening, is now standing with the owner of the gallery and with a woman she knows from the *Citizen*. "It isn't for profit," the gallery owner keeps saying. "This is for art."

Finally I get Maryse aside. She has been enlarged by all this, could squash me like Patrick's spider. "They're fascinating, but very sad," I say.

"I didn't really expect you'd come," she says.

"But you sent me an invitation."

"Well. You are family."

Family. Blood. Mine has seeped into hers and our misery is posted on these walls.

"Thank you for Patrick's goggles," I say. "I think they're an excellent idea. I'm just hoping against hope that he can stay as innocent as he is for as long as possible."

"He's seen the very worst," Maryse says.

"Yes." What more does he need to see? He saw me in the Kartouf video with my bones poking at my skin like tent poles and my eyes blinking, blinking against the light.

"I'm sorry about the hospital," I say.

"Forget about the hospital."

"I'm sorry about all of it."

"I know."

It's time to go. People are drifting away and need to say goodbye to Maryse and I have nothing more to add. Except one stupid, pathetic remark. "I'm getting better," I say, sounding like Patrick spouting off about his goggles. Hope against hope.

She turns to someone else. I know she doesn't want to hear it. I know it's the last thing in the world I should say.

Suddenly I need to go. I turn and push my way out the door, start looking for Joanne. For a moment I'm upset that she isn't here with a taxi exactly when I need her. Then I manage to relax a fraction, realize I've said nothing to her. So I turn. In a moment she'll recognize that I'm not there any more, will come out to find me.

But she doesn't. Where is she? She's got to realize that when I need to go I can't be standing around like this. It's like waiting for a twister to hit when you know it's coming. Those images, so innocent from a distance. They're not for me. I've seen all my eyes need to see for this lifetime. I don't need to give my brain any excuse to drag me through the shit all over again. *Where is she?*

Pacing, pacing. These goddamn parties. Why do people need them? You chat without saying anything and stand around and nibble and drink and the words fill the room until there's so much pressure but you can't leave, you stay there pretending nothing is wrong, it's all perfectly fine . . .

Damn! She's not noticing. I have to go back in. I barge back through the door. It's time to leave, for Christ's sake! Where is she? Towering over everyone in those ridiculous shoes. She should be easy to spot. But no. She's disappeared. Just gone. Jesus! How am I supposed to get home? She carries all the money. She gets the taxis. She's the one who talks to the fucking driver. What am I supposed to do if she's not around? *Where's she gone?*

Finally I see Joanne. Walking up to me as if everything's fine.

"*Where the hell have you been?*" I demand. Everyone's conversation stops at once. Too much force. "It's time to go," I say, trying for a more normal tone but achieving a stage whisper that echoes to the rafters.

"*Fine*," she says, turns and leaves. Bodies part for us, eyes peer through the window as we stand on the sidewalk. She hesitates, looks up and down the street, then thrusts fifteen dollars at me.

"This should see you home. I think I'll walk," she says. I start after her but even though she's a bit wobbly on her platform shoes she easily outdistances me in a few minutes. I don't call after her. If she's going to be this irresponsible.

No taxi comes. I won't wait. I can just walk. I know where I live. If I just take it slowly. I don't need any of them. Bloody leeches. Suck your strength. I don't need them.

It's dark and starts to rain and my hip becomes painful and these damn shoes, they don't fit my feet very well. It doesn't matter. I'm not an invalid. Some homeless man asks me for a quarter and I swear if he'd stuck his hand out I would've chopped it off. Don't mess with me. Don't mess.

When I get home I don't have a key to my own apartment, so I sit and shiver at the door, but no one sees me. I wait and wait. Finally something seeps through my brain and I take the elevator back down and call security. No problem. Something comes up, I solve it. I don't need anybody. I'm Bill Burridge. The world is my oyster.

The security guy is going to be here in fifteen minutes. When I get back to the apartment, I promise myself, I'll switch on *Abbott and Costello Go to Mars*, the one in which they actually go to Venus and are swarmed by beautiful, lonely women in gossamer gowns. I imagine watching it through foggy orange goggles with Patrick beside me slurping his drink, guffawing at every mishap, squirming at the mushy bits. Asking every minute, Is this true? Could this happen? Is there really a queen of Venus with a positronic brain?

Breathe and breathe and breathe until I get there.

7

I peer inside the room but my feet won't move. They didn't say it was going to be like this. It's too dark. I thought it was supposed to be a studio.

"Just in here," the technical guy says. He's maybe twenty-one, six-foot-five or taller, in long sloppy clothes with his hat on backwards.

"I can't go in there," I say. "I'm sorry. I thought we were going in the studio."

"This is the remote studio," he says. "It's okay. It gets light once you're inside."

"But I can't go in," I say, backing away. "This isn't what I thought."

He whacks his clipboard against his thigh a couple of times, looks at me like I have a mental disease. "Let me get Cheryl," he says. "You can just have a seat outside here."

I sit in the hall, a naughty boy waiting for the principal. The door to the room remains open – the blackness looms like the inside of a hood. A blackness I know too well. It's not what they said. I can't go in there. It's just asking for trouble.

—

Joanne should be here, or Derrick. I should've insisted. They could explain this. I can't be expected to sit alone in a black room. I've used up all black-room time for the rest of my life.

Cheryl comes back with the technical guy. She's maybe twenty-five, is wearing jeans, a blue shirt, sandals, and a headset. She also looks over six feet tall. I wonder, briefly, what's happening with the children these days. Too many steroids in the milk?

"Is there a problem, Mr. Burridge?" she asks. The technical guy's clipboard goes *whack whack whack*.

"I thought I was going to be in a studio, not a black closet," I say.

"It doesn't stay black," she says. "Actually it gets quite bright during the telecast."

"I can't do bright, either," I say. "I'm sorry. This wasn't explained to me."

Whack whack whack. Cheryl knocks her pencil against her thumbnail in time, *click click click*. "David, we have a problem," she says, but looking straight at me. It takes a moment for me to realize she's talking into the headset.

She moves off to explain the problem. The technical guy looks in the little closet as if noticing for the first time that it's totally fucking black. How's anybody supposed to go in there? It's 6:07. They're on air already and I'm supposed to be featured live at 6:11.

"Bill, how about if we keep the door open?" Cheryl asks calmly. She's been through this eight hundred times. Probably every single expert guest balks at going into that broom closet.

"Won't that ruin your picture?"

"It's fine. We can get around it. Why don't you just try the seat and see how it goes with the door open?" She turns her head slightly and says in a small, calm voice, *"We can't get Foster. There's absolutely no time."*

If Joanne or Derrick were here, I could say no. Derrick would sit in for me. Joanne would explain. There are some things you just can't ask. It's like getting someone to hold up a long metal pole in a flat field in the middle of a lightning storm. No fucking way. If Joanne were here I'd be able to say it. *No. Fucking. Way.*

But my feet move towards the little room. 6:09. The imperative of the newscast. How long can the interview last? Four or five minutes. They'll keep the door open at least. Breathe. Breathe. Elbows out, chin in. Breathe. I'm going to do it. I'm now going to grasp the long metal rod and hold it high in the air while walking barefoot through this flat field by the light of this thunderstorm.

"It's all right," Cheryl says, guiding me in the dark into the enveloping chair. In front of me is nothing – the abyss. I can hardly stand it. I breathe and breathe but half expect to smell the oiliness of the hood. Oh God. If her hand weren't on my shoulder, I'd have bolted.

"How're you doing, Bill? Would you like some water? It'll just be another few moments."

I shift in the chair, grip the rests, breathe and breathe.

"If you could just say a few things, Bill, we can get a sound level on you. What did you have for breakfast this morning?"

No words come out. I'm having trouble getting enough air. The problem is there's just the one hole barely big enough, every breath is an effort.

"Relax, sit back," she says. "Here's some water." I hear her through fog. My hand goes up, grasps the glass of water. I'm not going to be able to drink it. She knows that. Jesus. I really have to get out of here.

"Just another few moments, Bill," she says. Her hands press down on my shoulders now, keep me in the chair. A sudden pain flares through my chest and I think, this is it, what a stupid time to go. Everything pressing down on me now. Everything.

Then nothing. No pressure on my shoulders. I'm free to go. I start to rise and a light suddenly blinds me, *wham!* I turn left, right, but there's no escape. Behind me blackness and no Cheryl. She lied to me, of course. The door is shut up tight.

Then a voice comes down like the voice of God – a female God at that, from somewhere behind the light. The pain, the light, the voice . . . this is it, I think. It all makes sense now. It all . . .

"Joining me now is Bill Burridge from Ottawa," the voice says. "Mr. Burridge heads Freedom International, and also survived nine months of captivity in Santa Irene at the hands of the terrorist group Kartouf. Mr. Burridge, are you surprised at the events of the last few days? Did you think that Suli Nylioko would be able to pull this off?"

I stare transfixed at the light. Not death after all. Not yet.

A voice says, "Like everyone, I wasn't sure how this would play out. My fingers were crossed, of course, but one nervous soldier among thousands could've spelled disaster." Not a smooth voice, not polished, but quaking a bit. My voice. Coming from somewhere I don't understand.

"We have seen scenes of amazing jubilation today," the announcer says. "There was dancing in the streets as soldiers from both sides melted into the crowds, slipped off their uniforms, and joined Suli's prayers for peace. How did you feel watching those scenes?"

My voice again, saying reasonable things, heartfelt things, in interlocking thoughts, nice little sound bites. All while I'm trying to breathe, hang on. My heart going *boom! boom! boom!* My eyes must be bugging out of my head. But the words file along, little soldiers nicely lined up, uniformed and polished, marching *clip clip*. I can hardly feel my mouth move. *Sense of awe. Transfixed. Witnessing a miracle. Tremendous relief. They avoided a slaughter. Island passions. Time for healing. Tremendous challenges. Sense of history.* Those U.N. words coming from me, the same kind as the Danish delegate mouthed. Predigested, plastic-moulded, sterilized, child-safe.

"The country now has triple-digit inflation, and considerable infrastructure damage from the chaos following the assassination of President Minitzh," I hear the announcer say. "What sorts of challenges are awaiting Suli Nylioko, and does she have the experience to deal with them?"

I wait and, sure enough, my voice continues to come through. "I have to remind you," it says, "that Suli Nylioko, though immensely popular, is not an elected leader at this point and has no official mandate to rule. What she has done is defuse a potential catastrophe. She's now going to have to set up a commission to oversee free and fair elections. She's going to have to reassure International Monetary Fund officials that Santa Irene can reform its government spending and crack down on corruption, which is considerable. And she's going to have to keep these two factions of the military from overthrowing her and going for one another's throats." My voice authoritative, as if it knows anything about this at all.

As if I'm not shackled here, a prisoner, the Kartouf virus running round my brain.

". . . potential for disruption?" the announcer finishes, and I haven't been paying attention. I've been staring zombie-like into the light.

"As far as I know we've heard nothing from the Kartouf in all these days of turmoil and uncertainty," my voice says. Soberly. Legally correct but incomplete. There's something else that I'm not at liberty to divulge. That the Kartouf are still keeping me hostage. That they can blow me apart at any instant live on national television. An historic act. Burridge finally eliminated. No one knew. The virus was inside him all the time.

"But that could be another of Suli's challenges," my voice says, "dealing with a rebel group that fought for so many years against Minitzh and that probably feels it is owed a share of power." Secretly staring into the light of death. The man with the goggle-eyed stare. Probably they've backlit some comfortable scene. A book-lined office. The human-rights defender. Still held hostage. Now there's a headline.

The program shifts to commentary from a reporter on the scene, with, I imagine, shots of jubilation, of flower-draped tanks, of people praying and singing and dancing together, waving the abandoned uniforms of the soldiers like victory flags. I imagine, because all I see is the white light. In this chair I'm strangely calm. It's the middle of a twister, the calm place surrounded by chaos.

"Just to return to you, Mr. Burridge, how closely are you going to be monitoring the emerging human-rights situation in Santa Irene? With Minitzh dead, isn't it time to give the transitional régime some breathing room before being too critical?"

No words come out. I'm waiting for the appropriate response, but there is none.

"Mr. Burridge?" the Goddess voice asks. My jaw works up and down but no sound comes out, and suddenly I'm not in the calm middle of the twister any more, I've been booted out to the edge, spinning violently in the chair, gripping as hard as I can to hold on. My jaw works but of course now no words can come out, all language is swallowed in the intensity of the wind. The light collapses suddenly into blackness and then the door opens behind me and Cheryl is there but her words are indistinguishable from the rage of the moment and she and the techie have a hard time prying my fingers off the chair – they don't know, they don't realize if I let go, that's it, I'm flung off into oblivion. They pull and pull but I can't let go, it would be suicide and I've done that already, it doesn't work. I mean to tell them, but it isn't them any more. It's Josef, my keeper. We're back in the basement, we never left, I never got away. His black moustache, wedge face, all the same, the same as ever. And he has the video camera, that beautiful piece of machinery. He's pointing to me and I know what I'm supposed to say. I know but I've forgotten for the moment, all I can think is it's me on film, Burridge, but the Kartouf is hiding in the shadows, strapped with explosives, ready to take everything out in a moment. Whole city blocks. Lives of the innocent. Pedestrians and children and government figures, everyone.

I know what they want and I do it, as always. "Burridge O-K," I say, staring straight ahead. Such wind and noise. I know it's impossible but I can't let go till the twister is over . . .

Sad lights. Can't speak of how sad they are. Almost grey in their fluorescence. Or is that the medication? The medication, the medication. As if there were only one medication. I'm trying to remember the name of one of the drugs. It's tangled in the lint. If I thought clearly I could pull the name out of the mess, shake it briefly, hang it up to dry. It would be clear, identifiable. Just one.

I have a funny memory of a time in childhood. There was a gang of us on bikes, pedalling down a narrow path along a creek in the middle of the woods in the middle of the city. That creek by Billings Bridge. A strange part, quite wild for a stretch, although just a few hundred yards away were houses, streets, porches, sidewalks, a big mall. You couldn't see any of that from where we were, though. It was all thick brush and mud, strange insects, poking sticks, burrs and needles, weird-coloured water you wouldn't want to fall into. Wild urban creek water. God knows what lived in it. Strange species of fish and frogs and water spiders, toughened by chemicals and sewage backwash, toxic to touch, unkillable. A smelly place, wild in ways God never thought of, and this pack of boys on bikes disappearing from civilization to trace its dark turns.

I remember Graham falling in, how the other boys didn't want to go in after him. They were too frightened of the sludge, the bluish green metallic poisons we imagined would burn our skin. But there was Graham floundering, immersed in mud. I remember the suck at my feet, my anger at Graham, and at the others for abandoning us, the sense of panic, then relief when after all it was only mud, there was no burning acid, nothing to kill us right away. Graham laughing when my hand slipped and we both tumbled back. The cold and the grip of the mud, how easily it inserted itself between my clothes and skin, under fingernails, in my eyes and nose. Washing myself clean – *clean?* – with the odd water from the creek.

I remember pulling ourselves onto the bank, then walking home with our bikes in the rain. It might have been October – it was cold enough and we shivered badly, and our long wet clothes wrapped our limbs and weighed us down. The tight-ness and the mud. The effort of every step. Our shoes squelch-ing, feet plodding, heads drooping. Against the rain and up the hill and it seems to me now there was a wind against us as well, and our parents' wrath to anticipate all the way. But mostly the heaviness of the mud and our wet clothes.

It's the way thoughts are now. The way everything is. Here in this hospital bed. In this sad, sad light.

"You have to be careful, Bill," Joanne says. She looks like she's tripped into a wild urban toxic creek herself, is pale and small somehow, fallen into herself with worry and guilt.

"I will," I say. "You know I will."

"Well, you weren't!" she says unpleasantly, and the veins in my skull pulse just like that. I'm reminded that my head feels permanently bruised.

"You abandoned *me*," I say. "I'm not the one who walked off!"

"Bill," she says, holding her breath. It looks like an anger-management technique. "You said you didn't want me to come to the studio with you. You said you were fine on your own."

"That's a blatant lie!" I say, and another part of my brain gets bruised, just like that, hit by a rubber hammer.

Holding her breath then letting it out. Calming herself. Like she's dealing with some . . .

"We talked about it on the phone," she says, too calmly. "You said you wanted to go alone. You insisted. You sent Derrick off to Toronto to talk to the PEN group and you told me you were going to handle it all on your own. You said, 'I can do this now!'"

"Jesus! Why is everybody lying to me?"

"Don't get angry, Bill."

"Well, everybody's rewriting history here. How am I supposed to not get angry? Joanne, it's me. Me!"

"I know it is," she says, calmer now, and I cry against her.

"It's me," I say, "it's me, it's *me*," just so she'll know, so they'll all know. I can't tell them everything, but they'll know.

"You have to be careful," she says, in her right voice again, the one I hired her for – her flannel-sheets voice, her every-thing-okay voice.

"It's me," I tell her, brimming with tears again. "It's me."

8

There's a strange relief in failure, a release from the normal bonds of time and duty. When you've been in the hospital, sedated, insulated from the world, a week feels like a journey to the far side of the moon. When you've collapsed on network television, when your credibility has leaked away, when the phone doesn't ring . . . then the old sense of urgency relaxes its grip on your neck. Lets other things in.

Suli Nylioko. *Suli Nylioko.* The sound of her name insinuates itself between my bones and sinews, in the lighter passages of my mind, in the soles of my feet and the remaining roots of my hair. Suli Nylioko. This woman the world now knows simply as Suli. For a time she's everywhere: visiting the graves of the dead, holding hands with the wounded in hospitals, reviewing the troops, addressing a throng of well-wishers, praying alone in a square with a mere ten thousand others, the women wrapped in their *saftoris*, but only Suli in brilliant blue. Leading a revolution in prayer and song, in meditation and good thoughts. Good thoughts! Suli Nylioko. The sound of her name soothes through my body like an antidote, an incantation. *Suli Nylioko*. Stares the soldiers down and kisses away their fear. *Suli Nylioko*. Holds a child whose parents were burned in the Welanto fires. *Suli Nylioko*. Tells the aging white gentlemen at the IMF that they must allow her to pay for milk for pregnant mothers. A typhoon hits Kolaba in the north and Suli is there, setting up a hospital. *Suli Nylioko*. Rides in a helicopter to the scene of a ferry disaster and three hundred fishermen follow in their boats, scooping the survivors out of the water. Only twelve dead! It could've been much worse, but for Suli Nylioko.

At night in my apartment I practise my animals. Dragon, *lun*, *pang*, *mandarin*, snake, and ape. And now the bear: trap the punch, smack with the back of your fist, shuffle in and paw-punch once then twice. Knees bent, back straight, head high, chin in, elbows out, tongue on the roof of the mouth, eyes on the horizon. On Suli Nylioko. She stands in a bright light, dressed in blue, looking so dark and confident, her hair black as the night sky in fall. A strange energy coming from her. Suli Nylioko persuades the World Bank to fund the reconstruction of the island education system. Suli Nylioko sweeps the elections, then allows ten opposition members to sit in the *Kuente* anyway. Suli Nylioko prays with striking civil servants and they agree to return to work without their back pay. *For the good of the country and your neighbours. It will all be made good.* The People's President. Suli Nylioko.

There are walks along the river with Joanne, in rubber boots in the rain, water into water, summer gone, an old memory, autumn too sliding away so quickly. The leaves turn their colours and the sky deepens and one or two warm spells fool no one, the real weather is the rain and cold wind, dragging us down into winter. Every step, strangely, the name courses through my body. *Suli Nylioko*. A breathing thought, intravenous energy, hope, and grace. *Suli Nylioko*. The whole world watches the American president twist in the wind over his silly little affair, every apology getting worse and worse. He needs a name, a cure for his own staggering stupidity, something soothing in his veins.

Suli Nylioko.

Suli names her cabinet – half are women. Suli opens the first safe house for teenage prostitutes in Santa Irene. Suli cracks down on the sex trade. Suli knocks on the doors of the United Nations to ask for money to build a new police force, set up a system of health care, combat the drug trade. It all comes down to money. Possible now, perhaps, because Africa is so hopeless, money sent to most countries there seeps away and resurfaces somehow in Switzerland. And money sent to the rest of Asia evaporates in the economic free fall. But money sent to Santa Irene goes through Suli Nylioko, the beautiful woman in the blue *saftori*, whose bright light, by so many accounts, has transformed the whole country into a place of song and prayer and good works. She stood between the tanks and the soldiers melted, dissolved into boys who loved her. Everybody loves her. Suli. *Suli Nylioko.*

A political widow who plays the innocent, claims the high road. Too shining new to show any of the mud. I know this. And yet . . .

Say her name once and then again and it steals inside you like a spirit. Why not? Other spirits hide inside us all the time. Viruses lurk inside our organs, come out for a while to announce themselves, lure the drugs, then hide away again. Like the Kartouf camped out in the darkness of my brain. There's treatment but no cure. Burn one part of the forest and they move to another; destroy a mountain village and they reappear somewhere else. Like spirits. Why not a spirit of light? Why not an angel called Suli Nylioko?

A U.N. delegation becomes the first international group to visit a prison in Algeria and somehow they fail to talk to even one of the twenty thousand prisoners held for terrorism. Somehow they have nothing to say about the murders and bombings and other atrocities. The U.N. commissioner for human rights visits China but does not visit a single political dissident. T.J.'s cousin is not heard from despite my pleas to the prime minister, but one man does escape from a secret prison in Vavuniya, torture marks all over his body. He holes up in a church and is saved from the militia by a priest and by the police. The police!

The world turns in all its old ways. But now there's Suli Nylioko. "The difference is like night and day," writes a gushing columnist. "For a time we were killing one another and now we sing together every night, clean streets together, help in the markets and the fields. It is hard to believe the difference one person can make."

One person. Suli speaks on the radio and expatriate Santa Irenians double their foreign remittances. Suli brings inflation down to double figures from triple and then to single. Suli negotiates with Kartouf fighters and two thousand rifles and small arms are collected in one weekend. And yet where is Kartan Tolionta? He's nowhere and he's everywhere, in the back of everyone's thoughts (in the recesses of my mind), in a cave somewhere up north, in the jungle, in Welanto, safe in some village in Thailand – no one knows where the leader of the Kartouf is, and no one knows what he thinks of Suli Nylioko. One blast and he could bring her down. She moves without security, passes among the throngs, is as easy to spot and target as a bluebird in a field of snow. A bomb destroys a loading dock at the post office – no one killed, no one claims responsibility. Another bomb weakens a bridge at the north end of the harbour – but at three in the morning, no one was on it. No word on who might have planted it. These are minor blips in the celebration, reported and then mostly forgotten. It could've been drunken soldiers, some bad police, a gang of kids. The Kartouf is quiet, sleeping. Let them sleep.

I phone my son on his birthday. We talk about school and what Joanne bought for him in my name. I sit through an afternoon holding my father's cigarette while my mother gets her hair done, goes to a movie, reassembles her nerves.

No one from the media calls me again. My meltdown on the national news lasted only a few moments before the link with the famous human-rights defender became "unavailable." I hear nothing more about it, but no reporters call, I'm not asked for follow-up commentary. Santa Irene largely slips from view again anyway. The drama is over, Suli has won, the angry dogs have skulked away and peaceful days do not make headlines. But more than that, the word has gone out over the unseen network: Burridge is unstable. He's post-traumatic, can't be trusted. They brought him to the hospital. It was in the *Globe and Mail*. No letters arrive asking me to speak at conferences. Everyone knows. Derrick hopefully fills out the grant forms, but it's different now, the name has lost some of its magic. Burridge was like Suli in a way. There was an aura, not of grace but of the integrity of suffering. Now the aura has dimmed, the whiff has increased – mental illness, instability. Do we want to send money to someone who goes goggle-eyed on the national news? Who thrashes about in his chair and then goes blank? Even though everyone knows I was in the hospital before, that I tried to kill myself several times – it's well known – I went goggle-eyed on television and that's different. It's as if it has *really* happened now. Like Clinton apologizing on television. We all knew but now we *know*. The madness is official.

I finally write the note to my wife.

Dear Maryse,

The whole sky is mine tonight, there are no clouds, the last of the airplanes has just blinked by. I think of who might be up there: the young businessman coming back from a hectic day in Toronto, the maiden aunt who has been to Vancouver to visit her sister's bratty children and is relieved now to be heading back to her cats, to not have children of her own. The alcoholic newsman who couldn't write another original sentence if his life depended upon it – everything that happens now reminds him of something else that happened when he was younger and the world was more interesting and the details mattered and he wrote about it then anyway. All of them – the young mother with her two-month-old baby and the confused granny who couldn't buckle her safety belt without help and the professional athlete who's pissed off because his six-figure salary is in Canadian dollars not American – all of them are a few inches of metal from total oblivion and yet it feels as if they're sitting in their own living rooms. Or maybe they're not so relaxed because of Flight 111 that went down in Peggy's Cove – there's been so much coverage, so many of the passengers were U.N. officials and other accomplished types doing important work, and they too were sitting relaxed as if in their own living rooms, veterans of so many flights, no doubt, that went off without a hitch.

For us too the few inches of metal gave way, brought us into oblivion and yet somehow didn't erase us completely. Improbably, impossibly, we survived the fall, can even walk now, carry on, look more or less normal – at least you do, you still have life and beauty. My fall was further, I suppose, from outer space, but somehow I didn't entirely burn up upon re-entry. I can't say the angle was correct and yet here I am, a wreck, but a walking one.

I don't know why I'm still here, but we both know the reasons for our separation. Closing the door felt like another death, and yet also filled me with perverse relief – another responsibility I could leave behind, another room to shut off and ignore. Having eaten bitter for so long the smell, the possibility of sweet, was unnerving. I've said this before and will say it again – it was never you and Patrick, it was always me floundering in the bog. I've never gotten over the belief that it would've been simpler for all, better even, if I'd only died in my agony as I was supposed to.

And yet lately – the last few weeks perhaps? – something else has seeped into my soul which I wasn't prepared for. It's nowhere near joy, or contentment, or ease. Nothing bounding or extraordinary, no somersaults to land me flat on my back – just a few steps really on what feels like firmer ground. I don't know why, or perhaps I do and am afraid to say.

I'm not afraid to say that sometimes now I have small daydreams of being with you both – that time Patrick crawled into the laundry hamper to be among the warm clothes; that day I stayed home from work and we all played on the floor of the den in our pyjamas and when Patrick conked out we covered him with a blanket where he was and then slipped off back to bed ourselves.

I know that we had a life and then the inches of metal betrayed us and yet now in the ongoing chaos, the writhing and thrashing about after the fall, I find I can think the first unblistered thoughts about that life again. I have no right to hope, I know – I shut you both out and can blame only myself if the door now is closed on both sides.

But perhaps we can begin with something simple, a lunch maybe. I have a nice spot on Victoria Island. On a good day there's sun and shade and pretty water, wilderness to look at and civilization too. Maybe before winter there will be room for one warm hour. Call me?

Love, Bill

I spend long hours working and reworking the letter, polishing little phrases, cutting and adding and cutting again. Printing out and rereading, changing and rereading. They feel like the first and only words of hope I've ever uttered in my sorry life, and they fill me with dread and wonder. I sign and fold the paper, slip it in an envelope, then take it out and read it again, changing words, going back to the computer. On the screen the words are liquid, unimportant in a way – I can try them out like trying on different clothes. It's been forever since I've uttered such words. Of course, I can't send it. She'd turn in rage, fling the flimsy paper back in my face, file for divorce before I could take another breath. Where was I on Patrick's birthday? His first day of school? Could I bother to take him to the museum some Saturday – any Saturday in the last year? Where was I in soccer practice, or when he cried at night because I couldn't even answer a simple e-mail? Where was I when Maryse was mounting her show and needed help in the kitchen, someone to do a load of laundry, to pass a towel over a dish or two?

Words of love and hope. Flimsy, self-serving, pitiful words. Words of weakness and need, of ache and worry and problems down the road. Another wounded man looking for a nurse. Words of waste and reopened wounds.

Reopened envelopes. I read it again, fiddle, reprint, sign, and think. Of course, I can't send it. I've used up every chance. An honourable man would protect those he loved from further harm. I tear it up and then reread the words on the screen and print out the letter again, sign it, seal and address the envelope. One last chance. An honourable man would have to take it. Because I do have something to give now. Maybe?

It's just a lunch. It's just hope and love. It's just . . .

I put on my thick jacket and ride the overheated elevator down to the street, the real world, and gasp at the cold wind. What kind of wonderland have I been living in? I walk to the mailbox and then past, knowing I can't send such a letter. Just when they're healing and getting on with their own lives. Self-serving and pitiful words. Stupid. Broken eggs and spilled milk. Get on with it, man!

Past the mailbox and back, my hands cold in the raw wind. A picnic! Too late. Too little. Winter rattling at the gate.

Past the mailbox and I think, why am I here if I'm not going to mail this? I pull back the door and throw it in, am pulsed with immediate, burning regret. I almost reach in to try to retrieve it.

Long, muttering walk by the canal, the waves choppy from the wind even in this backwater. It will only bring more pain. Why couldn't I wait? Obviously I'm still unstable, will be the rest of my life. People never really recover from torture. They don't. They mutter to themselves and wet their beds until their brains have shrivelled and died.

When I get back to my apartment I'm cold through to the core. Joanne, who has let herself in, asks, "Where have you been?" but there's no time to answer. The phone rings and I freeze with fear – how did she get my letter that quickly? I snatch up the receiver before Joanne can get to it. I don't want her to know what a fool I am. (Who am I kidding? Of course she knows!)

"Mr. Burridge?" says a female voice, and for a moment I'm confused. Why would Maryse call me Mr. Burridge and speak with an accent? I fail to reply and so she must repeat my name.

"Yes?"

It's not Maryse. It's the Santa Irenian ambassador's secretary, calling to agree to a meeting I'd requested ages ago. Tomorrow morning, she says, nine o'clock. The ambassador is eager to discuss the situation in the mountains.

I reach Derrick later and ask him why the ambassador is suddenly so interested. It must be the new government, we decide. The ambassador, Waylu, is old-guard, but he's realizing that if he doesn't appear to change soon he'll be turfed out.

"Bring all your materials," I tell Derrick. "We'll slam him with documents!"

9

Waylu Tariola's office is dominated by a huge map of the tiny island of Santa Irene: a teardrop in the South China Sea, the capital weighing it down, green around the edges with spiny brown mountains in the middle. The ambassador is a wiry man with a sharp, angled faced and small hands. His eyelids are heavy and on the right one is a large black mole that makes it look as if blinking would be painful. But he does, often, anyway, and shifts his head in sudden excited movements, his lips and eyebrows gesturing, sometimes in anger and distrust, but this morning, apparently, in overwhelming welcome, as if this is all he has lived for, this very moment here with me.

"Mr. Burridge! It is such a pleasure at last that our schedules allow us to meet. I have been hoping for so long to have this opportunity," he says, offering his hand. It's such a barefaced lie I hardly know what to do – but I take his hand out of politeness and look away. For *months* we've been petitioning him to meet with us, and he has ignored us outright, while carrying on a campaign in the press to downplay, deny, or discredit any reports of human-rights problems in his country. I have in my briefcase a file of these clippings – AMBASSADOR DENIES KILLINGS; SANTA IRENE: GARDEN PARADISE; RIGHTS VIOLATIONS FABRICATED SAYS DIPLOMAT. I'd draw them out right now to confront him but he won't let go of my hand, has taken it with both of his own.

"I have read your gripping account, sir, and I must tell you what a thrill and an honour it is to finally meet with you. You are a prize of humanity, sir. I tell you this with an open and admiring heart."

A prize of humanity? I look questioningly at him, but he seems content with his odd phrase. I pull my hand away finally, as he is bowing. His three nervous assistants, all in ill-fitting suits, bow as well.

"I'm sorry," Waylu continues. "I have forgotten my manners. There is tea here and coffee, and all sorts of biscuits and sticky buns, fruit if you would care for it, juices of many varieties. Mr. Viranto, what choice of juices do we have? Guava, rambutan, lychee, mango, pineapple, we have fresh durian. Do you eat durian? It is – what do we call it? – an acquired taste. Please, you must have something, I am so anxious to speak with you."

"Nothing for me. Thanks." Derrick follows my lead and we take our seats around a low table.

"Please. Mr. Burridge, I implore you, you must have something. We have oranges, we have fresh bananas, *real* bananas, Mr. Burridge. I know you must have had them when you were in Santa Irene, not the pulpy things that pass for bananas in stores here. I have them delivered by diplomatic pouch. It's my one vice. All right, perhaps not my only vice. Please, a sticky bun?"

I take a small banana, just to get him to shut up, and Derrick tries the spiny durian, which fills the room with a fetid stink.

His face contorts for a moment, then he smacks his lips and says he likes it, but puts it down.

"Excuse me," Waylu says – having nothing himself, I note – "but I must ask you, out of awe and admiration, and please forgive me if I am treading on old ground or repeating what everyone asks . . ." He pauses for a moment, to untangle himself from his sentence. "But how in the world did you ever survive?"

I look at him blankly, dumbfounded.

"I am sorry! This is not an appropriate question. Clearly! I am so sorry. It's just that I am not alone in believing that you have achieved one of the greatest feats of human survival, and are a living testimony to the power of the human –"

"It was an accident, I think," I say. "All the way around. I wasn't supposed to be kidnapped and I wasn't supposed to survive and I wasn't supposed to make much of myself afterwards. But here I am, Mr. Ambassador, and regrettably I have many pointed things to say about your government's fundamental disregard for human life and the spirit you seem to prize so much. With respect, sir."

Down with the last of my banana. I nod to Derrick and he unloads the documents: the reports of the United Nations special rapporteur, and of the working groups on torture, on extrajudicial executions and arbitrary detention, on enforced or involuntary disappearances. The annual reports of Amnesty International, Human Rights Watch, the State Department. A special report issued by Fédération internationale des ligues des droits de l'homme. The summary report we brought to the United Nations. Our seven pages of recommendations. Copies for everyone. Waylu and his assistants take their seats, flip through the pages with apparent interest.

"Of course, of course!" Waylu says. "Let's not waste time

with formalities. But please, Mr. Burridge, you must accept my apologies for asking about what must be a sensitive matter. I cannot convey the true horror that all of us at the embassy felt during your ordeal. You must have heard how closely we worked with our Canadian counterparts to keep your family informed, and to spur on our Intelligence Service in its efforts to locate and free you finally."

I cannot bring myself to comment, but stare at him stonily, fighting to keep down the bitterness. My family wasted months dealing with an embassy that had no information whatsoever to provide. At last Waylu looks away in embarrassment.

I glance at my notes. "I thank you for seeing us this morning, *finally*," I say. "As for the your Intelligence Service – you will note in many of our handouts the abominable record of abuse associated with IS officers. But not to skip ahead. My assistant, Derrick Langford, will make the main presentation. Derrick?"

"Santa Irene," he says, "like many countries emerging from the shadow of oppressive and dictatorial rule, has a long legacy of human-rights violations that must be dealt with." His hands gesture in small, definite strokes. He looks concerned, emotionally involved, but speaks in restrained language. "The new government in Santa Irene must work to develop a climate of transparency and accountability. The state must work collaboratively with the United Nations and the human-rights and development community, both domestic and international, to put in place those institutions and practices that ensure a civil, democratic society in which fundamental human rights are not only safeguarded in law but in everyday practice."

The ambassador nods as if considering, weighing every word. He's a diplomat, of course. We can sit around this table politely discussing mass murder and it is all civil, understood. No matter what comes up there will be no display of bad manners. Or if there is, it will be a show, not personal, not real. It's a sickening game I used to have patience for, used to think I understood, but that was another lifetime.

"Accountability is the key," Derrick says. "For decades the police and the military have literally gotten away with murder. No one has been held accountable. Human-rights groups have documented over seven thousand cases of extrajudicial executions, estimate there are up to twelve thousand disappearances in the last two decades. Yet there have been no convictions of police or military personnel . . ."

Yes, yes, Waylu nods gravely. As if considering these things for the first time. He railed against the State Department report when it first came out, was quoted in the *New York Times* as saying that these figures had been concocted by Kartouf operatives and naively accepted by governments and non-governmental organizations. I have a letter from him from last year complaining about unverified statistics – the same month his government denied Amnesty International the right to visit the island and investigate allegations of atrocities. And now he has the gall to nod sympathetically when these same numbers are put before him!

"We are also recommending the establishment of a full-powered board of inquiry to investigate past human-rights violations," Derrick says, "in particular the campaign in the mountain regions to raze villages and persecute alleged Kartouf sympathizers. This board –"

He's still nodding and agreeing. Waylu Tariola!

"– would have the power and authority to investigate abuses of both the security forces and the rebel groups. It would be headed by a committee of independent observers prominent in the struggle for justice and peace –"

"Yes," Waylu says. He turns his gaze excitedly to me, then back to Derrick.

"The board members should in no way be implicated in the abuses of the former régime. They should have stature and authority and the trust of the people –"

"Precisely," says Waylu.

"It should not be a witch hunt," I add. "It should be fair but exhaustive."

"– in order to allow for healing, for justice, and the establishment of democratic institutions to bring the country beyond the rule and whim of individuals."

"No more demagogues," says Waylu, boring his gaze into my skull. "We have been too long under the thrall of particular personalities. You are absolutely right! Our institutions have suffered, our level of civil liberties has been – well, what can one say? – deplorable."

Derrick and I exchange glances. Waylu's aides are reading the reports as if they'll be tested on them later in the day.

"I have to admit, Mr. Ambassador," I say carefully, "nothing in your record to date has led us to expect this sort of reception. In the past you have taken exception to every –"

"The past is very much in the past, Mr. Burridge. These are new times. We have a fresh spirit in the country. As you know! Our new president is intent on sweeping out the horrors of Minitzh and his cronies. It is a new land! And this is very much the time for setting things right. This is why I have called you in today. Not to disagree with your reports, but to embrace them, as we must if we are to move on."

"Then I trust, Mr. Ambassador, that you will unhesitatingly bring these reports and recommendations to the attention of your government."

"*Already done, sir!*" he exclaims. His face is alarming in its exultation. "More than that. More than that!" he says. "Will you sit on the *Commisi vertigas*?"

"Sorry?"

"The Truth Commission! There is going to be one! Will you sit on it?"

I'm speechless. My leg snaps out and jolts the heavy table. The pain shoots through my shin.

"We need *you* to sit on this Truth Commission. To investigate the past abuses."

That heavy black mole drooping his lid, the rest of his face so twisted in a perverse look of victory. My God.

"I couldn't possibly," I say in a small voice.

"But you have said it yourself," he says, opening his hands. "We *need* a board of inquiry. If we are ever to heal from the barbarism of Minitzh. We need men of stature and fair hearts, who are not cowards. Who will stand up for justice and who the people will trust." Such hypocrisy! Throwing our words back at us. As if there was no blood on his own coddled hands.

"But you can't ask Mr. Burridge," Derrick says. He too is off-balance. This isn't what we expected.

"Who would be better than Mr. Bill Burridge?" Waylu asks, not moving his eyes from me. "He was taken by the Kartouf and yet he stands up and speaks for their protection in the United Nations. He has suffered the very worst and has dedicated his life to safeguarding the fundamental rights of common citizens. He is a giant in stature! And I say this sincerely, please, you must believe –"

"You are well aware of Mr. Burridge's precarious health," Derrick says. "His heart –"

"We would pay you, of course, in accordance with the rates for very senior U.N. posts –"

"*I can't fucking do it!*" I say, standing up suddenly, shuddering the table again. Jesus!

"I'm sorry!" he says immediately, rising, Waylu's face a mask of concern. He holds out his hand but I walk past it. Derrick rises and follows me. Which way out?

"Please, Mr. Burridge, please!" Waylu says, his hand on my shoulder. His advisers surround me as if they won't let me leave. Just try it! Raise your hand! I'll split your arm.

"What?" I say, whirling. "How can you even ask such a thing?"

Outside, in the taxi, I'm fuming. "Can you believe that shit?" I say. "Can you believe him suddenly pretending to accept our recommendations and then turning the knife to make it look like *I'm* the one standing in the way of justice and human rights?"

"Careful," Derrick says.

"I have never seen such blatant hypocrisy!" I rage. "He's a bloody murderer. He supported and protected Minitzh as much as anyone. And now to turn around and pretend to be on the side of human rights and democracy!"

"Calm down," Derrick says softly, patting me. What am I, a dog?

"I will *not* calm down. I am *livid*. This is *my* anger and I'm entitled to it!"

"Well, just be calmly angry," he says, then smiles nervously. He thinks I'm going to blow a heart valve right in the taxi. He might be right.

I stop flaring my nostrils, unclamp my jaw. He's right. Diplomats. They make their living slithering on the ground. I should know! It would be just like Waylu to try to give me a heart attack with this kind of invitation. Free trip back to the pit of hell. I can't even make it through the night without the fear of the Kartouf terrorizing my brain. How could they ask me to go back there?

"He's got me sweating at the palms," I say. "Look!"

"Don't think about it," Derrick says, patting me again. Where's Joanne when I need her? That's it, no more diplomatic meetings without Joanne.

"How can I not think about it?" I ask. "*He wants me to go back there!*"

"Just let it go," he says, eyes wide. He's scared. He doesn't think I'm going to make it through this cab ride.

Maybe I won't. I breathe and breathe but my heart won't slow down.

Joanne says it as well. "Calm down. It's all right. You don't have to go anywhere." I sit at the table in my apartment downing my pills.

"He had this look of triumph," I tell her. "He'd heard this human-rights crap for so many years and had finally figured out how to stick it all back up my craw –" Derrick stays silent. There they are, the two of them, waiting while their boss cracks up. "Don't you see? They're going to use my refusal to discredit me, make me look like a chickenshit advocate who runs away when he actually gets a chance to *do* something."

"Maybe," Derrick says. But uncertainly, as if he's only saying it because it's what I want to hear.

"Don't baby me!" I blurt. "For God's sake! I don't want to be surrounded by people who are afraid to tell me what they really think!"

I notice Derrick and Joanne exchange looks.

"I'm all right!" I say, too loud. Then softer: "I'm all right.

Derrick, what do you *really* think about all this? I need your clear head. You don't think I should *go*?"

"No. Obviously," he says. No hesitation.

"But if I don't, are they going to discredit me? Did Waylu set this all up?"

Like talking to the walls. Derrick looks at the floor, at Joanne, anywhere but at me.

"*What?*"

"Obviously you shouldn't go back there," he says again, finally looking at me. "But you have to remember, Waylu is part of the wind faction – he changes with the political climate. He would never act on his own in something like this. He speaks for the government of Santa Irene. That's who this invitation is from – Suli Nylioko. *She* wants you on this commission. Waylu is just the messenger."

He stops while I digest this.

"You're telling me this is a serious invitation," I say.

"All I'm saying is it could be taken that way."

"To ask a torture survivor back to the scene of his personal hell?"

"I think they see the head of an important new human-rights organization, someone who has profound personal knowledge of their little country. It's as Waylu said – the fact that you have tried to defend the human rights of the very group that terrorized you speaks volumes for your credibility. That's what they need for their commission."

I let him go on while I just stare.

"From our point of view," Derrick continues, "if you *could* go, it might be very good for the organization. It terms of coverage, profile. Repairing the damage." Of my meltdown on television, he means. "Suli is sexy right now. Politically, internationally. She's Corazon Aquino just after ousting Marcos and before she turned out to be so mediocre. Suli might be Nelson Mandela with a beautiful face. God knows. But she seems to want to do good things for her country. She'd love to drape her commission in your flag. That's what this is about. It could be good all around."

He shifts in his seat, looks away in discomfort. "I know how awful this could be for you, and for that reason, of course, I'm advocating that you refuse this invitation and stay home. Of course. But just look at another side. If you went, and if it worked out, this could do a lot for our funding." He clears his throat nervously. "I'm the *only one* thinking about money here," he says, still not looking at us. His face so red. "I'm sorry!" he says, rising, pacing. "Money is an evil word here, I know, no one wants to think about it. You're the organization, it's your face everyone knows, but I'm the one who signs the cheques and I'm the one who has to troop off to the bank to explain why so much is going out and nothing's coming in. I don't mind it, I can do it, I'm good at it. But I'm just reminding you, I'm the only one thinking of these things. I'm telling you, *don't go back to Santa Irene*. But if you *could* it might not be such a bad thing. For starters they've offered senior U.N. rates, right? I assume expenses would be included –"

He stops, sees the way I'm looking at him.

"I'm sorry," he says. "You'd rather not worry about finances. I know. And this is about much more than that. But you asked me to be candid."

"Nothing in this life obligates you to ever go back there," Joanne says.

"Obviously," I say.

Obviously. It echoes in my mind long after they're gone. As I sit by the window watching the city settle into sleep. I'm not supposed to go back. I was never supposed to go in the first place. I was never meant to be a diplomat and I paid for my bad luck – with my health and my family, my sleep and the great solid middle of my sanity. I *paid*. I owe no dues to Santa Irene.

Nothing.

And there will be other ways to rebuild my reputation.

This is all obvious. But why can't I just dismiss it? My mind doesn't work that way any more; it seizes on certain thoughts and plays them over and over obsessively. I wait for it to hit the press. BURRIDGE REFUSES POST ON TRUTH COMMISSION. The thought won't leave me alone. I don't have to go, but what if I did? What if going back to clean out the shit of that country helped me wipe this virus from myself? What if I could lie down and sleep the night through without dreaming of cut glass and burning flesh and being back there in the hood and the darkness and sweat and fear?

"Obviously you're not going to go," Joanne says to me. Days later and still I'm obsessed with this. "Put it out of your head." We're walking beside the scummy surface of the canal. A noisy paddle-wheel contraption churns past us, scooping up the masses of weeds that grow now that the water has been cleaned up.

"But it would be something," I say. "To be part of the healing."

"It's not worth the risk."

"To be in on a society that's making this kind of transition. Especially there."

"*Bill!*"

"I know!" I say. "I'm just talking. Just for debate. *I* could never do it. It would kill me. But somebody really pure of spirit. Gandhi. Mahatma, not Indira or Rajiv. It's something he would do. Be a torture survivor who returns to the scene and does something positive for that country."

"You don't have to be Mahatma Gandhi. Bill Burridge is good enough."

"But what if I did, what if going back to the valley of the shadow –?"

"The what?"

"To the heart of my own personal darkness. Maybe that's what I need."

"You need time and you need therapy," she says.

Churn, churn, churn. The boat struggles under the bridge, barely going faster than our shuffling walking pace. This is what happens when you clean things up. A new kind of murk descends. Nothing stays clear.

"I'm just talking. You told me it would be good to talk."

"With a therapist, Bill. You need specialized help."

I've tried three already. I thought we were done! I thought I'd never have to talk to another therapist –

"I could set it up," she continues. "I heard of this excellent woman. She does a lot of work with refugees and with battered spouses. She is booked for months ahead of time, but I know from a contact that she would make time for you."

How marvellous to be a special case.

"You don't have to decide right now," she says.

There is a world out there. I sit alone by my window and read an account of a Chinese journalist sentenced to thirteen years of reform through labour for "leaking state secrets" – reporting on Li Peng's family-planning speech the day before the official version was printed. He was taken to a dusty, grim facility in Heilongjiang Province and forced to work in a leather factory, barely clad, standing in vats of unknown chemicals, eating dirty rice and spoiled vegetables, meat once a month, letters never, thirty-one prisoners in a room, sleeping like sardines. "The guards sent prisoners to beat me when I failed at self-criticism. I would write: *I am very bad at understanding the politics of human terror. But now I am learning. I am learning so much.*"

It's like hundreds of accounts I've read, from China and Burma, from Indonesia, Guatemala, Chile, Pakistan, from too many countries and too many people. Their names mean nothing, the details blur. So-and-so had his leg muscles crushed, this woman was raped, this boy disappeared coming home from the union office where his father worked. They're just words on the page, and there's no reason to cry, but here I am, weeping, stupidly, alone and with no way to stop. I get up and I breathe, I wipe my face and roam the room, but my face is washed with tears whether I'm pacing or still. It isn't the story. That's the horrible thing, the story means nothing, less than nothing. Another atrocity in the endless list.

I'm just crying. For nothing, for everything. I wait for it to clear, but it won't clear. It's never going to be clear. Maybe that's why I can't stop.

10

"Ashes." The word hangs between us in this comfortable, professional, insulated air. I can see the garden out back – Maryse would know all those flowers. Purple ones, obscenely lush. The name will come to me in a minute. I should know it.

Irises. And the orange are tiger lilies, and the huge, red, floppy ones are poppies. There. Not such a bad brain. This is the house Maryse and I looked at in our other lifetime. A house just like this, with a ground floor stuck right onto the earth. Solid, brick, big rooms, hardwood, furnishings from around the world. This woman takes trips. A successful professional sitting opposite me in a long black skirt and a silky purple blouse that seems too dressy.

Maryse and I stood in a house just like this looking at oak cupboards with Patrick in her arms asleep.

"What do you mean by ashes?" she asks. Ashes? Slowly the word comes back to me.

"It's what I felt when I embraced my wife," I say. "When I got home."

We're digging through the shit of my life, which is necessary, somehow, part of my purgatory. I wonder, how long does this last? Not the therapy – I told Joanne I'd only stay an hour. But the churning, that seems to go on forever. In the hood, I thought I was being a hero by hanging on to strands of who I was in my old life. It was a conscious effort, I escaped the present every moment I could summon the energy. But when I got home –

"Bill? Can I call you Bill?"

Yes, of course you can call me Bill. You're going to bill me anyway. I start to smile and then I realize I didn't tell her the joke. I never said it. The words stayed in their distant orbit.

"I'm the world's worst patient," I say. "I'm really hopeless. I don't do well any more down on the earth. That sounds strange. But when I was shackled to the wall for nine months – it was a kind of reverse birth. That's how I thought of it. I felt like I was buried under the earth. I didn't know why it was happening and I still don't, but I thought my job was to get smaller and smaller and then die. And I couldn't even do that right. I was a fuck-up all the way along."

"So your surviving, that was a fuck-up?"

"Other people died because of me. Marlene, the Australian woman who helped rescue me in the end. The soldiers shot her down in cold blood. She knew too much, I'm sure that was it. And Josef, my keeper. Well, I killed him first, but it was a hallucination. The only time I actually *tried* to help myself, and it was all in my head. So I never tried after that. I was already part ghost."

"What do you mean?"

I can't talk about this. Most people don't understand, that feeling of being half here, half in some other reality. There are realms and dimensions far beyond what we know ordinarily. Places of refuge and torment, of other ways of being. I look around the room. Most doctors post their credentials. I see instead batiks and traditional cloths from some native group, God knows where. I see her professionally concerned eyes and her jade earrings and her wedding band and the pictures of her children on her desk. Her desk by the door by the garden.

There are tissue boxes everywhere. This quaint little countrified house where carrot juice is served and the windows are so new and clean.

"I'm sorry, I've only had time for a quick read of your book," she says. "It's very moving. Did you find that writing things out helped you to deal with them?"

"Absolutely."

She waits for more. She's very patient. She gets paid by the hour. She crosses her legs and leans in and fixes me with her therapist eyes tractor beam, trying to extract my thoughts. My precious thoughts.

"It helped a lot," I add, unhelpfully.

She crosses her hands on her crossed legs. Her married, successful, full-life hands. She ordered those windows. She paid for them from sessions like these with other sunken wretches. She paid for the trips and her husband is an architect, I put it together in a flash, their children are in private school, they go to Jamaica on spring holidays and Spain in the summer.

"Bill?"

"I need to focus." I say it before she does.

"Bill, post-traumatic stress is a tricky thing. It takes many people a lifetime of effort to overcome it. To keep the flashbacks in check, to get beyond the trauma, to generate some forward momentum in their lives. You have to be willing to talk about it, to revisit the worst so it will let you go. Your book is a powerful expression of what you went through. It must have been rewarding to write it, to get it out on paper. But you have to express it again and again, in many different ways, to really root out these demons. There's no way around it. If you close the door on these things they fester. You'll spend the rest of your life trying to keep it closed."

Those big, beautiful, professional eyes. No festering in her closet. Whereas I *did* fester, literally, for nine months I festered. It should be my name, Fester.

"Did I say something funny?"

She says it in an unfunny way, like a schoolteacher who's being laughed at. Well, children, let's all share the joke . . .

"Tell me about your ex-wife," she says, groping. *Wife*, I think. She's not my ex yet. Dr. what's-her-name gets up, a little irritated. I'm not taking this seriously. I'm scared shitless.

"There must be a lot of issues around the break-up," she says, hopefully. Issues. Yes, there are many issues. But not about the break-up of my marriage. That's not what I want to discuss.

She pours a glass of carrot juice from the tray on the table between us and offers it to me, but I refuse. In Santa Irene I lived on wood jelly and water. Sometimes I think that's all that's left of me.

"Say *something*," she says, but gently; it takes me by surprise. She leans in and caresses my hand. Not a professional thing to do at all. There must be a code of ethics. Or maybe there's just a bag of tricks. But it works. It gets me going. Goddamn her.

"My wife is not, was never, a really *nurturing* kind of person," I say. This is not what I want to talk about! That glass of carrot juice. If I won't have it she won't either. It's just going to go to waste. "She's an artist, she's a talent, she's exciting and beautiful and full of life, and I dragged her off to Santa Irene because of my career with the foreign service. And she stopped painting, you know, because of me, because of what happened. She stopped painting, she went white. Her hair was black as night except for one streak of white when I met her. You know, she had the face of an eighteen-year-old, but there was that streak of white in all that black. Am I babbling? I'm supposed to babble, yes? Babble is good. Then when I came back, from my little . . . time away, my trip to the dark side . . . she'd gone all white, her hair was – what do they call it? – a *shock* of white. A shock. It was. And there was one time . . . well, there were many times. I'll tell you about one time. I tried to kill myself. Uh, three times. It was really . . . disappointing for all of us, you know. Our hero survives worse than hell, and then . . ."

And then the words dry up because of the way she's looking, so satisfied on a professional level. Here is her famously taciturn patient opening up when other therapists failed to get him to communicate. It's written all over her face. The opening lines of her paper on treating Bill Burridge, torture survivor.

"Yes?" she says, hopefully. She has the air of – of what? Of an *irrepressible optimist*. But she wouldn't understand having your body broken, smothered, beaten, buried, forgotten for hopeless months but not giving in because of what's inside you, the universal force, the seed, the tiny sprout that pushes through asphalt. The pain and terror of that push. No other choice so you do it.

"Is the time up?" I ask.

"No. I don't want you to be concerned about time."

"Oh," I say, disappointed. If I wore a watch I'd be able to tell when the hour was finished.

"One day Maryse and Patrick came home," I say. Without thinking I pick up the carrot juice. It's unbelievably rich, it seems immoral somehow, far too much.

"Don't stop," she says. But without that look of professional triumph, so I keep going.

"They came home and Patrick saw some blood on the kitchen floor and he started screaming. I'd never heard such a scream. Well, I had, that was the problem, I'd heard it all too often. It was my own scream. The Kartouf used to hook me up to an electric-shock gizmo, a black box. They tried it everywhere on me. I think they were experimenting. Trying to get the hang of it. They'd had it done to them but they weren't so practised at doing it to others. They'd shock me right to the edge and then shoot me up with drugs to keep me for next time. They were incompetents. They didn't know what to do with me. That's why they held me so long and why they fucked me up so badly. They did, literally, they fucked me. And they burned me with cigarettes. Just the smell of the smoke as they approached. It drove me wild with terror. They put me through a mock execution. I knew they would, I'd already figured it out, I just didn't know when, and it doesn't matter, because when they do it you're terrified, every cell in your body screams in panic, nothing can prepare you for that. You see, I don't really have trouble expressing this stuff. I wrote it in my book, I took my skin off in public, I could talk all day about it. I could talk all night, and all the next day. I could never shut up and I'd never get to the end of it, you see, there's a Niagara Falls of shit here, an everlasting resource, and if I let it that's all I'll ever do with the rest of my life, process my own shit. And that's not what I want. I want to do something useful for other people. Which is what I do. As you know, with my organization. I'm processing misery for a lot of the world. I don't need to say any of this personal stuff. You know it and I know it."

"What about the blood on the floor?"

The blood on the floor. The blood.

"It was chicken blood. I'd tried to get dinner, only the chicken was fatty, I pulled off the skin and dropped some of the chicken on the floor. It was a big mess. In those days I started a lot of things and then lost heart and so there would be these projects in mid- . . . in mid-whatever. Mid-orbit. All over the house. I had jigsaw puzzles, and a windmill, I was building a windmill. It was a birthday present someone had given to Patrick, a model windmill, one of those hopelessly complicated toys people give to kids knowing their parents are going to have to put it together. Probably while the kid watches television."

I have the horrible taste of carrot juice in my mouth.

"So there was blood on the floor?"

She keeps bringing me back. Believe me, I can focus. All too well.

"I wasn't in the kitchen any more. I don't know what I was doing. Well, if I think of it I can tell you what I was doing. Is that important?"

"If you think it's important."

"I was . . . I was trying to fold socks. Laundry. It's very ordered and clean and it smells nice. Very satisfying. I'd reached a block with the chicken. You know, I'd started it but then things got bad, my head started to fester –" There's a good word, that's the word I'm going to remember from this afternoon. I say it again. "My head was *festering* so I decided to try something else. Just for a break. But that's when they came home. Patrick ran in first. He was always doing that. He was a running-in-first kind of kid. He saw the blood on the kitchen floor and started to scream. He thought it was me. I'd already tried to kill myself, he'd already seen my blood, all over the living room. He was scared for me and tried to protect me and I don't know why he ran in first like that. Maybe he *wanted* to see me all bloody. But he just started screaming. And he couldn't stop. Even when I walked into the kitchen with a clean pair of socks in my hands, normal as I can be. He screamed even more. And it was *my* scream, my scream from the black box, terrifying. He wouldn't stop. I held him and he wouldn't stop."

I have another sip of carrot juice just to quit talking. It's silly to go over it all again and again. I have better things to do. Not here. Not with this stranger in this fine house we could never have afforded in this life we never got.

"You're shaking," she says.

Well, of course I'm shaking. I have earthquakes inside me all the time.

"You say your wife is a not a nurturing person. Is that what you need now? Do you –?"

"I'm sorry, I need to go, is what I need. I'm sorry." I get up too quickly, nearly bump my head on her pretty, professional, leaning-in chin.

"I'd like to do some visualization with you –"

"Yes," I say, meaning no, never, I'd rather not visualize. I'm already walking out.

"I think that there's more –"

I turn, nearly furious. "With the black box," I say, "they attached the wires to my nipples. They attached them to my tongue, to my penis and testicles. And they shocked me. There's no way I can tell you what that felt like. No way in the world. They did it again and again until I passed out, probably long after I passed out. And not just once. It was days and days like that, and then they'd do something else. They'd rape me or they'd kick me. They stretched my arms behind my back. I lost my teeth. They kept me –" Now I really am losing it. I'm so angry and she wants this, it's what therapists do, they want to unleash the tears again and again. Well, I won't have it. *Breathe, breathe, calm down.*

I tell her, "You ask me, but that's all I can tell you and telling you means some part of me has to go through it over and over. I'm not a masochist!"

Time to go. Past time!

"Don't leave like that," she says. It isn't a steel voice but silk, so strong it stretches and binds, weighs nothing, but won't let me go. "We're getting you out of the pit, that's what we're doing. It means you're going to have to dig. You're going to have to reimagine the darkness and name the evil. You're going to have to see it again from the inside and outside, for what it was and what you thought it was. We'll work together, there are ways to do it safely. But you can't leave your heart outside the door. This is going to be as much work as your physical survival. There's no way around it."

I can't do it. She's asking too much. With no guarantee of anything but more pain. I've had enough of professional bull-shit and platitudes. I can't sit still and suffer any more. I have to go!

But where to, exactly? Joanne has been waiting for me on the porch, reading her novel. She has to phone for a taxi and so we have to wait. She looks at me with concern and at Dr. what's-her-face – Joanne knows her name, that's what's impor-tant – and she can sense what a disaster this has been.

"When's the next appointment?" she asks, trying for humour where there is none.

11

Days later, back at the apartment, Waylu calls. I'm still in a state, I hardly know what to say. "I am sorry, Mr. Burridge," he says, his voice softer somehow, not what I expect, "but I am calling in the hopes that you will reconsider. We did not really get a chance to discuss the proposal. Perhaps we could set a time. Perhaps you have specific fears and concerns that we could allay."

Perhaps, but I can hardly talk with him. The air leaves the room and I have to leave with it. "I support the establishment and the work of a truth commission wholeheartedly," I hear myself saying. That rational voice that seems to function no matter what the inner turmoil. "But for me a return to Santa Irene is out of the question. The issue is too personally charged. My health is too frail."

He starts to say something else, something polite and oiled and professional. I cut him off. "I'm sorry," I say. "I'm sorry. But I have to go out." And I do, there's no more air. I rush out and down the elevator and onto the street, crowded now with traffic, people hurrying home from their day. It's cold, I haven't worn a sweater, I pull my collar close and start walking anywhere. A woman holds out a hand and stops me from stepping off the curb against the traffic light. "Careful," she says, then ducks her head and steps out herself. But the light is green now.

I walk aimlessly and then I'm not walking, I'm leaning against a stone building crying like a fool. Weeping for nothing, but I can't stop myself. People hurry by, assuming I'm drunk, I suppose, a vagrant. It's cold and winter is coming, that's why I'm crying. I'm cold and I'm coming apart.

More days bleed by. In the silence of my sanctuary, my apartment in the sky, I watch the clouds shift as the afternoon drains away, an argument taking me this way then that, another replacing it, a voice, a possibility, a sense of importance and dread. Why can't they let go of me? Why can't I let this go myself?

The phone rings and I'm certain it's Waylu again. I shouldn't answer but I can't stop myself.

"Hello, Bill." Not Waylu. "Bill," Maryse says, "I got your letter." Letter? I think. Letter. Of course. My letter. It seems like a hundred years since I sent that letter. One more thing that was going to save my life.

"Yes, yes," I say, trying to recover. There is a long pause which, I suppose, I'm expected to fill, perhaps to restate what I said in my letter. But my mind is jamming.

"Well," she says finally, her voice now edgy. My fault, it's all my fault. My focus has been elsewhere. As always. I'm blowing it again.

"I meant it," I blurt desperately.

"Meant what?"

"What I said in the letter. I meant it."

Pathetic. I can't even sum up my feelings. I'm lying limp in front of her feet. As if any woman could be won back like that.

"Well," she says again. Reluctantly. Against her better judgement. "I guess we could come for a picnic."

"Yes. *Yes!* That's all it would be," I say. "Something civil."

"That would be a change."

"Yes." I let her have her dig. She deserves it. We make the arrangements and then seconds after I put down the phone it rings again.

"Hello?"

"Hello? Mr. Burridge?" An English accent, a woman's voice. "Mr. Burridge," she says, "perhaps you have heard of me. My name is Suli Nylioko."

"Yes. Yes, of course," I say, as if I'm not in shock, have been expecting her call all along. What time is it in Santa Irene? It must be two o'clock in the morning.

"Mr. Burridge," she says, and I'm struck by how ordinary her voice sounds. Just another person calling from the other side of the planet. "It is an honour to talk with you. Please accept my apologies for approaching you about participating on the planned Truth Commission. Mr. Waylu Tariola has reported to me your level of distress and I thought it perhaps appropriate for me to call. We had no desire to further your suffering. Indeed, many of us are mortified by what happened to you two years ago. Whatever our present troubles, there's no explanation, no way to condone the abominations that were visited upon you. Please believe me, I had no wish to compound your distress through this invitation."

I'm trying to find my voice but am suddenly swimming in emotion. She waits for me to speak, then when I don't she adds, "I know forgiveness cannot be hoped for, but I pray that someday you will find the peace that you deserve. Please know that even if you cannot be here in body, we know you will be in spirit. That's all that I am calling to say. Please accept my apologies."

"Yes," I say, somehow, and that breaks the dam so more words can come. "Yes, thank you, I've certainly been following your work and am a great admirer."

She says, "You know something, I think, of what I am trying to accomplish here. This is an ancient and very beautiful country trying to overcome the brutality of its recent history. We focus on Minitzh, the dictator, but it stretches back before him. We have been terrorized into feeling small and inferior, shown how to grind whole peoples into the soil without a thought for justice, for consequences, for what it has done to our soul."

"That's why you need a truth commission," I say. Safe enough, now that it's settled I won't be going. "You need to air the abuses of the past or the wounds will never heal properly."

"Precisely! It must be done right. Fair and thorough. It's going to be so difficult to find commissioners who are as untainted as you."

Untainted. An odd description for a torture survivor. And yet when she uses it I can see how it fits.

"The symbolism is so important," she says. "I know you know about that. How vital it was for *you* to speak out after what you had survived. This is what we need for our commission. Someone who can be the moral authority of the body."

There's a pause while I try to think how to respond.

"I appreciate your call," I tell her. "I feel badly I can't contribute more."

She says, "There will be a time, I hope, when you will feel safe enough to revisit this land. If we can heal this one corner, then think of what it will mean." She asks if she can call again to "consult" with me and I readily agree; she invites me to contact her any time and leaves her private number. When she hangs up I sit in an odd, breathless glow.

I walk to the window, watch the traffic stalled around late-season construction crews pawing at the streets in a desultory effort to finish before winter shuts them down. A man with a scruffy beard wearing a hard hat stands by the hole he's making with his jackhammer, smoking and talking with a friend.

It's settled. But is this what relief is supposed to feel like? I thought it would feel better. Like freedom is supposed to feel. But this isn't freedom. There are still eight hundred articles on human-rights abuses littered around my apartment. There's still no place for me to sleep. I pick up the phone to call Joanne and tell her, that's it, I've decided, but in the middle of dialling the number I think, well, of course, I had decided already. I had decided when I told Waylu to forget it.

So there's nothing really to say. I put down the phone.

I've got to get back on track. Tomorrow I will make my calls. To my contacts at Foreign Affairs, at the State Department, in Amnesty International and Human Rights Watch. To let them know it's me, I'm fine. It was just a little meltdown.

Slowly I become aware of a touch of smoke, a cigarette burning somewhere nearby. Down the hall? Strange. It smells as if it's in the apartment. Couldn't be. No one came in. But there it is again, stronger now. Not a Canadian cigarette, but spiced with cloves, harsher.

Stay calm. I walk to the kitchen, look in the bedroom. There's no one there. Of course not. How could there be? The door's locked. No one came in. But I should phone Joanne anyway. I walk back to the front room. Something's different. The smell is stronger.

"Hello?" I say, get spooked at the sound of my own voice. Stupid. Talking to myself in my own apartment.

I'll just phone Joanne. She'll be interested that Suli Nylioko called. That I've finally made up my mind.

"Who are you?"

It's dark suddenly, even though it should be the middle of the afternoon. The air so heavy and hot. Strange to have no one at the checkpoint. I'm driving, I don't know how, but I have to pay attention. The sad, huge, drooping leaves of the banana trees. Some kind of plantation by the highway. Deserted.

"Don't!" I say, because I know what's going to happen. But I'm ready this time. It's not going to be the same. I'm not going to hit the spike on the road. Have to keep my eyes sharp. But the car is going so fast. I try to slow down but the brakes are dead, the accelerator is stuck. Faster, faster. Men now, out of the corner of my eye, in bright colours. *Wham!* There goes the tire. But I'm not going to stop. I know better this time. Can't see them clearly, just bleeding colours on the edge of my vision.

The car slows. No! I can't figure it. I pump the accelerator and it slows even more. They must have switched the pedals. I try the brake too late. Now I'm stopped. I'm stopped, so I have to get out of the car. I don't want to but there's no other choice. I look around – no men anywhere. They've gone. It's different this time.

I open the door. One step, two. It's different. No men any-where. But it's so hot, just the roots of the mountains showing in the distance. It was clear the first time. So this is different, I think. If I go quickly I can finish before they get here. It's the back right tire. I open the trunk. This too is different – the tire irons, jack, and spare aren't where they should be. The trunk is too small. There isn't even the extra container of gas. I know I put it in there.

They've changed my car!

The spare is in the very back. A tiny wheel, but it's extraordinarily heavy. I can barely budge it. I pull and pull. So hot! I don't have time for this! I just need to get it out and on the car and away. They're coming, I know they are. Don't look! No time for that. Just pull.

I yank it free, turn, and there they are, fuck! A dozen of them, in bright, blurry colours, like a photograph not set properly, a glaring orange bleeding into blue and red. They're bigger than before. But I'm different too. I roar with rage, spin and fling the extra tire – light now, it dissolves into paper, they laugh at it floating past them. An arm comes out for me and I snap at it, the *pang*, how surprised he looks! *Crack!* His arm is twisted, broken, but I don't stop there. I jerk it towards me, strike his throat with the side of my hand then drive my knuckle into the same spot. He groans, gasps for breath, collapses.

They aren't going to take me this time! I push past several others, rip the car door open, slam it shut behind me, hit the autolock, and turn the ignition key. Concentrate. No jamming the gears this time. The engine roars, I feel for the clutch with my foot . . . but they've changed the pedals again! The accelerator is the brake, the clutch is reverse. I don't want to go back! Struggling, trying to keep hold of the gearshift, it's so slippery now with the heat.

Mustn't look. That was my mistake before, I looked and the tire iron came crashing through the window. That's when they got me. I looked.

Stalled! I try the key again, turn, and the glass explodes in my face. *Oh!* Unbelievable pain, the blood now filling my eyes, the skin on my face shredded. Hands pull me out through the window, the shards cut my arms, chest, legs as I'm scraped past.

It's different than before. It's worse. The boot lands in my kidneys and I cough blood right away. Again, and it's worse. They drag me on the pavement, it's so hot, it's been laced with chilli peppers, burns my skin and throat and eyes.

My eyes! I don't want to see this but I can't close my eyes. Everything through blood now. The trunk is so small. They're stuffing me in, they have to use the shovel to pack me in the corners.

Dust and gasoline and chillis burning my insides. It's worse than ever. I caved and they know it. Now there's no escape ever. I'm in the trunk bleeding from the eyes and it's just the beginning again.

12

There's a sliver of sunlight in late October. It falls upon the patch of grass by the water and warms the blanket I've brought. No wind here, and even the water looks warmer than it really is. Focus on this, I think. Breathe and focus on this. The cliff edge is russet with tinges of yellow and grey and black; the Gothic dull green towers of Parliament point impassively to a purple sky made more dramatic by the low sun. I look down at my silly picnic basket bought at an outrageous price from the tourist store on the Sparks Street Mall, the kind of store that sells ceramic Mounties and fake-furry beaver dolls and flimsy T-shirts that say I ♥ OTTAWA. I don't even know what foods Patrick likes, so I have brought as many different things as I could pack – three types of cheese, two breads, apples, bananas, pickles, olives, boiled eggs, fried chicken, Lebanese cheese pies, three juices, a salad. . . . The picnic basket comes with cutlery, plastic glasses, napkins, a tablecloth. I have red and white wine and flowers, a cutting board and knife, butter, mayonnaise, hummus. I've spread the blanket, laid out the food, am sitting with the sun gently warming my face, the grass breathing so softly, my dentures knocking together . . .

Three days since the twister. It only lasted the one afternoon and night really; I was up and functioning by the next evening. But the residue is particularly bitter, like lime and ashes have been poured into my blood. This is how it's going to be. The Kartouf are telling me. I refused to go back, and, far from being appeased, they've been spurred on. I'm offering no resistance so the knee will be in my groin more than ever.

Focus. The low light, the cliff edge, the bleeding colours. The approach of inevitable winter. Here I am shivering with not enough clothes. I have a sweater but not a jacket, and the ground is cold, the air chilly even in the sun. Stupid. A body like mine holds heat like a copper sheet.

I'm early, of course; couldn't face the entire morning in my apartment. What if the cigarettes came back? The sun passes behind a cloud and instantly the air is much chillier; even the wind seems to pick up. I huddle on the blanket, thrust my hands beneath my sweater. Bad news. Frail men like me catch pneumonia from biting little winds like this. I get up and shake my limbs, pace a bit, fall naturally into practising my animals. They're good for raising heat, calming the nerves. Dragon, *lun*, *pang*, *mandarin*, snake, ape, and bear . . .

"Daddy!" Patrick calls and breaks grasp with his mother, runs from the parking lot down the hill. Too impossibly tall; he seems years older than he was at the gallery. "What are you doing?" he asks when he gets to me.

"Trying to warm up," I say. "Here, punch me with your right hand."

"What?"

"Punch me. Nice and slow. Aim at my chin."

As his fist comes near I deflect the punch, bend the arm gently against itself, then pull him and catch his throat.

"Punch at me low," I say, and for a few minutes we pantomime the animals. I've been rehearsing what to say to him but this is finer.

"Careful of your father," Maryse says.

"He's beating *me* up!" Patrick calls back.

She has brought her own picnic basket, not a shiny new tourist version like mine, but an old family one that has done for generations.

"Wow! You've gone all out," she says, and I think immediately that I meant to get smoked oysters for her but forgot.

Patrick looks at the food but doesn't like anything except the peanut butter sandwich his mother has brought for him. He even hates all the juices – what kind of child doesn't like juice? – and the apples, though spectacularly ripe, are too firm.

"I have three loose teeth," he says, then points them all out to me and wiggles them.

"He really doesn't eat much," Maryse says. "Patrick, I think you're trying to be skinny like your dad."

It's choppy details like that. We both keep our attention on the boy. He can't seem to sit still for long but has to roar up and investigate the totem pole, run around and throw a rock in the water, come back for another bite of sandwich. Maryse is sensibly dressed in thick pants, a sweater and jacket. Her eyes look tired. She tells me the name of Patrick's teacher and I forget it. He likes numbers a lot but is slow with his reading. There've been some health problems – so many days he complains about a sore stomach, he doesn't want to go to school. She's taken him twice to the doctor but he can't seem to locate the problem. Stress, maybe.

I ask about his friends and she says he doesn't seem to have any. No one he wants to bring home. I ask about her art and she says the show was a critical success, which means, I gather, no sales. She's applied for a grant and there's a job coming open at the community college. Not looking at me. Hands busy with buttering the bread, pouring wine, wiping Patrick's face, plucking out an olive and pickle.

"It's pretty," she says, looking at the colours.

Patrick has brought a balsa-wood flyer, so we launch then chase it. It lodges in a tree and Patrick climbs it. Later the plane falls in the water and I snatch it out like a hero father would. Maryse sits on the blanket not watching us, her eyes trained on the river. After a time she pulls out her sunglasses and she looks like one of those glamorous starlets twenty years later, bundled and hidden and strangely human. Patrick has to go pee and I take him into the bushes. It starts to rain and we scramble to pack up the food and blanket, carry it all awkwardly to the car. Not a light refreshing rain but a steady daunting downpour, and we sit as if in a car wash, the windows fogging and obscured by water, this sense of being at the bottom of a lake. There's lots of food to nibble on and nowhere to go and a great looming subject or two I don't want to talk about. From the outside we look like any normal family.

"How are you doing for money?" I ask, and Maryse says it's fine, I've been sending enough. I don't tell her about Derrick's concerns. Why should I worry her? I'll feed them before I feed myself.

"I have to get Patrick back for piano," she says finally. "Can I give you a lift to your building?"

The rain is really lashing now so I accept. I didn't even bring an umbrella. She fires up the engine and even with the wipers and defogger on high the world outside stays blurry so the ride is slow and cautious. Not many cars are on the roads anyway. We pass several that have pulled over to wait out the downpour.

At my building the pleasant words come out. I have my hand

on the latch but don't leave. I can't think of what to say, of what I want. I open the door a crack and look at the rain and then close the door again.

"Could I come to the piano lesson?" I ask.

"What?"

"I've nothing to do this afternoon and would love it if I could just listen to the piano lesson."

Patrick roars with excitement and Maryse swallows her misgivings. But she drives much more aggressively across town and I can't tell if it's because we're late or she's angry at me. Small steps, I said, and now the picnic has turned into a piano lesson.

The lesson is in a private home in Ottawa South. "I usually don't stay," Maryse says, and deposits us both at the door. Mrs. Friendly answers, ushers us in, and Maryse dashes back to the car. Mrs. Friendly is in her late sixties, sagging in a comfortable way, with pasty skin and jiggling jowls. She has chocolate chip cookies on the table beside the piano. Patrick goes for them without asking. Geraniums and African violets line the windows and the furniture is old, quaint, impeccably clean. I sit on the sofa by the window and listen to the fumbling chords and the gentle voice, to the *chock-chock-chock* of the metronome. The piano is an upright Heintzmann; pictures of children and grandchildren crowd the top, in graduation gowns, prom dresses, clown suits, cowboy hats. The bookshelf is lined with Kipling, Tennyson, H.G. Wells, Churchill on the war, novels by Dickens, Thackeray, and Hardy.

"Sweetness, then tempo!" Mrs. Friendly says in her grandmotherly voice. "Stretch, don't look!"

I drink in the details as if this were my last supper.

I don't know the music. Something very light. When the lesson is over Mrs. Friendly effuses over Patrick's playing and I chime in. Then I praise Mrs. Friendly and she praises me for having such a wonderful son, so quiet and well behaved and diligent. It's a safe place, this piano room; it reminds me of my own grandmother's living room, and I'm in no hurry to leave.

We sit and talk about the deceased Mr. Friendly. He was an air-force navigator who missed World War Two and Korea – too young – but served for long stretches in the Arctic. In 1974 the army doctors told him he had a rare brain disease. "Such a long name!" she says. "None of us could pronounce it." But the CAT scan showed there wasn't much brain left; perhaps he had two months to live. So he went on sick leave and bought this house for his wife and kids – the back wing could be rented out to provide an income. After three months he asked his doctor if he could go back to work, since he wasn't feeling too bad. The doctor checked him over and agreed to part-time. He went back full-time instead, and never looked back. Died of lung cancer just three years ago.

"When he realized he had extra time, after those two months left to live, he started volunteering for everything," she says. "He headed up the Kiwanis for several years, was always out calling bingo, shovelling snow, cleaning highways, collecting blankets for charity. He was filled with the need to help others. Just to give thanks."

While she talks I'm filled with the need to believe in this story, in redemption, grace, second chances.

The rain clears and Maryse returns for us. "I waited for you guys to call," she snaps. Then more gently, "Patrick usually calls when he's through." Mrs. Friendly presses more cookies on me at the door and tells Patrick to practise a half-hour a day if he can.

Once we're back in the car Maryse pulls out as if she's in a big hurry. The wipers snap back and forth and she's completely absorbed in navigating through the annoyingly slow traffic. She can't wait to get rid of me. It's obvious.

"Listen," I say. I want this to be more private, but Patrick should hear me say these words as well. "I'm sorry. I'm so sorry for the way everything has turned out. You know that I love you – the both of you – as much as my rattling heart can any more." It's a pathetic attempt at humour, gets no visible reaction. "Anyway, what I want to say –"

"Bill," she cuts in, "I think we need to take the next step." Stopped at a red light, the cold rain washing us. I'm not sure what she means. The next step? I'm not ready to move back in. But her tone –

"We shouldn't talk about it here," she says, her voice lowered, as if Patrick hasn't just heard.

"No. Of course," I say. "The next step?"

Green light, but the traffic is still backed up from the next intersection. Maryse leans on the horn, but they aren't going anywhere and neither are we. "Oh, for God's sake," she says, and looks behind suddenly to try to get into the other lane. No good.

She doesn't mean moving back in. No, the next step is formal divorce. That's what she means. It's obvious, yet it hits me by surprise, like knocking your head on a corner you've avoided till now. The anger rises suddenly.

"Anyway," I say, "what I need to tell you is that I've been invited by the president of Santa Irene, Suli Nylioko, to serve on a truth commission to investigate past abuses. So for a lot of reasons –"

"*What?*" Maryse says. The light falls red but she swerves the van forward. I don't know how we miss a blue sedan on our right, but we do, somehow, make it, just barely, to the other side of the intersection.

"I've thought about it deeply," I say, my voice too loud, my temper getting the best of me.

"*What's Daddy doing?*" Patrick asks.

"Would you have to go back there?"

"I'm afraid there's no other way. But the president called personally. She's someone I really trust. I can't explain it but I think there might be a strong possibility of really making a difference."

"Bill, be reasonable!"

"What's Daddy doing?"

"A truth commission! Why do they need *you*? How could they even have the temerity to ask? Bill, you're not up to that kind of work. Be realistic. You can't go back there. It's just nuts. Call them back. Say you can't do it. God! Tell them your wife forbids you!"

It's an odd thing to say, and I look at her too long. What could she care? My wife. Who has just asked for a divorce. Who has not been my wife for years, it seems, and now is lost for good. The magnetic pull of our bodies and souls has been replaced by jagged spinning rock against rock with sparks flying, abrasion, heat without warmth. My wife.

Who doesn't have the Kartouf knee in her groin.

"You have to trust me," I say, trying to stay calm. "I've made myself sick thinking about this. I don't believe I have another choice. If there were any other way – of living, I mean. Not doing what I'm doing now, which is not living, it's twisting on a hook in a cold wind. I want to be free."

"Is Daddy going back where the kidnappers got him?"

"It's okay," I tell Patrick, reach back to hold his hand. He's shaking, brim-full with tears. "The kidnappers won't get me again. That's all over."

"But they got you last time. They almost killed you – you *told* me!"

"There aren't any more kidnappers," I tell him. "It's not the same place. They're trying to get better, and I have to help them, and maybe I can get better myself." I turn to Maryse. "Please listen," I say, quietly so she will. "I have to do whatever it takes to free myself."

"There are other ways you can be helped," she says, so angry.

"No, that's it," I say, "I can't *be* helped, we saw that, you did your best –" I fail to keep the bitterness from my voice, see it register in her eyes. "I have to help myself," I say. "It was all done to me, I was powerless. But this is different. This is *my* choice. A chance to *do* something. It's different and it's what I need."

I realize it now. This is the only thing to do.

"I'll write to you," I say to Patrick. "Every day, on the e-mail, you watch."

"Do you *promise*?"

Maryse looks at me, full of doubt and reproach.

"Absolutely," I say.

We talk for another hour, in the rain in the traffic and later parked on the street by my apartment. Back and forth, with tears and hugs and painful silences. But it's clear now for the first time in ages. It feels both sad and light, a relief and an ache for what's to come.

I have to return to Santa Irene. If it kills me, well . . . there would still be a freedom in that.

We talk it through in ever-tightening circles, until finally we are wrung dry and it really is time to go. Then I stand on the street in the diminishing rain and watch the spot where my family used to be.

13

The movie on the plane is a Chinese martial-arts extravaganza with English subtitles. I leave off my earphones but sit fascinated by the image on the tiny screen – the hero prince scales the wooden tower, fighting off ten, twelve, fifteen attackers at a time, then reaches the princess at the top only to find that *she's* a martial-arts master too, who boots him off when he isn't looking. Back up he fights, one hand holding flowers, and when he reaches the top this time they're joined by . . . *his wife*, also a martial-arts master. Now he must fend off attacks from both women, somehow explain to his wife why he's bringing flowers to the princess, and still woo the princess at the same time. *"You don't love me!"* the wife proclaims and leaps from the tower. Our hero goes after her, breaking the laws of gravity to catch up, grab her, and snag a ledge halfway down. Then the princess throws *herself* off the tower and so our hero must go after her as well . . .

The last few weeks have been a whirlwind of phone calls and negotiations, of doctors' visits and international briefings, meetings at Foreign Affairs and at the Santa Irenian embassy, of visa applications and last-minute packing, of scrawled messages, mass e-mails, hurried goodbyes. When I phoned, Suli agreed to forty-five thousand dollars plus expenses for three months – enough to pay me and Joanne decently and still make Derrick happy. I've left him back in the office with something to work with.

Oddly enough, after Maryse my worst argument was with Joanne – she still thinks I shouldn't have accepted, was even reluctant to agree to accompany me. But she's here. I finally convinced her I wouldn't have even thought of going if I wasn't sure she'd be with me. She's worried about her mother's health, too, but the latest prognosis was guardedly optimistic, in the short run at least.

Everything done under pressure, the rush of the decision and the hundred subsequent things to do. Now these hours on the plane seem unreal, a weird nowhere between the past and the future. The slow squeeze of time. Through the many trips up and down the aisle to spell my leg, through the rubber duck à l'orange and gazing at the floor of clouds, the little plastic packets of salted peanuts and chemical-cheese crackers and endless rounds of juice and tea and coffee and water.

Joanne has been uncharacteristically quiet. I ask her how she's doing and she says, "Fine," abruptly.

"Fine?" I say back to her.

She says it again, "Fine," without looking at me. She has a book turned face down on her lap and her eyes are half closed.

"Last time I made this flight," I say, "Maryse got a terrible headache. I think it lasted her whole time in Santa Irene. They recycle the air on these flights so it feels like the oxygen disappears."

Joanne doesn't respond.

"People were smoking on that flight, though," I continue. "All those Asian businessmen. What's your book about?"

"Damn!" she says, rising abruptly and hurrying down the aisle to the washrooms. She darts in front of a woman with a small child and into the next available stall. I crane to see through the gap in the headrests of the seats in front of me. The door stays closed a long time. The woman ushers her child into the cubicle beside Joanne's, and they finish and leave but Joanne's door stays closed.

I walk up and down the aisle, my leg feeling angry – it's the best way I can describe it, as if it needs to lash out at something. The warrior on screen is battling the many forces of evil while, for some reason, trying to keep his mother-in-law balanced on a pole in the courtyard.

I return to my seat, sit quietly and breathe. Tuck my chin in, fold my hands in my lap. Little sips of air, but controlled from the abdomen. Tongue on the roof of the mouth. What was it Wu said to me? That in ancient days in the night darkness men and women were like animals and stayed quiet so as not to draw attention to themselves. So they had plenty of time to learn how to breathe.

Joanne comes back grey-faced, her gait unsteady.

"Are you all right?"

She sits hard, puts her head down immediately, fingers on her temples.

"What is it? Have you got a headache?"

An old Mediterranean-looking man gazes across the aisle at Joanne then looks away. Joanne pushes her hands between her knees and keeps her head down.

"Joanne! What is it?"

I reach across to put my arm around her and in a minute a stewardess is kneeling in the aisle beside her.

"Are you all right, ma'am? Is there something I can help with?"

"I'm fine," she says. "I'm just getting worse and worse on airplanes, that's all."

She refuses juice, ginger ale, water, a warm blanket. "It'll pass," she says.

And it does, slowly. Somewhere over the Pacific, after the movie has ended and most of the passengers have gone to sleep, the colour comes back to her face, she breathes easier. I ask her if she's feeling better and she nods, gets up, takes a walk. Some minutes later she comes back carrying a cup of tea.

"Just a few more hours," I say. We're changing flights in Hong Kong, will head south to Santa Irene after that.

"Yes." But she doesn't look at me.

"It's a long trip."

She picks up her book, reads a few pages. I close my eyes.

"I shouldn't have come," she says suddenly.

Oh no. "What?" I say. "We discussed this."

"Look at me, I didn't even get my hair cut. I *hate* long hair in the tropics. I always get it cut before I go. But I didn't think you'd actually carry this through. It might be right for you but it isn't right for me. I've had this bad feeling for a while. I shouldn't have come."

"Are you worried about your mother?" I ask.

"It's that and other things," she says.

"What other things?"

The drone of the engines; a stewardess wanders by with extra blankets.

"I'm just not supposed to be doing this now," she says.

"What are you supposed to be doing?"

Sips of tea, fingers drumming slowly on the plastic tray in front of her. This drowsy, light, nowhere state.

"I have a weakness for running off," she says. "It's a bit of an addiction. The next crisis. All that adrenaline, it's a real high until you crash. Like Rwanda, that was a crash for me. I decided to change my plan after that. I wasn't going to run off. I was going to stick things out back home."

"This is only for three months," I say. "Besides, we discussed this."

"I know."

"You're mostly worried about your mom."

"No. Yes, of course. But she'll be all right."

Then it's someone else, I think. I've been so stupid.

"There's always the phone," I say. "You can send e-mails."

She doesn't want to talk about it. It's her private life, why should she? I've railroaded her into going, taken her for granted, been so self-centred.

Time crawling, endless clouds passing below. I try to think of what to say.

"You said you wanted to stick things out," I say. "Is there anybody in particular? Besides your mother?"

"There was the wrong guy," she says, still not looking at me. "I tend to go for the wrong guy."

I wait for more but she glances at her book, flips another page.

"What kind of guy is the wrong guy?"

She thinks about it for too long, until I'm not sure she's going to answer. Finally she says, "Boyish, unstable, dangerous types, into adventure, hardship. Impatient for the next flight out. Not good father material."

"So you want to have kids?"

Another thoughtful pause, before her reluctant reply. "Sure, I want to have kids."

She goes back to reading her book. I flip through a glossy in-flight travel magazine.

"I've got four younger brothers," she says after a while. "We were terribly suburban. My parents used to pile us into a station wagon at night in our pyjamas and we'd ride around looking at the lights. Everybody's normal except for me. Regular jobs, spouses, houses in the suburbs, their own kids growing so fast. I was the one who had to go off. But now I'm thirty-five and I don't want to miss out. You know, huddling over mouldy rations in a little tent in a cholera-infested corner of the world is not the best way to raise a family. Aid workers live the life for a while and then either it consumes them or they go on to something else. I thought I'd gone on to something else."

It's all she wants to say, so I get up and stretch my legs. This quiet, sleeping warehouse of people. The shades are drawn except for one window near the washrooms, bright sun beaming in.

When I get back she says, "I wasn't in Rwanda for the real horror." Her face tight, eyes on mine for a moment then shifting away. "You asked about it so I'm going to tell you."

"All right," I say. I didn't really ask, I think, but stay quiet.

"Things had calmed down when we went back in. There was a lot of . . . silence, really. Psychological clamping . . . because life keeps going, right? The rivers flow blood for a while but then you have to eat, you need a roof and somewhere to sleep. The darkness passes like something else you dreamed. Babies." She pauses at the word.

"Babies?"

"Well," she says, her voice faltering just a bit, "they keep getting born, don't they? The darkness comes and everything's turned upside down and it seems like the end of life as you've known it – the end of life, period, for so many . . ." She takes a deep breath. "The babies keep pushing out. They *demand* to get here. It's what I was doing in our little hospital outside Kigali. Delivering babies. Tutsis mostly, genocide survivors, now pushing out babies. It was like seeing the first green growth in an area flattened by forest fire. You know? It seems so desolate. And yet the next season there they are, the seedlings."

"Yes."

"I remember one birth, a breech, the mother was in terrific pain. I've never sweated so much, I felt like *I'd* given birth. She came out finally, backwards and purple, the cord wrapped round her neck. I don't know how she survived, or the mother, for that matter. A beautiful young woman, strong as rain. I remember she moaned. The African women I know didn't make a peep while giving birth, they were *silent*. So to have that woman moan . . . It really felt like we were on the edge of life and death.

"Oh God," she says. "Some nurse I turned out to be."

"You're a magnificent nurse. Where do you think I'd be without you?"

She looks at me briefly, turns abruptly away. "The local women usually gave birth in their homes. Without help, or just with their mother or sister or someone. I made it an issue to have them come to the hospital. Too many were dying, or the babies weren't getting their shots. There was one night we had fourteen babies with us. Fourteen. All collected together."

I just stay quiet.

"It was so stupid of us. Of *me*. We were thinking of security all the time and yet weren't thinking. I was so proud. Fourteen babies." Tears come down now and the words stop for a time.

"So in the night some men came. Probably it was men.

With machetes. They weren't particularly quiet about it and yet no one saw them. Or no one would say they saw them. Someone must've. There were so many rumours. That it was the Interahamwe militia attacking because these were 'genocide witnesses.' They were babies, for Christ's sake, they weren't witnesses. That it was the Patriotic Army attacking because they thought our guard had worked for the former government. Johnny. Jean Batiste Mbyanuwama. They hacked off his arms and legs."

Wiping her eyes. It always comes back to bad news, I think.

"And the babies?" I ask. Because I have to.

"They laid them out on the dirt road in front of the hospital," she says. "Their bellys had been split open and their guts pulled out."

I try to put my arm around her but it's awkward in these seats, and she has large shoulders. "I'm all right," she says. "I'm all right."

"You don't have to do this," I blurt. "You can go home if you want."

"And what would *you* do?" she asks, smiling suddenly, her face still soaked.

"I'd go back with you, of course. You know I could never do this without you."

"Well then, I'm screwed," she says softly. She goes quiet again, then says, "We need a safe thought for you. For Santa Irene, in case you feel a twister coming on. You'll need something to grab onto for protection, a mental life preserver. Have you got something?"

"Nothing that will work. A twister coming on is unstoppable. Once you reach a certain point –"

"But *before* you get there. One safe, rock-solid thought. Don't tell me, don't tell anyone, but fix it now in your mind.

Just hang it up where you know you can reach it in an instant. Can you do that?"

The only protector is Joanne. I look at her, her red hair and those gentle eyes. Joanne walking with me by the Ottawa River, Joanne coming through the door, Joanne any time, Joanne right now.

Joanne.

14

The heavens are unloading on us. Tumultuous rain on a black night, the sound almost more unsettling than the water. The air is sweating hot, heavy with the smell of rotting vegetation, of diesel fumes, and soaked black jungle soil, of too much life. Not the cold, raw, deadening wind of an Ottawa October. They've packed us in a military Jeep, the plastic flaps that pass for windows keeping out only part of the spray. Our driver laughs with every jolt. The guard beside him, a thin, sleepy-eyed man named Nito, smokes idly and drums his fingers on the doorframe. My personal protector! He looks as if he'd have a hard time fighting off a dragonfly.

But I feel surprisingly calm. It might be because of Joanne, who now has returned to her old self, laughs along with the driver and throws up her hands as if she's thirteen and this is a roller coaster. It might also be because we're in a convoy of about thirty military vehicles bristling with weapons.

Almost anything – the darkness, the slashing rain, the smoke from Nito's cloved cigarette, the mysterious flow of

Kuantij in male voices – could trigger a twister in me. And yet all is still so far.

"Sorry we could not send you a limousine," Mr. Tjodja says. He's squashed in the back, his black suit getting rumpled, muddy, and wet. I've already forgotten his title – minister of reconciliation? Perhaps that's it. He stood waiting for us at customs, waved his hand once and we were through. A small, broad man in tiny black Italian shoes. "Many of the government vehicles were burned in the uncertainties," he says. "The luxury ones, I mean."

"This is better than a limousine!" Joanne yells back at him. "Does it always rain like this?"

"We will soon be in the rainy season," he says. His hair slicked back, his purple tie flashing in the night, the tight twists of his mouth when he speaks and when he stays silent.

"Has there been any more violence?" I ask him.

"Very peaceful now!" he says. "I think you will find it quite a change. We're all pulling together. Suli has brought new co-operation to the people!" A gleam of near-malice in his eye – hard to see in the dark, so maybe I'm imagining it from the tone of his voice, parroting slogans. He seems cultured, looks rich enough to be part of the upper-class *lumito*, for whom everything was going great until the assassination. Maybe the collapse in the economy has meant he's had to snag a government job.

I'd forgotten the totality of this darkness at night, our headlights carving shallow tunnels, small buildings emerging then disappearing. No streetlights yet, though there is a sudden sign for Marlboro cigarettes and another for Kalio, the local soft drink. The company is owned by one of Minitzh's sons and was given a monopoly. The last place on earth untouched by Coke and Pepsi? Perhaps not for long.

The last time I arrived it was daylight. Peter from the embassy drove. Maryse sat still, holding herself, and Patrick watched everything, especially the guards at the checkpoints. The checkpoints are still here but we're just speeding by them.

Into the city now. I think we're passing through a section of Welanto. When I ask Tjodja he nods his head and starts telling us about the fires. We can't see anything in the black but there is an acrid smell, lessened but not quite washed out by the rain.

Nearly midnight local time, I don't know what time by my body clock. I'm longing for the solitude of the hotel room. Just a few hours to collect my wits. But at the hotel, the Merioka ("Prosperity," I whisper to Joanne), there's a reception planned.

"Don't worry. Nothing elaborate!" Tjodja says when he sees our faces. Then in a low voice, "You know it is our custom to have a ceremony on every possible occasion."

"We can't. I'm sorry. It's too late, we've had a very long flight."

"Yes. Yes, of course!" Tjodja says, as if he agrees completely. But then he insists. "It is just for a few minutes. Everyone has been waiting. It would be a terrible disappointment."

The Merioka is a gleaming high-rise down by the harbour, the most expensive part of town. I silently try to calculate the cost of our rooms. It used to be four hundred U.S. dollars a night, but those were better days for Santa Irene. With the violence and uncertainty tourism has disappeared and prices collapsed, I imagine.

Through the lobby, which looks subdued, or maybe it's only the hour.

"We can't go to the reception. Perhaps another time would be better," I say.

"Yes, yes," Tjodja says.

"You should show us our rooms."

"Of course." And we follow him . . . to a glitzed reception hall crowded with slow-moving people wrapped in smoke.

"*No!*" I say at the door. "I told you –"

"Bill," Joanne says, "I'm fine. If it's just for a few minutes."

"Yes! Yes!" says Tjodja, pinching my elbow, dragging me in.

"Mr. Burridge! What a pleasure to see you again! Happier circumstances, happier circumstances!" exudes a short, burly man in a tuxedo. He looks like he's been drinking for two days. Most of the others look that way as well. It's a debauch, an attempt at the old style, but far more tired and tawdry. "So fine to see you!" the man exclaims. "So fine!" Pumping my hand. "So . . . *fine!*" He turns to Joanne. "And your wife, Ms. Lorraine – *lovelier than ever!*"

"Uh – this is my *nurse*, Joanne Stoddart," I say. "Joanne, this is –" And I pause because I haven't a clue, although I should remember, I've seen him before. But the burly man doesn't take the hint. He's grasped Joanne's hand and gazes longingly into her eyes.

"– this is, uh –"

No help. Finally I say, "I'm sorry, sir, your name has slipped . . ."

"Of course it has!" he says too jovially. "I'm a slippery fellow. Burridge, I have to tell you, you *do* surround yourself with striking women!"

And you *lumito* men are still arrogant jerks, I think.

There are drinks on little trays held aloft by waiters who seem only slightly less intoxicated than many of the guests. A ragged-haired man in white tearfully renders "Love Me Tender" on the karaoke machine in the corner of the large room, by the velvet curtains. Several of the women in long gowns have formed a protective circle on the other side of the room and talk amongst themselves. A large semicircular banner in fluttery gold lettering near the bar reads, WELCOMMING YOU MR. BILL BURRIDGE.

"We have had a month of solid terror and uncertainty," the burly man says in a low voice, suddenly thoughtful and morose. "Everything was turned upside down! *But now you're here*," he says, emptying his glass. Cognac?

The crowd slowly awakens to the fact that the guest of honour has arrived. Several more tuxedoed men shuffle towards me and Joanne. Her red hair is like a flag of sexuality to them on this island of black hair. Drinks are thrust at us; twelve conversations start at once. The karaoke machine gets louder and a different drunken voice launches into "The Impossible Dream."

"Bill?" Joanne says to me, looking over several heads. "Is our two minutes up yet?"

"It must be!"

But we can't leave. An enormously wide man in a sloppy black suit wrestles with the microphone until the karaoke singer finally gives up. What follows is a twenty-minute soporific in Kuantij that the burly drunk sums up in just a few sentences. "He is welcoming you. You are such a hero to our people. You suffered so terribly the last time you were here. But now everything has changed."

"Mr. Alijo," I say, remembering his name.

"Franja," he says, correcting me. "Alijo has gone to Switzerland. No doubt he's climbing mountains as we speak!"

I met them both at a diplomatic reception at Minitzh's Pink Palace in the days before I was kidnapped. It seems a hundred years ago. Franja. He was a parasite then, like so many of Minitzh's hangers-on. Smiling, cultured, wealthy, spoiled men and women – who stage sudden, tumultuous, drunken applause. Hands push me forward. "No," I say, definite this time. I do not want to speak. It's too late, I've already stayed longer than I'd agreed. Where's Tjodja? I need to tell him, but he's disappeared.

"I'm not going to make a speech," I say, craning to find Tjodja.

"Please – just a brief few words!" Franja says, pushing me forward. "We've all been waiting!"

After a while it doesn't seem worth the fight. I wade through the crowd, shake hands, get thumped on the back. At the front I make a short meaningless speech thanking them for their welcome, asking for their help in the days ahead. It comes out as automatic jargon, barely better than Tjodja in the car. "And now," I say to their uncomprehending stares, "I look forward to some quiet rest, then the beginning . . ." The beginning of what? Several phrases present themselves: *the first step in the long road . . . the difficult process . . . the march towards healing and a chance at justice . . .* A chance at justice? I'd like to think it's more than that. I ponder some more and the phrase hangs incomplete – *the beginning* – until Franja starts the applause and everyone joins in and I don't have to worry about it. The beginning of what? Of what I've gotten myself into.

After the speech Tjodja reappears and takes Joanne and me to a huge penthouse suite on the twenty-third floor with a chandelier, grand piano, bar, and hot tub, the harbour lights flickering in the black distance behind the window, the bed large enough for a half-dozen restless sleepers.

"Where's the other room?" I ask the minister of whatever.

"I'm sorry?"

"Joanne is my nurse. We ordered two rooms."

"Ah," he says, his eyes telling me he comprehends – *appearances must be kept.*

"There is an adjoining suite," he says, showing us the way.

What looks like a closet actually leads to a small bedroom with a dresser, television, and bathroom of its own.

After Tjodja leaves, Joanne says, "Everyone thinks I'm your mistress."

"Not much we can do about it," I say.

"As long as Maryse doesn't think it."

"Maryse knows I'm incapable."

A quiet pause. Her sudden intensity tilts me off-balance.

"Some things get better," she says quietly. "You have to believe that. You know how I feel about working with chronic cases."

"Maryse has asked for a divorce, actually," I say, failing to keep the bitterness from my voice.

"Oh, Bill," Joanne says. "I'm so sorry to hear that."

"It's like there was a fire in the house," I say, slowly, trying to think of it exactly. "Even though you douse it early and the walls are still intact, there's been so much smoke and water damage, the electrical system is shot, the pipes are ruined. You might as well tear it all down and start over."

"Well, I'm sorry," she says again. "If there was one couple I thought might pull through this sort of disaster, it was you two." She squeezes my arm briefly, then shoulders her large knapsack, a swift, powerful movement, full of youth and life. "I'm turning in," she says and closes the door.

I sit on the bed. I have returned to the valley of the shadow and it looks like . . . every other hotel room on the planet. Not true. It's a luxury suite twenty-three floors in the air. Perfect for me. Either they did their research or it's a happy coincidence. I want nothing near the ground.

I lie back, blink at the ceiling, white stucco with glinting specks. Listen to Joanne running the shower in the other room. We could be anywhere. The Kartouf could be anywhere.

In my liver, blood, kidneys, brain. Behind my eyelids, in my marrow. A quiet cancer. Peaceful for now. Perhaps happy to have me back.

I don't sleep, of course, but it's a surprisingly peaceful sort of unsleep, not a twister, no disasters, not even acidic, regretful thoughts of my failed marriage. Just a quiet seeping of darkness into light. From my window I watch the sun levitate out of the depths of the ocean while hulking cargo ships nod at the dock and the gulls circle. It's odd to gaze from such a distance behind double glass – no sound, as if the volume has been lost on the television. The *tritos* begin to clog the avenues, multicoloured, chromed up, gleaming, outrageous, taxi-buses that dart from one lane to the next, nearly up on the sidewalk to win riders, men in untucked white shirts and loose black pants, and women in office skirts and blouses, others in *saftoris*. Farmers ride on jury-rigged mini-tractors, pulling their pineapples and papayas to market, little boys sleeping in the back, their faces deep brown with sun and dirt.

Joanne emerges rumple-faced and drowsy. "Oh God, what a horrible night!" she says. "I couldn't fall asleep until about four or five in the morning."

"Yes, I heard you."

"Well, you're used to it!"

She slogs off to the bathroom.

And suddenly I am certain this has been the right thing to do. I've returned to the valley of the shadow but I'm used to it, and there is a peace here at the core that could never be mine away from it. This is where my most terrifying, exciting, difficult, heroic, agonizing moments were spent. Where I was most *alive*. I was put to the fire and lived to tell. And now it's mine to put water to the fire. How could it be otherwise? I wouldn't miss these days for the world.

15

Breakfast is in the Kamus koriala – translated for foreigners as the "Happy Mouth Lounge" – a cheerless room decorated in a plastic bamboo motif with black velvet moonglow paintings of bucolic village life: a peasant in a cone hat leading ducks home across a bridge; a barefoot boy chasing a dog; two women bending low in a rice paddy. Joanne has weak tea and even weaker toast, and I try the fruit plate, which arrives in a swirl of colour, from the creamy white of the lychees to the scarlet of the local *huilo* to the greens and purples of unknown varieties. Our young waiter speaks no English, and we communicate by pointing to the pictures on the menu while he bobs and says "Huzza-huzza!" no matter what we've asked of him. Nito, our security man, quietly smokes in the far corner, near the door, watching but not watching.

I glance through the free copy of *The Islander* which has come with the food. On the front page, Suli Nylioko beams beside a newborn goat during a visit to her home village, and a fire in a brothel kills eleven, including three police officers. On page eight, beside the crossword, there is a brief article on the Truth Commission. When I talked to Suli Nylioko she was uncertain who would head it, but according to this article a retired supreme-court justice, Sin Vello, has been named chair. The third member is a Mrs. Grakala, who is the widow of the former ambassador to Argentina and has been active with UNICEF.

"It says here the commission is having its first meeting this morning," I say. "It starts at nine o'clock. What time is it now?"

"A quarter to," Joanne says.

I look around the deserted Happy Mouth Lounge. Besides Nito and us, there are no other diners. No one has been sent to meet us. There've been no instructions.

I throw the paper down and bolt from the table. Joanne follows, still munching her toast. Nito races to our side.

"Where is the Truth Commission meeting?" I ask him. "*Commisi vertigas.* Uh, *kaba, kaba?*"

He looks bewildered, so I point outside, scratch my head, say *Commisi vertigas* several more times until apparently he understands.

"*Justico kampi!*" he says, pointing in the same direction I was pointing.

"What's that?"

"*Justico kampi!*" He pulls us to the stand for private taxis, and then we pile in and Nito directs the driver.

"I haven't got my briefcase," I say to Joanne. "I haven't got a pen or paper. I don't even know what the agenda is!"

Nito, happy, I think, to be of some use, goes on at some length with the driver, who nods importantly. The taxi speeds us out of the hotel's walled compound and then into slow-motion, bump-and-grind traffic. Little Asian automobiles, farmers' tractors, *tritos* armed with boomboxes blaring the local auto-rhythm junk, young men on thin motorcycles with their wives or sisters or girlfriends sidesaddle on the back. Peddlers pushing carts of plastic watches, hairbands, combs, ribbons, swarms of squeegee boys darting from stalled car to stalled car. Other boys selling cigarettes and pop, newspapers, bottled water. Everybody on the street, the moving mall, except it isn't moving, or it moves only irregularly, like a sudden lurching sidewalk. It's exactly as I remember it – the traffic in Santa Irene is still hopeless.

The *Justico kampi*, the hall of justice, it turns out, is not all that far from the Merioka, but we're half an hour in this soup. The building is a grey, squarish monolith with hulking pillars and wide steps, a large lawn in front. Like many of the other buildings around it, mould, moss, waterstains, and creeping vegetation have erased most of the original colour, most probably a reddish brown, and replaced it with a sickly grey-green. Already the air has thickened. What seemed cool and fresh is now heavy with heat and water and the day's growing smog, and weighs upon us as we hurry up the stairs. What if I hadn't seen the notice in the paper? Were they ever going to tell me when and where?

Through heavy glass doors and into the massive lobby. High ceilings, a marble floor, not gleaming but not as dirty as some other public buildings I remember from before. Where is the meeting room? Nito has no idea. But a middle-aged man with a crooked nose – probably broken badly at some point, then healed over like a twisted tree trunk – recognizes us.

"Aya, Beeul Boo-reej!" he says, and shakes my hand enthusiastically. He and Nito talk, and then we walk down a hallway and up a flight of stairs to the large, airy meeting room. There are two solid teak doors that take some pulling, and four or five small birds scatter through open windows when we walk in. Long tables with empty chairs arranged in an open rectangle;

two immense ceiling fans, turning slowly; dark panelling, a frayed and dirty reddish carpet; microphones and headsets in front of many of the seats. Nobody else is here.

The man with the crooked nose shows us to our seats, pats his hands downward to tell us to wait, wait. Then he and Nito leave us, and we are left with the lazy fans, the still, heavy air. There's a chair set in the middle of the rectangle – it must be where the witnesses will testify. It looks so solemn.

"Do you think we're early?" Joanne asks.

By a half-hour at least, it turns out. I pace, gaze out the windows at the large lawn, the constipated traffic. They're open-style, island windows – no glass at all, just wide-spaced bars which keep nothing out, seem to have been erected so that spiders could hang nets across them at their convenience. There are nearly a dozen of them, some as large as my hand, red and black, yellow and black, or just black. Patrick and I used to watch beauties like these. They stay rock-still, then flash the instant prey appears, seize the bug before it has even begun to struggle, then rotate on a pair of legs and knit it up in a snug silken sandwich.

"Shhhh. Listen," I say to Joanne at one point.

"What?"

"Can you hear it?" I ask. It's faint at first, just a whisper nearly lost in the grind of the fans, the wind from outside, the distant traffic. *Tokay, tokay, tokay.*

"What is it?"

"Count," I say.

Tokay, tokay, tokay. Growing louder, not quite a croaking, rather proud, I think. Then it stops.

"It's saying its name," I say. "Tokay. It's a kind of lizard, it probably lives in the ceiling somewhere. Quite large, and it can be savage if cornered. But the Santa Irenians consider it good luck to have one. When you hear it you're supposed to count, and the more times it says its name, the more luck you'll have."

"I got six," Joanne says. "Is that good?"

"I don't know."

Eventually aides begin arriving in clumps of twos and threes, some bearing stacks of paper for distribution, all in Kuantij. One aide helpfully brings us a couple of pens. I try to introduce Joanne and myself, but the language problem becomes immediately apparent and mostly we end up waving hands at each other. One young man shakes my hand vigorously and says, "Pleasurably meet to speakably you!" Almost everybody motions for us to sit down again as soon as we rise. Mrs. Grakala, it turns out, is a lump of a woman who walks tentatively, her spine curved with age. But her limpid brown eyes seem to take in everything. Her hand is weak as paper when I grasp it in greeting, her skin tissue-thin. I try to offer a greeting in Kuantij, although as I'm speaking I remember that I have the form of address wrong, worry that I might offend her by using the wrong word, and so simply mumble. She smiles and bobs her head until I go away. She settles in the corner with her two aides and immediately begins flipping through the documents.

Some time later, in no apparent hurry, our chair, Justice Sin, arrives surrounded by aides. He moves like a limping piano, he's so corpulent, leans so heavily on his silver cane, takes such small, deliberate, wounded steps. His entire passage from the door to his chair at the head of the table is a drama of dignity, near-peril, astonishment, the capacity of the human spirit to create obstacles and then overcome them at least for a time. He looks damned but not yet delivered, powerful enough to bring us all down with him . . . and knowing it, and knowing that we know it.

Slowly, gingerly, like a dirigible trying to dock in a windstorm, he leans on the table and manoeuvres his body in position above the empty seat. Several hands reach out to help and the seat and the body are carefully aligned, as if there'll only be one attempt and failure will mean disaster. When all is ready he sinks inexorably, a boulder that once set in motion can't be stopped. Success! I'm mildly surprised at the lack of accompanying applause. He fingers through an enormous briefcase. Papers emerge and are passed left and right. More copies accumulate in front of me. The justice starts speaking and Joanne and I fiddle with our earphones for the translation.

Nothing.

The switch on the table in front of me has four channels. I try each in turn and fiddle with the volume. No luck. One of the aides says to try *janal ista*, channel two, but it isn't working.

I motion to him and point to the earphones. A number of people look over at me. Justice Sin continues with his opening remarks.

"It isn't working!" I whisper. The aide leans over to listen to my earphones, then leans over Joanne to listen to hers. He motions back to some other senior aide, who comes by to listen as well. Justice Sin interrupts his speech and, apparently, asks what the fuss is about.

The senior aide points to the headphones and explains. Several aides start talking at once. One young man abruptly leaves the room and that settles everyone down. Justice Sin resumes his speech. The man who spoke English to me before says, "Pleese to you uh . . . waiting waiting fix."

Waiting waiting. When Justice Sin speaks his wattles tremble and his eyes roam in an apparent drunken stagger, fixing on something for a moment, as if astounded by the wonder or stupidity of it, then moving on to something else. The sweat from his hands seeps onto the pages of his text, and even from across the room he smells of bad gas. The words roll in deep-throated rumbles that would sound impressive on their own without the woggling lips, the tiny nose nearly lost in the layers of fat.

I've nothing to do but fixate on his appearance, and wonder how these people view me with my jutting bone face and haunted gaze, the trembling I can never seem to ease from my hands.

Joanne takes a sheet from one of the documents in Kuantij, turns it over, and writes: *Do you need me here?*

YES! I write back.

She nods, turns over another sheet of Kuantij, and begins writing a letter home. I scratch on the first paper, *We'll bring the laptop for you next time.* There's no phone connection, but she could at least write her e-mails to send back at the hotel. She smiles and writes back, *And maybe a good book or two!*

I absolutely need her. Just having her here helps me to focus, stay calm. Though my leg isn't jumping this morning, my insides seem stable. No sign of a twister, yet. I suppose it's inevitable I'll fall into one sometime, but in the daylight in this great hall I feel much stronger than in a long while.

I keep waiting for the young man to return and announce that the translation service is working. The door remains ajar but no one comes in. Justice Sin rumbles on and many of the aides take notes, although Mrs. Grakala seems lost in her handouts, the enormous bifocals balanced heavily on the end of her nose. I look at my handouts, but can recognize nothing except the occasional reference to my own name.

Dear Mom, Joanne writes. We're sitting so close to each other, it's hard not to read inadvertently. *How are you? Better than me I hope. I'm trapped in a conference hall listening to what might be the most interesting meeting I'll never understand.* Her small, spidery writing. *Any word yet on the tests?*

Sin talks and talks and then, apparently, there is a break. There is no formal discussion of the justice's remarks – although the room explodes in conversation as soon as the break is announced. The justice remains in his seat, and when I address him in English he does the same smiling and bobbing routine Mrs. Grakala performed for me earlier. He tries fitting his earphones around his fat jowls and fiddling with the stations but it's no good, no one's looking after the translation.

"*Lumbi drongupta talios suling fan,*" he says, one of the few idiomatic expressions I know. Literally: "The water buffalo knows now is a good time to eat," meaning, I believe, that the rest of us are just going to have to wait our turn.

Waiting, waiting. "This sure is exciting," Joanne says, smiling, then returns to her letter. I pace to stretch my legs, watch the spiders for a while. Slowly people drift away.

One of the aides catches my attention finally. "*Suling fan!*" he says, and I nod, thinking he's saying we'll have to wait longer for the translation service. But he points out the door and then I clue in. Lunchtime!

Joanne and I follow the aide to the banquet room, which is in a more modern part of the building, is glassed-in and cooler due to the noisy air conditioning. Now there are fifty of us, five round tables of ten with white linen tablecloths and a band playing traditional Santa Irenian music on flutes, odd stringed instruments, and rapid small drums. Scattered among the men in their lounge suits are some of the famously lovely island women who seem to crop up at every official function: tall, lithe, raven-haired beauties in tightly wrapped gowns. All have golden-brown skin that seems to glow of its own light. Up close many are large-eyed, overly made-up creatures stinking of perfume, but one or two are impossibly vibrant and fresh, new orchids rising from a rainstorm. Their eyes pass over me as if I don't exist, that's how old and decrepit I appear, but they linger on Joanne. She's in light, comfortable cotton pants and a sensible shirt. "My God, it's a flower show," she says. "What a disappointment I must be!"

"They envy you your hair," I say.

"Give me a break. They're just gorgeous."

"And they think the same of you."

The midday feast is traditional here, and I gather that since this is the opening meeting of the commission we must all eat ourselves into stupidity. Round after round of dishes arrives: spicy meats, burning hot fruit and vegetable plates, odd-textured soups, fish concoctions, deep-fried mysteries. We try engaging our table mates in conversation about the food but the only words of English that emerge are "Harro!" and "Velly happy see-you!"

"Didn't you learn *any* Kuantij while you were here?" Joanne asks me.

"The Kartouf were not big on language lessons."

"And Foreign Affairs?"

"Ha! I was lucky to get a handout on what to bring."

Sizzling chicken strips with a fuzzy, piquant coating. Beans twisted in curlicues and glazed with brown sugar and something hot. A greyish unidentified meat, strings of which get caught in my dentures. *Supira*, the island firewater, for toasting, a sweet red wine for drinking with the soup, a heavy beer for simply washing things down. I taste and nibble but am careful about having too much. I launch into a long story for Joanne about some spicy *tarwon* sauce I had once that nearly killed me.

Several times I look back at the door, expecting Suli Nylioko to arrive. Surely she would have some kind of ceremonial function, opening the Truth Commission, greeting us. But there's no Suli. Instead a half-dozen men, some in natty blue business suits, others lounging in island casuals, stand up to make speeches. Each in turn is ignored by almost everyone in the room. I notice Franja at one of the other tables and he lifts his glass to me.

"He seems to be at all these functions," I say to Joanne.

"Maybe we could get him to translate?"

"You're right. He might be of some use after all."

But when I approach him he shakes his head in theatrical regret. "If only I could!" he says. "But my business interests keep me extraordinarily busy."

Heavy rain starts sometime in the afternoon and builds to the point where it drowns out the sound of the air conditioning, streaks down the huge windows until it feels like we're below decks in a glass-hulled boat.

It turns out that no afternoon session is scheduled. People begin to drift away after the spiced fruit and tea. I try a few of the aides but none can handle my fractured Kuantij. Franja, of course, has evaporated. Joanne hunts through the phrasebook, but it's hard to turn "What time is it?" into "What time do we meet again?" No one seems particularly concerned. Justice Sin limps majestically out of the room, an ocean liner this time, listing slightly but still powering forward. The aides and other guests disappear into the halls of the justice building or else into taxicabs. The young man with the best English says, "Pleese again tomorrow pleese."

A wall of rain, soaking through the awning above the arched doorway, bouncing up off the asphalt and splashing inside the open door. Against it Nito uselessly holds a single portable umbrella. We dash two metres to a waiting cab and jostle with the door just long enough for everything to be soaked through.

Then once we're inside the car immediately steams up. The wipers don't work and our driver proceeds on trust. It doesn't matter anyway; as usual traffic is halted everywhere. It takes fifteen minutes to insinuate ourselves onto the boulevard outside the *Justico kampi*, another twenty to make it a block and a half and turn onto another street. The rain continues unabated, the sewers running rivers, streets awash.

"At least it's warm," says Joanne. Her bra shows plainly through her soaked shirt and her hair drips down her back onto the vinyl of the seat. I have an aching memory of kissing Maryse in a cab like this when we were both wet and hot, the water running down our faces and into each other's mouths. It's so sudden it almost feels real, then seems unbearably remote and sad.

"There was a terrible traffic jam here some years ago," I say, looking but not looking. "I remember reading about it. A number of awful coincidences all at once. Construction closed the one bridge across the harbour arm, and a building collapsed from poor engineering. It started to slump in the morning and by mid-afternoon was crumpled across three main arteries. This happened during a heatwave – six solid days of over forty degrees Celsius – and there was engine failure in one of the two ferries that serviced the harbour. The other one had been commandeered by someone – Tinto, I think. He spent three days at sea gambling with Taiwanese businessmen. So all traffic had to go straight through the city. Horrendous plugging. Some people were stranded for three or four days. All those engines running to keep the air conditioning going. The smog building up, the heat, I think three dozen people died. There was no inquiry. The city just staggered on."

As I tell the story we move only a few metres further then sit. My leg gets anxious, I try rubbing it and then Joanne pitches in and that doesn't help at all. Now I can't avoid the smell of her, the closeness. Her strong hands work up and down my thigh while the driver leers into the mirror. Idiot, I think. I couldn't get excited if my life depended on it. Just as I think this I shift in my seat, look down involuntarily at my pitiful groin. My pants are even sticking up, that must be what he's leering at. It's just the empty fold in the fabric. So I pat myself down as surreptitiously as I can manage . . . only it won't go down, and it feels so unusual . . .

Oh, for God's sake.

I'm hard as a carrot for the first time in forever.

"Jesus!" I say, slamming out my leg to distract her. "I have to walk! I'm sorry. You stay in the cab if you like."

"Are you kidding?" she says, so she pays the driver and we hike off through the deluge, Nito bopping beside us trying to shelter us with the umbrella. We're just on Cardinal Avenue, the roots of towering glass banks and government buildings interspersed with sorry little crumbling shops, the tops of nearly everything lost to view in the rain. It isn't far to the Merioka. After a block we convince Nito to desist and we give ourselves completely to the rain. My tent pole has disappeared, but I'm exhilarated. Joanne laughs in the rain and looks near-topless in her soaked white shirt. I take off my sorry jacket and try to sling it around her, but she laughs it away. There are no other pedestrians, just steamed windows in car after car going nowhere, wipers flapping absurdly. The slick-tiled sidewalk is treacherous, the curbs half a metre high to keep the rainwater from flooding. After I lose my balance stepping down from one of them Joanne takes my arm and we proceed together.

The rain is so heavy that even with Nito we walk right past the Merioka then have to double back a block later. Staff members stare as we squelch through the lobby, and we laugh like children up the elevator. At the door we fumble, trying to pantomime to Nito to come back tomorrow, but he knows already anyway.

"Look at you!" Joanne says when we're safely inside.

"Look at me? Look at *you*! You're just as soaked as I am."

"No. Your pants," she says, and I think, my God, it's happened again. But it isn't that. I realize, to my horror, that I've shit myself.

"Jesus!"

"It doesn't matter. We'll clean you up. Come on to the bathroom." She says it in her nurse's voice, so I follow her, but once there I say I'll clean myself up.

"That's all right," she says, again in her nurse's voice, so comforting at other times, but right now I don't want to hear it. I was so hoping to be past that.

"I'll do it," I say, burning with disappointment and shame.

"Don't worry. It can happen to anyone. All this strange food."

She leaves and I strip down, shiver in weakness and sudden cold. My shit is runny as ever, parts of it black. Disgusting. I turn my pants inside out and hold them with me in the shower water as long as I can, then ring them out and toss them on the floor. In the hot water the shaking should stop, but instead it increases. I turn up the heat and think ruefully of our Pope joke as I gaze down on my own unemployed, which look a hundred and twenty years old. And those knobby knees, the wet black hair of some starved animal, not a man, not a young man. I soap myself from top to bottom, the water now as hot as the dial will go, but I'm still cold. I know this cold, that's what's so frightening about it. It's life seeping away.

I can barely stand, the shaking has gotten worse and worse. I turn off the water and wrap myself in a huge purple and gold Merioka towel. Close my eyes, lean against the counter.

"Joanne!"

Trying for breath. Relax, relax. Let the air enter. It can't reach the lungs if it doesn't go down the throat.

"Joanne!"

"What is it? What's wrong?"

If I shift my weight I can stay against the counter and not slump to the floor. It takes all my energy. What's happening? It isn't a twister. It's something else. Heart attack? As soon as I think of it my chest constricts from a dozen needles pressing at once.

"Bill! Open the door!"

No. Not now. This is not the time. Please God, I hear myself praying. I still have things to do. Please. Not now.

I reach along the counter and unlock the door. Joanne is half-dressed, her hair tied up in a towel. I feel my breath returning. It's all right. The needles are slowly extracted. One by one. But the shaking remains. I don't trust myself to say very much.

"I need to lie down." Then, at the bed, "Please hold me."

The warmth of her spreads along my back, her arms around me. Maryse and I would lie like this before going to sleep. Just a few minutes. She could never stand it long – her arm would fall asleep, she'd always withdraw. "I need a small place for myself," she said one time.

Not me. I want no small place, but to be swallowed whole, remade, given another chance. To just stop this shaking, this cold, rest a time. To breathe and love. To be loved and made warm.

Strange to be so cold in the tropics. Is the air conditioner on? Maybe we could turn it off. Just this once. I think the thought but it's hard to make the words come out. Nice with a pair of arms around me again, to feel and hear someone else's breathing. To close my eyes.

I had strange travels before. There were places I fled to in rest, in my head, in dreams. Cold places sometimes because I was so hot, sweat seeping out of me, bag of bones that I was. I remember shaking like this. I remember.

New snow. Like fine, clean dust, but under that is hard, old snow that goes *crunch crunch* when we walk. Dad doesn't wear a hat but I don't know how – my ears get cold even with my ski hat. We walk with our sticks and skates hanging over our shoulders.

When we round the corner the rink isn't white and snowy in the distance as I thought it would be, but a gleaming silver, the new ice pulling in every bit of light from the dull dawn and magnifying it. Even before we're there I can tell it's a perfect sheet of ice, so slippery and hard that my little wrist shot is going to skid all the way across to the far boards and then bounce back like a bolt from Bobby Hull.

Dawn, and the change room is locked. "Somebody cleared the rink, then watered, then went home to bed," Dad says, stopping to look out at the immaculate surface.

We sit on a snowbank to put on our skates. The air is so cold our fingers freeze a minute after we take off our mitts. Dad does Graham's skates, squats in front of him and fusses with the laces. Graham looks cold and somehow almost still asleep, sitting so small in his ski jacket. I get my left skate on then have to jam my hands back in my mitts to warm them up again. When I take off my mitts my hands get cold again and I shake them but it doesn't help. My foot won't go in my skate. I push and push and then the skate shoots out and spins across the ice. Graham laughs suddenly and Dad turns around to watch the skate.

"Better go get it!" he says.

So I clump on one skate and one boot, take two steps then end up on my bum. I *knew* it was slippery ice! When I get back my hands are cold still, even in my mitts.

"Dad, can you get this skate on me?"

"You can do it yourself." He's finished now with Graham and sits down on the snowbank beside me to pull on his own skates.

"But the laces are frozen –"

"Stop talking and just do it."

I don't say anything, but pull till I don't know what I'm pulling, if it's tightening or loosening the stupid laces. Finally Dad comes over and impatiently squats in front of me. In a minute it's done. The skate that he tied feels snug and firm and the one that I tied is loose and flimsy. But before I can ask him to do the other one he skates away. I have trouble picking up my hockey stick with my mitts on, have to get down on my knees and take off my mitts to pick it up and then put on my mitts again as I get up.

Glide squish, *glide squish*, *glide squish*. That's what it feels like with the one good skate tightened by Dad and the one loose one tightened by me. Besides that, I'm a frozen ice chunk skating around, I'm so cold.

Dad passes me the puck. I feel it on the end of my stick, move it back and forth, concentrate. It's so cold! I try my wrist shot just to see how it goes on this ice: the puck spins and skids then bounces on a few bumps and stops before it reaches the boards. So much for Bobby Hull.

Here's how I warm up: we're skating down the full length of the ice, practising our long passing, and Graham passes it to me but it's so far ahead I have to skate really hard to get there. When I start I'm cold and just before I reach my stick out to get the puck I'm hot, my hands almost burning and my hair wet from sweating and the inside of my jacket feels like there's an electric heater. Just like that. I pass the puck to Dad and skate off to the other end of the ice and then I take off my hat and loosen my jacket because everything is boiling.

Boiling and different. It's late now, so late, Maryse has been out with some of her girlfriends. I've been waiting here for her, waiting, the light on downstairs. Lying on her side of the bed. She knows I can't sleep without her. I hear the sound of the car downstairs, her feet in the hallway, the fridge door opening while she considers what to have. This is her time, the dark side of midnight. She's in no hurry now, it isn't the rush of the day, she doesn't want to go to sleep either. I'm stretched like a cable listening, waiting. The soft turn of pages. Please, not a *New Yorker* article. Something short. She has a glass of warm milk to slow herself down. Don't go to your studio, I think. It's too late. You'll be up all night. Feet on the stairs, please. Quiet feet. Yes.

She pauses by Patrick's door. The soft kiss. Gentle fingers tuck and soothe, turn out the hall light.

Barefoot on the carpet. Buttons. The skirt slides off. Small pile on the bedroom floor. I stay as still as I can. Stretched like a cable. She doesn't turn on the light. Opens the drawer for a T-shirt, but there's no need, it's so hot, leave it for tonight. I move my leg a bit and she sits on the edge of the bed.

Still.

The lightest touch. Just on the outside of my foot. Around the ankle. I move my leg slightly and she continues up the calf. So slowly. To the thigh and then down again, to the other foot. Playing her after-midnight game.

On the back and shoulders, down my arms, her body so close but not pressing. I move to get closer but she pulls away, then touches me again.

"Are you awake?"

"Hmmm."

Shoulders, neck, lips, cheeks. With her fingers and then her lips, and now she does press against me, it's been so long, it feels like forever I've been stretched like this, aching and waiting. I turn and pull her against me and she laughs, pulls back, says, "Slowly," so soft and low I nearly lose it.

"You've been waiting for me," she whispers.

"Yes."

"When you should've been sleeping."

"Could've."

"Yes?"

Straddling me, pressing, opening, her fingers guiding me inside.

"Maybe."

Half-asleep. Rocking at sea, crying salt tears, it feels like it's been forever, like nectar, like you could take away everything else but this, or the memory of this. To keep it somehow, it's all I'd need. It's been so long. I'd forgotten, blocked it out. Now to be back, to find every nerve has memorized this feeling, has soaked in it so that it would be there all the time, I just had to ask.

Everything's here. The smell of her, the night's sweat and her lipstick and the vague traces of cigarette from her artist friends and the wine she's had. Her impossible softness. Muscled but soft, how is that accomplished? The turbulence of hair and suddenness of want, of her wanting me . . .

The suddenness of losing her.

Everything, all at once – smell, touch, sight, oh the sight of her, gone, taken, about to be taken. It can't last. Even stored inside me it can't last. It isn't now. She couldn't want me. That was a hundred years ago. Before I fell down the rabbit hole. A hundred million years gone by.

"Bill?"

I'm sorry. I try to say the words but they won't come out. It's that kind of a dream. I know the words to say but my mouth won't co-operate.

"Bill?"

I try to get her back. Just the light touch was enough. In the darkness, the sound of her clothes sliding to the floor, the soft approach. Just to get that back. The anticipation. I used to be part of a life with anticipation. And love. I used to yearn for it, live for it. But when you're a hundred and eighty years old no one will . . .

No one.

"Bill?"

Eyes open. Strange light. What place is this? Not before, not . . . *back there*. . . .

Yes. All right. I know.

"You slept," Joanne says, like it's a minor miracle, which it is, I have to admit. Just the word – *slept*. It has such an exotic feel.

She's about to tell me it's morning. She's going to say what's planned for the day. All my directions will line up in just a moment.

"Good dream?" she asks in her wicked-innocent way and I know, immediately, that she knows. She couldn't have been looking in my head, but she knows anyway what was there.

16

Day two is quickly soured with a bad feeling, an anxiousness and growing anger that's hard to place at first, but there's plenty of time to think in the hearing room at *Justico kampi*. We go through a carbon copy of the day before – Justice Sin begins his remarks; I fiddle with my headphones and complain about lack of translation; aides appear concerned, check the equipment in apparent amazement that it could still be malfunctioning, then leave to do, it seems, nothing.

I don't have this much time to waste. Sin Vello, Mrs. Grakala, and me – we all look as if we could expire at any moment. But Sin Vello seems happy to pontificate; Mrs. Grakala reads till her eyes droop. And I sit here, silent, stewing, understanding nothing. This isn't a show for me, not with my heart the way it is.

As with yesterday there is a sumptuous luncheon. This time we're seated with a number of township mayors who have no connections to the commission at all, but appear to have used the excuse to come to the capital. There are photos and toasts and phony smiles, and through it all the veneer of my courtesy becomes more brittle. I make a point of crossing the room to corner Minister Tjodja and inform him that the translation service has been useless so far.

"Mr. Burridge, please do not worry yourself over such technical difficulties," he says. "My staff is fixing them as we speak. Have you met Junta Gund from the Chamber of Excellence?" Junta Gund rises from his dessert and I give him the barest nod before turning back to Tjodja.

"Well, until the service is up and running, perhaps *you* could provide summary translation for me for this afternoon's session. Your English is excellent, Mr. Minister."

He blanches. "If only I had the time," he says. "But we are fortunate that there is no afternoon session planned for today, and I am certain everything will be functioning tomorrow. It's all formalities, anyway, Mr. Burridge."

"What do you mean?"

"I mean so far. Justice Sin has been setting up the administrative workings. It's nothing for you to concern yourself with."

"Then perhaps I do not need to attend," I say sharply. As I expect, he backs off.

"Tomorrow will be very different," he says quickly. "But please have patience with us. We are just a backward country. What would be done with a snap of the fingers in the West is much more difficult here." His head droops slightly as he delivers this last spineless comment, but I manage to leave before I say anything insulting.

"You're awfully quiet," Joanne says in the taxi back to the hotel. We're stuck in traffic again. We could have walked, but even yesterday's wall of rain was more inviting than today's oppressive heat and pollution. The cloudburst will come later. For now the air is sweating and breathless and mildly poisoned, and it presses down on us heavily.

I tell her about *liir*, island spirit. "It's a funny term, meant pejoratively –" As soon as I mention the word both Nito and our driver turn and smirk, although they can't follow the rest of my explanation. "There has been such a parade of colonial powers through here – the Spanish, Dutch, British, Americans – that for centuries it's been considered a patriotic duty to make sure nothing runs smoothly. So when Tjodja dips his head and tells me I can't expect a functioning translation service in such a backward country, he's really expressing a perverse sense of superiority. *All these rulers have never changed us – what makes you think* you *will be able to get anything done?*"

Joanne grins. "You've just described most places on this planet," she says. "The trick is to figure out how to keep from having that whatever – *liir* – swallow you up."

Our driver tries to turn left at an intersection, but no one will let him through and we get caught. The light turns red but we can't clear, it's jammed up ahead. We can't go back because a *tritos* is trying to bull through behind us. The oncoming traffic fills up whatever space was left. Now the light cycles fruitlessly: red, green, yellow, it doesn't matter. We honk and the *tritos* honks and everybody else too. We inch forward and stop, inch forward, stop. A man on the corner wades into the thick of it and waves people on, stops others, yelling instructions and collecting tips. Inch and stop and inch and honk and pay and inch and stop again.

"Where there's a will there's commerce," Joanne says, shaking her head.

In the evening we are invited, suddenly, to a gala folk-dance performance at the Minitzh Arts Centre. The name is yet another reminder of his legacy, like the airport, like the soccer stadium, and the Minitzhi katra dinga, the central post office. There is little time to prepare – a messenger delivers the invitation just as we're finishing dinner in the Happy Mouth Lounge. I've brought nothing as fancy as a tuxedo, and have given up even on neckties, so my batik island shirt will have to do, and Joanne wears a simple black cotton travelling dress with a string of pink coral bought at a stall outside the hotel. We ride this time at high speed in a black limousine along avenues that seem to have been cleared of traffic for the event. Nito is much more nervous than in any falling-apart taxi we've been in so far. He glances frenetically out the various shaded windows at the tropical darkness. I see nothing but shadowed buildings, checkpoints, soldiers in armed Jeeps patrolling the side streets.

"It looks like they're getting ready for a coup," Joanne says nervously.

But it's not that, it's a night out with the spoiled upper-class *lumito*. The Minitzh Centre stands glittering and new, flooded in purple and pink lights, the one corner that was blackened by fire in the riots looking in this light softened, like a bruise. We leave our limousine and walk arm in arm past a phalanx of photographers. Everything is excessive – the jewelled and sequinned gowns, the slicked hair, the perfume, the teetering shoes and tinkling chandeliers and delicate glasses of champagne handed out with the programs as if the country were overflowing in riches.

We sit front-row centre, drawn and pressed here by the crowd, stuck to this spot. The dance is a solo by Marika Contala, the most brilliant *feriko* dancer of her generation – it says so in the English insert of my brochure. So why can't I get translation for the commission? *Feriko* is a complex series of sudden, sinuous movements brought to a periodic halt, the pose held five to ten drumbeats before the dancer melts into other movements, hands and arms snaking, legs twisting and stretching, eyes doing most of the communicating. Only one story is told in this type of dance, but in several variations, of the attraction between the pure Princess Tarlan and Gnotka, the horned ruler of the underworld whose heart has not held love since Mother Earth abandoned him as a young man. In some versions – again, according to the program – the innocence and purity of Tarlan wins out, and in others Gnotka's darkness envelopes them both. Marika plays all the parts, soft and slight yet tall as Tarlan, a rigid and powerful little toad as Gnotka. Joanne quickly becomes entranced by the performance, but I can't relax. I feel oddly complicit. They need me here, I think, to validate their opulence amidst suffering and poverty. I look around, wonder if Suli Nylioko will make an appearance. But later, when she doesn't show, I realize that the People's President wouldn't come here. Not even Sin Vello and Mrs. Grakala came. I was the only one and this is my last time.

It's hard to stay awake. The music seems strained, difficult, the clues and messages of the dance too obscure and coded to pick up. When it's finished – Tarlan has won, I gather; Gnotka has been transformed into a shining prince – there's a reception, but I plead fatigue, try to keep the disgust out of my voice.

My bad mood carries over to the next day. Joanne has a hard time marshalling me through medicines and breakfast, and we arrive late at the *Justico kampi*. Sin Vello is already talking to his assembled aides; Mrs. Grakala is already nodding in her seat, the papers piled around her. I walk directly to my regular seat and snap on my earphones as I sit down. That familiar deadness. It's not working. They've done nothing. I jam through the channels: *janal lito*, *janal ista*, *janal trikos*, *janal kolian* . . . Dead, dead, dead.

"I'm sorry, I'm sorry, I'm just . . ."

"Calm," says Joanne beside me, but I can't stay calm. I smash my fist on the table and rattle my headphones.

Mrs. Grakala starts awake and looks to see what the disruption is. Justice Sin opens his palms in a gesture of monumental concern and powerlessness, and two aides rush to my side to fiddle with the connection, as if that's the problem.

"*You haven't got anybody translating! Don't treat me like a bloody idiot!*" I start to gather the new papers – no, for God's sake, they're all in Kuantij! So I scatter them in the open area in the middle of the room, where our witnesses are supposed to testify. If we ever get around to calling any.

A clamour, of course. Aides rise, try to smooth the feathers of the ruffled foreigner. But none of them can speak English! The minister, Tjodja, appears, not the least bit embarrassed about having told me yesterday he was too busy to deal with the commission. "I need a full translation service," I tell him, trying to keep my temper from going completely off the rails. "I'm not going to sit here and validate what I can't even understand. And I want to see your president today, or else I'm going home!"

"*Bill*," Joanne whispers, her hand on my back.

"But Suli is not available!" Tjodja says. Squeaking in panic.

"Well, maybe I'll have to make *myself* unavailable!" I say and storm out, Joanne in tow, papers dripping from my briefcase, who cares?

Tjodja begs me down the hall, but I tell him, again and again, what my conditions are. I'm not here to see this commission become a joke. I'm not lending my name to a sham and a farce.

In the hotel room Joanne sits reading a novel and I steam, pace, fume, mutter.

"You gave your conditions," she says, turning the page, not looking up.

"I did. I made a stand. This whole situation is ridiculous."

"Absolutely," she says.

I slam the bed with my foot. Several useless stacks of commission paper jump, then settle back.

"Why don't you do your animals?" she asks languidly.

"I can't. I can't relax."

"But I thought the animals were supposed to *help* you to relax."

"They're to help me kill people who attack me," I say. "*Then* I can relax."

"Listen – the ball is in their court and it might not come back for a while. Who knows where Suli is or how long it will take them to get the translation service working?" She doesn't look up, but sits engrossed in her book, stays infuriatingly calm, like some wife who's been thinking rings around me for years.

How long am I prepared to wait? Through room-service lunch, the fruit plate that's already growing tired, and stale bread that seems purposely unappealing, as if part of a larger conspiracy to make me leave. What's the point of staying in a luxury suite if the food is bad? Through the long afternoon of nothing but fuming and self-doubt. Through the sun sinking back into the other side of the ocean, but false somehow, like a cheap effect liable to fall over at any moment.

"Look, you're driving me nuts!" Joanne says. "Would you stop that pacing?" She's finished her book, is suddenly much more aware of my restlessness. "You're starting to remind me of Dennis."

"Dennis?"

"Just sit, will you? Would you be of some use? Can you play the piano?"

I stride over to the gleaming grand and hammer out "Chopsticks." Then I return, push her feet off the sofa, and sit down.

"Tell me about Dennis," I say. "Make it last several hours."

She doesn't want to at first, but I insist. If she won't tell me about Dennis I'm going to start pacing again.

"Okay, okay!" she says in mock panic. "Dennis was our driver in Sudan. I forget where he was from. Michigan? He'd left a program in international relations so he could get some field experience. And he was an All-American lacrosse player. He really wanted to see the world. So there he was, our driver, in this little camp covered in dust. The end of the world. Jerry, an Australian doctor, came up with that. It was so hot and barren, everything was covered in fine grey dust, you couldn't escape it. Dust in your eyes and your mouth. We breathed it in even through handkerchiefs. There was dust in the water.

"Just boys in these camps, from the south. The lost boys. They'd been kidnapped by the Muslims, brought north and made to fight against their own people. These ones had escaped somehow and walked back south to find their families. Only their families were gone. The boys were starving, many of them were going to die. Some had only the strength to lie on their cots hooked up to an intravenous. The others would sit in the shade and stare at nothing. Such silence. I've heard it twice, in southern Sudan, and in Rwanda when all those Tutsis were force-marched back from Burundi. The scale of it kills something inside you, or makes you feel like something's been killed. Silence and suffering times tens of thousands. All those fifteen-year-old boys internally shut down, seeing but not saying a word. Beyond words. Beyond anything that can help. I lasted three months and then I swore I wouldn't work in those conditions again. It was the hopelessness. I felt the words get sucked right out of me, a vacuum of silence and any sound, any thought or feeling I might want to express would be drawn out and dissipate into nothing. In the face of all that. A few drops of water in a bone-dry desert."

She looks down at the rug, her fingers drum absently on her shin.

"What about Dennis?"

"Oh, yeah, Dennis, the driver. We didn't stay in that camp. It wasn't safe after sundown. We didn't have the security. So every evening Dennis picked us up and drove us back to our own camp, which was twenty kilometres away. The militias took over the refugee camp at night. We had no control over what went on. We didn't know and we didn't ask, and nobody talked about it. It was one of those things, you know, beyond our control. God grant me the wisdom. In the morning we'd drive back, very slowly, because different groups mined the road at night. The village kids would mark the mines with little sticks for us. Every so often we'd have to all get out of the truck and check to see if it was a marker or just a stick. And when we got to the camp in the morning sometimes there were bodies. Well, in the morning often there were bodies. We couldn't always tell if it was the malnutrition or the dysentery or the militias. We didn't look too closely, to tell you the truth. We just focused on what we could do in the present moment.

"But Dennis had a hard time with that. He brought in our supplies and had to deal with the militias more than most of us, and of course he was the one driving over that mined road. Sometimes the food got through and sometimes it didn't. There was a lot of pressure and Dennis had such a great image of himself, you know, All-American jock. But this was another universe, this was everything tilted and upside down. He started raging against it, he couldn't stay still, he wanted us to take on the militias, arm ourselves, do something! God, he was scary. There was huge Dennis armed with a butcher's knife in the mess tent, and wiry little Jerry. He was mostly bald and laughed at everything. He talked so softly, and finally after two hours he led Dennis out and put him in a straitjacket. We all watched. It was awful. It was the very lowest point."

Tap, tap, tap, her fingers against her shin.

"The moral is," she says, smiling, a real Joanne smile, "you have to play cribbage. That's what we decided. Dennis never played cribbage with us in the evenings. So he thought about all the crap too much. That kills you in this type of work. You have to play cribbage."

She gets up and goes into her room, returns a moment later with her medical bag and a deck of cards.

"Meds first, then we'll play." And out they come, the rattling little bottles of pills. We go through the ritual silently, and I swallow everything down with practised gulps of the bottled water provided by the Merioka. Quick and painless.

"Where's the board?" I ask.

"There's no board in this type of cribbage. You have to keep track of your own points in your head. And your opponent's. If you find he's cheating or has made a mistake, you call him on it."

"How can you tell?"

"You have to be sharp. It doesn't allow you to think of anything else."

She shuffles the cards like a Vegas pro.

"I haven't played for ages," I say. "How do you score?"

"I can see you're going to have a great time," she says. "Maybe we need to add some money to make it interesting."

I'm awful at it, but it *is* interesting, and keeps my circuits full until nearly midnight, when Joanne goes to bed. I play a few more hands against myself, completely absorbed, when the phone rings. A male voice says, "Suli would like to see you. You can come now?"

I'm groggy with the late hour, with fatigue and indignation and too much mental cribbage. It doesn't occur to me right away that my walking-out stunt might have worked.

"It's awfully late," I say. "Perhaps in the –"

"A car is downstairs. You can come now?"

I knock softly on Joanne's door and tell her the news.

"She wants you now?" she asks.

"It does sound odd, doesn't it?"

"Say you'll see her in the morning."

I go back to the phone to set up a meeting for tomorrow. But Suli herself comes on the line.

"Bill," she says, strangely familiar, as if resuming a conversation, "I know this is unusual, but it looks like my schedule has changed for tomorrow and then I'm travelling for the next while, so I'm not sure when I'll be able to meet with you properly. And it's important that we do meet right away. If you're not too tired."

"No. Of course," I blurt.

"You'll find my personal guard waiting outside your door. You have nothing to worry about with them. They would step in front of a train to protect you."

"Let's hope there are no runaway trains."

"Yes, of course." Her words are clipped, slightly hurried. I think I hear someone in the background going on in Kuantij.

I tell Joanne the details through the door and she asks if I want her to come with me.

"I should be all right," I say. "You get your rest."

She opens the door. She's wearing a long T-shirt too thin to hide much of the fullness of her body. Those long naked legs. "Listen," she says. "How are you feeling?"

"All right," I say guardedly.

"No, really," she says. "You were losing it most of today. You collapsed in the bathroom yesterday. Bad things happen when you get overtired. Maybe you should rest."

"I'll be fine. It feels all right. So far." I knock on the wood of the doorframe. I don't know where to look, she's so beautiful. My life preserver. Here's my safe thought: Joanne in this T-shirt. Finally I turn to go.

In the hallway I find three hulking, grim, fit-looking men in island casual-dress loungewear. Their hair is military short, though, and they all wear the same style of pointy, polished brown or black leather shoes. The fourth man is Nito, grubby, small, and out of place beside them. Just for a second I imagine one of these elite guards lunging at me and me coiling forward with the dragon.

Wordlessly down the elevator then through the lobby. The desk clerk looks on impassively. I can't actually see any weapons on these men, but they look armed. How do I know? Maybe I'm just hoping they'll be able to protect me. The five of us crowd into a white van that roars down the deserted avenue. I look back but no one is chasing us. Maybe they always drive this way. The rain has slackened but the streets are slick, the blackness even more profound. My guards smoke soundlessly as we rocket along.

I know the smell of those cigarettes. It used to mean utter terror. But I'm oddly calm.

We wheel around to a back entrance of the Pink Palace. I wasn't sure that Suli would take this as her residence, but perhaps it makes sense: a symbolic seat of power, and it's nicely guarded by a heavy wall, with room for a battalion of soldiers if it comes to that. In the darkness the pink is barely discernible, but for a moment I think of Minitzh and his faded régime. All those glittering parties, his own Versailles for the *lumito*. How ironic that their skins have been saved by the widow of an assassinated opposition leader.

We walk up a back staircase, then along a hallway lined with carved teak panels. The lost art of the Watabi? The artist race wiped out by the British. It was Franja who offered to show Maryse and me his collection. Originally bought with blood. The carvings show scenes of village life revolving around rice cultivation and maintaining a fabled valley of ter-raced paddies that climb up the mountainsides in gleaming slivers of water. I've seen pictures of the terraces and of these carvings, but the effect in the hall is disconcerting, as if I've wandered into the valley floor and find myself surrounded by fragile layers of brown water and mud that could easily slide down to swallow me.

Suli's office is at the end, on the right. The three elite guards remain subdued, but little Nito, eyes wide, rubber-necks the whole way. They leave me at her imposing, solid-teak, half-opened door. My eyes have a hard time adjusting because of the low light – candles only, perhaps fifteen or twenty spread about the high-ceilinged room. They cast deep shadows on the shelved books, the stacks of files, newspapers, and letters, the large bamboo desk that seems naked without a computer perched on top. She blends in so completely I miss her at first, but there she is bent by a candle at the desk, quietly scratching with a fountain pen, one hand supporting her cheek, her short black hair sharply framing her face. She looks up.

"Mr. Burridge – Bill, thank you so much for coming," she says, rising but staying tiny, coming out from behind the desk in her famous blue *saftori*, her body lean and light and straight. "I'm sorry for all this cloak-and-dagger stuff. Sometimes the day's schedule gets beyond me, and this is the only way I can meet people. Can I pour you some tea or *supira*?" Her voice, in person, at this late hour, is lower than I expect, not quite the same as on the phone, satiny somehow, unsettlingly familiar and intimate. She closes the door. No aides, no advisers. This must be the personal style that Suli is becoming known for.

"*Supira* would be fine." I don't know why I ask for it, except that the situation seems to call for something stronger than tea.

Clearly she wants to speak, to make this her meeting. But I blurt my piece nervously. "I feel I have to come forward, for the good of this commission," I say. "I've put everything on the line to return here, to contribute. Yet communications within the commission are very poor. The first day no one informed me about the schedule. I had to read it in the newspaper – which was wrong, as it turned out. Now I find there's no translation service, so I have no idea what anybody's saying. We agreed I wouldn't get buried in details, but this is preposterous." I sputter on the word, deliver it like an actor who doesn't know what's coming next. Settle down, I think.

She's extraordinarily beautiful. Her cinnamon skin, ageless, her deep brown eyes, the stillness that surrounds her. Her thin shoulders that have borne so much, seem so ready to be embraced.

"Please, sit down," she says tranquilly, making me feel I've made a poor first impression. I try a low, carved teak double-seater by the window. It's ornate and undoubtedly expensive, but straight and hard as a prison bench. All the seats are similar. I suppose guests are meant to be impressed, and not stay long.

Suli walks into the shadows – even, measured, balanced steps – and emerges in a moment with two delicate, bulbous glasses half full of the golden-brown liquid. I take mine but put it down immediately.

"You must understand what this means to me," I sputter. "My time is limited. I cannot be days and days sitting in a hearing room understanding almost nothing of what's going on. That's a complete –"

"I have ordered funds for a full translation service to be created," she says.

"– farce as far as I'm concerned. I'm sorry to be so blunt but . . . What did you say?"

"A full translation service will be created. It will take a few more days, but please understand, you have my complete backing for this commission. We just aren't quite ready for you yet. You weren't expected to attend these first few meetings, since they are devoted to administering bureaucratic details. We're happy that you've taken such an interest –"

"But nobody *told* me!"

"I think," she says, "more from embarrassment than any-thing else."

It takes a moment for this to sink in, and for my own embar-rassment to flush through my face and up my scalp.

"I want to be involved in the details," I say. "That's what I'm here for. How are we choosing our witnesses, for example? What's the scope of our inquiry? What powers of investigation and enforcement are we going to have? Will anybody be bound by our decisions?"

Suli takes a deep breath, then a sip of her *supira*, and leans back against her desk. "Again," she says, "there was going to be a proper briefing on this. We do things more slowly here. But you are quite right to ask. You have to understand, this commission is central to our national mourning. The commission will be our official means of examining the past, finding our way to justice, and of burying our dead. So it must be seen to be fair and thorough, and I do not want anyone to feel they are being excluded. So I have recommended to Justice Sin that you open the doors as wide as possible, in the beginning at least, simply allow anyone who feels the need to register and then testify. There will be a prescreen, of course – officials will take preliminary testimony and schedule the witnesses according to groups: whether they are from the same village, for example, or were affected by one particular atrocity."

"Just in the beginning?"

"You will have to see what the reaction is," she says. "I suspect there will be somewhat of a national outpouring, that for logistical reasons you may need to limit testimony later on. But for now it's essential that no one feels excluded."

"Some commissions in other countries have been circumscribed as to what they can investigate, how far back they're allowed to go," I say.

"Yes, and again, for logistical reasons, it might be prudent to do that at some point, when focus becomes important. But for now the field is wide open, and you will have the freedom to investigate as you feel fit. You can call your own witnesses and they will be bound by law to testify. You will have what we call *trilanto godin*, the power to instruct the courts and government. It's not the power to convict individuals or pass laws, but it can't be ignored either. It's a wide mandate, Bill. You can travel, you can investigate, and like all of us you could be shut down any moment by the military. But that would be a coup and all rules would change then anyway." She smiles wanly. "There are some people, of course, who wish to derail this commission, and me as well. But not to worry. If there is anything you need, just tell me. I can't be seen to be too close to the process, you understand that. This is not to be Suli's vendetta against the murderer of her husband. But I am vitally interested. You must accept our apologies for not being better prepared. We are in many ways a backward country. I beg your patience."

She draws a chair from out of the gloom and sits near me. I think of *liir*, but she's so gentle with it, just the slightest trace of irony.

"I haven't answered everything," she says, "but perhaps that will help for now. What I should have said right away is thank you so much for changing your mind and agreeing to sit on the Truth Commission after all. I am overwhelmed by your dedication and courage. How are you feeling now? Are your accommodations up to standard?"

"They're fine. Luxurious. More than I expected."

"Good! Well, I'm glad about that!" she says. She looks at me too long, not at all overwhelmed.

"I'm feeling well," I say. "I was anxious about my return but I seem to be handling it. I've brought my personal assistant, Joanne Stoddart, to look after me."

"Yes, I know. Good!"

Cautiously I sip the *supira* – one small taste races sharply across my tongue. I swallow, manage to avoid coughing. I should have more questions but my mind is suddenly in neutral. I've been raging about, when if I'd only stayed patient . . . The lull in the conversation stretches into my own discomfort. "Do you always work this late?" I finally ask inanely.

"Usually," she says, folding her legs up in the large chair in a feline motion. The movement is familiar, unofficial. "I never learned to sleep very well after Jono was killed. You know I was there when it happened. I turned to look at a red banner. *Teriala kojinda Minizhi lundafilo.* 'The Minitzh airport wishes safe journeys.' When I looked back Jono was on the floor beside me. Half his face was ripped away. There was blood on my stockings and bits of his teeth hung onto threads of skin. It was utterly silent. I didn't hear a thing. But there was my husband and there was the banner: *Teriala kojinda Minizhi lundafilo.*"

Her voice so quiet, flickering slightly as if with the candlelight. A strange and sudden intimacy. She has opened up completely, without any apparent hesitation, in a way that seems natural and effortless and stunningly human.

"This happened in 1983?" I ask, trying the *supira* again. Much smoother this time.

"April seventeenth," she says. "I shouldn't be functioning, I know. I should be in the asylum." Her tired smile again, but sly as well, as if this is a private joke, meant mostly for herself. "I pray, I meditate, I sing, I rest. But sleep was no longer the safe place so I let it go. Maybe someday it will be all right again."

"Yes."

Maybe someday, but this is now and time has turned liquid, stretched itself and slowed with the quiet of the hour. She tells me about reading my book in a small country library in Kent, with a cold rain outside and tears washing down her face. "It was as if every bit of rage and sadness in my body was stored in those pages and written directly for me. I read by the window from ten in the morning until almost ten at night. The whole day I didn't move except to turn the pages. I felt your captivity. I sat so still the staff forgot I was there and closed the building behind me. When I stood finally it was as though years had passed. I'd practised fasting before and been still through meditation, but this was different. It was being caught in someone else's torment that bore the scent of my own. I thought about contacting you. Finally it boiled down to just one main thing. After reading your book I realized how thankful I could be that Jono's death was so quick. He couldn't have been in pain long, if at all. It's not such a bad way to go. The Intelligence Service could have put him through agony."

She holds my gaze for too long, but it's not uncomfortable. She connects with people, I think. This is where her genius lies. She's the president of her country and yet she wins you through her vulnerability and willingness to open up, makes you feel like you could ask her anything and it would be all right.

"Is that who killed Jono? The IS?"

"Nothing is certain," she says. "Maybe that's something you'll find out. There was never an inquiry, of course. I believe the man who pulled the trigger is either a wealthy landlord in the back country by now or else *doslin terda*."

"*Doslin terda*?"

"Literally, 'feeding maggots.'"

A pause stretches into the shadows of the room.

"You said there are people who want to derail this commission. Do you know who? What do I need to do?"

"Nothing is certain," she says again. "But it is possible that Barios is still in the country, and he has a lot of support among Minitzh's old guard. Have you heard of Barios?"

"The former vice-president?"

"Yes. He should have stepped in when Minitzh was killed but disappeared instead. He has been seen in some of the villages. A large man, fat as a cow, it's hard to mistake him. What we've learned – and nothing is confirmed – but it's possible he has joined with some of the Kartouf groups. He also has extensive contacts with the *djotkas*."

"The drug lords?"

"They have enormous money and grew very comfortable while Minitzh protected them."

"But why would the Kartouf join with Barios? They were mortal enemies."

"And sometimes the lion lies down with the lamb." She pauses, looks briefly at her hands, then fully meets my gaze again. "There are things that you need to know. Many factions of the Kartouf are no more than armed thugs happy to work for the *djotkas* anyway. Whatever it takes to get rich. Only certain portions of the Kartouf want anything to do with helping peasants or overthrowing corrupt governments. Once you look closely at the pattern of villages destroyed by Minitzh you'll see that it looks much more like a Kartouf turf war than any crackdown on an opposition group."

It takes time for the words to sink in. My mind feels webbed by her soft voice, the *supira*, the late hour.

"There are army members who actively support certain Kartouf groups," she says. "The few groups that wanted Minitzh out were never very powerful. Most of them desired a share of the drug profits. That's what it was about. That's what you fell into. And that's what I now have to deal with."

She seems so candid, yet from her tone and the look in her eyes I suddenly feel that she's keeping back important things. Things I didn't want to know, and yet now that I'm here I must ask. If I didn't it would be like coming to the edge of the water then turning back.

"Do you know who kidnapped me?" I saw my keeper, Josef, and the others shot by the army helicopter during the rescue, but it was never clear exactly who was behind it all and what they wanted, or why they held me so long.

"Nothing is certain," she says.

"No. But what do you know?"

"I don't *know* anything," she says. "That's what you're here for, to find out as much as you can, as certainly as you can."

"But you've heard things."

"We've *all* heard things, Mr. Burridge."

The formality of the name seems to bring things near an end. Suddenly I feel the exhaustion of the day. She *knows*, but she won't tell me. She's been playing me, winning me over without giving anything away. But then just as I'm thinking this she confides something else.

"You must be careful of Justice Sin," Suli says.

"Why?"

"He was close to Minitzh. I fought to keep him out of this, but I'm balancing between Tinto and Mende Kul and both insisted on him. He'll try to protect his cronies, so I'm hoping you'll be able to work with Mrs. Grakala. She has a strong record working behind the scenes for issues of social justice. I fought hard for her. And for you too."

I'm surprised, and pause before speaking. "Mrs. Grakala has been very reserved so far," I say.

"Appearances deceive." She leans in to press her point. She's playing me. The Angel of Kalindas Boulevard. She uses everything – her beauty, vulnerability, soft words, the steel hidden behind them. "Mrs. Grakala has a strong record. And Justice Sin can surprise us all. He is his own man, or I would never have finally agreed. And if I don't agree, no one gets on the commission."

Then it's as if a switch has flicked. Clearly the meeting is over. She rises and moves across the room to her desk. I find myself standing, not sure what to do with the remaining *supira*. It's already weighing heavily in my head. I put my glass down on a side table and start to thank her for seeing me. She looks up from something at her desk as if surprised I'm still here.

"Justice Sin will contact you when the translation service is available. You'll have to watch him closely. But Mrs. Grakala will be your ally, I'm sure. And you *will* make a difference."

Suli and I say our goodbyes, then I walk down the hall, surrounded by my guards again. Outside it's still night, although it feels as if many hours should have passed. The air is filled with mist, and a drowsiness enters me. We ride back in silence and I nod my head with fatigue, too tired to look out the window, too strained to really sleep.

17

Back at the commission meeting room in the *Justico kampi*, two days later, and the translation service is up and running. It comes through the headphones in the form of an unemotional female voice, in competent English, only slightly hurried, with most of the island singsong taken out of her accent. The room feels overflowing with staff, but there are no reporters allowed, only limited seating for the public. Most of the men in the room are smoking; the pall hangs over us as a visible, choking reminder of the gloom that enveloped this country for so many years.

Our first witness is a villager with only one name, Tangul, who survived the Lorumptindu massacre of three years ago. He sits in the middle of the room surrounded by the rectangle of our tables, telling his story. His hair is grey and dishevelled, his clothes ratty, still bearing mud from the fields.

"And when we came to the checkpoint at Lorumptindu," the voice in my headphones says, "soldiers boarded the bus. They had guns and ordered us all out of the bus, and separated the men and the women. We were the men, we were on one side and we could hear the soldiers yelling and saying abusive things to the women but we couldn't see because the bus was in the way. They made us cross over the ditch and then walk into the jungle, it wasn't very far, there was a clearing where some men had been digging. I asked where they were taking us and one of the soldiers took his *waloo* rod and slashed it across my ankle. I fell in the mud and then he hit me three or four more times and told me to get up or he was going to shoot me right there. I got up and limped a bit further and then they gave us all spades and said we had to clear the land by digging a large hole. Someone asked why should we clear this land and the soldier said it was a special peasant tax, this was our labour. But we knew there was no peasant tax, they just wanted us to dig our own graves and then they were going to shoot us."

Tangul pauses to elaborately sip from a mug of tea, his hands shaking badly. Sin Vello asks him to continue.

"We could hear also some wailing and commotion from the other side of the road by the bus. There were no shots yet but it seemed clear that soldiers were raping the women. I considered then that I was a dead man and I thought, do I want to dig my own grave first and let these *jiroptas* rape our women or do I want to bring some soldiers with me while I die? For others, I could see they were afraid and wanted to hope that really we were just clearing land and the commotion from the other side of the bus was not soldiers raping our women. I whispered to one or two of the others we must die like men and then there were shots. I didn't know what was happening. I thought they'd started killing the women, and so I turned and swung my spade at the nearest soldier. He saw me coming and pointed his gun, but he was very young, perhaps only fifteen, and scared by the shots, he froze and my spade caught him on the side of the head. As he fell I grabbed for his weapon. I don't know how I thought what to do. I'm a farmer, not a fighter. But now shots were coming from everywhere and I ran as fast as I could into the jungle. I believed any moment I would get hit, but I guess no one followed me in the confusion."

"How long did you spend in the jungle?" Sin Vello asks.

"Two nights. I climbed a rinko tree and waited in the leaves. I had the soldier's gun ready in case anyone came for me and I slept only in small . . . only in little bits."

"What happened when you got down?" Mrs. Grakala asks. Her voice in Kuantij above the headphones is broken and faint.

"I started to feel weak from hunger and thirst, and there had been no sounds, so I got down from the tree and walked carefully back to the bus."

"What did you see?" Sin Vello asks.

"Where we had started digging the grave there were many bodies. They smelled like dead animals and were covered in insects and maggots. They were only partly in the ground."

"Were they your companions on the bus?" Sin Vello again. He clearly wants to play the lead. Tangul turns in his chair to speak directly to him.

"Some of them were, and some were the soldiers who had ordered us off the bus."

"What about the boy you hit with the spade?"

"His body was there. It was right where I had hit him."

"Was anyone alive?"

"No."

"Was the bus still there?"

"No."

"Did you look on the other side of the road where the women were taken?"

"No."

"Why not?"

"When I first saw and smelled the bodies of the men I fainted."

"And that's how the soldiers found you?"

"Yes."

"They thought you were dead?"

"Yes."

"What happened when you woke up?"

Tangul looks away, rummages in his pockets and pulls out a stained blue cloth, wipes his sweat-soaked face, then sips his tea again.

"The soldiers were sprinkling lye and gasoline on my body. I was on top of several other bodies and they were going to burn all of us. I cried out and tried to get up. The soldiers were so afraid one of them shot at me but missed. Some others ran away. They thought I was a *huloika* come back to revenge them. But the commander told them to help me out. They washed off the lye and gasoline."

"I'm sorry!" I say, waving my hand to Sin. "What's a *huloika*?"

Sin puts on his headphones, whispers something to an aide, writes on a piece of paper. Tangul looks at me in real fear – imagining I've asked something serious, no doubt. Finally the translator's voice comes through in my ear: "A *huloika* is a spirit. A ghost."

I nod my thanks, wave okay to Justice Sin and Tangul.

"Where did they take you?" Sin asks.

"I don't know."

"You were unfamiliar with the area?"

"I was blindfolded."

"Was it a military base?"

"I don't know."

"But the men who interrogated you were soldiers?"

"They wore black. I didn't recognize them."

"Where were you kept?"

"It was a small room. Very cold at night but hot in the day."

"Were there windows?"

"No."

"Was there a cot? A toilet?"

"No."

"Did they keep you blindfolded?"

"Most of the time."

"What did they ask you?"

"Who killed the soldiers. What happened to the bus. How I survived. Whether I was part of the Kartouf. They thought I'd told the Kartouf where the soldiers would be. I said how could I know where the soldiers would be? I didn't know I was going to be pulled off the bus. They said I was lying and . . ."

"Yes?"

"And beat me."

"How did they beat you?"

"With *waloos*, with their hands and feet. There was also . . ."

"Also what?"

"A black box. They attached me and gave me electric shocks."

"Were you naked?"

"Yes."

"Did they sexually molest you?"

Silence.

"What else did they do?"

Silence.

"Do you want to take a break?"

Silence.

Silence.

Tangul stares at the floor, his eyes swollen with tears. Sin Vello asks him several more questions, but he has stopped responding. Finally a dignified elderly woman in a red and blue *saftori* – his wife? – walks slowly to his chair and touches his shoulder, brings him out of his trance. He lights a cigarette distractedly. Together they walk out, his eyes on the floor, hers ratcheted on Justice Sin's.

They take the air with them – *swoosh!* – and suddenly I'm gripping the table, trying to breathe. It's as quick as that: while the words were coming out I was fine, but his halting, agonized gait has taken all the air. I know about the black box. I know about being raped. I gasp, feel the choke-rope at my throat, *God*. There's something I can do, I think, but the darkness is coming, it's too late, they'll get her if I think of her, I can't, I won't, it wouldn't work . . .

"Bill!" Joanne says, puts her warm hand on my shoulder. "*Breathe!*" she says in my ear. And then there's just a glimpse – Joanne in the doorframe that night. She turns into Joanne in the rain, soaked and laughing. I'm dizzy, but in a minute I feel the spell passing, a lucky near-collision. Hundreds of eyes are on me but it could be worse. The table is still there, the air isn't oily black, the footsteps and the cigarettes belong to now, not then.

"It's all right. It's fine!" I say. Sin Vello calls a break anyway and Joanne walks me to the grand lobby and fresher air. A large crowd has begun to assemble on the lawn of the *Justico kampi*. Not locals but people from the villages, arriving with bags and sacks of belongings, with food and umbrellas against the rains that will come later in the day. Come to testify.

"That could have been horrendous," I say to Joanne.

"Did you use your safe thought?" she asks.

"I did. Eventually. Yes, I think it helped. You helped."

"The next time will be easier," she says.

Three different officials, including Sin Vello, inquire about me, but I assure them I'm fine, I want the hearings to continue.

When we are reassembled a young, quite fair-skinned man in a blue suit is ushered in. Again Sin Vello takes the lead in the questioning, and asks him to state his name and occupation.

"My name is Dorut Kul, I work as a reporter for the *Islander* newspaper."

"When was the first time you heard of Lorumptindu?"

"It was in March 1995."

"How did you hear of it?"

"I was told by some contacts that something had gone very wrong at the checkpoint."

"What contacts?"

"I cannot say."

"You cannot say or you will not say?" Sin Vello presses.

Silence. Dorut Kul looks at the chief justice with an odd mixture of defiance and equanimity.

"Mr. Kul, if we are to weigh your evidence we must be able to evaluate the source."

"And Justice Sin, I must be able to close my eyes at night."

"So you will not co-operate with this commission?"

"I will tell you what I saw, not what I heard or from whom."

The thin young man and the corpulent chief justice staring one another down.

"Then tell us what you saw."

"I went to the area called Lorumptindu. My photographer was with me. We had not received military clearance."

"Why not?"

"Because if I waited for military clearance I would never make it out of my office."

"So you proceeded illegally to Lorumptindu?"

"I went with my photographer, Davu. I did not expect to be let in, but the soldiers were in a state of panic. There was confusion, no one stopped us. We drove right to the site."

"In a military Jeep?"

"Yes, I had access through a contact."

"Whose name you cannot reveal."

"I see no need to endanger him, Justice Sin. I have seen too many bodies already."

I watch Sin Vello closely. There seems to be a history between these two – Sin is much more antagonistic towards him than towards Tangul. Perhaps Dorut Kul wrote about the chief justice at some point? The reporter does not seem overly awed or out of his league, but remains composed, focused.

"Were you wearing military uniforms?"

"Not regulation, Justice Sin."

"Where did you get them?"

"My friend had extras in the theatre where he works."

"So you impersonated members of the armed forces?"

"They were not regulation uniforms. We bore no insignia."

"And nobody stopped you?"

"There was great confusion. We drove straight to Lorump-tindu and found about twenty soldiers carrying limbs and pieces of bodies, digging in the ground, preparing to burn them. Davu started taking pictures immediately and no one stopped him."

"They thought he was a military photographer?"

"No one stopped him. I took out my notebook and asked a soldier what had happened."

"And the soldier talked to you?"

"He said there had been an ambush on the checkpoint by the Kartouf, that thirty-one people had been killed, mostly civilians from the bus."

"Was the bus still there?"

"It was blocking the road. Yes."

"We heard testimony earlier that the bus was gone. How do you account for that?"

"Davu took pictures of the bus. There were bullet holes in the side."

"Did you ask how the people got off the bus?"

"The soldier said the Kartouf had stopped the bus and taken the people off, that the soldiers from the checkpoint had been shot right away. He said the Kartouf executed all those people."

"Were there any Kartouf bodies?"

"I couldn't tell."

"In the article you wrote on this incident you said that the soldiers seemed to be proficient at disposing of bodies. How did you come to that conclusion?"

"It was just an observation."

"An observation based on what?"

"I was surprised that the soldiers were burning the bodies, making no attempt to get in touch with the relatives of the dead. It also seemed to me that they were working very efficiently."

"But you said earlier that they were in a panic, that there was confusion?"

"Yes."

"Was it efficient confusion?"

"I suppose so."

"That makes no sense."

"In the middle of the confusion they seemed to be working efficiently, as if they'd had a great deal of practice already at this sort of thing."

"At disposing of bodies?"

"Yes."

Sin Vello pauses to write some notes, and I take the opportunity to speak up. I can see myself relegated to window dressing if I don't.

"What happened to the females?" I ask. Dorut Kul turns to

me and answers in perfect English, while around our rectangle of tables people scramble to pull on their headphones.

"Davu and I noticed across the road that part of the ground had been dug up recently. So we scraped with our boots and found bits of bodies and clothing, some only a few centimetres under the dirt."

"Female bodies and clothing?" I ask.

"Yes."

"How could you tell?"

"There were brighter colours. There were some . . . other parts."

Sin Vello interjects. "You are very composed giving this testimony, young man."

"I'm trying my best, Justice Sin."

"You have written a book, is that right, Mr. Kul?" Sin continues.

"Yes."

"What kind of book is it?"

"A novel."

"Fiction?"

"Yes, Justice Sin."

"Stories you simply dreamed up, fabricated, is that right?"

"I suppose . . ."

"But this story you have told us about Lorumptindu, this is not a fabrication, is it, Mr. Kul?"

"No."

"What happened the day you filed your story?"

"Several agents came to my office after I gave the story to my editor."

"Who is your editor?"

"It is – was Kali Jukmahindza."

"What happened to him?"

"I do not know."

"He disappeared?"

"His wife says he was taken from their home at two o'clock in the morning by special agents. She has not seen or heard from him since."

"This was the day after you filed your story?"

"Yes."

"What happened to your photographer?"

"They found Davu's body on the beach in the harbour two weeks later. His hands and feet were bound in barbed wire and his eye sockets had been burned black."

"You don't know who did this?"

"There was no investigation."

"What happened to you?"

"The agents took me from my office and shoved me in the back of a white van. It's the kind of van everyone knows is used by the IS. They pushed my head to the floor and pulled black tape over my eyes."

"So you don't know where they took you?"

"It was a secret detention centre."

"Were there others there?"

"I could hear screaming sometimes."

"Describe the room where they held you."

"It was small, dark, entirely concrete. There was no furniture, nothing to sit or lie on, no windows. It got very hot during the day and cold at night. It's the only way I could tell the difference."

"How long were you held?"

"I think only three days."

"Were you tortured?"

"No."

"Not tortured?"

"I was mistreated, but I can't call it torture. They interrogated me but I was never hit, burned, or the like. I was scared witless, but not tortured."

"Do you know why you were released?"

"I think so. Because of my family connections. Someone must have gotten word through and the agents thought twice before harming me."

"For the record – your family connections?"

"My great-uncle is Mende Kul, the chief of the armed forces."

"Do you get along well with Mende Kul?"

"No."

"But you think he stepped in on your behalf?"

"I think the agents were afraid to harm me."

"Did you ever publish an account of your treatment?"

"In the U.K., yes, and in Germany."

"But not in Santa Irene?"

"No."

"Not in Kuantij?"

"No."

We break for a short lunch, then listen to testimony through the afternoon and into the early evening. Back at the hotel room we order in and read over the morning's testimony, which has been translated and word-processed already. It comes in faint blue dot-matrix type, complete with pauses, strange spellings, and bracketed inaudible patches. I take my meds and read through the flurry of e-mails that Derrick has sent on – other business, which somehow now seems remote and unimportant. Except for one item: the initial ten thousand dollars that the government of Santa Irene was supposed to deposit in our bank account at the beginning of my contract has not yet arrived. Could I check on that and get it expedited?

I make a note and Joanne drubs me in cribbage and then I fall into bed and fail to sleep. But it's a safe lack of sleep. It's full of Joanne dealing me sevens and eights, of her soft voice and a story she told me about going fishing with her grandfather, how at dawn they would creep up to the stream on their bellies to avoid scaring the fish. "He used to tie his own flies," she says, in my warm unsleep. "And he'd cut off the barbs – what was the point of fishing if you weren't sportsman enough to cut off the barbs? That way you had to waltz the fish in so gently, and a little brook trout could keep you going for half an hour. And I remember him laughing at me whenever I got tired or hungry or fell in the water. He had a saying, it was almost like a zen koan: 'No use complaining, because this is what is happening!'"

This is, I think, in my tired unsleep. This is what is happening.

We spend three days on Lorumptindu, then two more on a similar massacre at Hindluv, and then three on the burning of a village called Toygoptu. Through it all Sin Vello leans forward in his chair, cutting in with his questions, sometimes apparently trying to discredit witnesses, other times drawing them out. I interject from time to time, Mrs. Grakala less frequently, appearing usually to be either deep in thought or asleep.

The testimony is relentless.

"Where were you when the helicopter arrived?" Sin Vello asks Vegu Lat, an unusually dark-skinned young man with nervous, roaming eyes. He's another villager in the capital for the first time.

"I was in my shop in the village."

"You are a silversmith?"

"Copper, silver, bronze. I make jewellery and some tools."

"Had helicopters arrived before?"

"Never."

"What did you do?"

"I left my shop and saw that the children were running to greet the helicopter in the square. I yelled at them to stop, stop, but they couldn't hear me. They just ran right to it. I could see the soldier in a white helmet behind the gun. He had dark glasses. He didn't look like a man. No man could kill children like that."

"He shot them down?"

He pauses to stare empty-eyed. I remember the helicopters during my rescue. I remember the little boy in the village a few feet away from me. How he turned and held his hip, then twisted violently and fell in the mud. How his body came apart when I reached for him. I glance behind me at Joanne, who has been listening raptly to the testimony. My life preserver.

". . . and then the women who ran after the children and the men who ran after the women," Vegu Lat continues. "We all ran to the helicopter to be shot. When I close my eyes now there is blood everywhere."

"But you were not shot?"

"I was hit in the shoulder and my father dragged me away. We stayed in the jungle for seven days after the fire. I was in a bad fever and should have died. My father carried me to the next village where there was a clinic."

"Have you been back to your village?" I ask, as much as anything to keep myself here, not to dwell on my own blackness.

"No."

"Do you know why you were attacked?" I ask.

"No."

"Did your village support the Kartouf?" Sin Vello asks.

"We fed some starving men who came to us. That was months before. We also fed soldiers and some of our daughters went away with the soldiers."

Sin Vello's eyes narrow with this last detail. "Did they go willingly?" he asks.

"Some of the soldiers paid money . . . for some of the daughters."

"You sold your daughters to soldiers?" Sin Vello presses.

"Some did."

"How much did they pay?"

The man's cracked nails beat nervously on the table.

"It was uncertain."

"Different prices for different daughters?"

"Some people were very poor."

"But not you?"

"My daughters died in childbirth."

"Had the soldiers come back to get more daughters?"

"When they came to get daughters they came in Jeeps."

"So this was different?"

"They came to kill us."

During a break I look through the bars on the window at the line-up outside the *Justico kampi*, which winds now like a fat river all through the parking lot, across the great lawn and onto Cardinal Avenue. Whole families camp here, waiting to testify: grandmothers in torn clothing looking after babies wrapped within an inch of their lives; middle-aged men squatting in twos and threes and fours, smoking, drinking homemade beer sold in the street by the glass; mothers cooking flatcakes over tiny fires, burning wood that must've been stripped from the few remaining trees in the downtown core or else carried with them. Ever since the first day, they've been arriving in family clumps, disgorged from *tritos* or buses, or sometimes come on foot, erecting lean-tos of bamboo and plastic sheeting to shelter them from the rain, putting out bottles to catch the water, shitting and bathing and cleaning their food and dishes all in the same stream that passes a few blocks away and empties into the harbour. The press has a name for them: the *sorialos*, "shadows waiting to speak."

They won't leave until they've been heard. That's the wondrous, frightening thing – they all want to be heard, and we're proceeding at a snail's pace as it is.

"When did your son disappear?" Sin Vello asks, impatient to get to the important details now that our pile of testimony is beginning to grow. The new witness, Mrs. Dindympte, is a plump woman in a satiny purple cocktail dress – her best outfit, no doubt – with yellow pumps and a sequinned brooch in the shape of a butterfly.

"October third."

"What year?"

"1994."

"Can you tell us what happened?"

"We never heard a thing."

"Was he taken away?" Sin Vello presses.

"Of course!"

"Who took him away?"

"We never learned."

"When was the last time you saw your son?"

"He had just come home from school."

"Please be specific."

"And he said he was hungry, so I served him his dinner early."

"Yes?" Sin Vello's eyes widen incredulously.

"He ate everything."

"*And what happened?*"

"He studied very hard."

"Yes?"

"He always worked very hard."

"Yes. But can you tell us – ?"

"He was going to be a travel agent."

"Mrs. Dindympte –"

"We never discouraged him. He always believed he could do it."

"Was your son taken away by soldiers or the police?"

"I think he must have been."

"*Tell us what happened!*"

"We did receive a card once, but it could not have been true. He would never have married without our permission."

"What did the card say?"

"It said Sonny had moved to the Philippines, but we did not believe it. It was his handwriting, but I don't believe he would do that to us."

Joanne and I go over the stacks of testimony in the hotel room every evening, the day's work spilling over in a natural rhythm. I need her mind to help me keep the witnesses straight, the incidents and explanations, the various versions, the place names and timelines. On the wall by the piano she tapes a huge map of the teardrop island and within days it becomes covered with sticky notes crowded in her tiny writing. On many nights we find the telephone system either down or too sluggish to bother with, but when it's working she handles most of the e-mails – by mid-evening now my eyes are too tired to cope with the computer.

But one night she erupts. "You don't listen to anything I say!" she says. "I might as well be a piece of lint on the wall!"

"What?" I ask, startled.

She gets up, snaps the laptop shut, paces. "I need to get out of here!" she says.

"What's the problem?"

"Did you get back to the ministry people about the pay back-up?" she asks. "Derrick is apoplectic."

"Tell him to speak to the bank people again," I say, tired, uncertain how to deal with her sudden anger. "The money is coming. I've had assurances."

"The bank people won't move unless *you* talk to them."

"Fine. I'll talk to them."

"That's the *third* time you've said –"

"I'm sorry," I say, exhausted. "There've been a few things to do."

"And you will write Patrick, yes? Just a quick note. It would be good for him to hear from you."

"Yes. I will." As soon as the pace lets up, I think – but I don't say it because I know what she'll reply, that the pace isn't going to let up. It's just begun.

"What about cribbage?" I ask after a time.

"*You play*," she says, and snaps the cards in front of me. "*I need to go out.*"

In a moment she is gone, the luxury suite resoundingly empty without her. A terrible mess, I suddenly realize: stacks of testimony everywhere, my bed covered by the remains of our dinner – plates of pineapple burgers and french fries with a sickly sweet "ketchup" sauce made from bananas and food colouring.

I'm unsettled by her sudden moodiness. But of course she doesn't want to be here. These demons that we're exorcising, they don't belong to her. They're mine.

I call home. The phone rings just once before it's picked up.

"Hello?" I say.

"Grey?"

It's my father. "Dad," I say. "Hi. How are you? It's Bill."

"Grey?"

"No Dad, it's Bill. How are you? It's so good to hear your voice."

"Time to come in for supper," he announces. "Where's Grey?"

"Dad, it's Bill on the line. I'm phoning all the way from Santa Irene. How are you? What have you been up to?"

"Your mother's getting angry 'cause it's spaghetti. Just wanted to tell you. Time to get back to the house."

"Dad —"

"And tell your brother." The phone goes dead.

"Dad!"

I call again immediately but just get a busy signal — it could be anything: the hotel operator taking a break; the overseas network overloaded somewhere; Dad playing with the phone on his end. *Grey.* He was thinking of Graham.

At midnight, when Joanne still hasn't returned, I begin to worry. I go down to the lobby but don't see her anywhere. I return to the room and pace. I need to talk to Maryse and Derrick, try my parents again. But suddenly I can't think of what I would say. Tomorrow.

Joanne comes in after one. I am propped up in bed, flipping cards. "It's not safe!" I say immediately. "You shouldn't go out on your own at night!"

"I know," she says, calmer now. "But I needed to get out of this room, Bill. Are you all right?" When I nod she says, "Good. I'll see you in the morning," disappears into her room, and we don't speak of it again.

Every daylight hour, new clumps of *sorialos* arrive. After the first week the lawn in front of the *Justico kampi* is completely full, so the tent city leaks onto Cardinal Avenue and no one dares move them away. Suli arrives one afternoon with rice and kerosene and the pace of arrivals picks up. Most of those who've had their say stay on because this is suddenly a happening, an event, there's an air of anticipation. But what can we do? The testimony gathers in great stacks of paper, details upon details that serve mainly to blur, it seems, rather than clarify. We know already about the killings, the disappearances, the massacres. We don't know who ordered them, who to call to blame.

From my chair in the corner I gaze for a moment out the window in the late-afternoon sun down on the *sorialos* stretching below us, a lake of quiet humanity going about their business of eating and sleeping, shitting and loving, talking and playing. I can hear, somewhere in the ceiling above me, our good-luck beacon: *tokay, tokay, tokay*. Six, seven, eight. On the lawn a boy and a girl pull on a piece of cloth, and in between some of the tents a strange game of soccer breaks out, the ball a lumpy mass of wire and plastic that bounces erratically off the sides of the various dwellings, the kids racing and laughing, nearly upending someone's chamber pot, tripping over a pole then scrambling up and running on. For a moment I imagine the ball smashing over a kerosene stove and setting fire to a tent, the flames leaping up and igniting other tents then others. We have the makings of a disaster right here at our feet, but no one can bear to move them on, to tell them they can't be heard.

There's no fire. The ball bounces off an old man who turns, smiling, and kicks at it awkwardly. Two other men join in and one spills his glass of beer stretching for the ball. The voice behind me continues and the stacks of paper grow and I wonder, how long will this take? My contract is simply for three months. I have no doubt this national grieving could continue a year, or two, or five, for that matter. But Joanne won't stay past the three months, and I won't stay without Joanne.

"State your name," Justice Sin says, and another ragged witness sits before us to have his say.

18

"Maybe we should have gone by helicopter after all," Joanne says with a rueful smile when the Jeep gets stuck in the mud for the sixth or seventh time. We're all covered in it, red-brown, soaked in everlasting rain, on this road now for five hours. I was the one who didn't think we should arrive at Hoyaitnut by helicopter, like the soldiers who burned the place down. Bad optics. Symbolism isn't everything we're about, but it's something.

But maybe this is worse: *Commission mired in mud*. Someone simply could've spoken up, said we couldn't get there by road this time of year. I wouldn't have insisted if I'd known. Mrs. Grakala decided to stay in the capital – the conditions in the mountains are too rough for her. She said she would eagerly await our report.

We climb out of the vehicle, step as carefully as we can onto the soggy grasses away from the mud, and watch while the soldiers winch us out. Ten minutes later we're stalled again. This time it's Sin Vello's Jeep, and the road is so narrow there's no way past. We're in the mountains, though it's hard to tell, the visibility is so poor. But there is a slight chill in the air, which seems joyously fresh, a relief after the stultifying heat and smog of the city. And a good diversion for Joanne – even with the mud her spirits have improved remarkably since we left the city. Maybe it's her traveller's soul, I think.

We shelter under some enormous-leafed trees and soon are joined by the American Dr. Parker. He must be six foot-five and at least two hundred and fifty pounds, white-bearded and pink-skinned, his light blue eyes peering out of rain-fogged glasses.

"We're within ten klicks," he says.

"Does the road get any better?" Joanne asks.

"It wasn't this bad coming down."

We stand quietly for some minutes. Parker seems happy just to listen to the rain, watch the soldiers pull and pry the Jeep. The justice remains in the back. The faster the wheels spin the more liquid the road becomes beneath him.

"Helicopters aren't much fun in the rain either," Parker says finally. "I lost three crew in Guatemala in a helicopter crash. Went right into the side of a mountain. This way at least we can walk in if it comes to that."

Joanne asks him about Guatemala and he shakes his head. "I've never felt more frightened for my staff. These were medical people, and I trained them in forensics myself. One of them had spent much of his career falsifying reports for the army – covering up torture, helping to keep political prisoners alive for more punishment. More than anybody else he knew what to look for. That was his problem – the army didn't want him working for me. Velasquez. They hanged him in the village square, threw his arms and feet to the dogs down the road."

This little smile on his professorial face, as if he isn't saying the words he's saying.

The soldiers attach three different winches, strain like horses. One loses his footing and falls face-first into the slop; another pushes from behind and is sprayed by the spinning tires. Sin Vello sits in the back apparently unaware, a briefcase on his knees, files open.

"Did you ever fear for your own life?" Joanne asks.

"Not as much as I should've, probably," Parker says. "I had my American passport. I thought, stupidly, they'd never dare do anything to me. It was supposed to be part of the reconciliation anyway. Then when they got Velasquez . . . Some men go home, you know, and some lash out. But I got very calm, and tried as hard as I could to keep it on a scientific level. They're not used to it – it's one of the things missing in so many of these countries. They've no investigatory skills. Instead the police just seize and terrorize people till they talk. They never think they'll be held accountable."

Lower, lower in the mud until I'm sure the Jeep will never move again, and then improbably the winches take effect and Justice Sin's Jeep is pulled free. Now there's a rush of activity getting us all back in our vehicles before they bog down again. Our driver slams the gears, swears, bounces us off trees, but somehow we keep going despite the rain and mud.

We arrive at Hoyaitnut much later in the day, after the rains have stopped but still with the humidity so thick we seem to be living in a cloud. There's not much anyone would call a village here now, although Dr. Parker's advance crew has erected several tents, and in some areas of intense green foliage there's still evidence of charred remains. It's only a few minutes to six and sundown happens in an eyeblink, but Parker takes us anyway to the old church ground. The area is so small I have a hard time imagining what sort of building might have stood here – perhaps a one-room shack, hardly space enough for ten people, not the sixty or seventy who supposedly crowded in for refuge.

"Nobody was buried here," Parker says soberly. Luki, the young woman who translates for the aides – Justice Sin didn't walk up the steep slope – is hardly higher than Parker's elbow. It's her voice behind the earphones in the hearing room. In Kuantij she is velvety smooth. Parker points back to a clearing barely the size of a couple of driveways. "That's where the helicopters landed," he says. "The soldiers ran up the hill to get here. We scoured the area but all the spent casings were here. They seemed to know where to go and what they'd find."

Rubble, collapsed walls, charred wood. The jungle already growing over a good part of it, well on the way to wiping it clean.

In increasing darkness we head back down the hill to where the soldiers have been erecting our tents. I'm wet and dirty and bone-tired just from sitting all day as a piece of baggage. But it feels good to get out of the hearing room and away from the silent expectation of the *sorialos*. I hadn't realized how relentless the pressure was becoming, as if somehow our little commission is going to relieve the pain of thousands.

The tents are grey canvas, ripped in some spots with no floors and therefore no real refuge from mosquitoes. Fortunately we're high enough to be out of malaria danger, but Joanne has us on anti-malarials anyway. What's another pill among the crowd? I hang my kerosene lamp from the centre pole and try to weigh down the bottom tent fringes with rocks and bits of luggage. It's pointless, I know – Santa Irenian mosquitoes drill you, then move off quick as houseflies, so you rarely get the satisfaction of killing them.

Fortunately Joanne brings a mosquito coil and lights it for me. Then a soldier arrives with a pan of hot water and some towels and I wash myself, retrieve some clean clothes from my luggage. Such a simple act, and yet I feel renewed, like Joanne's Hindu woman on the train. I extinguish my light, then grope for the tent flap and step into the night. Joanne's tent is next to mine; I find her outside it in a yellow rain jacket, seated on a wet log with her knees pulled up, eyes closed, face covered in mist and turned skyward. The whole encampment has a ghostly look to it: the white tents disappearing in black shadows, the lamps glowing eerily in the mist, the press of the jungle, sky and mountains all around us, swallowed in black.

Some soldiers stand around a fire, their weapons leaning teepee-fashion a little ways off. I hesitate, but pass on.

"I used to have visions of a place like this," I say.

"What's that?" Joanne asks.

"In captivity. They gave me drugs and I had visions of a mountain encampment like this – the fire, the weapons leaning like that, the blackness. I remember a really light feeling – like flying, hovering. And Josef was there. My keeper. He kept telling me I was dead, to leave him alone. It was just like this. Only there were children quite often. It was a Kartouf camp, not army."

We find the mess tent – circus-sized, almost, with eight or ten tables surrounded by metal chairs. Justice Sin, changed now into a newly pressed safari suit that looks big enough to clothe a tank, motions for us to join him at his table. We pull up chairs, and Luki, the translator, frees herself from talking with a young, mud-covered soldier and sits between us and the justice. The conversation is light and friendly – "What a day!" we say in various ways, laughing and nodding. Dinner is some sort of spiced stew with a bean sauce and *supira*. I ask for water, but the cook insists I try a type of jelly instead. As soon as I see it my stomach convulses.

"God, Bill, what is it?"

"Take it away. Take it!"

The cook starts to explain what it is so I grab the plate and hurl it off the table.

"I'm sorry! But I can't have it. *Damn!*"

Sudden rage blotting out everything else.

"This is not harmful. This is –" Luki starts to say.

"*I know what it is!*" It seems impossible to explain so I rise and leave, fists doubled, face on fire. Jesus! One of the soldiers looks up from his meal and for a moment I imagine my thumbs at his throat. I surge past him, through the flaps of the tent and into the darkness.

"Bill!"

Jesus.

I keep walking, but they won't let you. They keep after you, so I turn suddenly and knock her down. Joanne scurries back in the mud and I try to breathe, calm myself.

"Bill, it's me."

"Yes."

"Are you all right?'

"Yes."

"What are you doing?"

A crowd of soldiers around me now. Even Sin Vello has made it to his feet to see what's happening.

"It's nothing. I'm sorry."

"Why are you breathing like that?"

"Like what?"

"Like you're about to go to war."

"It's nothing. I'm fine."

Slowly, slowly, I loosen my fists. I won't let them get me. Clearly I won't. It's not going to be like last time.

I make it to my tent, sit inside with the poison of the

mosquito coil. This flimsy cot. At least it's off the ground. I've done my share of sleeping on the ground.

They leave me alone for a while and then Joanne comes. "Bill?"

Breathing. For days and days I've forgotten my breathing.

"I've got some food. Why are you sitting in the dark?" I don't answer. She brushes aside the flap. "Can I come in?"

"Have you brought the straitjacket?"

She steps in and puts the tray of food on the ground, then fumbles for a moment and lights my lamp. The suddenness of it strains my eyes, makes everything overwhelmingly white for a time. Another reminder. This wasn't such a good idea after all. I should've stayed in the Merioka where practically nothing would remind me of this country.

She hands me the tray, then sits beside me on the cot and we nearly tip it. When we're righted she puts her hand on the back of my neck. "You never need to hit me," she says.

"No."

"You *never* do. It's just me. And you know what else?"

"What?"

"If it happens again I'll sue you for millions."

"Yes."

"Not *loros* either."

"U.S. dollars?"

"Huge ones."

The smoke from the mosquito coil poisoning the air. The smell of the lamp. Darkness pressing in from outside.

"They served me *linala*," I say. "That jelly stuff. It's made somehow from tree bark. Try some. It's not completely taste-less, but it has so little taste it's revolting. And there's no nutri-tion. Zero. For months it was the only the thing the Kartouf fed me."

"Did you use your life preserver?" she asks.

I'm looking at it, I think. Of course I used it. If you hadn't been there – "Yes. It could've been worse," I reply, and I ask her to tell me a story.

"What story?"

"I don't know. One of your stories. The one about the Hindu lady."

"I told you that already."

"If you can't think of another one then tell me that again. I just want to sit here and breathe poison and listen to your voice while you rub my neck."

"So it doesn't matter what I say, just how I say it?"

"You know I'd fall apart without you."

"Would you?"

Breathing the smoke deep into my lungs. No mosquitoes going to get me, hoo boy!

"I'd be dead or in the loony bin. I've no doubt."

I spoon in the food, chew it joylessly. After a few minutes I put the tray on the ground, careful not to spill the glass of water.

"Tell me about one of your boyfriends. The most important one."

"Oh God," she says.

"Was it Jeremy? The guy who abandoned you in Lagos?"

"No," she says, sighing deeply. This might not be the right thing to ask about. But she responds after a moment.

"There was a New Zealander," she says, "a young doctor, Daniel. Tall and wiry with bright hazel eyes and beautiful hands. A pianist's hands – long, tapered, strong fingers. He played the piano like he was born to it."

"I hate him already," I say, and she laughs. My hands are thin but not graceful, not skilled.

"We were a team. I met him in Mozambique, and we were together in Sudan, and went travelling in Nepal. I visited his family in Auckland, and he came to Ottawa in February, hated the snow. It was very, very intense. Everything gets magnified, you know, when you're dog-tired and filthy and stretched past what you think you can do. That's just how he wants his life. He got sick in Nepal, but wouldn't slow down. It turned into pneumonia and he still wanted to trek in the Himalayas. He couldn't turn anything down, it was all experience."

"But he was all right?"

"Oh, he survived. He always does. But he had a hard time turning down other women. He has a very magnetic personality, shall we say. The first couple of times I figured it was the stress of the situation. But he could be relentless. Especially after you break up with him."

She goes quiet, the hiss of the lamp, her soft breathing.

"So it took some willpower to keep the separation?"

"It was the hardest thing I've ever done," she says. "But I had to seize responsibility. That's what I told myself. It sounds like something from a self-help book. But it's true. If you keep making bad decisions you can't expect your life to turn out."

There's a lot more she could say, I'm sure, but she lapses into silence.

"Where is he now?" I ask.

"Bosnia. I didn't want to make the trip."

No. You came here with me instead.

I change tack. "What about your first kiss?" I ask, and she knocks my shoulder sharply.

"I can't talk about that," she says. "It's too painful!" But she does anyway. "Danny McDougall. Oh, he was beautiful. Long wispy blond hair, blue eyes, those high cheekbones. His skin was so smooth. I wanted to have his skin. Grade five."

"You had your first boyfriend in grade five?"

"He was a choirboy, had this crystal-clear voice. He got to do all the solos. But I desperately wanted to sing 'Silent Night' in the Christmas pageant. There was an audition. I remember my mother came and I had on a green velvet dress with white ribbons, my hair was in braids like Anne of Green Gables. And Danny McDougall came up to me a minute before I was supposed to go on. He just put his hand behind my head and kissed me as if he'd been doing it for years. Then I stumbled onto the stage, flustered, and sang dead flat. Mrs. Dorchester at the piano actually stopped halfway through the first verse and had me start again, but I couldn't get it. He was perfect, of course. And he never spoke to me after that. Years later and I still couldn't figure out if I wanted to break his teeth or have him kiss me again."

"Could you sing it now?" I ask.

"Oh no," she says and looks away, a little flustered.

"Please." I put my hand on her arm.

"I wouldn't be any better."

"Sure you would." She takes a deep breath, silently pleased, I think, at the invitation. And then she sings, quietly, beautifully, her eyes soft and happy, mouth round and full and tender-looking.

"Thank you," I say, and applaud, and she turns down all other requests, lays me down on the cot instead and starts to rub my back.

"What about your first kiss?" she asks.

But I tell her a different story. I tell her about the time my brother Graham fell off the roof on a construction job, how he stayed in mid-air all night long, or at least that's what it felt like. He was in Edmonton, my parents in Ottawa, and I was in Kingston going to school. My mother phoned to say Graham had fallen off a roof but she didn't know how bad it was, she and Dad were just getting on the plane, she'd call in the morning. So all night long Graham was floating in my mind. I didn't think to call the hospital. In a way I wasn't in a hurry to know. If he was dead he'd be dead a long time. This way at least he was still possibly alive.

I talk stupidly about the girl I'd met that evening at a party, of all things. How I was distracted by the news of my brother but not distracted enough that I didn't find her attractive. Only I didn't follow up on it right away. It was only much later, at the end of the school year, the day before my final exam, that I saw her again, in a laundromat. She'd remembered my talking about Graham and had asked how he was, and I said he was making a full recovery, isn't that great? Some really lucky things happen in life. She was wearing a tank top and short shorts and was reading Hegel. And all the way home I thought, why didn't I ask her out this time? Because it was the end of the year and I was graduating and it was too late. . . . I got all the way home, dumped my laundry, and ran back to see her, but she was gone by then. This silly question of timing. Of knowing when to do the right thing.

I tell the story and Joanne rubs my back and I think, what if I turn over and pull her towards me? It seems as if it would be the easiest thing to do. Well, if the cot were bigger or more stable. I imagine myself rolling over and dumping us both. Would that be so bad? We'd laugh and then I could pull her towards me . . .

I think about it but can't make myself move. There's every reason not to, starting with the fact that I'm married – still married, it still means something to me. Doesn't it? But such a simple act – turning and reaching. Men fall in love with their nurses all the time; sometimes nurses with their patients. Sometimes.

"You've stopped talking," she says, leaning close so I'm filled with the smell of her. Nothing store-bought – just pure, alive, mountain-camp woman. There's a right time, I think. It can't be missed.

"Are you asleep?" she asks.

Breathing, breathing. There's a right time and it can't be missed.

She rises, extinguishes the light.

"Joanne."

"Yes?"

Breathing, breathing. In the next moment everything will be different. One way or the other. I turn and was right – catch myself tipping. Joanne bends down to help and I pull her so that she falls on top of me.

"*Aak!*" she says, starting backwards. I let go reluctantly.

"Did I hurt you?" I ask. We scramble to our feet clumsily in the dark. There's a right time and it can't be missed . . . but this isn't it. Words come out – *fine*, *okay*, *sorry* – and the moment passes. Joanne steps on the plate and knocks over my water. It doesn't matter. Her haste to leave. I step towards her and kick over the cot by mistake. We could never fit on it anyway. Stupid.

"Good night," she says while I'm struggling with the cot. I don't have any matches either to relight the lamp. I mean to ask her but shouldn't – just let her go.

I pee into the waterglass and fling it into the darkness outside my tent, lie on the cot rigid, breathing poison, listening for mosquitoes.

19

"When we've located the field," Dr. Parker says, "the first thing we do is mark it off with cords and pickets. In this case, because of the rain, we've put up the tent to keep the ground dry. We don't want people running around, digging indiscriminately." His voice becomes oddly modulated when speaking to us, as if he's narrating a nature show, talking to a camera. He pauses and Luki fills in the Kuantij for Justice Sin, who is balanced in a canvas field chair – I'm not sure how it supports his weight.

"We scrape off the entire overburden first," Parker says. "The first several inches – grass, shrubbery, loose sticks. Just enough to expose the soil. The key is to make sure nobody roars ahead and starts digging up particular spots. It must be done systematically, like an archaeological dig."

There's an odd light in this huge tent. It's raining outside and grey, but the tent glows, and Parker, especially in his khaki clothes, looks almost fluorescent. He has several assistants with him – young master's students who dress in jeans and old army shirts, the men all sporting new beards, the one woman striking-looking with a beaked nose, long, greasy blonde hair, and large-veined hands.

"You can tell by the way the soil is drying just where the graves are," Parker says. "The older soil is greyish on top. The earth that was disrupted more recently has a darker tinge to it. It isn't settled and packed in the same way. Can you see that?" He points to a faint oblong patch in the dirt. Once my eyes get accustomed I pick out seven or eight similarly discoloured areas in the space around us. "No picks, no shovels, no hoes. We know where we're digging. Slow and steady, trowels and brushes. We don't disturb anything, we're just – exposing it." Parker bends as he talks, whisks at the dirt with a small brush. Two of his students join in. Nothing happens quickly. It's even slower, in a way, than listening to testimony. My legs start to tremble, so I walk for a bit then come back, stand while they poke and whisk. Some while later I have to go out again, and when I come back this time something starts to emerge from the dirt.

"All right, we have a ribcage," Parker says finally, his voice still calm, still narrating the documentary. "Notice that we don't pull anything out. We want to leave everything as intact as possible. Notice too that we're being very careful to observe every small piece of evidence in the vicinity. Is there a bullet nearby? Is there anything that will give a clue as to the cause of death? If we want to put the perpetrators away we need evidence. It's as simple as that. Don't get too close."

The ribcage seems small, the bones stained with black soil and some green mould. They're only down a foot or two, but the dug-up dirt is already accumulating on the side. One of Parker's students combs through it to see if anything has been overlooked. It takes so long, but this time I can't pull away, I'm chained here, fascinated, as the skeleton slowly emerges –

twisted, shrunken, strangely peaceful, a deflated person with stained trousers, bits of shirt, belt still intact. The sandals made from old rubber tires. The blue kerchief still tied around the eyes. Parker marks down everything in excruciating detail – the name and position of every bone found, the numbers of the photographs his assistants take, the condition of the artifacts.

"Note the twine that we've found down here, the position of the hands and wrists. How do we know that it's a male? By the arch in the iliac crest of the pelvis, the narrow sciatic notch, the triangular pubis. In the cranium the large mastoid processes, the strongly developed nuchal musculature ridges. We can tell that the victim is left-handed because of the relative length of the left upper-extremity bones compared to the right. As well, note the extra bevelling on the scapular posterior glenoid rim which is not evident on the right side. Now, when we look at the cranium, we can see from the bevelling here that the first bullet entered in the posterior left parietal. . . ."

Parker's voice narrating on and on, his students scratching down every word, like notching scars into bone.

Then his voice stops and we all watch his fingers prying loose something else, stopping to whisk, prying again. In a minute he has it, a tiny bronze medallion. "Some relative will look at this . . . ," he says, his voice breaking, narration forgotten. Tears come and I turn and nearly vomit. I expect Joanne's hand to hold me up, but she too has stepped off a ways and seems to be fighting off nausea.

"The bones belong to real people," Parker says simply.

Sometime later the helicopters arrive. We're on the third excavation and my stomach is sick and hungry at the same time but I feel I can't leave, it would be sacrilegious somehow not to stand by, as if there are people who might be rescued

alive, like victims of a building bomb. The sound of the helicopters changes all that, fuses my spine. I catch Joanne's gaze
and know she's thinking the same thing: that it's soldiers come
to repeat the atrocity, bury the commission in the same soil
as the villagers. The wind of the rotors picks up the sides of
the tent and blows sticks and glops of mud through the air. I
rush outside with the others to see a military cargo helicopter touch down in the small landing space, while two others
hover some way off. A gunner points straight at us and looks
emotionless as an insect behind his dark glasses. Two other
soldiers disembark, guns at ready, and I stand gaping, shocked,
until finally Suli Nylioko steps off, a thin woman in blue
holding her hand out for steadying. The two soldiers and Suli
hurry towards us, bending low under the chopper blades, and
the wind picks up again as the helicopter lifts off and another
moves into position.

It's the press, of course. It takes fifteen minutes to disgorge
them all, a few dozen men with notebooks, tape recorders,
cameras. They overrun the camp, swarm us, change the pro-
ceedings from a solemn disinterment to a circus act.

The young man from *The Islander*, Dorut Kul, approaches
me dressed in loose-fitting black pants, slick shoes, and a white
silk shirt with the sleeves rolled up, smokes in the shirt pocket.
He asks what the commission has discovered to date. I give
him a two- or three-sentence no comment but he presses me.

"Have you found mass graves?"

"Dr. Parker and his crew are excavating systematically. They
have found a number of skeletons so far. The people were
apparently executed with shots to the head. But it will take
time to fully determine . . ."

We have no press strategy. I have no idea how much I should
say in response to his questions.

"Why have you heard testimony from no military, IS, or police sources?"

"I believe that we have a number of such figures slated for later in the . . ."

"Do you feel that Sin Vello is truly acting in an independent manner? He was appointed by Minitzh and has many connections to the old régime."

"The chief justice is doing a wonderful job as far as I can tell. I've been very impressed by Justice Sin and I'm sure . . ."

"How do you feel about the entente signed between the government and the Kartouf? Do you agree with the limited protection from prosecution offered as part of the deal?"

I stare at the young man, his pen making tiny flick marks on his pad but his eyes fixed so intently on mine.

"This is the first I've heard of –"

"So Truth Commission members were not consulted before the limited immunity was offered?"

"I was not consulted –" He scratches the words down, for once waits for me to finish my thought. But I've nothing more to add.

Suli begins making a speech at the entrance to the excavation tent, so all reporters and cameras are drawn to her. They're a motley bunch, irreverent, hasty, as journalists are everywhere, it seems. Yet they're the ones who'll tell the story. Their eyes, their words, their opinions are the ones that matter. Suli leads them into the tent and they follow, the whole clatter of them, with their lights and battery packs, tape recorders, attitudes. Suddenly I have no stomach for it. I stay outside, drift to a rock outcrop down the hill, past the last of the utility tents. There I sit and watch as the sun makes a rare appearance, burning between cloud banks suddenly to show a glimpse of mountains, the valley far below. A good place to watch and breathe.

In a while I hear Joanne's approach, the strength of her steps, sure but light. "I was wondering where you'd gotten to," she says.

"I couldn't see anyway."

"You could pretend to be a member of the commission."

"Yes. I suppose. I'd have to have an ID card."

"Would you?"

"Probably. Probably they wouldn't put you on a commission without an ID card."

She sits beside me on the rock. A funny phrase comes to me – "a little bit of all right." Who wrote that to me? Leanne what's-her-name from Amnesty International in London. She was writing about the new house she'd bought with her new husband whose new job meant they could afford something better than the miserly flat they'd been living in. "Now this is a little bit of all right," she wrote.

So I say it to Joanne: "This is a little bit of all right."

"Is it?"

Sitting in fresh air, in rare sunshine, quietly, beside someone I love.

"Yes."

Little tingles of energy up my spine. Sips of breath. Some small sense of wellness breaking through.

"I just, uh, I thought maybe I should explain about last night," I say.

"Oh." Startled. *Oh.*

"I thought maybe you might have come to some wrong conclusions."

"Wrong conclusions?"

"About my behaviour."

"Oh listen, Bill –"

"You listen first. You might have thought from all my stumbling around –"

"Really, Bill –"

I stop talking and then she stops. Far down below a big bird – eagle? hawk? – circles the treetops, disappears into a stretch of cloud, then reappears.

"You might have thought from all my stumbling around that I was trying to make a clumsy pass at you. I just want to put to rest any sort of misconceptions you might have had. I wasn't trying to make a clumsy pass at all. I was trying to be –" Choosing my words, not looking at her but down at where the big bird disappeared. "– smooth and subtle and . . . attractive. I just felt . . . probably you would need that interpretation since I was in fact hopelessly clumsy. Just so there's no misunderstanding."

No big bird. I look and look but it doesn't reappear. Clouds move in on the sun again and the air picks up a fresh scent of rain, which in a moment I can see closing in from the right, sweeping up the mountainside, steely grey and inevitable.

"And I love you," I say, for punctuation.

"And you love me?"

"Yes." Not looking. Trying to keep the breath regular, to keep that tingle in my spine. It's a funny feeling. Just as I think of it, it moves across my skull and parks on my chin. I reach for her hand, squeeze it, don't look.

The patron saint of lost causes. A funny thought. Is there one?

In a moment the helicopters start up again, the wind nearly blows us off our rock. It's the reporters heading out to post their stories in time for the evening's news or tomorrow's edition. I feel oddly lightheaded – relieved, I suppose, to tell her and to know that I don't have to labour under my illusions any longer.

"I don't know what to say, Bill," she yells into my ear as I get up.

"It's okay. You've said it!" I yell back, like something someone would say in a movie.

If I walk it'll be better. She won't have to say anything.

So I walk. It's funny, all the breath has gone just like that and my whole body feels on the edge of a spasm. But one step and it's less, one step and then another. That's how you get past things. A step and a step and another.

I'm surprised to find Suli has not left with the reporters but stays talking to Sin Vello outside the excavation tent. They're quite a pair, the enormous chief justice and the wraith-like president. He leans on his silver cane, perspires from the simple act of standing, while she balances lightly, her spine straight, her shoulders a fraction of the width of his. When she sees me she looks at me – how? With rapt attention, as if I'm someone she has been eagerly awaiting.

"How are you, Bill? Ms. Stoddart, how are you both? I've been getting such good reports about the commission –"

"Have you?"

"Yes! It's been such a relief for people. Well, you've seen the crowds waiting to talk to you."

"The *sorialos*. Yes."

"I'm getting such mail. Two thousand pieces a day! So many people are writing in –"

"But what about this deal with the Kartouf?"

"We just signed it today. It's historic. Finally we have peace on the island after nearly twenty years of war."

"But we're not supposed to prosecute Kartouf members?"

"Except for human-rights crimes," she says hastily. "Which you define. If it's serious enough you can recommend prosecution."

"Why would they agree to something like that?"

"Because they want peace, Bill. Finally!"

The conversation extends into the mess tent where we sit like old friends, Suli making a point in Kuantij to Justice Sin, another in English to me and Joanne and Dr. Parker. Luki scrambles to keep up with it all. Suli, vibrating like a bow of energy, fires off her ideas, observations, questions on everything: micro-banking, shelters for women, programs to reduce child poverty, education grants for girls, clean-up crews for public works, rehabilitation schemes for first offenders, international trade missions, what to do about homelessness and poverty.

"They're killing us," she says at one point. "The currency speculators. Every time we try to launch something, they feed on us. How can we do anything if our money isn't worth its weight in banana skins?"

Later: "Did you know that murders have gone down 35 per cent since the elections? Do we have more police? No. It's a sense of peace. I don't know how else to describe it. The people have a sense of peace and co-operation. Suddenly we're all poor but we're building together. It's just an idea, but even the drug dealers have stopped killing one another. Can you imagine? What's going to happen if we don't deliver? Bloodbath. And it'll be my head for betraying them."

And on the police: "They're tiptoeing around, have you noticed? Even the traffic cops have been polite lately. It's your doing, the commission. They know certain questions are going to be asked and they're afraid and ashamed of who they've been and what they've done. So now they're consulting on everything. Do I want so-and-so arrested? Should they proceed with this trial? I tell that coward Fulika it's his department, his responsibility. You can't keep asking the president whether to arrest somebody for shoplifting. He's petrified of an inquiry."

Sin Vello laughs when the talk turns to Fulika, the chief superintendent of police, and he tells a long story that gets briefly translated as being about Fulika's four mistresses ganging together to stop a rape charge levelled by a pregnant teenager. The four argued in court that they kept the chief superintendent so tired he couldn't have had enough energy to commit rape even if the desire were there. Finally the young woman accepted a settlement: a cash amount, monthly stipend, apartment, and guaranteed tuition for the child at the foreign university of his choice.

"He knows such stories!" Suli laughs, pointing her thumb at Sin Vello, a sign of disrespect in this culture but meant affectionately, it seems. I watch them closely – either they are consummate actors, and can hide their mutual distrust brilliantly, or they get along much better than Suli let on that night when I met her in her office.

Sin Vello tells another story about the personal interest Minitzh would take in certain trials. In a famous one, Santa Irene's foremost cricket player was accused of accepting bribes to lose to Sri Lanka in an important match. Minitzh had lost a small fortune betting on the outcome, and phoned Justice Sin to make sure the cricketer fried in hell.

"But, Mr. President," Sin supposedly said, "it's up to a jury to decide whether or not he is guilty."

"And if he's not guilty," Minitzh supposedly said, "then you will bowl the next match and the fans can rip your limbs from your body."

Joanne asks what the justice decided and Sin looks down slyly. The translation comes slowly, long after Sin, Suli, and

Luki have had their laugh. "Fortunately for everyone the man escaped to Sri Lanka before the verdict. It's the only time I've ever found the CIA useful."

Supira, laughter, serious talk, hours stretching into early dawn, Suli picking up energy, others drifting off one by one until Suli and I are alone with the sound of cicadas in the jungle, the glow of the kerosene lamps, the discomfort of the metal chairs. I want to move, find my tent, catch some sleep, but I also want to stay here with Suli, I don't know why – to let Joanne know that there's no reason to worry about me and our conversation before, that I won't be imposing my clumsy body on her again. But also because of Suli, her sense of spirit, this intoxicating talk of rebuilding an entire country, the whiff of power and responsibility, of history surrounding this woman. It's heady stuff, and there's an old sense too that, since she's a woman, a small one at that, she could use my help – as if I have anything to offer. I'm surprised to find myself thinking this way, yet there it is. Maybe everyone feels this way: she's no arrogant, untouchable General Minitzh, but tiny Suli Nylioko, brave as an angel but she needs our help, she can't do it alone . . . and so we give it freely.

"Have you heard from your family?" she asks, a question that catches me off-guard.

"I get e-mails from my son," I say. "He's only eight. He isn't a particularly informative correspondent." And I don't often remember to write back, I fail to say.

"I lost my son," she says. "After Jono was killed. I tried so hard to hang on to him, but I lost him." The clear eyes, calm hands, her face so suddenly sad. "Nothing could be right again for him. The harder I tried to hold him to me the more he pushed away. You know how adolescents can be. He went for everything that would take him away. The friends, drugs, interests . . . it was all designed to add distance. My daughter stayed with me. My daughter became my closest friend."

I ask where she is now and she searches through her handbag, comes up with a photo of a dark, sinuous young woman holding an infant, beaming, with a tired-eyed white man standing behind her, his hand the size of her shoulder.

"Safe in England. Living a very conventional life. Happy, happy life. We talk nearly every day."

"And your son?"

Eyes down, hands spreading out on the tabletop, fingering the edges of the photo.

"I don't know where Jacob is. It's a terrible, hollow feeling, not to know. Except that I have a sense that I've lost him, that it's irrevocable. I don't know why. I suppose there always should be hope. But I don't feel it. What I feel . . . I think it must be close to what a woman here feels who has lost a son or husband or father to the IS, only there was no news, it was simply a disappearance and they won't even admit to having taken him. It's just – empty. Their struggle is with the IS but somehow mine is with God. I had a husband who was a brave man and we were steps away from safety, so why didn't God give us those few steps? And I had a son I loved more than . . . more than God, and I think I got the Old Testament God, you know, the jealous one who couldn't stand to be second in any way. That is not the God I pray to, but I fear it's the God who took Jono and Jacob because I loved them too much.

"I'm drunk, you see," she says, "so you mustn't remember any of this. But part of why I came back to Santa Irene and stood up when it was time was to show Jacob that I'm still here. How could I face those soldiers? Was it prayers to the God who took my family? No. Not all of it. It was partly too to have my face and name sped around the globe so Jacob could be proud. He doesn't have to be ashamed of who he is."

Breaking down now, this tiny iron-willed lady. I stand, nearly totter over myself from stiffness and the need to pee. "Come on," I tell her, gently pulling her out of her chair. "You should go to bed. Where's your tent?"

"I don't think I have one. I didn't mean to stay. I don't sleep anyway. I just need to sit." Small voice, not the fireball of earlier in the evening but a deflated, tired soul.

We step out of the tent into the grey light of a chilly dawn. A black and yellow spider knits the last strands of an elaborate web stretched between a tent rope and the ground; a lizard flashes for cover off the path ahead of us; overhead a bird stops its song as soon as we come into view. I take Suli to the rock where Joanne and I sat the day before. Down below the valley is sunk in mist, but the first gold bands of sunlight are poking between mountain peaks.

"Stay with me," Suli says.

"I'm exhausted. I need to find my cot."

"Stay with me."

She folds her legs beneath her, straightens her back, closes her eyes as the sunlight soaks her face. I sit much less formally, my knees drawn up, and look not at the valley but at her. If I had a camera and could capture this light, then here's my Gandhi at the spinning wheel – Suli in meditation. The lines on her face soften, her shoulders relax, she clasps her hands in front of her, almost, but not quite, in prayer. I need to pee badly now, there's no escaping this mundanity, and I don't know why she doesn't have the same need – unless she does and this is all a show, like arriving here yesterday with the reporters, like visiting the *sorialos*.

I leave her finally, sleep fitfully, and when I rise for breakfast she has gone, back into the maelstrom of nation-building.

20

"And what did you do then?"

We have returned to the *Justico kampi*, to the endless testimony, but for now we have moved on to questioning some men from the military. Sin Vello takes his great head off his hands and pulls a glass of water to his mouth. Mrs. Grakala's eyes flutter from behind her spectacles and I wait for her body to slump, completely asleep. I've been waiting for her to fulfil the promise Suli predicted, but so far she's been a void in this commission, has barely shaken herself to utter a word. So the chief justice and I take turns with the questioning and Luki tries to keep up with the translation. The man in the centre chair is a helicopter gunner not so different, perhaps, from the one who pointed his machine-gun at us in Hoyaitnut. He's young and wiry; his moustache is thin enough to look painted on. Without the glasses and helmet, though, he loses the look of cold efficiency – he's just a skinny young man now, scared to be here.

"Answer the question," Sin Vello says. "What did you do then?"

"I opened fire on the women on the hillside."

"As you had been ordered?"

"Yes."

"Who ordered you?"

"Captain Velios."

"He was your captain?"

"No. He was from a special unit."

"What unit?"

"He was part of the IS."

"How did you know?"

"Everyone knew."

"Did he give you this order in person?"

"No."

"Did you ever meet Captain Velios?"

"No."

"But you knew that the order had come from him?"

"Yes. That's what we were told."

"By your commanding officer, Major Tuk?"

"Yes."

"Why was a major taking orders from a captain?"

"I don't know."

"But you felt that since the orders had come from Captain Velios it would be all right to shoot down these women on the hillside?"

"I was following orders."

"Did they look like terrorists?"

"No."

"What were they doing?"

"Gathering wild yams."

"For terrorists?"

"I do not know."

"What did you do with the bodies?"

"Nothing."

"Nothing?"

"We flew away."

"So you have no idea if anyone survived?"

"They were all dead."

"But you flew away?"

"They were all dead."

"And it's all the fault of this Captain Velios?"

"I followed my orders."

Captain Velios. In a week of questioning military personnel, this shadowy figure emerges as the villain of nearly every abuse. It was Captain Velios who ordered the slaughter at Hoyaitnut, the poisoning of the wells at Tylios and Gumptavinka, the kidnapping of union leaders in the capital. Velios who said to take no prisoners, Velios who ordered the execution of the village boys, Velios who said to drive over the journalist Ho Kionga with the van. Velios who commanded the secret special operations unit about which nothing is known. Velios who made the plans, gave the orders, knew exactly where to attack, when and why and how.

But no one has met him. Not Major Tuk; he only heard Velios's voice on the telephone. Not Colonel Loros; he received his orders from Velios via General Kuldip, who died last month of a heart attack. Why were a general, colonel, and major taking orders from a captain? Because Velios was understood to be the voice of President Minitzh.

Who's also dead.

It is my turn to question. The corporal sits small and uncomfortable in the witness chair, his uniform faded and wrinkled, his shoes ragged runners instead of proper military footwear.

He leans to the left – probably only one speaker in his head-phones is working.

"Corporal Tiu, what unit do you work for?"

"The special operations unit, sir."

"That's part of the IS, the Intelligence Service?"

"No sir."

"It is not at all affiliated with the IS?"

"It is a special branch of the presidential guard."

"Under the orders of the president, then?"

"We operated under orders from Captain Velios."

"Did you meet Captain Velios? You worked with him?"

"Many times."

"What does he look like?"

"He has black hair and thick eyebrows. Not a large man."

"How old is he?"

"Not old."

"In his twenties? Thirties? Forties?"

"Not old."

"You don't know?"

"Not old."

"Corporal Tiu, you must answer my questions. We have been looking for this Captain Velios. Do you know where he is?"

"No."

"When was the last time you saw him?"

"Before the troubles."

"Before what troubles? The assassination of President Minitzh?"

"Yes."

"He disappeared after that?"

"He did not come any more to the office."

"But you heard from him on the phone?"

"No."

"Not a word?"

"No."

"Corporal Tiu, what does the special branch do?"

"It is involved in secret activities."

"Such as?"

"I do not know."

"You work there, but you don't know what the unit does?"

"I am a clerk in the supply room."

"And everything is secret?"

Silence. He rocks sickly in his chair, his face down, either terribly ashamed or on the verge of vomiting.

"Corporal Tiu, we have heard from several witnesses about the sordid activities of Captain Velios. We have heard that he ordered the slaughter of villagers, the murder of a journalist, various kidnappings, that he oversaw a ring of secret detention centres throughout the capital and outskirts. Did you know Captain Velios to be in on any such activities?"

"No."

"But you have no idea what he *did* do? As part of special operations?"

"He liked very sharp pencils," Corporal Tiu says.

"I beg your pardon?"

"Most days he required three or four very sharp pencils. Sometimes he sent his office clerk and sometimes he came himself to pick them up. He brought us sticky buns sometimes."

"Is this all you can tell us about the notorious Captain Velios, that he liked sharp pencils and brought you sticky buns? Did people talk about him? Were there stories about what special operations was all about?"

Silence.

"You knew about these murders, Corporal Tiu, didn't you?

You knew about what went on in the detention centres. Don't come here and tell me about pencils and sticky buns!"

Silence. Not vomiting, but not looking anyone in the eye. Here is the one man we've been able to find from special operations. A clerk who says he knows nothing!

I press, cajole, threaten, humiliate, but Corporal Tiu will say nothing more, not to me, not to Sin Vello, not to the rest of the world.

I walk back to the Merioka with Joanne, both of us holding umbrellas against the hot sun, Nito staying a few paces behind. The exhaust fumes seem particularly bad today, and we edge away from the street as far as we can. Diesel fumes from unregulated vehicles, sickening, but not bad enough that we can't breathe. These day-to-day poisons we learn to accept. Joanne has missed most of this week's testimony, has been working with the *sorialos* instead. I seem to be handling the hearing room better, and there's a great need for public-health people in the sprawling encampment. I tell her about the sticky buns but she seems preoccupied, not really listening. I tell her I've requested a meeting with Suli to iron out the money problem, make sure we start to get paid. "Derrick will be happy," she says curtly. All week she's been like this. We haven't talked about Hoyaitnut, what happened or didn't happen between us. But she still reviews the testimony with me in the evenings, we still share our late-night cribbage. I'm happy to retreat, forget – just be as we were. I was stupid and greedy to hope for more than that. And I need to tell her but can't find the moment.

A day slides by. I meet Justice Sin and Mrs. Grakala in Sin's office after testimony. It's a grand room with an oceanfront view, a carved desk the size of a small boat betraying an extraordinary lack of clutter. The walls are lined not with books but with colourful oil paintings of splendid flowers I don't knows the names of – purple-spiked, white-rimmed ones, others lined in crimson with flashes of yellow, some black and gold like a sunset, some silvery and soaking in metallic blue water. I ask who the painter is, and Luki says Sin Vello himself.

We sit at the small table by the window, Sin taking up most of a couch, Luki perched on the remaining edge, and me and Mrs. Grakala in ornately carved, hard-backed island chairs like the one in Suli's office. At Sin Vello's request, we are meeting without aides. Joanne has gone back to the hotel early; Mrs. Grakala seems nervous without her staff present.

"The IS or the presidential guard or I don't know who – somebody is going to have to produce this Captain Velios," I say. "Everything's pointing to him. But what happens if we can't find him?"

"I am certain we will be presented with a Captain Velios," Sin says after the translation. "They are packaging one as we speak." Mrs. Grakala says something to him and they have a back and forth. When I look to Luki she shakes her head, not important.

"Packaging one?" I ask.

"I am certain," Sin Vello repeats. "What is less certain, perhaps, is who this Captain Velios will be, and what he has done." He smiles, somehow taking joy in the subterfuge. "Everyone knows IS has played a key role in our island's problems for many years. We need someone to blame, but we don't know who. Now we are being given a name."

"Has Captain Velios been invented?" I ask. When the translation comes Mrs. Grakala nods and her chin waggles affirmatively. "He is being packaged and prepared," she says, "the one man responsible."

"The IS is packaging him?"

"Since Minitzh and through all the changes," Sin Vello says, "the IS has remained the same men in the same positions doing the same poisonous things."

"What are we going to do? Just be made fools of?" I ask.

Sin Vello smiles, looks to Mrs. Grakala, rubs his thick hands together. He knows more than he's saying. I can't tell if Mrs. Grakala knows as well. "The IS generally gets its own way. But maybe there's something we can do," he says.

"What?"

"Let's sleep on it." He says it jovially, not at all like a man who needs to sleep on anything, but who knows already. At first I'm offended, expecting to be taken into confidence. Is he uncomfortable with Mrs. Grakala present, I wonder? I remember Suli Nylioko's remarks – there might be some sort of distrust between the two. Or perhaps he's uncomfortable with Luki present. She's an extra set of eyes and ears; maybe she's even an IS plant. But she's so young and earnest, works so hard, is so intent to please. The gawky arms, bony body, toothsome smile, the bad facial skin. I look at her closely, as if for the first time, and notice her wedding band. She seems very young, but of course she must have finished her schooling, is competent in her translation. But not only that, I also notice, for the first time, that she looks pregnant. It seems outrageous to have missed it, although she isn't huge, probably never will be, but there under the stretchy fabric of her skirt is the beginning of either a pot-belly or a baby. And her face is visibly puffier than before – glowing? I stare at her until she stares back, red-faced, and I look away. Justice Sin has been talking and I've missed it. But in a small way too the world looks different just because I've opened my eyes.

Would a pregnant, happy, young married woman be an IS operative? No. Clearly not. Clearly?

As Nito and I are leaving the *Justico kampi*, several powerful young men suddenly surround us. For a moment I'm worried, but then I recognize a few of them as my escort from my late-night meeting with Suli. "*Haha, Suli!*" one of them says, pointing outside, and I realize that they're taking me to see her. We were going to meet Joanne for the walk home, but they hurry me into a white van instead – government issue, I know now, maybe even an IS vehicle. Nito stays behind; he'll let Joanne know that I'm safe. As we drive past the *sorialos* on the lawn I strain to catch a glimpse, but can't see her.

It's full rush hour, yet cars make way for us, even without a siren. Everyone seems to know about these white vans with the polarized windows. We race through the downtown, quick snatches of the harbour glinting at me between skyscrapers. When the Pink Palace comes into view it looks dull behind the shading, but once I step outside the stopped van it's vibrant and glaring in the naked late-afternoon sun, garishly unreal to my northern eyes, like a mammoth candy-floss castle liable to blow away in the first wind. But there near the gate is a gaping, blackened hole – it must be from the assassination of Minitzh, I realize. The bakery truck that blew up. I must have missed it when I visited here that first time at night.

This time I'm not taken to her office but to the garden in the central courtyard. It's a humid square packed to jungle density with lush, sweating, perfumed vegetation: a mass of glowing green leaves, some as huge as elephants' ears, others spiky and small, and everything in between, the blossoms purple, orange, white, and red, the rich black soil fed by bur-bling streams and rockpools teeming with fat tropical fish, some red and white, some the same pink as the palace, some blazing gold, crimson and black.

Suli is sitting alone, cross-legged, on a stone bench behind a towering palm, her back straight as the tree trunk, face composed, eyes closed. In her blue *saftori* she looks as strikingly elegant as any of the jungle flowers. My escort withdraws when they see her, and I am left to approach her alone.

"This is my quiet spot," she says, opening her eyes and smiling – tired but welcoming. She rises gracefully and takes both my hands with hers, kisses my cheek quickly in greeting. It's an effortless motion that seems to acknowledge immediately that we know one another better now, can get beyond the stiff formality of a business meeting, this small matter of my getting paid.

"Let me show you," she says before I can say anything, and pulls me along the path. Her hand fits perfectly in mine; it seems normal and acceptable, somehow, that it would stay there while she points out the flowers she loves, the medicinal roots, the birds and lizards and insects. "Minitzh used to spend hours here every day," she says. "He had it built according to exact specifications, consulted with tropical horticulturists the world over. It's frightful to think of how much money he lavished on it. When I first saw it I thought I really must take off the glass roof – such a terrible thing to keep everything captive like this. But it really has been designed with care to be self-contained. I find myself taking refuge here more and more."

"It's very beautiful," I say.

When the tour part is over she lets go of my hand and says, while still walking slowly, "Your money is being held up in a special account by Talios Hind. He's a corrupt bureaucrat from Ludapa district, the banking sector. He earns interest on it, you see, and so is loathe to release it. He's a bit of a robber baron, very powerful in his little kingdom, and has strong friends in the military, who also are benefiting from this situation. I'm sorry I haven't worked it out yet, but it's normal for this to take time. There are many other considerations – favours that are owed, special projects for Ludapa that are being held up by other corrupt bureaucrats for their own particular reasons. It exasperates me no end, and yet it also reminds me of what I read of the U.S. congress, how public-health legislation must be rolled into a bill on highway expenditures and liquor taxes in order to appease all the politicians along the way. I believe it's called log-rolling. This is the Santa Irenian variety."

"It sounds more like a kleptocracy."

"Yes. Perhaps that is accurate," she says. "Even though Minitzh is dead, the system he so carefully nurtured is still with us. It will take more than a few months to deal with the many remaining Talios Hinds. Please accept my apologies, but you must have faith – you will be paid, with interest. I personally guarantee it."

The moment passes when I could rant, express my disgust, threaten to pull out and go home. As usual, she has undercut my anger.

"There is something else we need to discuss," she says. "I have to tell you that the danger to my personal safety has increased. Factions of the military are unhappy with the pace of change – and not that it's going too slowly, I can assure you. I cannot give details, but it's possible there will be an attempt on my life. It would make no sense. Many of the most power-ful players in the military realize that with me as the face of Santa Irene we are doing very well with aid from the wealth-ier nations. But bombs and guns, and the men who use them, do not always make sense. I'm taking every precaution."

The tendons on her neck are rigid as she speaks. She looks frightened, as if she needs someone she can trust. We are now back at the stone bench beneath the tall palm. She sits, draws her feet up and, almost childlike, holds her knees to her chest, tucks the hem of her *saftori* under her feet. There is not much room for me to sit so I hesitate, but she shifts over slightly, inviting me to sit as well. When I do we're no closer than we were on the rock that day, and yet it seems more intimate here.

"Not to alarm you," she continues. "These threats won't affect the good work of your commission. Although you've upset some people with the questioning of security forces personnel. Don't worry, you will not be interfered with. Calmer heads realize that this inquiry must proceed. With prudence, of course."

"Prudence meaning what?" I ask her. She looks away thoughtfully before answering.

"Meaning just that we are all feeling our way here. I know that you and the other commissioners won't do anything rash, that you won't dwell on allegations that are unfounded or unproven, for example. It's hardly worth mentioning."

And that seems to be all she will say about it, so I pursue another topic. "I was surprised," I tell her, "at Hoyaitnut, how well you got along with Justice Sin. You told me before you fought to keep him off the commission. And yet you seem to be friends."

"I have *developed* a great respect for Justice Sin," Suli says carefully, and suddenly it occurs to me that the two are meeting regularly. Of course. Suli would not want to give up control. Just the *appearance* of it. "In the same way," she continues, "that I have developed a great respect for you. I always knew you were the right man for this commission."

"I haven't contributed much," I say.

She gives me a long, unwavering, intense look, as if there are things she means to say but can't.

"You have given much more than you know," she says simply. Then suddenly: "Perhaps when there is a break in your work we could go to my village in the mountains. I'd like so much to take you there. It's so different from the city – titles and positions fall away. Here it's so easy to forget who we are inside."

"Yes," I say, trying to understand what she means.

"Forgive me. My life is not my own these days, there is so little time. I'm sorry, I have to go, I have such a crushing schedule." She stands, and I follow her lead, then she steps too close, looks at me again with such intensity, such apparent longing, I'd swear she wants me to embrace her.

But – "I'm sorry to have to rush off," she says then, and turns away. "My men will take you back. Please be patient about the funds."

"And you keep your head down," I tell her. She steps away quickly, deep in thought, turns back once with the same look.

"I'm sorry I'm late," I call out when I get back to the suite at the Merioka. "I had a sudden meeting with Suli Nylioko about the funds. Listen, though, Luki is pregnant, did you know that?" I expect Joanne to tell me that she knew this weeks ago, where have I been? But instead it's quiet. The bed has been made, my things arranged. I walk to Joanne's door, which is ajar, knock on it quietly then walk in. No one. Not only that, no one's things – her bag is gone, I'm certain of it, even before I look in her closet, fling open her drawers.

I run back to the main suite, turn around, look in the bathroom, race back to Joanne's room. Empty. I pick up the phone, try to ask the front desk when she left, but can't make anybody understand me. I try calling the airport, but the woman at the hotel switchboard can't understand. What's the word for airport? I pull out the telephone book, but of course if I don't know what the word is then what the fuck good is any of this going to be?

Damn! I hurl the phone book into the bathroom, my breath ragged, head suddenly burning with pain. I don't believe she'd do this, just leave without a word. Then I notice the note on my bed and my body starts to tremble. My first instinct is to back away from it, the residue of this abandonment. Joanne has traded herself for this sheet of paper. I've been such an idiot. *Take it back*, I think. *Rewind the tape.* Say nothing. Just sit on that rock and keep your bloody mouth shut and then this paper wouldn't be on the bed, her bags wouldn't be gone, she'd be here still. This whole week she's been so quiet, so distant.

I don't want to touch it. Silly, I know, but somehow if I pick up the letter then I'll be accepting this reality and there'll be no other choice.

There *is* no other choice.

I read the goddamn letter.

Dear Bill,

In a rush. Just got a message at the hotel about my mother. I called my Dad – the cancer is metastasizing and they need to operate right away. There's a plane in an hour and I have to be on it, otherwise I lose two whole days.

So – I'm sorry to flee. You have your medicines, I've left my logbook, but you know the drill by now. You have enough to last another month, and by then I should be back or I can send more if you find you don't need me. You're doing so much better – you know that anyway.

Don't go off your meds, though. Bad scene if you do. Remember to continue with the anti-malarials for three more weeks.

Racing out the door. I'll call you.

One other thing –

I love you too.

Don't really know what I think about that.

Yours,

J.

Down the elevator, out the doors, into the first taxi. The driver smiles and I scream at him, "Airport! Airport!" When he doesn't seem to understand I try louder, then spread my arms and make buzzing noises till he gets the idea.

It's after sunset: why is there still so much traffic? The *sori-alos* are blocking up Cardinal Avenue, everything else is that much more congested. The police don't dare move them and I'm not in a white van any more, am I? So I have to sit here, inching forward. Stewing.

I love you too.

Don't really know what I think about that.

What I think. God, what do I think?

"*Katti-katti!*" I say, suddenly remembering the word for "fast." The driver looks back, mutters something in disgust, leans on his horn, which starts everybody else blaring as well. Hopeless. But he does manage to wedge between a tractor and a *tritos*, then change lanes behind a motorbike and scoot up an alley that leads to another street where traffic is actually moving. When it stalls again, inevitably, he doubles back across four lanes and up another alley to God-knows-where. But at least we're moving.

I love you too.

Much more complicated that way. Harder to breathe, think straight, be normal and lonely.

I love you too.

At the entrance to the airport highway we stop at a military checkpoint. The driver discusses things with the guard, then turns to me and says something I don't immediately understand.

"*Porbasso!*" the driver says, pantomiming something with his hands, opening and closing.

"*Porbasso?*"

More Kuantij. The guard shines his flashlight in my eyes. "*Porbasso!*"

My passport. I don't have my passport. "*Jut porbasso!*" I say. "*Jut condo porbasso!*" Of course I didn't bring it. I haven't any money on me either. Because Joanne carried all the money. So I can't bribe this stupid guard. I can't even pay my taxi fare.

Now they're both talking at me.

"*Jut condo porbasso! Yiu-yiu ripunta!* I'm sorry!"

The light leaves my face, but the passbar doesn't rise. Instead the soldier motions to others to join him. They want us out of the car.

"No," I tell the driver. "Don't get out of the car!" I know what they do if you get out of the car. "Just take me back to the hotel!" I scream it at the driver, but it's no fucking use. Soldiers swarm us now, they're everywhere, sub-machine-guns pointed, flashlights scrambling me. The door opens and too many hands start pulling at me. How did I get into this? Joanne! My leg kicks out. I don't mean it, but a hand goes crack across my jaw and I freeze, just like that, freeze on the seat of the taxi, don't breathe, don't move, face jammed into the vinyl, still as stone.

"Boo-reej! Boo-reej!"

Of course they know my name. They've been through this before. Any second now the tire iron is going to come smashing through the window. Hands will pull me out, shove me in the trunk. Don't look! That's always my mistake. When I look the glass sprays in my face. Then the hood and shackles, the cigarettes and the black box, the needle when I'm truly damned.

Breathe all you want. Close your eyes or open them. Kick out, shit yourself, stay quiet, scream, doesn't matter. Realer than real. They're attaching the wires, leaning in with their cigarettes. Make your heart like a scared rabbit, can't take it, poor little cardboard and tinfoil heart, not made for this again, once was enough! *I love you too* she wrote right on paper realer than real *Don't really know what I think about that.*

Grapple with *this* reality, I think. Boo-reej this, Boo-reej that, they're saying. *Commisi vertigas.* They know me. It isn't the Kartouf coming out of hiding. It's soldiers. Why so many? Are the Kartouf really soldiers?

Joanne in the doorway turning her eyes on me. My life preserver. I choose what to cling to.

This reality. I'm not going to the airport. I'm not being shoved in the trunk with the extra gasoline and the shovel. I'm sitting in a military Jeep, surrounded by soldiers who return me to the Merioka. Up the front stairs, through the lobby, the staff staring, officers looking like they're going to shoot someone. Into the elevator, back to my room. When the door closes I know they keep standing outside because it's still a trap, just velvet-lined, with a huge bed and television and an ocean view, a hot tub and a piano and a note, one-page, to somebody else, whose life I sometimes step into.

21

Morning. It isn't a hangover, but has something of that feel: the skin of reality is still wet, too delicate to jostle. A full headache is one bad thought away – a bright light, harsh noise, one wrong food for breakfast. My hair hurts, skin feels grated from the inside, eyes cut by sand.

No Joanne. This is the emptiest cavern without her. I wander bereft, still dazed, aching from this abandonment. I wasn't going to be here without her. That was one of the guiding principles. I would never have come without her, don't want to stay now that she's gone.

But how long will she be gone?

There's no message on my phone. She should have called by now. She would have changed flights somewhere, in Seoul or Hong Kong or Tokyo. But no word. I try to call Derrick, but the line is busy, for fifteen bloody minutes it's busy.

I find the cash that Joanne has left, take my meds, gingerly shower, shave, and dress myself. There's my passport in my drawer, right where it's supposed to be. I stick it in my back pocket with my wallet, then take it out – too easy for pickpockets. Into my shirt pocket, the one with the button flaps. Everything in slow motion. I try Derrick again, but this time the line just rings and rings. Either he hasn't left the machine on or there's a bad connection somewhere in the thousands of miles that separate us.

I don't want to stay here without Joanne. I have no heart for it. I wish I was on the plane with her.

Nito is waiting for me outside the door. It's time to go to breakfast. "Did you see Joanne?" I ask him. When he doesn't quite understand, I just repeat, "Joanne!" until he nods his head. In a minute of gesticulated Kuantij he helps me understand that he took Joanne to the airport yesterday afternoon, while I was meeting with Suli. He pretends to write something on his hand and I nod yes, I got the note.

But I don't want the note. I want Joanne.

Eventually, we ride down in the elevator in silence and I step quietly into the Happy Mouth Lounge while Nito inspects the lobby, part of his security routine. I sit at a table, pick up a plasticized menu. Then I realize I left it to Joanne to do all the ordering for us, I haven't learned the words. Except *kofi*, which I don't want. I stare at the choices. I just want toast. Some juice. They're simple words. I did know them. But my brain isn't working so well.

"*Merika*," I say, pointing to the selection where I see the word. The waiter asks me something detailed and I nod yes, okay. Agreeing is easy. The American breakfast. It'll be too much food but at least there'll be some toast and juice.

The waiter brings *The Islander*. The rest of the tables are empty; three staff stand by the cash register in a strange trance, not talking, not looking, not doing anything in particular. A small piece on page twelve catches my eye.

TRUTH COMMISSIONER FLEEING COUNTRY?

19 November 1998
Dorut Kul

Truth Commission member Bill Burridge was spotted last night headed for Minitzh Freedom and Prosperity International Airport, according to sources close to the Interior Ministry. Burridge, the Canadian who was appointed last month by President Suli Nylioko to the Truth Commission, was apparently trying to leave the country, but turned back after failing to produce his passport at the Trilaka checkpoint.

The Interior Ministry source declined to comment further and would not agree to be cited by name. IS spokesman Kajob Telinde stated that the IS continued to wholeheartedly support the work of the Truth Commission and does not wish Mr. Burridge to leave. Burridge could not be contacted for this story. A source connected to the Merioka hotel, where Burridge is staying, said that soldiers returned the Canadian Truth Commissioner to the hotel last night. "Burridge looked *sutu i kondapa*," the source said.

I can't go now, I think, staring at the stupid report. It's clear: anyone reading between the lines will jump to the conclusion that I'm fleeing the IS.

"*Sutu i kondapa?*" I say to nobody. The three motionless staff remain in their trances. Beautiful. Burridge tries to flee country. Burridge is *sutu i kondapa*, whatever that means. Going out of his mind?

I force myself to stay for breakfast, which arrives finally, after a wait of decades. At least I guessed right: the American breakfast is three fried eggs, bacon, ham, sausage, a small steak, hashbrowns, toast, a pancake, syrup, coffee, and a bowl of sliced fruit. Enough to feed a small village. But no juice. Doesn't matter. The toast is as usual white, light, thin, tastes even more than usual like . . . Styrofoam? Is that possible? I try the local version of butter – it spreads fine but tastes sour.

Sutu i kondapa? Not complimentary, whatever it means.

I love you too.

She wrote that to me. *Don't really know what I think about that. Yours, J.*

Yours.

Not *Love.* She already said that. *Yours.*

But she's probably still sitting in a plane over the Pacific Ocean. *The cancer is metastasizing.* She knew we both shouldn't have come.

I have all these calls to make, but it suddenly seems overwhelming, I can't bring myself to return to my room. I have money, my passport. A hundred thousand e-mails are waiting on my computer. A hundred thousand reasons not to check in.

I sign the bill, walk through the lobby – cavernous, deserted except for a half-dozen staff standing in the same trance as the breakfast crew. I step into the heat of the day, not really knowing what I mean to do. Return to the *Justico kampi,* I suppose. I'll have to tell Sin Vello and Mrs. Grakala, probably even Suli herself. Tjodja will have to set up the airline ticket. No, forget that, it'll take months. Derrick can arrange it. We must have some credit left.

Nito reappears by my side. Normally he gets the taxi but this time a black car is waiting for me. Luki steps out, carefully, like a young woman who's carrying a baby inside her.

"I'm supposed to pick you up," she says. Then her eyes

really see me, but the worry that registers there doesn't form into words. She looks to Nito then back to me and asks if Joanne is coming.

"Joanne has gone back to Canada," I say, my voice sounding strange, as if I'm lying. "Her mother is ill. She left suddenly yesterday."

Evidently Luki hasn't read today's *Islander*. She takes my words at face value. Why shouldn't she? They're true, although somehow they don't feel as true as the *Islander* report. *A published report.* It must be true. Surely I was trying to flee the country.

We get in the back of the black car, a Mercedes, which pulls away powerfully, the way you'd expect a German car to pull away. The traffic is unusually thin, which suits this black German car, not meant to go slowly, to be interrupted. The driver is wearing a chauffeur's uniform. In Santa Irene? Nito sits silently beside him.

I'm thinking of the details. It's just a matter of explaining that I can't carry on, my health is at risk without my personal assistant. But I suppose I can last a few days without her.

"Luki, what does *sutu i kondapa* mean?"

She looks at me strangely, seems at a loss for a moment. Then she says, "Walking on his eyeballs."

"On his eyeballs?"

"Yes." She turns her gaze out the window, the mouldy, sloppy buildings of Santa Irene whizzing by at uncommon speed.

"What does it mean?"

"It's used for drug addicts."

Wonderful. Burridge on drugs.

Much later, it occurs to me that we aren't on our way to the *Justico kampi* at all, and I ask Luki where we're going.

"Justice Sin has received a tip about a secret IS detention centre. He is already on his way there and we will meet him to demand an inspection. It's in the mandate, we have every right to be given entrance. The neighbourhood is called Aaden."

If Joanne were here I'd tell her to stay behind at the Merioka. Long minutes riding behind tinted glass, the Truth Commissioner, *sutu i kondapa*, walking on his eyeballs. It's true in a sense – I've been here for weeks but am isolated, don't really know what's going on. We ride past dozens of makeshift dwellings, people apparently camping out on the sidewalks. What's that about? Children playing in rubbish, groups of men sitting on old tires, women hanging clothing out to dry on twine stretched between parking meters. I ask Luki and again she looks at me for an odd pause before replying.

"They are *manglop*, blind vagrants," she says.

"Are there more of them than usual?"

"They're flooding in from the countryside because of *kontra qitaos*."

"*Kontra qitaos?*"

"The economic disaster. They cannot afford basic food and supplies, so have come to the capital to look for work."

"And these are different from the *sorialos*?"

"Sometimes the same, sometimes different. You know the *loros* lost 200 per cent this week?"

"Yes. Of course," I say.

Small, tidy houses with whitewashed security walls topped by broken glass, the gates lined with bars, dogs and children in the street, an old man sitting on a tiny stool, a boy in tattered pants leaning on a telephone pole. Bright pink flowers sprouting out of the side of one wall, a cactus pushing through the pavement near the sidewalk. We stop at the house labelled 24. Justice Sin is already there with three aides, a similar black sedan parked nearby. At the gate Sin leans on his silver cane and talks to someone on the other side. When I get closer I see it's a tall, unhappy man in a brown suit. The holster of his pistol is visible behind his jacket. Luki hurries to Sin but doesn't talk to him, she simply listens, then turns back to me to explain.

"This man says number 24 is government property, but he will not let us in until he has authorization from the minister. Justice Sin has sent two staff to the back of the house to make sure no one is being taken out secretly. He insists they must let us in immediately, but the man says his superior is right now phoning the minister."

How long can it take to phone the minister?

Forever. Sin's aides bring a folding chair from the back of his black car. Luki and I go to the back and wait with Sin's men. Nito stays near me nervously eyeing the surroundings. Who does he work for, I wonder? IS? The wall is too high to see over, the glass too jagged and sharp to try any climbing. There doesn't seem to be a back entrance anyway. Unless a tunnel connects to other houses, the only way out seems to be through the front. We return to find that the minister still can't be reached.

"Perhaps if you got written permission from the minister and returned another day," the man at the gate says.

Sin pulls out a cellular phone, punches some numbers and waits, mops his face with a cloth, each bead of sweat instantly replaced with another. It's not a sunny day but steambath hot, the air itself perspiring. A short conversation, then Sin makes two more calls and we wait. Kids gather from up and down the street: two boys who were playing with sticks, a girl with scabbed knees, some young teens selling cigarettes, bottled water, and magazines. The unhappy man in brown gets even less happy with this crowd and yells at the kids to leave, but the chief justice tells them they can stay, so they do. Then a number of other cars and vans arrive – the press in some, IS members, I suppose, in others. The press are generally in more relaxed dress, IS members look both sterner and more confused. None of this is supposed to be happening. The IS guys mingle and take notes. Dorut Kul pushes to the front and immediately hurls questions at Sin.

Several IS men from the house gather inside the gate now, grimacing and conferring, turning their backs to make phone calls, gesturing to the kids and reporters to clear out. Sin answers Kul's questions patiently, turns to other reporters now thronging around him.

Kul catches me and asks for a statement about my attempt to flee the country. I give him as thorough a denial as I can, explain that I was trying to get to the airport to see off my assistant, who has returned to Canada for personal reasons. He probes further, asks if I plan to stay without her, but I tell him that's all I can say for now.

"So you might return to your home prematurely?" he presses, and I squirm. Just what I need, to have the press go off half-cocked.

"I have no current plans to return to Canada," I say carefully, and am grateful when he lets it go.

"What are you expecting to find in this house?" he asks.

"We have received a tip that this is a secret IS detention centre – where IS members take people they've abducted. From testimony in front of the commission it appears these detention centres are used for torture and murder, and are kept secret so that the IS can deny having custody of particular people and avoid being called to account. We simply want to inspect the premises, but we're being denied access."

A stand-off in the heat. The IS has the advantage: a roof over their heads. As the humidity builds we all know what's coming, a torrential rain that will drive us away. The minister isn't going to phone. That's just a ruse to win time. Sin confers quietly with me and Luki, several reporters' microphones leaning in to catch the conversation. Then he nods to one of his men, who walks back to the car and reappears with a huge crowbar. Sin takes it and steps up to the gate, jams it into the small lock before anyone in brown can stop him. Several pistols appear at once and Sin pauses, his large hands on the crowbar, a dozen cameras poking around him, all of us looking on.

A tense exchange. Sin doesn't lower his eyes but neither do the IS men. The moment hangs and hangs, then the first drops of rain fall, fat and warm. We only have a couple of minutes before the deluge.

I don't know how we all know, but somehow the advantage falls to Sin. Without a word he leans his bulk on the crowbar and the lock snaps like plastic. Instead of rushing the gate, however, he pushes it open gently and the IS men don't resist. Their guns stay pointed, but these men aren't going to shoot the chief justice in front of all these reporters. We walk in uninvited, but unimpeded as well.

A drab house, on first glance surprisingly domestic-looking, with a mat by the door to receive people's shoes, a living room off the entrance, a batik hanging of a small boy, sitting on a water buffalo, playing a flute. The ceilings are high, in the local style, and in the living room four plain wooden chairs are gathered around a table covered in cards, ashtrays and tall beer bottles. It smells of sweat and old cigarettes, and the further in we get the dirtier it seems, almost in the way that an animal's den will be – I sense the occupants will put up with the filth for ages, then decide to move on rather than attempt to clean.

We sweep past the kitchen: blackened, grease-stained walls, a dirt floor, a brown rat scavenging on the cluttered counter, pausing to look at us but not alarmed enough to move away. It feels like a dream, like stepping into layers of darkness. Sin pushes open one bedroom door: nothing. No furniture, decorations, or people, just heavy drapes on the one window, a dark stain in one corner, the stench of old urine. The same in the next bedroom, except the stench is stronger and there's a rough bench of sorts, under which is something I recognize – a black box, about the size and weight of a car battery.

"Take it," I say, pointing, barely able to get the words out. "*Take it for evidence!*" Luki relays the message to Sin's men, who are behind me.

"You should wait outside," I say to Luki.

"It's all right," she says.

"No, it isn't. There are some things you don't want to see if you don't have to. Believe me."

She wavers, but I put enough force into my voice and gaze that she obeys. Most of me wants to follow her retreat. But I don't. Down the corridor. The third bedroom. The smell much worse. The door is locked and Sin Vello steps aside while his aides kick at it. The IS men are behind us and watching but not stopping us; they've fallen aside like the Berlin Wall. Two, three, four kicks and the door gives way.

Nothing.

Grey light; the pounding of the rain on the window, no curtains this time, no dark shades. A small bed, a mirror and dresser, a huge mouldy poster of the Rolling Stones, Mick Jagger looking like a revivified corpse.

A handprint on the wall, some Santa Irenian magazines in the corner – porno, bad colour, the reds bleeding into the greens.

Nothing we need.

But the stench is gut-wrenching. The stench of failure. They've cleaned the place out. Someone's tipped them off. We've come too late.

The IS generally gets its own way. I remember Sin Vello's face when he said that: urbane, cynical, knowing. Not his face now – it's purple with indignation and anger. He flings the bed across the room, a surprising flash of speed from such bulk. His aide checks the closet, but clearly there won't be anything left. A few hangers, a mouldy set of clothes.

All of the air rushing out of our balloon.

I step into the corridor, crowded now with IS men, short, bulky, silent, most with moustaches, one with a red rash on his neck. Where's the smell coming from? It doesn't make sense. The house looks bigger from the outside . . .

"They're here!" I say to Sin Vello, as if he can understand me. "They're still here. There's another room!" I call it out excitedly, looking for the secret door. There must be one, right? This is a secret detention centre – there must be a secret door. A basement room? Back dungeon? Where's the stench coming from? I run around tapping the walls until Sin's men get the idea. Some of the reporters join in, push the IS men out of the way, although it occurs to me that most of them stand back, and some haven't even entered the house. We have to find it. We have to!

Tapping, searching, calling. This damn smell. It's not from using the wrong disinfectant. Something evil's been happening in this house. I go back to the living room, upset the card table, tear down the water buffalo picture. Then to the kitchen, rip open the cupboards. The smell is revolting. The rat has moved on but the decaying food he was feasting on is still mouldering on the counter.

Pull open the fridge door. There's no light. The fridge is full of darkened, blackened, bloodied . . .

Heads.

Decapitated heads, some wrapped in plastic bags, some in brown paper, some simply . . .

I stand transfixed.

There are some things you don't want to see.

An IS man stands in the doorway, his hand on his pistol, pointing. What am I supposed to do? Close the door, walk away? Dorut Kul pushes past him as if he weren't holding a weapon at all, as if he has shrunk to three feet and is fast disappearing. As soon as he looks inside the fridge he calls out – ecstatic, a cry of triumph, and his photographer pushes past the IS man as well. There it is, tomorrow's front page, a fridge full of heads. More and more cries of triumph, bodies pushing into the kitchen. Kitchen? I stumble out, crash against the wall twice while reeling down the corridor. Slashing rain outside, even heavier than that day Joanne and I abandoned our taxi. Years ago. Decades.

Another life.

I kneel in the courtyard, hold a small railing, the water flooding around me like an ocean tide. What are we going to do about the IS? A small part of my brain still functioning in that old way. There's a houseful of them, armed to the teeth. How are we supposed to arrest them? But even as I'm thinking this the police arrive. Called by Sin Vello, no doubt. *He is his own man*, I remember Suli saying.

His own man.

And police are arresting IS, who stand around in shock, demoralized, some now vomiting in the rain beside me. It's as if this discovery has taken them by surprise, that it wasn't real before. A fridge full of heads!

It's the guillotine. They always knew it was there. That someday the crowds would come. The heads would be their own. That's why they're vomiting, being led like sheep into police wagons. The heads in the fridge are their own.

22

"I was coming down the right side and started to fall over? So I shot my first slapshot. Ever! But it wasn't a raise. It went right along the ice and into the net. Everybody came out and mobbed me."

"I wish I'd been there."

Patrick tells me more about the hockey game, his voice so young, almost pushing everything else out of my head. Almost. Except for the stench in that house – it's clinging to my clothes, skin, imagination. I am back in the safety of my suite at the Merioka, a full day has passed, but nothing can scrub off the stench. Where are the bodies? The police are investigating. They're going to find them somewhere, and there will be marks of torture, of unspeakable things done in that little grey house in that peaceful little suburb in Aaden.

"Why didn't you write me any e-mails?" Patrick asks.

"I'm sorry," I find myself saying, hollow little words, nothing against the disappointment in his voice.

"We saw your picture," he says. "What were you doing in the rain?"

The whole world has seen my picture. Kneeling in the deluge, grasping that railing, almost prayer-like in supplication. For one day the one picture shown everywhere, in every newspaper.

Reporters are waiting for me downstairs, have been feeding from me all day. Not just locals, but international journalists flying in from everywhere. A new twist to the story of Suli Nylioko and the Santa Irenian miracle: a fridge full of heads, a houseful of IS men arrested, led away like cattle.

Maryse comes on the line. "Are you all right?" Her perennial first question, and how she must hate to ask it. What we never seem to get past. Am I all right?

"Yes. And you?"

"You're amazing for getting headlines."

As if that's all it is. Whole blocks of arguments rise like icebergs suddenly tipped over so that the huge base is now forty storeys in the air, supported by the tiny tip that usually never gets wet. Ignore it, ignore it. It's the only way.

"Things are happening. It wasn't me, really. I was just the one in the picture."

"The paper said more than that."

"Yes." Easier to agree. Breathe and breathe. She asks about Joanne and I explain about her going home and how I haven't been able to get in touch with her, or Derrick, for that matter.

"When was the last time you talked to him?" she asks.

"I don't know. It's been quite a while. I'm afraid I haven't kept in touch the way . . ." Blah blah blah. She picks it out of my voice and changes the subject.

"It's just I didn't get my cheque this month."

"Ah," I say. "I guess I know that, and I'm sorry. There's been a delay in the payments here, nothing to worry about, the money should be on its way soon. I've got the president of the country working on it."

"Well, maybe the president could phone my landlord, get him off my back." For a second I think she's serious.

"I suppose I could ask –"

"It's a joke," she says. Then – "I'm really scared for you, Bill. Have you done enough? When are you coming home?"

"I know, I know," I say. "I am planning to come home, maybe very soon. It depends on Joanne, I just have to talk to her. I won't stay here long without her. I do need her help. I recognize that. Anyway, I didn't think you'd be that concerned."

"What's that supposed to mean?" she asks.

"Nothing," I say, but bitterly, I can't help it. Simmer down, I think.

She doesn't take the bait. "Don't wait too long," she says instead. "I'm really worried. And certain members wait by the computer worshipping you. I'm not nagging, you know, I just don't know how else to say it. But a quick note now and again would mean so much to him."

"I'm sorry about the e-mails," I say, too angry to really sound sorry. "I've been so caught up."

"*Yes.*" She could say something gentle to let me off the hook, but she doesn't.

"Before I left, you said something about taking the next step. What does that mean exactly?" I ask.

"We don't have to talk about it now," she says. I know the way she's looking, her jaw clenched, her eyes so narrow and hurt.

"Do you mean a divorce? You want things finalized?" My heart suddenly pounding in my head.

"I'm not going to talk to you about it on the phone," she says, managing to keep control of her voice. "When you're back. It's just – life isn't standing still here."

"What does *that* mean?"

"Bill," she says, and I try to calm myself. "Just come back safely. Soon, all right?"

In a small meeting room off the hotel lobby I meet with journalists from the BBC, Reuters, AP, AFP, and *South China Morning Post*, among others. No Canadian journalists – they'll get the story off the wire feeds. And no big names either. For the most part young, informal, hungry types, earnest, insistent in their questioning, as if truth can be levered out of memory and consciousness. Reporters can be levered out, anyway. One good photo and the Merioka is back in business, no doubt charging their old rates in fat American dollars.

"How far can the Truth Commission go in healing the wounds of this society?"

"Do you trust the police to properly investigate abuses by the IS, and would you trust the IS to investigate the police?"

"Who is there to investigate the military?"

"How much leeway has your commission be given in its work?"

"Now that the IS has been directly implicated in atrocities, do you fear for your own safety?"

College-educated questions that I try to answer patiently, as if my own thoughts can have some bearing on reality.

"The day before the IS detention-centre bust you were reported to be trying to leave the country. Can you comment on those reports and what your participation in the commission has meant to you personally?"

Personally.

Words form like they do in these interviews, well-shaped responses, apparently thoughtful, one sentence leading to another. *Atrocities . . . abuses . . . extrajudicial executions . . . natural justice . . . corruption . . . time for healing and redemption . . . institution-building and renewal.*

I go slowly, do my best to push some sort of light into dark corners. But shine one way and something else falls dim. Nothing stays clear. *Life isn't standing still here. My first slapshot. Ever! I love you too. Don't really know what I think about that.*

Don't really know.

The reporter stops writing, looks in some surprise. Not one of the young men, but a grey beard, balding, heavy, wearing too many clothes for this climate. "Pardon?" he says.

"I don't really know what sorts of conclusions we might reach," my voice says, "or how all this is going to help in the end. But holding perpetrators accountable for atrocities is important. Don't you think? If we ever want to move beyond these cycles of violence."

Cycles of violence. Another handsome phrase. Sounds like a particularly vigorous bicycle race.

Not like the stench of that house. Where are the bodies? You can't have heads without bodies.

"I'm just not certain what's beyond the cycles," I say.

"Do you mean what it takes to break the cycle?"

I love you too. Don't really know what I think about that.

"I haven't been able to move beyond the cycles myself," I say.

"You yourself are caught in the cycles of violence?"

I keep thinking of a bicycle race. I can't get off the course. Shoes locked to the pedals.

"Yes, that's right. Because of what was done to me, you see. I'm still caught in cycles of violence."

Pens scribbling, tape recorders turning, eyes watching, questioning, but not understanding. They could never understand. I see it now clearly. Whatever they write from this, whatever story gets reported and read around the world as if the closest to truth we can get – garbage. Clever phrasing. It can't approach the darkness of that house. The utter darkness.

After the session I rise and walk to the elevator, encased in the same weariness I felt getting off the plane in the wheelchair, home from the Kartouf. It's as if it all hits me again, the strangeness of this journey, the withering knowledge once more of what we can do to one another.

Back upstairs, there's a call waiting on my phone. I retrieve the message and feel of flood of relief to hear Joanne's voice. "Bill!" she says. "I'm calling from somewhere over the Rockies – I was hung up in Sydney, it's a long story. I can't tell you how frustrated I feel, not being home yet. But I saw your picture in the paper this morning. My God, I nearly spilled breakfast all over myself. Are you all right? I wish I could talk to you. I'm so sorry to leave like this. I'll try to call Derrick when I get in, but you can get me at my parents' home in Toronto." She's left the number; I scramble for a free piece of paper, the back of someone's testimony, and scribble it down. "Look, I'll call you when I know more. My mother's hanging in there, but it doesn't look good." There's a series of crackles on the recording and she says, "Turbulence or something. Talk to you later!"

I try to call Joanne's parents' home in Toronto, but the international circuits are busy. I try Derrick's number too, but can't get through there either. Sometimes the phones just don't work here.

Nothing to do but wait. This is the problem. Stuck in now, waiting for later, through the aching stretch of darkness. Last night I sat for hours by the window wide-eyed, peering into the black, trying to keep the images from my mind: that rat in the kitchen, the black box, the look of triumph on Dorut Kul's face. The kids waiting in the rain by the fence, peering through the gates of hell.

Those IS men vomiting as if they didn't know.

The door of the fridge. My hand on the grubby handle, pulling it open.

I have to replace them all one by one. Joanne in her T-shirt, her long legs, her eyes. Joanne leaning over the menu at the Happy Mouth Lounge. Joanne cradling me in this stupidly luxurious bed after my collapse that time. Her feel, her smell. It's insanity otherwise. The filth in that kitchen. The stench that I can't seem to wash off my skin.

There's a mountain of things to read, but I shouldn't do that tonight. I need to keep a clear head, safe thoughts.

I need to go home.

I try the phones again and again through the night, finally doze restlessly near dawn. Luki tells me later at the *Justico kampi* that sometimes the telephone grid malfunctions on windy days – the wires can't handle the vibrations. But it's not particularly windy here. Perhaps somewhere else.

"We just wait," she says, "until the system is working again."

I'm distracted in the hearing room, have a hard time following the testimony of a colonel who apparently had no idea what anybody under his command was doing most of the time. Sin Vello gets him to admit that his parents bought his commission for him, and that he spent much of the year at the family villa at Bolo Beach. Dorut Kul seems particularly interested in the testimony. He takes copious notes from the tiny visitors' gallery, several times makes eye contact with me.

My mind is stuck on the thought that I shouldn't be here.

Joanne won't be returning soon, I'm sure of it. But I should actually talk to her before I make my announcement. I'm bone-tired listening to the colonel, but the idea of returning home is so compelling I'm almost ready to tell Sin Vello.

In the afternoon an IS commander scheduled to testify fails to appear. During the wait I try to call Joanne's parents from Minister Tjodja's office, but the phones still aren't working. I tell Tjodja that I'm strongly considering returning to Canada because of Joanne's departure.

"But I can provide you with any number of personal assistants, Mr. Burridge!" he exclaims.

"It wouldn't be the same," I tell him. Then when he gets really anxious I relent a little, say that my mind is not completely made up. "I have to talk to her, that's all," I say. "Before I can really know what's going on. But my health is precarious, as you know."

"We will do everything in our power to help you, Mr. Burridge."

I think of telling him he could start by paying me, but I shy away – he might get the idea I'm leaving over money. It would take a whole other conversation to extricate myself from the room; I'm too tired to deal with it now. Instead I thank him, return to the hearing room filled with the certainty that this is the right decision. I gather my papers, wait, ready to approach Sin Vello and Mrs. Grakala with the news. But Sin Vello has been called away on something urgent; Mrs. Grakala has already left. The afternoon's session is postponed.

On the *Justico kampi* steps, as Nito is getting our taxi, Dorut Kul approaches me in some agitation. "We need to talk, Mr. Burridge," he says quickly, under his breath, without quite looking at me.

"About what?" I ask.

He thrusts a padded envelope under my arm. I'm already burdened with too many papers.

"Not now," he says and walks away. In my surprise I drop the package, bend over awkwardly to retrieve it. So much for secrecy, I think. If that's what he wanted.

I return to my hotel room tired, distracted, suddenly weighed down by details. If I'm to leave I'll need to buy an airline ticket. Perhaps Luki can help me out. What about money? Do I have enough credit left to purchase the ticket? If I go home now I may never be paid for the work I have done. I'll need to talk to Derrick. But the phones are still out. Must be a hell of a windstorm. I could start packing. What will I do with all these documents? I'll have to talk to Tjodja about them.

Stymied, I turn to Dorut Kul's bulky envelope. No explanatory note, no return address, just a videotape and several sheets of what looks like a transcript typed entirely in Kuantij. Fortunately the luxury suite comes with a television and VCR, so I plug in the tape, though it takes several minutes to hit the right combination of buttons to get the two machines to work together.

Blurry picture, at first entirely out of focus. It sharpens slowly, looks like a long-distance shot through leaves and some sort of screening. Zoom, zoom, not much clearer. Finally a small woman and somebody huge – Sin Vello? It's hard to think of anybody else that big – standing on what looks like a verandah, surrounded by green. A country place? Somewhere in the jungle? The two are talking and there's a lot of background noise – rain, I guess, coming down pretty hard. I turn up the volume and at maximum I can just barely detect voices. Sin Vello and some small woman, speaking in Kuantij. I look at the transcript and see Suli's name up and down the pages. Suli and Sin Vello.

What does it mean, a tape of Suli and Sin Vello talking on a verandah? If it is them in the first place. Nothing's very clear; it could easily be a fake. Where did it come from? When was it made? Will Dorut Kul testify as to where he got it?

In front of Sin Vello?

Too many questions. I don't like the look of this. Why did Dorut Kul give *me* the tape? He knows I don't understand Kuantij. He could easily have done his own translation. And published it himself.

Dorut Kul said we needed to talk. Perhaps I should just wait for him to contact me again. Maybe tomorrow. This might be nothing, I think. Dorut Kul and his half-baked reporting. He thought I was trying to leave the country. That cry of triumph when he saw the heads in the refrigerator. Bloody journalists.

Maybe he wants me to take it out of the country.

I eject the tape from the machine, put it back in its case, then return the letter and case to the original envelope, which I hide in the sleeve of my suit jacket hanging in the closet. Nothing to do until tomorrow, but it's so hard to get this out of my head. Suli and Sin Vello. What are they saying to each other?

The afternoon drains away. I pace, make a stab at reviewing testimony, try the phone again and again. I go down to the Happy Mouth Lounge to order dinner, then have it delivered upstairs so I can avoid the reporters who need more news. Back in my room I eat the local version of flatcakes – slightly sour-tasting, with various vegetable- and meat-paste dips, some mild and palatable, others too spicy for me to digest. The sun sets quickly, sinks like a ship. No lingering sunsets here.

When the phone rings I nearly jump out of my skin.

"Hello?"

"Hello, Mr. Burridge? I'm sorry to disturb you in your rest."

"That's quite all right, Luki," I say.

"Justice Sin has asked me to call you. We have just received word that Captain Velios has been found."

"Are you sure? Captain Velios?"

"Unfortunately he is dead. Justice Sin is hoping you will go with him to examine the body."

My heart plunges at the thought of more bodies. Why did I have the feeling this Captain Velios would never survive to talk to us?

"Yes, of course. Does he mean tonight?"

"We will send a car shortly."

I'm halfway out the door before it occurs to me the phones are working again. I go back, try Joanne's parents' number – it's the middle of the night in Canada but this is an emergency. The ring sounds strange, though. I don't think I've gotten all the way through to Toronto. Finally a busy signal cuts in – another bad connection somewhere.

No time now. I leave it reluctantly, pick up Nito on my way out. Luki arrives in the same black German sedan as the day before. Are these windows bulletproof? I ask Luki to tell Nito exactly what's going on. I want him alert and effective. The night is blacker now than ever, streetlight after streetlight either barely flickering or completely out, shadowy forms on the sidewalk beyond the tinted glass.

"Where did they find him?" I ask Luki.

"In Welanto. He was left in a hotel."

"Tortured?"

"I do not know."

I stop myself from asking if his head is still attached. What was I thinking? Of course bodies are going to turn up. This is the underside, full of maggots and slugs and wet black earth nourished by blood.

If I can just hang on for a day or two, I think, I'll be out of this, on my way home.

"Luki, how long till your baby is due?" I blurt, conscious that after all this time I don't know much about her.

She smiles suddenly at the unexpected question. "The twenty-seventh of February."

"First child?"

"Yes."

"What does your husband do?"

"He works as a travel agent. At least he did."

"Has he changed his work?"

"His company does not exist any more. There is not much travelling these days."

"*Kontra qitaos?*" I say, remembering the phrase.

"*Kontra qitaos.*"

"Does that mean you're the breadwinner these days?"

"The pay would be fine if the *loros* was not evaporating. And if the pay would actually arrive."

"You're not getting paid?" I ask.

"Not yet. There are delays processing the cheques. No one else has been paid yet either, so it's not so bad."

Not so bad? Recipe for disaster, I think. So I'm not the only one. "Does this happen often?" I ask. "People not getting paid?"

"Just in the government," she says. Then she smiles again. "It's all right, we have faith in Suli. She is bringing great changes."

I ask some more questions and she tells me about her father, a postal clerk, and her mother, who sold flatcakes in the market for years to raise money to send Luki to a school where English was taught. She studied evenings and weekends, glued to foreign broadcasts to improve her accent. Her husband is

Kaylun Wel, from a fishing family that moved to the capital twenty years ago.

"And Nito? I don't know anything about him really. What's his background? Could you ask him for me?"

"He trained with the militia and received his class-one marksman's certificate, but he did not serve with the regular army. He was personal bodyguard instead for Naloya Bintillo, a plantation owner in the north. His brother was taken and killed by the IS, that's why he would not serve in the regular forces."

"Tell him I'm sorry," I say.

Nito nods gravely, explains further.

"He says we all lost someone in the bitter years." *Rinda gutra*, I recognize the phrase. "He will not let anything happen to you. You are making things better."

I thank him, and he keeps talking, now that I have asked.

"He has three daughters, all of them getting married this year. The youngest is marrying his best friend, Binte. They trained together, and Binte's wife died four years ago of dysentery. The eldest is marrying a Malaysian businessman, going to be very rich, and the middle daughter is marrying a boy from her high-school class." Nito shakes his head, smiling through a false grimace. "He will be in debt for many years," Luki says, "trying to pay for all these weddings. But this is the way on our island. Nito hopes you will come to all three!"

"I will if I can," I tell him, and extend my hand, which he grasps with feeling.

Then I ask Luki if Nito is getting paid for his services, actually receiving his money. It turns out he has a family connection on his wife's side to Minister Tjodja, and is being well paid for his work.

We speed through the night, no traffic now, just strange

shapes in the shadows. Bodies? Live ones. Most bodies are alive, I think.

"How many translators does the commission have?" I ask Luki.

"Five of us."

"You must be working tremendously hard to keep up with all the documents."

"The others are envious," she says, smiling again, "because they are back in the office while I have the opportunity to go with you to the field."

A strange term – of all the things it is, Welanto is not a field. Sometime in the ride it occurs to me that we're surrounded by grubby little desperate dwellings made of tin sheets, cardboard, plywood, car parts, plastic sheeting, each shack webbed to the others with electrical wires balanced daintily on jury-rigged poles, lighting naked bulbs and dully flickering television sets. Through the tinting of my window and the cathode glow I see unshaven men sitting in undershirts and women in *saftoris*, with children on the floor or in the doorways, watching. A young woman looks up from a neighbourhood pump and a dog barks at us. A rooster tethered to the side of a shack, young men squatting around a game, women cooking over an outside fire. The car barely reaching walking speed now. It seems to take forever. I don't particularly want to find this body, but I do want to have it over with.

Blocked now. People in the road, which isn't a road any more, so narrow it's more like a path between dwellings. The driver honks his horn and we sit, idling, while swarms try to peer in. Are all the doors locked? More honks. He revs the engine, moves forward slightly, but people either ignore the car or slam their hands down on the hood and make rude gestures.

"How close are we? Do you think we should get out?"

Luki asks the driver for me. Then Nito, Luki, and the driver talk at length.

"It is not too far," Luki says finally. "I will go with our driver and you stay here."

"I can walk."

"It might not be safe."

"It'll be safer for all of us if we go together."

More discussion. Finally we push open the doors. Faces in the glass, hands reaching to feel the inside of the car. Somehow we get out and close the doors before anyone can get in; the driver locks them with his remote. Now what? Luki, the driver, and Nito start talking to everyone around us, and soon I hear the words "*Commisi vertigas*" and "Boo-reej! Boo-reej!" People give way, a path of sorts opens up. We walk among the stares, some sullen, most just curious, with the odd hand reaching out to touch my shoulder, finger my hair. I follow the others, try to keep track of the twists, the little landmarks – that one shack lit up in neon, is that the corner store? A sign on another shows a beautifully painted set of teeth and bears the inscription *Ligi-ligi*, which I gather means "dentist." Soon I'm lost and irritated – I don't like being so imperial any more, so dependent.

Strange, circuitous route. Finally we enter one of the larger buildings, a two-storey concoction of odd planks, rickety stairs, panels taken from old billboards. Half of a huge Marlboro man peers at us: one eye looking away, a blond moustache, smoke trailing from a giant cigarette tip, the top of a cowboy hat sloping into view. The air feels thin and hot, reeks of too much humanity and . . . something else. This is the right place. People milling all the way up, but fewer in the actual room. The body is on the floor, wrapped and taped in green garbage bags. The stench in the room almost as bad as at the IS detention centre. I fight the dizziness. We're the first officials to arrive. Where's Sin Vello?

"How did it get here?" I ask, looking around, anywhere but at the body. I'd send Luki out of the room but I can't talk to people without her. "Who owns this place? Luki, can you find out?"

She turns to a wizened, baldheaded man next to the door who looks like he knows what's going on. He shakes his head and points to a young woman leaning on the bed. At first glance she seems undisturbed, but her hands, though clasped tightly, are shaking. Luki questions her then turns to me.

"This was not the man staying here. He disappeared two days ago owing money. When she looked in his room she found the body."

"Wrapped like this?"

Luki asks the question. "Nothing has been touched," comes the reply.

"Then how do we know it's Captain Velios?"

The woman hands over a clear plastic bag. Inside are a wallet and a plasticized ID card with a blurry picture of a bearded, sad-eyed young man, VELIOS printed underneath it, and a stylized insignia in the corner – an eagle grasping crossed sub-machine-guns in its talons.

"The ID card was sitting on top of the body?"

Luki asks the question again and the woman answers yes.

"So no one has actually looked at the body?"

No one.

"Why haven't the police been called?"

The woman hesitates, then tells Luki that they have been. Instead of coming themselves, they told her to call the Truth Commission.

"Oh, for God's sake!" I can see a set-up. "Call the police again. Jesus. What am I supposed to do with a body?"

The woman leaves the room and I wait. For the police, for Sin Vello, for somebody to come and relieve me of this burden. But they're not going to come. Somehow it dawns on me. This body is meant for me – I'm the one supposed to deal with it. Unwrap the plastic. See what's been done.

But I'll be damned if I will. It may be meant for me but I'm not meant for it. I agreed to hear testimony, to consider evidence in a hearing room. Not to stand in the stench and heat of a Welanto firetrap with this sacrificial victim, this gift-wrapped Captain Velios, supposed author of all state atrocities. The police and IS are waiting for me to peel back the plastic, but I can wait for them, they've no idea how long I can wait. Man of bone, still as a rock beneath a lizard. I will not be moved.

No one else will either. Nothing happens. We're all stuck here. Time has stopped. The rickety stairs are not meant for this press of people. All looking in, watching me, the walking embodiment of the Truth Commission. Waiting for me to do what I'm supposed to do. Damned if I will. I can wait them out. They don't know who they're dealing with. I waited out the Kartouf. Starved, tortured, beaten. I waited them out. This too will pass.

Eyes peering in. The wizened old man, two young toughs with scraggly beards, an obese woman with thick lips and something growing on her eye. Children now poking their heads between people's legs. "Get them out!" I say, pointing to the kids, yelling it two more times until they leave. "Luki, where are the police?"

"They would not answer the phone, Mr. Burridge."

"Well, where's Sin Vello?"

"Justice Sin is supposed to be here already. I do not know

where he is." Her face is sickly, the stench now getting to her. Her knees wobble and she braces herself against the flimsy wall.

"All right. All right!" I say. "We can't wait here. Tell some of these men to pick up the body. We're going to bring it in the car with us."

Not a popular command. The young toughs melt away at the suggestion. No one will come forward.

"Where are Nito and the driver? Get them up here!"

I give the command but everything takes forever. Well, I'm not going to open that wrap. Damned if I will.

Nito and the driver finally arrive. I bark the order at Luki and she hesitates, then tells them. They don't look at her, or at me, but stare transfixed at the lump.

"Pick it up! Christ!" I stamp my foot and the floor buckles. Rotting plywood. Sin Vello would fall through.

Down the stairs, the multitudes parting more quickly than when we arrived. Nito and the driver struggle with the load, switch from shoulder to shoulder to get around corners and squeeze between onlookers. The street now even more jammed with the curious. Not a policeman in sight. No goddamn Sin Vello. What was he talking to Suli about in that video?

There's blood on their hands. I know it suddenly in my gut. Whose blood?

Later, I think. One problem at a time. Right now I don't know where the fuck I'm going, have to wait for Luki, Nito, the driver, and the corpse. Captain Velios. Who is it really? Some village boy stolen from a bus? The plastic bag with the blurry ID and wallet is in my hand. Eyes of the damned.

"Where's the fucking car?"

I have to follow them now, the body bumping, slipping off their shoulders. Nito is hardly strong enough. Whoever hired him as a bodyguard?

"Where's the fucking car?"

I say it over and over, out loud and in my head, broken record. "Is it this way? Somebody must remember. For God's sake!"

We go down one alley, up another. All the buildings and passages look identical – rundown, grubby, deeply shadowed. Crowds everywhere, silent, jostling to get a better view. And the further we go the more the body slumps. Despite myself I look – the garbage bags have started to come undone.

"Jesus! Luki, could you ask somebody? Everybody here knows exactly where our car is except us!"

Little bits of hair start to poke out. I look away; it's hard to focus on anything else. We change directions. Some men in the crowd say that way, then some others say no, the other way, we turn around and around . . .

"Luki – get the driver to use his remote to honk the horn!" She doesn't understand at first, but then she talks to him. He takes the body off his shoulder and the corpse falls roughly to the ground, slumps against a set of stairs; a little more plastic gives way. He checks his pockets. It's a nightmare. Everyone looking in, the darkness pressing in on us like a thousand feet of ocean.

The driver says something to Luki, looks at me in fear and guilt, starts going through his pockets again. Oh my God, I think. This isn't happening.

"I'm sorry, Mr. Burridge," Luki says.

"Oh come on, I don't believe this."

"He has lost his keys."

Luki and the driver talk now, a hundred miles an hour, and Nito joins in. Now everyone's talking, the crowd included, taking all the air. My head is pounding. I don't need to be here, I think.

"I'm sorry, so sorry!" Luki says, near tears. "The car has been stolen."

The body has started to slip out of the plastic bags. It's black as hell and hundreds of people are crowded around staring as the head pokes out. No, I think, this isn't happening. How could we have lost the car? Where are the police? I am not going to look at this poor boy –

This poor boy with no eyes. The eyes have been burned out. Blackened like charcoal, and the rest of the face is purple in this infernal light, and Luki is right there looking. I turn her away. Too late. Too goddamn late for anything.

23

"Where's the nearest police station?"

It's the only thing I can think of. We're stuck in the middle of Welanto with a corpse and no car, no Sin Vello, and no police.

"I don't know," Luki says.

"Then *ask*, goddamn it!" She dissolves immediately into tears and I apologize, try to get hold of myself. I'm shaking.

Luki recovers, asks the people crowding around. The driver kneels on the ground and vomits. The head of the corpse lolls to one side, and for a moment I expect it to roll right out of the bag, but it seems to be attached.

"There is a police station this way," Luki says, pointing.

The driver won't get up to carry the body. For a moment it infuriates me. "Get up!" I scream, "Get up! Get up!"

He covers his head, waiting to get hit, like he's being terrorized.

"Mr. Burridge!"

"*Get up!*"

"It's all right, Mr. Burridge – I'll take him. I'll do it." Luki's face strained with fear. She bends down uncertainly, tries to hoist half the corpse to her shoulder.

"Luki, put it down."

"It's all right, Mr. Burridge." Struggling, losing her grip.

"It's not all right, Luki. It's so far past all right I don't even know what it is. But you put that down. I'll take it. I'm *meant* to take it."

My shoulder so much higher than Nito's. I'm at the back with the weight, the lolling head. The body slopes down to Nito at the front, holding the legs and feet. I can't believe how heavy it is. And the reek of it, so much worse like this than even a few feet away. I stagger a step and another, nearly pull us all over, but catch my balance. Is my heart going to take this? I don't know, yet somehow it seems clear that I am meant to do this. This body has been put here for me.

The crowds watching. Who knows where we're going? I've no idea. Nito is in front. He's following Luki's directions. We're going somewhere, I've lost track of where. My brain knows. Step after step into the darkness, one alley becoming another, maybe the same one we passed ten minutes ago. I will not fold. The brush of this boy's ghoulish hair against my face and shoulder. It's my body, I realize at some point, hours and days later perhaps, step after step into the darkness. I'm bearing my own body. I'm Captain Velios. I'm the one who had to be killed.

"Here is the police station," Luki says in the dream. It is a dream, yes? This darkness, the heaviness of my limbs, the pressure in my chest, the strange disconnected faces all around me.

I look up. Of course it's a dream. This is no real police station, it's a dreamified one: dark, sorry little claptrap building completely closed up. No police here. Never were. Couldn't be.

Luki pounds on the door. This small pregnant dream person. Yelling in Kuantij, but I understand perfectly, so it is a dream. She says, "Wake up! Wake up! We have a body!"

Nito puts his end of the body down, but it seems too soon. I'm perfectly willing to carry it farther. How else can I get rid of it if I don't carry it the whole way?

Finally a tired old man in a nightshirt opens the door holding a lamp. Now that's in a dream. This isn't a policeman. He jumps back comically at the sight of the body, of me still holding the head to my chest. The poor boy's head. Luki explains it all to him, but I can follow exactly what she's saying, so it is a dream. He doesn't want to take it. Of course not. I have to carry it farther. All the way. How else can I get rid of it? But Luki pushes herself into the station house. It changes completely inside – there's a desk with papers and record books, doors leading to rooms in the back where prisoners, and corpses, I suppose, could be kept. The outside station house doesn't correspond to the inside one.

The body goes down to the floor – dirt, cold – but I keep hold. The poor boy. Marks on his neck, black welts in the purple skin.

"We need to see the whole body," I say. Luki looks at me. I'm not crazy. This is a dream, but I'm not crazy. "We need to see the whole body and to make notes, and this man must sign in the register that he received the body."

He doesn't want to do it. You see, I knew he was going to be difficult, not a real police officer at all, but a skinny old man standing in his nightshirt with his spindly legs sticking out.

"Does he have a knife or some scissors?" I stretch the body on the floor, the boy's sorry head lolling again but staying on. It is a dream. In real life the head would come off and we'd have to put it in a refrigerator.

Luki hands me some scissors. "I have to do it," I say. "You get a notebook and mark things down. But *I* have to cut it open."

Quiet, relaxed. Still as a rock beneath a lizard. The plastic slices so easily, the tape more difficult – duct tape. A thousand and one things you can do with it.

"Start with the eyes," I say. "Burned out. Mark that down. A deep scar on the neck, like a knife wound. I don't know how old it is. There are burn marks down the arms and some of the fingers are missing. On the right hand – half the index, and the whole middle finger, half the pinkie. On the left all of the ring finger and the other one – what's it called? – the fourth one." Like Dr. Parker's voice but with informal terminology. "Burn marks on the nipples and abdomen, and a gash across the belly, it looks like it's been roughly stitched up. Testicles –" and here my voice fails, I have to fight, stay in the dream. "There are no testicles. And the legs have been lacerated and there is no left foot."

We turn it over, make note of the welts on the back and buttocks. No bullet wounds. No puncture marks. A strange lack of blood, as if the body's been bled already. I have the policeman check among the garbage bags for the missing foot. He does it because it's a dream. None of this makes sense otherwise.

"Have him make a photocopy of your notes and sign this body into the register."

Luki tells him, but there's no photocopier. Of course not. So Luki copies out her notes by hand, signs both copies, leaves one with the officer. I watch him write something down in the register, his hands shaking.

It should be the end of the dream. I should wake up now in the luxury suite at the Merioka, or back at home – where? Wherever I'm supposed to be. I wait, but the dream doesn't end. We stand staring at the body on the floor, the cut garbage bags, the blood on my hands and clothes – now where did that come from? It wasn't there before.

"Have him call for a police car to bring us home again," I say. She asks and he explains, frightened, as if we're going to have him beaten, that there is no police car at this station. They just use bicycles.

"Have him call one from another station," I say. And he replies – again, almost in a panic – that the radio is broken and the telephone lines have not worked since Tuesday.

"I'm not staying the night here! For God's sake! Get him to find us a taxi!"

Luki yells at him now too and he withers, the old guy, the fake policeman in his nightshirt with his spindly legs and Adam's apple gulping every breath. When Luki yells, he leaves and we wait, alone in the police station with the body. What happens if he doesn't come back? It's that kind of dream. Nothing is going to work out. I'm going to have to wrap up the boy again and hoist him on my back and carry him to another –

The taxi pulls up in minutes and we leave the body at the station.

Silence on the ride back. Everything so dark – no streetlights on now, none. No shop lights, a blackout. It makes perfect sense. This is a black night. The city deserves to be in darkness.

"I'm sorry," I say to Luki. "No job is worth what you've seen tonight."

She stares ahead in silence, her hands folded on her lap, resting against her growing belly.

"I have something else I need to show you," I say. "I'm sorry. My instinct is to order you now to clear out, go find something else to do. But there's no one else I can ask."

"I'm all right," she says dully. Eyes transfixed by the darkness.

When we get to the Merioka no lights are on. It makes total sense, since no lights are on anywhere else, but my brain is preternaturally slow processing the information. There's been a total blackout – no electricity in the quarter. The young man on the steps explains it to Luki but stares at me, the Truth Commissioner washed in blood.

"How long has the power been out?"

Most of the night. The elevators aren't working. My room is on the twenty-third floor. I tell Luki to go home to her husband. What I have for her – the video – can wait. Luki asks the young man if there's a room on the main floor I could sleep in tonight. But I want my own place. A change of clothes, water to wash with. It's only right. I'm meant to walk up all those stairs. Nito comes with me, silent, holding the flashlight, and I have a sense that we're making our way up from total blackness into something else. Not daylight, but something else.

I couldn't have done this three months ago. Somehow I'm getting stronger. Or else I'm fooling myself, and it's going to kill me. My abused heart. I try to relax everything, just use the muscles that have to be used – in the thighs, calves, ankles, feet. We climb a flight and rest, climb a flight and rest, the air getting hotter the higher we climb. We smell so bad, Nito and I, rank with the stench of Velios, as if we are still carrying him.

Finally we reach the twenty-third floor and I find the lock with my key. Eerie darkness, just the impotent poking beam of Nito's flashlight. I open the door and Nito shines his light into the blackness. It doesn't feel like my suite at all. Seeing it this way, the narrow beam showing files here and there, my stuff so messy, the bed even. . . . The bed wasn't like that when I left, and neither were those chairs. I reach for the light switch instinctively, but of course it doesn't go on. I grab the flashlight from Nito, shine it crazily around the room, but everything is in the wrong place, as if my brain can't order the information any more, the pictures come in randomly with no sense. My briefcase overturned, papers dumped, the mattress sideways, my clothes littered on the floor, the lamp bent and leaning against the bureau, that body face down as if crawling out of the bathroom . . .

I scream and Nito yells something a split second later, an animal shriek. *How did Velios get up here?* For a moment I'm stuck with the thought. *It should've been me.* I drop the flashlight and kick it in my confusion and it goes out, I have to feel on my hands and knees, crash into things, I can't control anything now. *Breathe, breathe.* But I can't, I have to get the flashlight first. Nito searches beside me, curses in Kuantij. Then I've got it again, turn it on, and hold it still with every muscle in my body. This beam carving in the darkness, as if we're in a cave a thousand feet underground, everything not in the beam lost in irrevocable night. Nito walks towards the bathroom reluctantly, his limbs stiff with fear. There's the body. No garbage bags. Why did they put Velios back into clothes? All this blood pooling in the bathroom.

Then Nito kneels, turns the body face up. It isn't Velios. It's Dorut Kul. The back half of his head has been blown off and something – brains? – are clumped in the blood on the floor.

I fight my nausea, step to the closet with the flashlight, leaving Nito for a moment in the dark with the body of Dorut Kul. There's my suit jacket still hanging, untouched. Thank God! I reach in the sleeve – nothing. In the other sleeve . . .

"Come on! Let's get out of here. Come on!" I yell, shining back on Nito, his face struck with horror. "*Now! Come on!*" I yell.

Out the door, down the stairs, two at a time, three and four, the light bouncing crazily off the walls, this endless, oven-hot stairwell. They killed Dorut Kul. They took the video and the transcript. Savages. Bloody savages. I bash my knee against a post and then I trip, roll for a moment then right myself, keep going. Nito runs behind me. They shot Dorut Kul right in my bathroom. Because of what was on the video. They would've shot me. Yes? If I'd been there. No – they sent me out to Welanto to deal with the body of the boy they're calling Velios. They did it to get me out of my room. So they could shoot Dorut Kul.

Slow, I think – slow. Your heart can't take this. It's too much. Everywhere I turn, nightmare. They shot Dorut Kul. Right in my fucking bathroom. Executed him and stole the video. It must be Sin Vello. He sent me out to Welanto then never showed up. Forever and ever these stairs, hot, airless, black as hell. Down and down and down, this one flimsy light with its narrow beam, bouncing.

Ground floor finally, no time to think, don't *want* to think. "Car!" I yell at Nito, like a loud American tourist. "CAR! GO!" And I turn my hands as if on a steering wheel, make honking gestures and noises. I do know the right word but I can't access it now, everything has to be dead simple or my mind is going to melt. He runs off and I wait, gasping, in suspended animation, a portrait of panic but with nowhere to go, nothing to do but wait for the car. What car? Where's Nito supposed to get one at this time of night? I've no idea, but he must find one. There's nothing else that can happen. I will it with every nerve in my body.

"What's happening?" asks someone in the shadows. Sleepily, in casual English. It's the older, grey-beard journalist, getting up from a couch in the lobby, his suit wrinkled. "What the fuck?" he says when he sees me.

"Do you have a car?"

"What's happened to you?"

"*Do* you have a car?"

"Are you hurt?"

"Answer my question or I'll break your fucking neck. Do you have a car?"

Shakily: "I rented one. Yes."

"Then give me the keys."

"You have tell me what's –"

"*Give me the fucking keys!*"

I'm in my cat stance. In two seconds if he doesn't move I'm going to –

He hands over the keys.

"Where's the car?"

He stands rooted, dumbfounded, till I bark at him, "*Take me there. Go!*"

His feet lurch and I kick him in the back of the leg – a poor kick at that, off-balance, barely glancing him – but he whines like a frightened dog and hurries along uncertainly, my light illuminating just a few feet ahead of him. I don't know what I've become but it's something low to the ground, pure instinct and adrenaline, crouching in that murky space between killing and being killed. I haven't room for thinking where we're going, just for trusting that we'll get there. My eyes on the light, on every step of his weathered shoes. No room for extra thought, for anything I can't use.

The next thing I know, I'm in the car, driving in the pre-dawn, alone. It's been ages since I've driven myself, but my body knows, if I just surrender to it, submerge, it's fine. But I can't remember getting in the car. I don't know what I did with the journalist. The flashlight bounces in the seat beside me.

Too fast. The sky lighter, a greyish tinge, another sunrise in

hell and I don't know where I'm going. But I do. I've been there.
I wasn't paying attention but my body's been there so it knows.
If I just shut down my brain, think with my body. That animal
in me that knows what to do. Life on this side and death on
the other. Time immemorial. Part of me knows what it's doing.

Again, no memory. Each moment passing one to the next
but nothing sticks. But here's the Pink Palace. I knew I could
make it. I get out of the car, walk to the soldier at the gate.

"*Commisi vertigas*, Bill Boo-reej! Suli Nylioko!" I yell.

An AK-47 levelled at my chest.

"*Commisi vertigas*, Bill Boo-reej! Suli Nylioko!"

If I move like a flash I could bat away his weapon and break
his neck. I know the move exactly. He's suspicious, but scared
too. The blood on my clothes. He knows who I am, but I'm
not acting as he expects.

"*Commisi vertigas*, Bill Boo-reej! Suli Nylioko!" I jump up
and down. He's either going to shoot me or let me in.

I want him to kill me. I'll die with my hands on his throat.
Come on!

"*Commisi vertigas*, Bill Boo-reej! Suli!"

Either way it's the same to me. I'm way over the edge. Fuses
blown, kill or be killed. This is blood on my hands. My clothes
reek of decaying corpses. They're piling up. One of them
should've been me.

"*Commisi vertigas!*"

I am just about to move. One lunge forward then that's it.
The soldier takes a step back. How does he know? As soon as
his foot starts to move I'm nearly overcome with the need to
crack him. That first sign of retreat. Why don't I move? His
eyes look away. Just for a moment. He's lost. I know it. If I just
stand still, don't move a muscle, I've won.

It feels like the hardest thing I've ever done. I want to crack him. I want him to have to shoot me. Put me out of my misery.

Breathe and breathe and breathe. *I love you too. Don't really know what I think about that.*

Don't really know.

He phones, comes back out of his little hut, his weapon still pointed, left hand patting the air as if trying to get a pit bull to calm down. Talking to me now in Kuantij, soothing words I guess. *Wait, wait,* he says. I don't want to wait. I want to crack him so that he has to shoot me.

But I don't move, just stand in my cat stance, left foot forward a bit, weightless, hands relaxed but ready by my waist. I could probably step and grab the gun right out of his hands. Then what?

Then what?

Several more soldiers arrive. They walk slowly, calmly, like men approaching a bomb. Their hands pat down on the air as well, silently soothing the beast. I hear myself snarl, feel the hair stand on the back of my neck. I can't see them all clearly, but sense their movement, some behind me, outside my peripheral vision.

The first touch I'm going to explode.

But they don't touch. It's gentle phrases in Kuantij, with Suli's name sprinkled throughout. She's the one I need to talk to.

Their gentle sounds and my snarls. I want to lash out. I want to go down breaking someone. It's the one thing I never did with the Kartouf, it would've changed everything. They would've killed me early. I would never have had to go through all this shit.

I love you too.

I wouldn't have –

Someone moves and I lunge and the blow to the side of my head doesn't kill me. I have this distinct thought as I fall – I'm not dead. They hit me but I'm not dead.

24

From far down the road I see Patrick running, chasing a red Chinese dragon kite so elaborate I wonder for a moment who possibly could've made it. It dips and swirls with the wind, swoops down, its magnificent head so well engineered that the jaws swing open as they get closer to the boy. He runs, laughing at the jaws, which do look funny in a way, gaping open and lurching, the tongue dangling out, hiding the teeth. From where I'm sitting I can see him perfectly, far better than I want to: the way his legs scissor forward, the ragged mop of hair, the undone shoelace, his hands grasping the string that isn't restraining the kite at all. No, the dragon is well ahead of the string, swooping down on my boy, who isn't watching properly, he never does – crossing the road, riding his bike, he doesn't pay proper attention.

He doesn't even see me. I look his way, but I'm in a strange position. I can't yell out, he'd never hear me, and I can't raise my hand, I don't know why. I just can't. And it gets hard to hold him in view. One moment he's racing just ahead of his dragon kite and then when I look again . . .

When I look again he isn't there. I wait, because Patrick and the dragon should come into view. I'm moving and they're moving, it's a matter of angles. Soon enough they should come into view again. But they don't, and I have that sickening feeling. As I round the corner they should come back in view.

But nothing.

Nothing.

Slowly I fade back into this version of reality. I'm in the back of an army truck, the cover up because of the rain. Not tied, not bound, but it's as if I've been encased, in a sense – my body doesn't feel as if it can move without permission. Two soldiers are sitting with me. One keeps his eyes fixed on my sorry frame; the other's head bobs as he lurches in and out of his own sleep. I don't know how long we've been climbing, but it seems like yet another version of eternity. The road behind is mud-slick from the rain. I can just see a receding bright circle of it out the back opening of the truck.

Still in my bloody clothes. I've had a chance to wash a bit but don't have my meds, they're back at the hotel, in that other world I can't return to. Doors have closed, it's better to run for now. I should be fine for a couple of days. And then, who knows? It all feels oddly remote, except for the heartburn. I shouldn't have had the papaya and pineapple they offered at breakfast. Maybe better simply not to eat.

We're climbing, climbing, I can only look backwards through this receding hole. I have a vague notion that they're taking me to see Suli. I don't know why we have to go this way, so far into the mountains. The gears labouring, one soldier staring at me in his own trance. I could reach across, seize his weapon, and kill the both of them, I think dully. Only I couldn't possibly move fast enough. My arms would float as if in water. Heavy as sausages. I'd never make it.

This is my last trip into the mountains, I think. Whatever happens. Either I'm going to make it out or not, but I'm not coming back.

I have an odd thought of Nito's face after I'd left him in the dark with the body of Dorut Kul. The shock, like in a bad movie, but soundless and forever human. Nothing we could ever get used to. Alone in sudden darkness with the cold and heat of death. On our way down the jaws of the beast.

The village appears gradually, down below us for some reason, peeking between trees and clouds, the road having taken us along mountain edges higher than we needed to go. With each switchback of the mountain road I see clouds and the tops of trees far below the cliff edge, sometimes the skeletons of old trucks abandoned at the bottom. I think of something I read about ages ago – the Indian army driving from Kashmir to occupy Ladakh, a long line of trucks proceeding so cautiously in the fog, following the rear lights of the troop truck ahead . . . twenty of them shooting off into the abyss with military precision and passivity into soundless doom.

Soundless Burridge, as if my vocal cords have been cauterized by the shock of the past few days. Wrapped and still and soundless, no anger left, no fear.

No fear.

It doesn't feel like what I thought it would. It feels less alive than before, when I was a mass of fears. It feels dead but not quite gone, hovering, impassive. Like Joanne's lost boys in Sudan. Maybe. Numb from shock. Bodies shutting down. Low gear, slowly, slowly down the slope.

Stopped finally. A shock to move my legs and arms, to rise and crouch in the back of the truck, then have to step down into mud. My legs trembling still from climbing all those stairs in the Merioka.

The Merioka.

Dorut Kul lying in his own blood and brains.

And now Suli here to greet me, her face sombre, her bare feet and the hem of her *saftori* spattered with mud. "I am so sorry," she says, embracing me like a mother.

"I have some questions," I say, trying to remember my lines.

"Not now. I must clean you." Not a request, not an order, but a statement of reality for which I'm grateful. I need statements of reality. She folds her arm into mine and we walk along the mud of a pathway, soldiers ahead of us, some villagers as well, looking at Suli and the bent foreigner. The rain has stopped and the clouds for a time look like they might clear; the air feels fresh after the long, confined ride and the city smog. It isn't much of a village, it seems, just a collection of huts on stilts surrounded by trees, perched on the side of this mountain. Hardly anyone around, either – no children that I can see, a few elderly women tending chickens.

"Can you climb?" she asks, and rather than speak I step onto the broad ladder and slowly draw myself up into the hut. It's surprisingly spacious and airy, with a thatched roof, woven bamboo sides, a sturdy plank floor worn smooth, I imagine, by generations of bare feet.

"What is this place?"

"Lie down. Rest. I will return."

The mat is thin but comfortable, with a pillow made of sturdy cloth stuffed, it feels like, with soft feathers. I drift near sleep, feel my body relax so completely it seems as if I'm rising off the mat, hovering, looking down. This odd sense of safety I sometimes got with the Kartouf. It was the drugs, the needle. Maybe they've shot me up again. Maybe that's it.

No panic. It feels all right. Just to hover, be still.

I don't hear Suli re-enter, don't feel her peel off my bloody clothes. What I do feel is the water – coolish at first, then fine. Such an elemental thing, washing me clean. Forgive me, Suli, for I have sinned. I can't remember what I did, but I must have sinned or why would I be so bloody? She rubs my shoulders now with scented oil, my back and legs. I'm naked before her but it doesn't feel like the usual world. Nakedness doesn't matter. Blood, pain, sweat, filth – doesn't matter. Not in this world. She turns me over and I see her face glistening with tears. They suit her – I can't imagine anything more beautiful. The grieving widow. I see her for a moment kneeling in the airport, panic around her, her grief so perfect and profound.

It isn't the usual world.

I say, "Dorut Kul has been murdered. He showed me a video of you and Sin Vello talking. The video has been stolen."

She says, "Shhhhhh. Not now."

Calmly. Everything is peaceful. Her hands are small but strong and warm. Wherever she touches on my body feels better instantly. My buttocks and legs and feet, oh my feet.

Like being with Joanne. *Joanne*. From that other reality I must cling to.

"He was shot in my suite at the Merioka. The back of his head blown off. His blood and brains were on the floor. And somebody took the video and transcript."

"Just be still," she says. "Everything will become clear."

Her soothing hands on my belly, my wretched stomach, fragile chest. Everywhere she touches.

"Some boy they called Captain Velios was killed in

Welanto," I say. These things I have to hold on to. I'm a Truth Commissioner. I haven't come all this way to forget. "He was wrapped in garbage bags. He'd been mutilated."

"Don't think about it now," she says. The fragrance of the oil. Sandalwood? I'm never going to leave this moment. Eternal comfort and relief. It must be some sort of death.

"I carried the body all the way to the police station. With Nito. Luki said she'd do it but I said no at that. Some things I said no to."

"Yes."

Her fingers on my scalp, rubbing the oil through and through, working down my forehead, across my eyes, down the line of my jaw. Like Wu. For a moment I could be back with him. None of this happened. Of course I didn't go back to Santa Irene. Ridiculous. I've had enough punishment for one life. Wu's fingers on the back of my neck, down my shoulders again. Pulling out the bad energy.

"What were you and Sin Vello talking about that was so bad?" Of course I have to ask it. I'm a Truth Commissioner. It's why I'm here.

"Not now. Stay still."

"Was it Minitzh? Did you plot to assassinate the president?" It's the worst thing I can think of. What makes the most sense.

"Shhhhhh."

"Why else would you kill Dorut Kul?"

"Everything will become clear," she says. "Now we have to get ready."

She rises and my body turns cold, just like that, grace has been withdrawn. I can't move, lie here still as a corpse. Of course. If she had Dorut Kul killed then she'd have me killed too. It's probably already happened. I've been killed and like so many other things it isn't what you expect. I'm lying here unable to move, cold as death, but still sensing, still thinking.

"We carried the body all the way to the police station, and I would've carried it up the stairs too at the Merioka, but somebody else had already done that."

When she puts her hand on my shoulder again I can move. As simple as that. Reanimation, warmth flooding in. I sit up, then stand, and she wraps me in a long, patterned brown cloth – ginkos running up and down the trunks of trees. It hangs loosely around my shoulders, snug around the waist, falls nearly to the floor.

"For the man it's called a *golung*. Yours is from the Upong, my old tribe. This one belonged to my husband."

"Somebody else had already carried the body up," I say. "The refrigerator was full of heads."

Sunshine, the first really brilliant dose of it since coming back to the island. Dully, some thought from the past about my meds, how I shouldn't spend time in full sun. But I'm off my meds anyway. Still, a hat would be useful, and sunscreen. Page one, *Your Visit to the Tropics*. When walking along a mountain ridge in the full sun carrying a chicken for hours, wear a hat and sunscreen.

The chicken has gotten used to my carrying it. At first it squawked and flapped wildly, but now I have her cradled from below with my hand at her throat. Comfort and death. I'm sweating like a water sack. Suli is leading a goat and some of the soldiers have turkeys in bamboo cages. Why didn't I get a cage for my chicken?

It doesn't matter. We're just walking. The *golung* is light and cool, doesn't seem to be falling off. I'm hungry though, and the pressure is building in my head. I didn't think there would be headaches in death. Somehow that seems too earthly. But then again this is a journey back. An impossibly colourful bird sings at the top of a tree and then for a while the path swings to the edge of a rice paddy and I see the other paddies tiling down the slope, then up the next, filling the whole valley, liquid silver layers. We *have* to stop to look – you'd have to be dead not to pause in awe, and so I know I'm not dead yet. There's more I have to go through.

Small steps, blood working through my body, the chicken hot against me but still calm. The path turns into the wooded area then back to the open, affording another clear view of this valley of tiled water. It isn't the fabled Watabi Valley but like it, I imagine. The path is slick in most places and my cheap rubber thongs swim in the muck, flap against my heels when I step forward. Down and down, over a rickety log bridge, past a small village like the one where Suli met me, huts on stilts, a few cooking fires smouldering. Then finally to a larger village, all of us collecting like small streams coming into a river. Old men with gnarled ceremonial walking sticks, some in red *golungs*, some in brown. Women in blue or green, draped in lavish garlands of flowers, and children too in bright colours, many of them leading goats, dogs, carrying chickens. Trickling down, the colours blending and mixing, voices like water. Shadows deep and cool when we reach them, sun so bright, overpowering in the open.

We pool on a flat field on the far edge of the village. A large, low platform has been erected under the shade of three enormous trees, and in front of it, on the ground, the families are swirling, gathering, talking, sitting. Hugs and laughter, kids skittish, sitting for a time then running, pausing to whisper then darting off.

"Is this a wedding?" I ask.

"No. A funeral," Suli says.

She's greeted now not like a president but as a favourite returning daughter. The soldiers are soon garlanded and Suli is enveloped and carried off like a flower in the current. I'm left with my chicken, which is anxious now; it doesn't like this crowd of people and all the other animals they've brought. It scratches and flaps and I let it go for a time. It darts from between legs to open patches, then stops and eyes us all nervously. One of the soldiers corrals it for me and holds it, and when Suli comes back we sit on the ground twenty or thirty feet from the platform.

"Who died?" I ask.

"Her name was Kulika Lo, which means the mother of Lo. She had twelve other children, eight of them survived. Those people up on the platform are her family, her brothers and sisters and their children, her own children and theirs." Over a hundred people in all, it looks like, squatting, sitting, kneeling on the mats on the platform, some with heads bowed, others talking casually, some young girls sleeping with their arms around each other.

"How old was she?"

"Probably not yet sixty, though aged for around here. She was sick for a long time. Nobody paid attention to her then. But now that she's dead she's become very important."

"Why's that?"

"She's part of the *huloika* now, the spirit world. She can intercede on behalf of her friends and relatives. When she was sick that meant she'd angered the *huloika* somehow. She must have deserved it. But now she has crossed over and it's important to let her know that she is well respected."

For a long time it appears as if nothing is happening. More and more people dressed in finery arrive from various paths, fill up this open space bearing baskets, food, animals. We talk and don't talk; the family members on the platform look at us and look away. I'm slow to become aware of the music – soft bamboo flutes, long stringed instruments on gourds, drums of various kinds, a rhythmic tapping device festooned with bottle caps and empty tin cans. Gradually people move forward to the platform in twos and threes, and pull out lengths of cloth, jugs, jewellery, household items.

"Presents for Kulika Lo," Suli says.

They bring out the finery and show it to the family, who watch or don't watch, talk or stay silent, it doesn't seem to matter. The gifts are presented then laid at the foot of the platform in a growing mound. Ages pass and then it dawns on me that the body of Kulika Lo is underneath this mound.

"You mustn't hold back when giving to the dead," Suli says. "You must be extravagant in order to win favour."

Machetes, carving knives, carved masks, baskets, woven cloth, fancy hats, *saftoris*, figurines, wooden bowls, decorated sandals, pots of food. The first goat is brought up and now the family notices. Long speeches are made which I can't hear and of course wouldn't understand, but no one in particular seems to listen. And then the goat is slaughtered right there in front of the family, in front of us all. A skinny boy holds the rope and a young man in brown with a ceremonial cloth hat wound high on his head swings a machete through the goat's neck. Blood spurts immediately on the boy and the young man as the goat goes down, its back legs kicking up for an instant, as if fighting might be a possibility. The boy smiles and steps away with the head still on the rope, blood now down his front and dripping on the ground. More whacks and a leg is presented to the family, whose members applaud but don't take it.

Suli brings me some local beer in a carved wooden goblet. It's warm and plentiful and sweeter than I expect, and every time I look my goblet is full again.

The slow tide of families. Each in turn brings their offerings, adds them to the pile. Some of them have beaded hair and red dye on their faces, anklets of animal teeth. A muzzled monkey is brought forth and held up for the family, briefly tries to escape before being clubbed to the ground with the back of an axe. Two boys hold the arms while a father pauses to smile, then swings through one shoulder then another, twists the limbs off and holds them aloft. Again, there's no effort to avoid the blood – it spurts over much of the nearby crowd; the mist of it hangs in the air like salt spray. A dog is chopped but survives, cries out piteously, and there's confusion as blow after blow glances. Half-lame, the dog starts to crawl off but is pursued until a gush of blood brings a roar. Knives flash, and the sorrowful dog is soon reduced to bloody sections, each presented to the family then taken off to one of a dozen cooking fires behind the big trees.

Then Suli stands and motions to me and I rise, my legs stiff from being crossed so long. We walk slowly to the front, Suli talking to everybody, not in Kuantij, it seems to me, but some tribal language, the words sounding even stranger than usual. Hardly anyone pays attention to me, and I wonder if it's because I'm sick – I must've offended the *huloika*.

No sun now, but thick clouds and building humidity, my *golung* soaked with sweat, the heat of the day and of all these people trapped in the bowl of this clearing. Near the platform the ground is soaked in blood. Suli slips off her sandals, motions for me to do the same, my toes slide and squish in the hot mud. Then she begins a chant of sorts, her voice reedy, fragile. At first it's just her and then others join in, from the family and from the field. A low chant, simple – *boru'ut ki gan da gan da tu na*, it sounds like, over and over. I sing along, close my eyes, feel my body swaying, feet in the blood-soaked soil, the smell of rotting flowers, meat, perfumes, incense, of death and life filling my head. *Boru'ut ki gan da gan da tu na.* It could be anything or nothing, but it sounds to me like the most profound poetry. It seems to vibrate through my body and I don't want it to end. It builds and builds till thunder fills the valley, till every voice is with her, every body stands and sways, louder and louder and then suddenly, all at once, low as a whisper: *boru'ut ki gan da gan da tu na.*

Then I'm slaughtering a chicken. A soldier brings it up, the same one I carried so far under my arm, and holds its head and body down on the great chopping block while I raise a machete. One slip, I think, and I'll slice off part of this man's arm, maybe even catch him in the neck coming down. I pull my swing and miss completely, to the roar of the crowd, their hilarity, the soldier jiggling with silliness, Suli doubled over, the family rocking on the platform. I raise the machete again but the soldier laughs too much, he can't hold the chicken still, it seems inevitable I'm going to get his hand. This time I can't pull away, I try to focus.

Slash! The shock of it rockets up my arm, the machete sticks in the block as the chicken falls away in parts and the soldier rises, blood-soaked . . . lifts the chicken for everyone to see. His hands still fastened, head still on.

After my measly chicken there are more goats and dogs, then a water buffalo the size of four men. When the blade strikes its flank the blood sprays out over all of us, comes down like rain for a time, washes in our hair and sweat. We're all drinking now, *supira*, the local version, far more powerful than what I tasted before. I know I shouldn't drink this much, but that was from the old days, when I took medicine and was a Truth Commissioner. This is a new time, an in-between time – nothing is quite real and nothing is unreal. In fact, I come to realize, we're all on our way to death, every one of us, children to grandmothers. Just slightly behind Kulika Lo, but not that far. This is the waiting lounge, in a way, the place to say goodbye and to wish for favours from the one who's leaving, because we'll be going there soon ourselves. Every one of us. The blood falls on us all.

Food, feasting, music, chanting, wild dance, more slaughter and sacrifice, talk and more talk. Suli never stops, spills *supira* on herself as if it were blood, kisses the children, feeds the grandmothers, teases the young boys with their big feet and thin shoulders. She seems like a president now too, a president and a returning daughter, someone to curry favour with here, in this life. I watch her and eat, regardless of the food, vast quantities returning now from the many fires, spiced with fruit and burning peppers, strange sauces, cool jellies, more *supira*, always more *supira*. Every time I look up it seems more crowded, the air hotter, less room for any of us and our cumbersome bodies. Dancing now on the platform and in the field, dancing under the blackening sky, dancing crazily as the rain comes down, slashing, rivers of it, all heading here, in the pooling place, the waiting lounge, where we meet before death. Soaking the flowers and food, the fine clothes, the gifts, washing the blood into mud and the mud into blood that covers our feet and legs, splashes up our clothes the more we dance, soaks us all, washes us in the same blood-mud we came from, the same we're heading towards.

A young woman loses her *saftori*, stepped on by someone: one moment it's there and the next she is naked in the blood-mud. I'm startled, but she laughs, the others laugh. An older

to know about Dorut Kul. Why was he killed? What
discussing with Sin Vello in that video he was so dis-
out?"

I step into the water, let the filthy *golung* fall from
hing, aging body. Limbs back to their familiar trem-
ach in its usual roiling state.

you were going to explain everything."

verything will become clear."

" Immersing myself in the water, sickly warm. I
t diseases are lurking here, what leeches and snakes.
u to the *onjupta* ceremony so that you would know
very close to life and death here, to the *huloika*. It's
tronger part of our reality than it is for you. But
seen some of it. You've been part of it. And it is

conspire to murder General Minitzh?" I ask.
why Dorut Kul had to be killed.

enemies massing against us from every corner."
nd Sin Vello plot to kill the president?"

shades of truth and night that do not bear too
tion," she says. "They wipe out everything else.
k nothing else matters."

ve Dorut Kul murdered?"

st me, as if she's somewhere else.

ou want me on your Truth Commission? To
good? A hobbled torture survivor who wouldn't
ing things too closely? Why did you fuck me?
k these questions?"

ore answering, then simply repeats, with mon-
There are shades of truth and night."

des of Suli Nylioko, too, that do not bear too
ion. My will for it evaporates, like the mist

man on the other side of the crowd hoists his *golung* in the air
and then there are others. It seems exactly the right thing to
do in this mud, in this rain, with this music and the *supira* and
blood. Several women start laughing and calling because one
of the men has an erection. It looks like a penis gourd from an
old *National Geographic*, but no, it's the real thing, the women
laugh and point and the man is dancing, strutting. I turn to
look at Suli, to ask her, *Is this what your folks do at funerals?*
Where is she? We are all whirling and singing. I see her for a
moment and lose her, then she is right next to me, her face
filled with laughter. She bends to scoop up an armful of the
blood-mud and hoists it at me, splashes my chest. I do the same
to her, and then we're rolling in it, blood-mud in our hair and
faces, up and down our bodies. She pitches me onto my back
and I see her now as an animal. I am erect as that other man,
as all the men, and quick as any wildcat she pulls me inside her
and before I can breathe or think I stream so painfully I cry
out. She lurches off me, stays gasping on her hands and knees
when another man washed in blood-mud approaches her from
behind. I rise in a fury, throw him off, and then Suli turns on
me again and drives me on my backside, spitting and laughing,
the rain falling in torrents now so that I can hardly see what
other writhing bodies are doing.

What other bodies are doing doesn't matter. We kick and
spin, circle, swim, laugh and ache and reach for one another
again and again as the rain slashes and we are washed in tides
of mud and blood and longing for this life and the next and
the lives we've left behind.

25

At the community lagoon, not long after sunrise. A great flaming tree with red and orange blossoms overhangs murky brown water that smells of the rot of too much life. I feel it too, within my body, and it's not just the ache of overindulgence. I've spent too much of my life too soon, and what's left is tired and sore and brittle and badly used.

"You must turn your eyes away," she says as she wades into the pool and begins unwinding her *saftori*. It strikes me as the first really funny thing I've heard in a long while. "I'm not kidding," she says. "The villagers take this very seriously."

"After last night men and women can't bathe together?"

"That was different," she says. "Turn your eyes away."

A sleek grey snake lies quietly on one of the upper branches of the flaming tree. At first I think it's a vine, then I notice its flickering tongue. Not looking at us, not looking away.

"Last night was not entirely part of our world and is treated as something separate from the traditions and decorum of everyday life. Did you notice any *huloika*?"

"No."

Her thin brown body glistens in
straight, her throat and neck –

"Turn your head away!" Emp
were dancing above us. I could ju

This terrible sadness, a bitter
the devil, with a blood-soaked an
from me the last ounces of m
redemption, dignity, for this go

"Who are they?"

"The *huloika* don't always
knew them. They're someth
thought was Jono and my fa
me, to be together again afte
pened in a very long time fo

"Being with your father a

"Being with their *huloik*
lunatic." The sound of h
gently splashing and dripp

"I didn't see any *huloika*
get back on my meds." \
huloika. Not last night, b
must have floated over t

"We'll take the helico
can turn your head now

Her hair pulled back
light she looks fragile
sending out powerful
to embrace her, damn
the sadness I feel in
she'd reached out w
dominate, spoiled as
her, eyes down.

"I nee
were you
turbed ab
Silence
my own a
bling, stor
"You sa
"I said e
"It isn't.
wonder wha
"I took y
that we live
all a much s
now you've
part of you."

"Did you
Surely this is
"There are
"Did you a
"There are
close an inspec
Make you thir
"Did you ha
She looks p
"Why did y
make you look
be up to examin
So I wouldn't a
She waits bef
umental calm, "
There are sha
close an inspect

from this scummy lagoon, like any forward momentum this country ever generates. I turn to watch her step away, her head erect, body swaying slightly, looking now like a twelve-year-old village girl walking back from the community lagoon.

Fresh clothes, a brown batik shirt and light pants, my rubber thongs cleaned of all the mud and blood from yesterday. The villagers move slowly, as if the air has been made gelatin and gravity increased. The grounds are littered with chicken feathers, animal fur, soiled clothing, fly-infested remnants of food. My stomach is in disarray, my head held together by cellophane.

Suli Nylioko killed President Minitzh. The angel of non-violence, probably in concert with – why not the Kartouf? Why not? Anything is possible. She evades and distorts and so it's probably true. I haven't a lick of evidence – a film and transcript I couldn't understand and no longer possess, a dead body in my suite, a lover who will not deny any of it.

A lover.

Who sees spirits, stands in front of soldiers, calms thousands, makes me turn my head away. Who brings me back to life and turns it sour.

A lover.

Who'll probably have me killed. Why not? Death is so close here anyway. What's one less Truth Commissioner?

Lover.

The word turns over in my mind as we lift off in the presidential helicopter and the village becomes a spot of brown nearly lost in the monstrous green surrounding it. And the delicate silver terraces – from up above they're sheets of mica glinting in the sun, whole mountains' worth, art not food. If I were a god looking down I'd want to pluck the entire valley as a jewel.

A lover. Reanimating my body, but with a trick of mirrors, I wake up in the morning and my spirit's been sliced open. There were *huloika* all around me but I couldn't see them. All I've been able to see is dead bodies: heads in refrigerators, bodies wrapped in garbage bags, brains on my floor. I couldn't see the *huloika*. The other side. Where the mud and the blood meet, food and death and sex and rain, pouring rain, flowers and filth and the stink of it all. My battered body. I've been through everything, I think. There's nothing else that can be done to me. Kill me? That's nothing to fear. Not any more.

The lint now closing in on my brain. It's been days since I've had any medication, I've been through too many shocks. Is this why I feel so oddly detached, why my chest feels like it's being gripped in a vice? Why I can't hate myself for what I've done with Suli Nylioko? She and Sin Vello had Minitzh killed. Minitzh the dictator, Minitzh the bloody murdering tyrant. President for life – he wasn't going to leave any other way. So she had it done, and she put her own body between the tanks, filled us all with the hope and glory of peaceful revolution. And somewhere along the line a reporter got hold of a tape that would have shattered the dream completely. And he gave it to me, so he was sacrificed and left in my suite as a warning.

A Minitzh-style warning, from the Angel of Kalindas Boulevard, or else from the IS, which now serves her, or wants to discredit her, or both. Or maybe the IS wants to frame *me* for the murder. Anything's possible. The mud and blood are never too far away.

Now, from the clearest blue sky I've seen in my whole life, I look down on the island paradise. Where is all that rain? No sign of it today. Jungle and mountains, and we're close enough to the coast to see the beaches, mile after mile of winding white sand, and the water a thousand shades of blue and green. Such water! Tiny fishing boats, specks of white gull, a mile-long wave breaking on the shore, smoothing out then sucking back. Suli sits up front, near the pilot, spends the whole flight gazing out the window. She doesn't look at me but at the splendour below. Really, what is there to say? This is God's perfection, this tiny corner of this tiny world. A fridge full of heads? Microscopic. A couple of stray electrons in the giant scheme of things. We writhe in the mud and blood and are practically invisible.

It isn't a long flight. Far too soon, it seems, the capital comes into view, a cancerous brown smudge on the edge of perfection, the air so hazy, like a mistake, like Patrick trying to get rid of something from his page using a bad eraser. The closer we get to the ground the greater my feelings of disappointment. This inexorable tug back into the filth.

Coming in for the landing. I see a small fighter plane first out of the corner of my eye, a flash of silver whose wave of pressure bounces us like we're on a life raft in the wake of a much larger boat. Suli doesn't notice but turns her head to look at me finally – the lover again. There's no mistaking those eyes. Not just for last night. We've been lovers since her long day in the library in Kent. I see it now. She doesn't turn away. Doesn't regret a single thing she's done.

The plane flashes by again. It must be some sort of escort. I think to ask Suli if this is normal – it doesn't make sense with the ground so close – but the words don't make it from my throat. Suli is looking at me and then she isn't. There's a flash of light and heat and the helicopter disappears. For the longest moment I'm alone staring at the most extraordinary infinite blue. Soundless, my face pressed against it, I can't peer beyond but seem to get lost in it. It's clear and forever and I have the most wonderful feeling of being free of my body –

flying, finally, effortlessly, I've left behind my broken-down shell. . . . But it should last longer than this. An odd thought. Forever shouldn't pass nearly this quickly. Yet it changes like that, gets cold and dizzy. I turn back to look for the blue, but once it's gone it's gone, it turns into a sickening rush of darkness. If only I'd been able to stay on my meds, but I couldn't, it wasn't my fault, and now this pull is wrenching me back to my wretched body. . . .

I don't want anything to do with bodies. Not live ones, not dead ones, certainly not severed ones. I'm sitting in the centre seat in the hearing room at *Justico kampi* trying to make Sin Vello understand. But he isn't listening. He hasn't plugged in his headphones. He's whispering something to Mrs. Grakala but I can't make out what they're saying.

And then it smells awful, burning rubber and scorched plastic. Fumes so bad it's hard to breathe. What's happening? There's no hearing room any more, it's black smoke and this sudden silent, slow-motion confusion – trucks passing, people screaming but making no sound. "Don't touch me!" I yell to the wrinkled little man staring at me on the tarmac, but he can't hear, doesn't move. I'm looking now for before the hearing room, for the endless quiet blue, but it's gone, you can't get it back, it turns brown and black and smothered in smoke. Soldiers running everywhere, but slowly, as if they're all pushing through water. Helicopter wreckage twisted and steaming.

This silly wrinkled man stares at me then falls to his knees.

Suli Nylioko has been killed. I don't know how long it takes before the thought penetrates my addled head. They meant to kill us both, but instead they've just killed her and somehow I've walked away from a helicopter crash. Fire now, burning oil, the black smoke wiping out every trace of that infinite blue, water arcing from pumps and men in silvery spacesuits man on the other side of the crowd hoists his *golung* in the air and then there are others. It seems exactly the right thing to do in this mud, in this rain, with this music and the *supira* and blood. Several women start laughing and calling because one of the men has an erection. It looks like a penis gourd from an old *National Geographic*, but no, it's the real thing, the women laugh and point and the man is dancing, strutting. I turn to look at Suli, to ask her, *Is this what your folks do at funerals?* Where is she? We are all whirling and singing. I see her for a moment and lose her, then she is right next to me, her face filled with laughter. She bends to scoop up an armful of the blood-mud and hoists it at me, splashes my chest. I do the same to her, and then we're rolling in it, blood-mud in our hair and faces, up and down our bodies. She pitches me onto my back and I see her now as an animal. I am erect as that other man, as all the men, and quick as any wildcat she pulls me inside her and before I can breathe or think I stream so painfully I cry out. She lurches off me, stays gasping on her hands and knees when another man washed in blood-mud approaches her from behind. I rise in a fury, throw him off, and then Suli turns on me again and drives me on my backside, spitting and laughing, the rain falling in torrents now so that I can hardly see what other writhing bodies are doing.

What other bodies are doing doesn't matter. We kick and spin, circle, swim, laugh and ache and reach for one another again and again as the rain slashes and we are washed in tides of mud and blood and longing for this life and the next and the lives we've left behind.

25

At the community lagoon, not long after sunrise. A great flaming tree with red and orange blossoms overhangs murky brown water that smells of the rot of too much life. I feel it too, within my body, and it's not just the ache of overindulgence. I've spent too much of my life too soon, and what's left is tired and sore and brittle and badly used.

"You must turn your eyes away," she says as she wades into the pool and begins unwinding her *saftori*. It strikes me as the first really funny thing I've heard in a long while. "I'm not kidding," she says. "The villagers take this very seriously."

"After last night men and women can't bathe together?"

"That was different," she says. "Turn your eyes away."

A sleek grey snake lies quietly on one of the upper branches of the flaming tree. At first I think it's a vine, then I notice its flickering tongue. Not looking at us, not looking away.

"Last night was not entirely part of our world and is treated as something separate from the traditions and decorum of everyday life. Did you notice any *huloika*?"

"No."

Her thin brown body glistens in the water, her shoulders so straight, her throat and neck –

"Turn your head away!" Emphatic. Then calmer: "They were dancing above us. I could just catch sight of a few."

This terrible sadness, a bitter fatigue. I've laid down with the devil, with a blood-soaked angel, and it's as if she has pulled from me the last ounces of my hope. Hope for what? For redemption, dignity, for this godforsaken country.

"Who are they?"

"The *huloika* don't always connect to people exactly as we knew them. They're something like amalgamations. One I thought was Jono and my father. They were so happy to see me, to be together again after so many years. That hasn't happened in a very long time for me."

"Being with your father and husband?"

"Being with their *huloika*. I'm sorry, you must think me a lunatic." The sound of her light steps approaching, water gently splashing and dripping.

"I didn't see any *huloika*," I say. "But I'll *be* one soon if I don't get back on my meds." What I don't say is this: I was part *huloika*. Not last night, but in captivity. I was so near death I must have floated over the line sometimes.

"We'll take the helicopter back to the capital in an hour. You can turn your head now. The water is yours."

Her hair pulled back and sleek, face fresh but tired, in this light she looks fragile, losing the battle with age. She's also sending out powerful female waves of longing – she wants me to embrace her, damn whatever the villagers might say, damn the sadness I feel in my bones. Her pull is as powerful as if she'd reached out with her hand. It's a selfishness, a need to dominate, spoiled as everything else this morning. I walk past her, eyes down.

"I need to know about Dorut Kul. Why was he killed? What were you discussing with Sin Vello in that video he was so disturbed about?"

Silence. I step into the water, let the filthy *golung* fall from my own aching, aging body. Limbs back to their familiar trembling, stomach in its usual roiling state.

"You said you were going to explain everything."

"I said everything will become clear."

"It isn't." Immersing myself in the water, sickly warm. I wonder what diseases are lurking here, what leeches and snakes.

"I took you to the *onjupta* ceremony so that you would know that we live very close to life and death here, to the *huloika*. It's all a much stronger part of our reality than it is for you. But now you've seen some of it. You've been part of it. And it is part of you."

"Did you conspire to murder General Minitzh?" I ask. Surely this is why Dorut Kul had to be killed.

"There are enemies massing against us from every corner."

"Did you and Sin Vello plot to kill the president?"

"There are shades of truth and night that do not bear too close an inspection," she says. "They wipe out everything else. Make you think nothing else matters."

"Did you have Dorut Kul murdered?"

She looks past me, as if she's somewhere else.

"Why did you want me on your Truth Commission? To make you look good? A hobbled torture survivor who wouldn't be up to examining things too closely? Why did you fuck me? So I wouldn't ask these questions?"

She waits before answering, then simply repeats, with monumental calm, "There are shades of truth and night."

There are shades of Suli Nylioko, too, that do not bear too close an inspection. My will for it evaporates, like the mist from this scummy lagoon, like any forward momentum this country ever generates. I turn to watch her step away, her head erect, body swaying slightly, looking now like a twelve-year-old village girl walking back from the community lagoon.

Fresh clothes, a brown batik shirt and light pants, my rubber thongs cleaned of all the mud and blood from yesterday. The villagers move slowly, as if the air has been made gelatin and gravity increased. The grounds are littered with chicken feathers, animal fur, soiled clothing, fly-infested remnants of food. My stomach is in disarray, my head held together by cellophane.

Suli Nylioko killed President Minitzh. The angel of non-violence, probably in concert with – why not the Kartouf? Why not? Anything is possible. She evades and distorts and so it's probably true. I haven't a lick of evidence – a film and transcript I couldn't understand and no longer possess, a dead body in my suite, a lover who will not deny any of it.

A lover.

Who sees spirits, stands in front of soldiers, calms thousands, makes me turn my head away. Who brings me back to life and turns it sour.

A lover.

Who'll probably have me killed. Why not? Death is so close here anyway. What's one less Truth Commissioner?

Lover.

The word turns over in my mind as we lift off in the presidential helicopter and the village becomes a spot of brown nearly lost in the monstrous green surrounding it. And the delicate silver terraces – from up above they're sheets of mica glinting in the sun, whole mountains' worth, art not food. If I were a god looking down I'd want to pluck the entire valley as a jewel.

A lover. Reanimating my body, but with a trick of mirrors, I wake up in the morning and my spirit's been sliced open. There were *huloika* all around me but I couldn't see them. All I've been able to see is dead bodies: heads in refrigerators, bodies wrapped in garbage bags, brains on my floor. I couldn't see the *huloika*. The other side. Where the mud and the blood meet, food and death and sex and rain, pouring rain, flowers and filth and the stink of it all. My battered body. I've been through everything, I think. There's nothing else that can be done to me. Kill me? That's nothing to fear. Not any more.

The lint now closing in on my brain. It's been days since I've had any medication, I've been through too many shocks. Is this why I feel so oddly detached, why my chest feels like it's being gripped in a vice? Why I can't hate myself for what I've done with Suli Nylioko? She and Sin Vello had Minitzh killed. Minitzh the dictator, Minitzh the bloody murdering tyrant. President for life – he wasn't going to leave any other way. So she had it done, and she put her own body between the tanks, filled us all with the hope and glory of peaceful revolution. And somewhere along the line a reporter got hold of a tape that would have shattered the dream completely. And he gave it to me, so he was sacrificed and left in my suite as a warning.

A Minitzh-style warning, from the Angel of Kalindas Boulevard, or else from the IS, which now serves her, or wants to discredit her, or both. Or maybe the IS wants to frame *me* for the murder. Anything's possible. The mud and blood are never too far away.

Now, from the clearest blue sky I've seen in my whole life, I look down on the island paradise. Where is all that rain? No sign of it today. Jungle and mountains, and we're close enough to the coast to see the beaches, mile after mile of winding white sand, and the water a thousand shades of blue and green. Such water! Tiny fishing boats, specks of white gull, a mile-long wave breaking on the shore, smoothing out then sucking back. Suli sits up front, near the pilot, spends the whole flight gazing out the window. She doesn't look at me but at the splendour below. Really, what is there to say? This is God's perfection, this tiny corner of this tiny world. A fridge full of heads? Microscopic. A couple of stray electrons in the giant scheme of things. We writhe in the mud and blood and are practically invisible.

It isn't a long flight. Far too soon, it seems, the capital comes into view, a cancerous brown smudge on the edge of perfection, the air so hazy, like a mistake, like Patrick trying to get rid of something from his page using a bad eraser. The closer we get to the ground the greater my feelings of disappointment. This inexorable tug back into the filth.

Coming in for the landing. I see a small fighter plane first out of the corner of my eye, a flash of silver whose wave of pressure bounces us like we're on a life raft in the wake of a much larger boat. Suli doesn't notice but turns her head to look at me finally – the lover again. There's no mistaking those eyes. Not just for last night. We've been lovers since her long day in the library in Kent. I see it now. She doesn't turn away. Doesn't regret a single thing she's done.

The plane flashes by again. It must be some sort of escort. I think to ask Suli if this is normal – it doesn't make sense with the ground so close – but the words don't make it from my throat. Suli is looking at me and then she isn't. There's a flash of light and heat and the helicopter disappears. For the longest moment I'm alone staring at the most extraordinary infinite blue. Soundless, my face pressed against it, I can't peer beyond but seem to get lost in it. It's clear and forever and I have the most wonderful feeling of being free of my body –

flying, finally, effortlessly, I've left behind my broken-down shell. . . . But it should last longer than this. An odd thought. Forever shouldn't pass nearly this quickly. Yet it changes like that, gets cold and dizzy. I turn back to look for the blue, but once it's gone it's gone, it turns into a sickening rush of darkness. If only I'd been able to stay on my meds, but I couldn't, it wasn't my fault, and now this pull is wrenching me back to my wretched body. . . .

I don't want anything to do with bodies. Not live ones, not dead ones, certainly not severed ones. I'm sitting in the centre seat in the hearing room at *Justico kampi* trying to make Sin Vello understand. But he isn't listening. He hasn't plugged in his headphones. He's whispering something to Mrs. Grakala but I can't make out what they're saying.

And then it smells awful, burning rubber and scorched plastic. Fumes so bad it's hard to breathe. What's happening? There's no hearing room any more, it's black smoke and this sudden silent, slow-motion confusion – trucks passing, people screaming but making no sound. "Don't touch me!" I yell to the wrinkled little man staring at me on the tarmac, but he can't hear, doesn't move. I'm looking now for before the hearing room, for the endless quiet blue, but it's gone, you can't get it back, it turns brown and black and smothered in smoke. Soldiers running everywhere, but slowly, as if they're all pushing through water. Helicopter wreckage twisted and steaming.

This silly wrinkled man stares at me then falls to his knees.

Suli Nylioko has been killed. I don't know how long it takes before the thought penetrates my addled head. They meant to kill us both, but instead they've just killed her and somehow I've walked away from a helicopter crash. Fire now, burning oil, the black smoke wiping out every trace of that infinite blue, water arcing from pumps and men in silvery spacesuits with heavy masks, this little man on his knees, he won't get up. Soldiers scrambling, but slowly somehow, guns at the ready. Someone's going to shoot me. I stand here waiting. I saw it all. The plane that shot us out of the sky. Suli murdered. I was supposed to be too. So it really is my time. It really is.

Yet except for this one man everyone ignores me. This is the strange part. It's as if I'm invisible, have become a *huloika*, only he can see me. I stand for the longest time waiting to be shot, to be run over by the emergency vehicles. But nothing happens. The man gets off his knees and pulls me off the tarmac, towards the airport buildings. The ground jolts beneath my feet, my limbs tremble now worse than ever.

There's burnt skin hanging off my arm. Like I'd held it in a fire. Cooking meat. That's me I smell.

It's happening right now – the chaos, the sudden speed, my God, it's as if the panic button has been hit and what was dead slow before is now a rip of wind and noise. Too much to take in. A blur of racing trucks and soldiers, sirens screeching – too loud and fast, the ground shaking with commotion. The smoky air scratching at my throat and lungs as if I'm trying to breathe in too much.

This whole country is about to tear itself apart. The ring has been pulled and this is the detonation.

Suli Nylioko is dead. And I'm lurching through the airport where Jono was killed and Suli looked up to see that sign. What was it? The moment I think the thought I glance up to see the sign: *Teriala kojinda Minizhi lundafilo.* "The Minitzh airport wishes safe journeys." Did Suli know it was still here?

Word is just getting around. Passengers are becoming alarmed, soldiers run this way and that. Alarms are sounding. It happened just minutes ago. Not everyone knows. Someone asks, in English, very clearly, "What's going on?" The beautiful girls behind the ticket counter have deathly white faces, their make-up seems to harden and crack at the news. The men in their customs uniforms don't know what to do. I pass straight by them. They don't see me. It's as if I'm a *huloika*, but I'm not. I feel the pain in my arm, the trembling in my limbs, this odd sense of distance. If I had my meds, I think, I'd be all here and terrified like any normal person.

I walk around the metal detector and no one notices. Wailing sirens, shots now, people diving for cover. The chaos has started. This whole country is heading for a meltdown. Suli Nylioko is dead. The angel of Santa Irene. The murdering bloody angel.

If I run the spell will be broken, someone will notice me, I won't be invisible any more. I feel this clearly and yet must hurry too, so I walk faster. No time to think, to try to read signs, to reason it out. I just have to know where to go. This way not that. Down here. No ticket-taker at the post. The velvet rope just dangling. Which way? Down here. Everything a blur around me, but if I just walk then the time will stay slow. Like face to face with that blue. That kind of slow. Infinite, calm. Step after step. Down the little corridor. This way to the plane. Some people ahead of me. But if I run I won't make it.

The door closes. If I say a word the spell will be broken. I'll never make it. If I run . . .

The door opens again. I reach my hand in, squeeze through. Someone pulls and the floor immediately begins to move. Everything jumbled. Passengers cowering on the floor, others glued to windows, overhead compartments open, staff in a panic. I lurch down the aisle, the plane already lumbering along the runway. Soldiers, smoke, military vehicles. Burning wreckage. I collapse into a seat, any seat, and the plane gathers speed . . . too slowly. It won't make it. Not like this. Slow motion. I wait for the explosion. We're going to be shot down. I was just in a helicopter that was shot down. It's going to happen again. They can't let me leave. I know too much. I'm a Truth Commissioner and I know too much.

Lifting, people loose in the aisles, bodies slam into seat backs, into each other, suitcases fly open, pants and shorts and someone's panties whip past. . . .

Climbing, climbing, into that blue, there it is again just outside the window. The infinite blue. Who knows where we're going? Anywhere away. The last commercial plane out of Santa Irene before it descends into hell.

I was shot out of the air and walked away, I think, as the plane levels, the bodies stop slamming, the luggage comes to rest wherever it comes to rest. *I've been shot out of the air but by some miracle allowed to walk away.*

"You're bleeding," a woman says beside me. An Australian accent. Her face large and red, breath coming in great gasps. We've all just escaped the jaws of the beast. "Let me wrap it," she says.

"No." God knows what I look like. Her eyes so large, lips quivering.

"But you're bleeding!"

Of course I want it wrapped. I give her my arm. She tears some fabric from a runaway shirt and starts to wind it around my arm, which hurts now tremendously, I can't believe how much.

"*No*," I say again, because of the pain. But what I mean is this: I'm even now, back to zero. I've known the claws of hell and the kiss of grace, and they both hurt more than I could imagine.

We put down in Darwin, Australia, in the middle of a violent storm – harsh winds, lightning, slashing rain. On the approach I watch the ocean roiling purple and grey, pounding the white beaches of the town, with the dark green tropical trees leaning precariously, branches blown back. I clutch the armrests, ready for another cataclysm, but the touchdown is surprisingly light and sure. The flight's original destination was Sydney, but we left Santa Irene with only a partial load of fuel and now this storm has forced us to land.

Emergency vehicles flash their lights in the darkness of this strange afternoon: an ironic cavalry of ambulances and fire trucks now that we're out of the worst danger. The injured are taken off first: a woman in a torn blue dress has broken her leg; a young boy is strapped in a neck brace; an old man, his glasses twisted but still on his head, holds his chest and can't seem to stop crying.

A little girl in a seat behind me says to her father for the seventh time, "I saw a body in the grass. There was blood on his face. I saw it."

I'm in pretty good shape, considering. I have to sit straight to calm the pain in my chest, and my shaking is worse than usual. A paramedic looks at my bloodied clothes and bandaged arm. "We'll take you to the hospital, sir," he says, but I tell him no, there are others worse than me. "It's all right, there's plenty of room." His Australian accent – *aw ride, plinty a' rume.*

"No. No, I'm fine," I tell him.

"You look like you've been through a hurricane!" he says, insisting, so I go with him. They want me to sit in a wheel-chair but I refuse.

A forlorn, drenched stewardess stands on the tarmac in a meagre plastic rain suit handing out black umbrellas for the short walk to the main building. I take hold of one but as I open it the wind wrenches it from my grasp and sends it pitching and rolling. The stewardess laughs suddenly and starts to hand me another but I wave her off.

"I'm soaked anyway."

It's only mid-afternoon but the dark sky makes it feel like nighttime. Inside the main building the paramedic says we'll head for the hospital as soon as I've picked up my bags and passed through customs. I tell him I have nothing – no luggage, no papers, no money, no identity or credit cards.

"How did you get on the plane?" he asks – *git on the pline* – and I tell him, "Just lucky." I didn't think about it. I was half *huloika*. My feet knew where to go.

He shakes his head and grins, this strong young man with the bushy eyebrows turned blond from the sun. Groups of travellers talk excitedly of the mad scene, the escape. A television suspended from the ceiling features a cricket match until someone changes channels and scenes of military Jeeps, of fires and looters appear. A female announcer's voice is saying something about renewed rioting in Welanto, but it's the headline in white print at the bottom of the screen that alarms me. SANTA IRENIAN PRESIDENT SULI NYLIOKO DIES IN CRASH . . . CAUSE UNCONFIRMED . . . ALSO AMONG THE DEAD CANADIAN HUMAN RIGHTS ACTIVIST BILL BURRIDGE.

"I have to get to the phone," I tell the paramedic. He tells me I can call from the hospital, but I say no, now, I need to get to a phone. "My family thinks I'm dead." So he points me to a pay phone on the wall beside the washrooms.

"I don't have any money," I repeat and he grins again, like I've just told him a joke.

"That's all right," he says. Then he puts his hand in his pocket, fishes out some money, and asks me where I'm calling.

"Canada," I say.

I walk over to the phone, deposit a kangaroo dollar, then dial the operator, give her my parents' number, and ask her to reverse the charges. The wind is driving the rain against the windows just a few feet away. It's the middle of the night in Ottawa, I think; at least they'll be in. The phone rings a dozen times and then a man's voice comes on, gruff, drunk with sleep.

"*Collict call from Bill in Darwin, 'stralia. Will you accipt the charges?*"

"Huh?" the voice says. It's Dad, he won't understand.

"Hi, it's Bill," I say.

"*Do you accept the charges?*" the operator asks again.

"Bill! Yeah, sure!"

"Dad," I say, surprised at how much better he sounds. He was so disoriented that last time I spoke to him. "How are you? You won't believe what's happened."

"Bill, it's Graham," my brother says.

"What? Did I call Calgary instead?"

"No, I'm here," he says, meaning Ottawa. "Listen, we've been trying to get in touch with you."

They haven't heard, thank God. No one has called them with the false news.

"I'm sorry, Graham, I'm going to need you to send me some money and to help me out. There's a toll-free line for Canadian consular services, maybe you could look it up for me. It's a long story, but I've left Santa Irene, and I've got nothing here, not even my own clothes. I need you to call Maryse and Derrick at my office, tell them I'm okay." I'll call Joanne myself, I think.

"Bill," Graham says, "I'm trying to tell you something."

"I just got out. I don't know how, it was blind luck, but it's chaos back in Santa Irene. The president has been assassinated. You might get a call from somebody saying –"

"Bill, Dad's dead. He fell down the stairs last night, that's why I'm here. Mom's pretty bad. How soon do you think you can get here?"

Just raging against the window. I lose my breath for a moment, have to lean against the wall. I look up and see the paramedic walking towards me, this young strong man, his grin unshakeable, like he can take on the world no matter what's thrown at him.

26

We leave the house at ten-thirty in a driving, biting wind, the ground covered with a full foot of snow, the steel-grey sky promising more. December in Ottawa. It's a shocking contrast to the heat and humidity of Darwin and Santa Irene, makes the body shudder and revolt from going outside. Graham has put on weight, doesn't fit very well in his flannel pants. His daughter, Leah, is out of diapers now, has changed so much I didn't recognize her. She nestles at her mother Alice's shoulder, the two twinned in dark outfits with their long straight black hair tied back with red ribbons. My mother is in shock. I watch her leave the house and lean into the bitter Ottawa wind, step nervously down the walkway as if holding a too-full cup of just-boiled coffee.

The doctor in Darwin put me back on medication, and Karen Wong, an old friend from Foreign Affairs now stationed in Canberra, moved heaven and earth to get me here in two days. But I'm still dizzy from the rush of travel, from this saddening news, from the frustration of not being able to talk to

Joanne. I don't know when I'll see her. I left a message on her parents' machine in Toronto.

And here are the reporters. They've been camped out here since six this morning, stand in frozen clots praying to large Styrofoam cups of coffee. The weather has taken all their sting – they lob their questions listlessly, *pro forma*, betray no interest at all in what I might reply.

"Mr. Burridge, do you buy the engine-failure story, or do you think Suli Nylioko was murdered by the military?"

"Was the Truth Commission anywhere near issuing a report or reaching any conclusions?"

"Do you feel that Mrs. Grakala is simply a figurehead appointed by the military or did she engineer a coup against Suli?"

This is the stunning latest development: the military has appointed Mrs. Grakala as interim leader. I hardly know what to say – it's all shadows and blood games. I know now that I've never had a good sense of the reasons or the rules.

"No comment," I say. "On this day, especially, please leave us in peace."

Graham asks my mother if she wants to sit in the front or the back. She hesitates, looks at me in confusion. I open the back door for her and she gets in creakily, fusses with her dress and jacket, then announces that she's forgotten her purse.

"I don't think you'll need it," Graham says. Wrong answer. I say that I'll go get it, but this too is wrong.

"I'll get it! For God's sake, what's wrong with you people?" Mom says. Fussing, clambering, fighting her way out of the car. "Look! You were going to let me leave without locking the house!"

She goes back in alone. We wait, shuffle our feet in the hard wind while the reporters watch us uncertainly, wishing we'd leave so they can too. My gloves and coat are too thin for this cold and my arm still aches from the crash. There's nothing to do but wait until she finds her purse and walks back out, determined to do it alone, to face what has to be faced.

Silence on the drive. The heater coats us too soon with thick, hot, dry air, and I start to cough, a deep rattle, the worst I've had since my release.

My release. When was that exactly? I can't remember being released. I'm nowhere near released now. Bloody useless words. We waste little time on them during the ride. I accept a cough drop from Alice then sit in rigid silence, concentrate on defeating this cough.

The streets, sky, grass, buildings, clouds, faces all so grey, passing like a grainy picture from the 1930s. A young man sits on the sidewalk with his sweater pulled round his shoulders, his head slumped forward, baseball cap turned up in his hand. A woman walks past him, nearly steps on his sneaker, ignores his request. Leah sings herself a song from daycare, something about a caterpillar and a garden hose. Her voice so small.

"There's parking in behind," my mother says finally.

"I'm going to park here, Mom," Graham says, and steers the car into a vacant spot across the street from the church.

"But there's parking in behind."

"This is perfect, Mom." He shuts off the engine.

"It's not perfect. You have to pay the meter. There's free parking in behind!"

"I don't mind paying the meter, Mom."

"Don't be stupid! They said there was free parking in behind!"

"Graham," Alice says, in an unsubtle tone, and without

another word he starts the engine again, then steers us back into traffic.

"It's one way," he says in a minute. "I can't get there from here."

"You'll have to go around the block, dear," Alice says.

We stop at a traffic light, then encounter construction.

"Oh, for God's sake, we're going to be late!" Graham says.

"Then park in the old spot!" Mom says. "*Just make up your mind!*"

"I *did* make up my mind! And I *can't* turn around . . ."

Slowly traffic clears. I think of saying something about Santa Irenian gridlock but the words don't come out. I'd rather not think about it. When we get around the block we find the church parking lot is full, then when we swing past the first parking spot, it's taken as well.

"You let us out here, Graham," Alice says. Superb control in her voice – in command whatever the contingency. "We're going to be late."

"Be *careful* getting out," Graham says. "Alice, watch the child, for God's sake!"

"I *am* watching the child, and the child has a name."

Slowly, a sad parade across the street. My mother so old-looking. I take her arm and she leans on me. Leah runs ahead and pulls on the heavy door but of course needs Alice to help her open it. Then into the darkness, the smell of old polish and wet carpet. This place of refuge and silence.

"I think the minister asked us to wait with him in his chambers, Mom," I say.

"It's too late. It's time to start."

"It doesn't matter."

"Funerals start on time," she snaps. "You can be late for anything else."

Tired steps up the aisle. A smaller crowd than I expected. Could be the weather? The short notice?

White hair, a tall straight man with tired eyes, looking with such sadness at my mother and me. Whispers, nods of recognition. People who knew Dad, people I don't know, who've been shoved out of my brain by other events. A lady in a dark purple dress with a black coat and fine papery skin, powdered, deflated. A young man in enormously baggy black pants with an awkward haircut and a ring in his lip, his tie crooked, worn under protest. A woman stands suddenly when she sees us, puts her hand on her boy's shoulder for support – exactly the same sort of gesture that Luki would have used and so I think for a moment that she must be pregnant although nothing is showing.

And I see Luki in my mind sheltering with her family, waiting for this latest madness to pass.

Maryse at the front with Patrick. Patrick? Taller yet again, strangely mature in his blue jacket and tie, in this wrap of sadness. His eyes find mine and there's no leap – a hint of recognition, but no welcome there. It's unspoken but devastating. I realize it right away – I stayed away too long. The slight chance I had in the summer is now frozen shut.

All my words feel locked away in a cold cellar, huddled, inconsequential. I go to hug Maryse and she takes a step back, nearly trips in the pew. She's trapped and so we embrace, and I hold her too long, feel her squirm for release. Release! There is none. As soon as I think it I start to sob. Stupidly, for no reason, I unleash upon her a flood of choking, inappropriate tears. I can feel her, she doesn't want to hold me, doesn't know what to do. No one knows, least of all me. I try to let her go but the tears increase. I can hardly breathe; it's as if I'm underwater. She pushes me, gently, but a push still, so I have to straighten up. I hate this! Everyone looking. Through a blur I see Patrick staying back. He'll have none of it and so I don't try. My hand brushes his shoulder and he ducks his head almost as if I'm going to hit him. We shuffle into the front pew, Mom kneels immediately and so I do too, still crying, reeling from the awkwardness.

The organ music, the deep brown pews, solid; the arches and the red carpet and the gleaming candle holders, the blues and reds of the stained glass. Christ and his sheep. My father's unknown friends. His unknown life. I dry my eyes, breathe, breathe, regain some sort of composure. The minister comes out in his white robe with the black trim and the large golden cross, and I think of carrying that body, how heavy it was, how it stank in the streets of Welanto. Streets! Passages. That policeman in his nightshirt. The page of notes I had Luki copy out. For the record.

For nothing.

Riots spreading everywhere, the police back to their raping and pillaging, Welanto in flames again. But there's no second Suli Nylioko. It's Mrs. Grakala propelled from behind like some Mao-puppet. It's about power and death and I don't understand it. After everything I've been through. I talked in the darkness with the woman so much of the world is intent on making into a saint. She told me she was praying to the wrong God. That the Old Testament God could have given her husband a few more steps and he would've been all right, they would've made a new life. She told me this and then she took away the few steps from other men. I don't know this for a fact. I just believe it. Sometimes saints are dripping in blood. And sometimes they can still be good people.

The organ music changes, all of us stand. I feel it first in my body before my mind knows anything. *No*, I think. *Not this one.* I have the order of service right in my hand. I should've known it was coming. But once again I'm taken by surprise. Graham arrives at my side, out of breath, still annoyed.

> *Abide with me; fast falls the eventide;*
> *The darkness deepens; Lord with me abide.*
> *When other helpers fail and comforts flee,*
> *Help of the helpless, O abide with me.*

My throat catches mid-sob and I can't stand it. Mom leans against me and so does Graham. My shoulders jerk, breath comes in short clutches. *Help of the helpless.* It's too much. Five verses, on and on, music too strong. Not what I wanted. I wanted to stay frozen. It's too much.

Then we all sit and Graham goes forward. It's too much. I lasted through blood and mud and rain, chickens and goats, *huloika* dancing above us, bodies writhing, all of us soaked and washed in it. But not this.

Don't take my father from me.

Graham's voice is shaky, but it still works. "The Lord is my shepherd," he reads; "I shall not want." My tears streaming. *I shall not want.* It's all I do, want and want and want. For peace, for life, for sleep and rest. These heartbreaking words. I can't withstand them, am a slobbering mess. I fight, but there's nothing I can do. "Yea, though I walk through the valley of the shadow of death . . ."

The valley of the shadow. Stop it. It isn't fair.

"I will fear no evil: for thou art with me; thy rod and thy staff they comfort me . . ."

More hymns and prayers but the damage is done, and now I'm supposed to speak. Brought down to this. Breathe and breathe and breathe. The softness of the carpet. *The valley of the shadow.* I know it. If anything, I know it. It's nothing to fear. But this –

I can't look at anyone. Now I'm supposed to account for it all. Now I'm supposed to –

"I don't remember my father," I say. It isn't my voice. It's some croaking, beat-up imitation. But we're all here and something has to come out.

"I didn't know him very well. Many of you . . . knew him better than me. I look at my son and I think of him stepping up here at my funeral, whenever it's going to be –"

I lose my thread.

Breathe and breathe. Something of my voice comes back.

"I'm sorry. I tried to write out a speech."

I take another moment, breathe, compose myself.

"He worked so hard," I say. "He took himself off every morning to a government job that he stopped believing in decades before his retirement. But he kept on with it. Until he got sick. He kept on."

I pause again. All their eyes are on me.

"There was one time, I remember, it was Christmas when we were very young. Graham and I were fooling around with the paper dessert hats. I took mine and stuck it around one of the candles. Then Graham did his, and it burst into flames, just like that. The whole table could've gone up. But my father took the fire in his hands. He had such big hands. He moved in an instant, clapped them together and the fire disappeared. Just like that."

I see it now, bright as anything, as if it's all happening again.

"That's what I always wanted to be able to do for my family," I say. "I wanted to be able to take the fire in my hands and make it go away."

I try to continue, but there's no more air. As I raise my eyes I swear I see him in the second row, looking at me as if he'd like to take me out back and tan my hide for making such a spectacle. I blink and it's him, blink again and it isn't. He becomes some other old guy in a blue suit with hands that can't stay still.

The minister puts his hand on my shoulder and I step down. Silence.

On with the rest of the service. There are hymns, the minister intones his familiar words. I breathe and breathe. Graham examines his knuckles; Mom is holding herself very still, trying to be composed; Alice keeps Leah close to her, whispers in her ear from time to time.

Filing out. The family first. All those grey faces.

We stop at the doors and unbearably Mom decides she wants to greet everyone, tell them about the reception at the golf course, even though the minister announced it.

Worn faces, knobby hands. Dad wasn't as old as many of these people. They don't look at me. Thankfully. Kind words for my mother, it's what she needs, what we all needed – kind words, soft tones, gentle reminiscences. I should've talked about his silly jokes, his tirades at the news, the way he loved my mother. I see them now in the morning standing in the kitchen just looking at one another, a thousand miles from the rest of the world.

"Bill, this is Liam. Liam, I'd like you to meet Bill." I look up to see Liam blocking half the hall. Liam with square shoulders, too manly a grip, his left hand pressing on my sore arm. I barely squirm free. Liam with the hulking diamond ring set in gold.

"I'm sorry for your loss," he says, right out of a television show. Liam, who looks like he owns a car dealership. Who has his hand on my boy's shoulder and stands too close to my wife. Maryse looks at me all shot through with the emotion of this moment, and so I know. We won't talk about it now because it is now, the day of my father's funeral, standing at the gates of hell, greeting the mourners. We'll save it for later, but at least I know.

Liam, who looks big enough to wrap all the way round the both of them and protect them. How did I miss him before? I must've walked right by him.

"I understand your pain," the minister says to me. An older man with a heavy head and eyes too clear, it's hard to look away. He understands my pain. I don't understand it at all but somehow he does and now he's told me.

I step into the grey wind. There's the reception at the golf course but I can't go now. I can't stand with a glass of wine and a napkin and oyster-cheese spread on crackers making conversation. I can plead illness or I can just walk, head down, wherever. I choose the latter. Someone will figure out I'm missing, but it doesn't matter. Graham is there and Alice will tell him what to do and my mother will obsess over the cold cuts and –

"Bill!"

– and people will try to drag me into this morbid after-death party when the man is gone, his brain died a long time ago. Maybe he's with the *huloika*. Maybe he's with Suli Nylioko, the saint of non-violence, in the blood and the mud and the rain of the valley of the shadow of –

"Bill!"

I turn, startled. "You got your hair cut," I say.

"Yes."

She looks utterly different, like her pictures from Africa, and immediately I know. I know and I liked it better when I didn't figure things out so quickly.

"You're going somewhere," I say.

"Wait."

"That's why you got your hair cut. You're going away!"

"I'm so sorry about your father," she says.

"And your mother. Did she –?"

"Not long after I got back. I tried to call you –"

"And I tried –"

She stands a few feet back from me so I know. I know about Liam and Maryse, and now I know that Joanne's going to fling herself back into some famine or other.

"Derrick's frantic," she says, this funny shorthand. I know already what she's going to say and she knows what's coming from me.

"He's been great," I say. "He's setting up a meeting at the bank this afternoon. I've been a lousy manager but we'll keep it together. There's so much more to do. Don't go back to Africa."

"Honduras, actually," she says. "It's only for two months. Hurricane Mitch."

"Don't go for two hours. Stay with me."

This cold wind. Graham now walking towards me, pissed off because he's supposed to drive us all to the reception at the golf course and what the fuck am I doing?

"I'm afraid I'm committed. It's only –"

"Don't go. You cut your hair, that's okay, I'll forgive you. But don't go. You'll get cerebral malaria. Your plane will crash. You'll catch cholera, locusts will descend. *Don't go!* Scorpions, rattlers, killer bees, bandits, looters."

"Bill!"

Two of them at the same time: Graham stopped at the red light yelling at me to come along; Joanne shaking her head at me.

"I'm telling you – nothing hangs together. The plagues of antiquity rise up. The vessel crumbles, the centre will not hold –"

"Bill, just shut up!"

"I can't! If I keep talking then maybe you won't go."

Graham gets to us, asks me, livid, what's going on.

"I'm not going to the golf course," I say. "And *she's* not going to Honduras!"

He looks at Joanne and I realize they haven't met. The moment passes when I should introduce them, but I don't.

"You're not going to the golf course?" he asks finally.

"No. I don't believe in it."

"You don't believe in what?"

"Golf courses!"

"You're fucking nuts!"

"Yes. I am!" Two brothers yelling in the grey wind. My mother now walking towards us. It's just going to get worse.

"You have to go to the golf course," he says, as if it's written on a stone tablet.

"I don't and I won't."

"What's going on?" my mother yells from across the street.

"I'm not going to the golf course unless she agrees not to go to Honduras."

"This is ridiculous!" Joanne says.

"I didn't walk away from a helicopter crash to have my father die and my wife and son taken by a used-car salesman and have you go to Honduras. I didn't and I won't."

"It's all right. Calm down."

"It's not all right and I won't calm down and you're not going to Honduras."

"You cut your hair," Mom says to Joanne. Beside us now. Brilliant.

"I have to get my way sometime," I say.

"Why can't we just go to the golf course?" Graham asks.

"*Because I have to get my way sometime!*" I yell, and if I say it long enough, if I repeat myself and stamp my feet and ignore that cold grey wind and *will not give in* then the lady will stay.

The lady will stay and it's the only thing left that will make a difference.

"Why don't we all go to the golf course?" my mother says.

Strangers now stop to look at this clump of family arguing on the street.

"*It isn't what I want!*" I say, like a two-year-old raging at the universe.

"What golf course is that?" some stranger asks, stupidly.

"What *do* you want?" Graham asks.

I have to think about this. I'm not in the mood, but it seems inescapable. "I want what I've always wanted," I say. "I want to be part of making things better. And I want Joanne to stay here with me and be part of it too and not go to Honduras."

"It's only two months," Joanne says lamely.

"I'm not a wreck any more!" I say, and see immediately how pathetic I look in their eyes. But I'm too far gone. "And I love you!" I say. "And you told me you love me too!"

"Bill –"

"*Don't really know what I think about that.* You wrote it."

"She did?" my mother says.

"You run away," I say. "It's what you do, remember? Well, don't do it this time!" I'm out of control, saying anything. Stop it, I think.

"We don't have to decide right now out in the street," Joanne says.

"Yes, we do! We have to put the universe in order right now!" I scream it to grey Ottawa, where such things are never done in public. The universe is never put in order in the street in the cold wind during working hours.

"For God's sake, let's go to the golf course," Graham says, shaking his head. "Everybody's waiting."

And like that my tirade drains away, victim of the most sensible thing. We all have to go to the golf course. Because everybody's waiting. Joanne takes my arm and Graham walks with Mom and the universe is not going to fall in place just for me, just because I need it to at this very moment. It never does, and the bitterness rises in me, a hard, burnt electrical taste. But not worse than that, and it doesn't last long.

"When are you supposed to leave?" I ask Joanne in the car. Quietly, hoping for privacy. Then – "Don't answer that." Holding her arm. "It's not right away. It's not today."

"No," she says. The old sound of her voice – warm flannel. "Not today."

"And you are coming back."

"People are dying. I have certain skills."

"And you are coming back?"

"Yes," she says, and looks at me finally the way she's supposed to when she says yes. There's everything to tell her. I watch as much as I can as my heart goes *hammer hammer*, it can't slow down. Buildings, streets, hills, sky, it all appears so permanent, and yet I know there's no glue, nothing stays fixed, it could fall apart from one moment to the next.

I fall for a moment into a memory. It's late, late, one of our first nights in Santa Irene. Maryse and I are lying in the darkness in bed, wide awake, jet-lagged, naked and quiet, sweating on the sheets, it's so hot. Exhausted and yet still roiled from the trip. This feeling: *We've done it, we've travelled across the world and now here we are.* Then suddenly, from behind the high ceiling, come the sounds of a terrific battle – two animals having at it fiercely above our heads. We don't say a word – it's frightening but distant. The way they're thudding and screeching I think they might come crashing through the tiles right on top of us. And yet it seems safe, somehow; we're in our new home, we don't bother to move. I'm more concerned for Patrick, who's in the other room.

Then it gets very quiet, and I hold Maryse's hand, and we hear it. *Tokay, tokay, tokay.* We don't know what it is, but it sounds soothing.

It will never be like that again, I think now. We were different people and we've been reassembled and it won't be the same. And yet, this has something of that same feeling. I've just crossed the world and here I am. This is what is happening.

I close my eyes and listen.